# The
# WOLF

❦

## JEAN JOHNSON

BERKLEY SENSATION, NEW YORK

**THE BERKLEY PUBLISHING GROUP**
**Published by the Penguin Group**
**Penguin Group (USA) Inc.**
**375 Hudson Street, New York, New York 10014, USA**
Penguin Group (Canada), 90 Eglinton Avenue East, Suite 700, Toronto, Ontario M4P 2Y3, Canada
(a division of Pearson Penguin Canada Inc.)
Penguin Books Ltd., 80 Strand, London WC2R 0RL, England
Penguin Group Ireland, 25 St. Stephen's Green, Dublin 2, Ireland (a division of Penguin Books Ltd.)
Penguin Group (Australia), 250 Camberwell Road, Camberwell, Victoria 3124, Australia
(a division of Pearson Australia Group Pty. Ltd.)
Penguin Books India Pvt. Ltd., 11 Community Centre, Panchsheel Park, New Delhi—110 017, India
Penguin Group (NZ), 67 Apollo Drive, Rosedale, North Shore 0632, New Zealand
(a division of Pearson New Zealand Ltd.)
Penguin Books (South Africa) (Pty.) Ltd., 24 Sturdee Avenue, Rosebank, Johannesburg 2196,
South Africa

Penguin Books Ltd., Registered Offices: 80 Strand, London WC2R 0RL, England

THE WOLF

A Berkley Sensation Book / published by arrangement with the author

PRINTING HISTORY
Berkley Sensation trade edition / April 2007
Berkley Sensation mass-market edition / April 2008

Copyright © 2007 by G. Jean Johnson.
Excerpt from *The Master* by Jean Johnson copyright © 2007 by G. Jean Johnson.
Cover art by Franco Accornero.
Cover design by Annette Fiore.
Interior text design by Kristin del Rosario.

ISBN: 978-0-425-22087-0

BERKLEY® SENSATION
Berkley Sensation Books are published by The Berkley Publishing Group,
a division of Penguin Group (USA) Inc.,
375 Hudson Street, New York, New York 10014.
BERKLEY SENSATION and the "B" design are trademarks belonging to Penguin Group (USA) Inc.

PRINTED IN THE UNITED STATES OF AMERICA

10  9  8  7  6  5  4  3

# ACKNOWLEDGMENTS

I'd like to thank my three lovely beta-ladies for another outstanding job: Stormi, NotSoSaintly, and AlexandraLynch. You're still making me look great, and I appreciate it. (Not to mention how fun it was to meet Stormi and her husband in person!) My thanks also to others who've put up with my pestering them at odd hours around the globe, especially to Alienor, Stellarluna, and Just-Jeanette for letting me bounce ideas off their heads, and to Pern_Dragon for cold reading this novel and letting me know it wasn't too confusing to read on its own, without having to read the one before it first.

And as always, many thanks to the Mob of Irate Torch-Wielding Fans for toasting my toes with your impatient demands for more! All are welcome at my website, http://www.jean johnson.net, or join us at http://groups.yahoo.com/group/MOITWF (18 or older only please).

# ONE

❧

*The Second Son shall know this fate:*
*He who hunts is not alone*
*When claw would strike and cut to bone*
*A chain of Silk shall bind his hand*
*So Wolf is caught in marriage-band*

lys of Devries pulled back from the pool, answering the call that had interrupted what she had been doing, though she didn't want to answer. "In here, Uncle!"

Without hurry—never hurry, which would suggest there was more going on than she could let anyone know—she glanced back down at the volsnap pool. Only the fanged, finned creatures swam in its water. Only her own reflection rippled back up at her, as one of the horrid creatures riffled the surface with a close pass of its body.

"Have you finished feeding the tanks?" Lord Broger inquired, descending the steps of the chamber.

"Almost, Uncle; I just have this last pool." She stooped, picked up the bucket of entrails, and tipped it over the pool, pouring quick and high as it splashed, for the volsnaps lunged out of the water, jaws gaping for snatches of the offal. They would snatch at her, too, if she was ever foolish enough to come within reach during feeding time. There were charms to keep them in the water at other times, so long as she didn't touch the surface of the pool.

Lord Broger eyed his niece. The girl had shaped up nicely in the past three years, ever since the influence of those cursed brothers had gone. "I have bad news and good news. The bad news is, the Nightfall fools have managed to do something to thwart my scrying attempts. They have done so too well to even use what I learned back when I sent the wyverns. And I dare not send any more wyverns, lest the Council detect their presence."

Alys wished he would, so that the Council could. She turned away from the feeding-churned, stone-lined pool, her expression passive but polite. "And the good news, Uncle?"

"The Baron of Glourick has paid me handsomely to marry you. Literally, so there's no wriggling out of this bargain, for you."

Not even by a flicker did her bland expression change. She wanted to run screaming from the room. Especially since the baron in question had hygiene habits that made a volsnap's dinner look good and had the temperament of her uncle when it came to how he treated other people. Not to mention the baron was past sixty years in age . . . and that she was never going to be in love with him or any other man her uncle sought to force her to wed. The warning she had been given in the reflection of the no-longer mirror-smooth pool seemed all the more urgent to heed now, but she couldn't even hint at what she had to do. Not if she wanted to do it successfully.

"I thought I would be on hand when you finally crushed the Nightfall fools," Alys finally offered, shrugging.

"That pleasure is mine—as was the pleasure of killing their uncle, that fool Daron. Who was 'only holding the County until the Prophesied Disaster is past'—*fool!*" Broger spat, with a twist of his head, literally dampening the stone of the wall next to him, where he stood on the next to last step. He mustered a smile after a moment and stepped down onto the floor—not for his niece, but for the creatures imprisoned by iron, stone, and spell around her. "But my pretties will have their fun, and so shall I . . .

"What are you doing, still standing here?" he demanded, looking at her as she stood there, hand clenched around the handle of the feeding bucket. He flicked his dark brown head at the stairs and the door. "Go. The caravan leaves in two hours. You'll be at Glourick Castle within a week, and wed as soon as you arrive. No arguing, or I will bring you back and feed you to the mekhadadaks. The baron was willing to pay the most money and land of all, and I will not disappoint him in this barter. *You* will not disappoint him. This time, the bargain has been struck and *will* be completed."

"If you truly think this is the best alliance and price, Uncle, then I will obey," Alys murmured and took herself away. Thankfully, her uncle was in too good a mood to cuff her as she headed up the steps.

Returning to the slaughtering room up beyond the stairs, she rinsed out the bucket, washed her hands, and removed her protective, slightly bloodied apron with unsteady hands. While Broger's mind was still deciding something, deciding the fate of her hand in marriage, she had been able to sway him. *I don't think he's really your type of ally, Uncle. . . . How much did he offer? That much? He cheated you, Uncle! . . . He doesn't have enough magic in his veins, Uncle—do you want to pollute the bloodline with something inferior? . . . If I go to that man, Uncle, will it not make a powerful enemy of this other?*

She wasn't surprised he had finally made up his mind; she had stalled him for three years—really, for the nine-plus years he had borne the unwelcome care of her after her parents' accidental death. She knew it was an accident, too; Broger would never have burdened himself with a child. He had even neglected his own son, too, until the boy showed signs of magic, whereupon he had taken Barol under his unpleasant tutelage. Her cousin had learned his lessons well, once he became interesting enough to Broger.

But she was very, very glad Morganen had contacted her just now, especially with those three precious words. *"It is time." Time for me to flee this place! Thank you, Kata, Jinga, for answering my prayers!*

Her childhood friend's message was practically a gift sent by the Gods, given the news she had finally been sold to the highest bidder. Leaving the butchering room—which she hopefully would never have to see again—the twenty-four-year-old woman wound up the stairs of the hidden fortress, buried inside one of the mountains ringing Broger of Devries' original home, and entered his study. Stepping through the mirror-Gate, eyes closed tight against the disorientation, she emerged in his workroom in Corvis Castle.

That was how he maintained his "precious pretties," the vicious, magic-created beasts in his hidden menagerie. Two mirrors, cast back-to-back, split apart by his power, and forever linked as a doorway to each other. Linked only to each other, too; they weren't registered with the Mage Council, and since they only linked to each other and were constantly active, there was no unexplainable rise or fall in the energies of either location for the Council to notice.

She was tempted, as always, to turn and smash the frame. That would shatter the mirror in the only way it could be broken, permanently tied open and thus surfaceless as it was. But she didn't.

Leaving the workroom instead, she paced through the halls she had played in as a young girl, heading to the room that had once belonged to another. The servants avoided her. Not because she was the niece of their new lord, but because they knew their lord didn't care for her and by now undoubtedly knew she was being sent away. Exiled as surely as the original sons of this hall had been, if for a different cause.

Broger had married the sister of Lord Saveno's wife. When Lord Saveno had died—shortly after his wife, the Lady Annia, had passed away in childbirth—and then his sons had been exiled, Saveno's brother Daron had taken over the County of Corvis. As next in line to the seat of the county, the man had no offspring and there were no other kin; Daron was vulnerable. Broger had assassinated him so carefully, only his gloating in front of his niece had been proof the deed was by his own doing. The Council certainly hadn't been able to tell.

Stepping into the vacuum of power two months after the sons had left—Saveno's sons had been decreed the Sons of Destiny and exiled for the crime of being targeted by a powerful Seer many years before—Broger had then paid dearly for paintings of the ancient castle on the island of Nightfall. That was where they had been exiled. Broger intended to use those paintings as scrying aids, for porting in beasts to torment and hopefully kill them. He had always longed to be rich and powerful, and though the Council and the King and Queen had declared him to be only a "Count Pro Tem," he was determined to exterminate the rightful line and make himself fully the Count of Corvis and his son the next rightful heir, instead of the eight sons living in exile.

As she reached her room, Alys again wondered how Broger's youngest brother Tangor, her father, could have wound up so nice and wonderful. Even after nearly ten years, she missed her parents, still wished they hadn't been swept to their deaths in a flash flood while crossing a river near their home.

Tansia, one of the few servants who had befriended Alys, was directing the others, Maegra and Kelvin, in the packing of Alys' things in the room that had once belonged to Saber and Wolfer of Nightfall, when they had been young boys. Tansia spotted Alys and flung herself at the other woman. "You poor thing! You poor dear! I'm not even allowed to go with you."

Alys hugged her, then set her back. Her emotions held tightly in check, she soothed the maidservant. "It's all right, Tansia. It is better that you stay here. There is no telling what this Baron of Glourick is like as a master. Uncle is bad enough."

Tansia shuddered. "I've heard enough rumors to know I don't *want* to know."

The other two nodded mutely, folding up Alys' clothes. Alys eyed the garments being folded and knew she had to do some of the packing on her own. Crossing to one of the chests, which was not opened, because it was already more or less packed, she opened it and palmed a silk pouch—she could leave behind her clothes, her meager jewelry, everything else that was hers, but not this one item.

The moment the pendant inside touched her flesh, her escape could finally, successfully begin. Tucking the small sack down the front of her dress, between her breasts, she began assembling the things she could do without in a pinch, but would be better off if she had. A knife, tucked under her gown as well, a full cloak that could serve as a blanket or bedroll, since it was thankfully summer, cloths for her moon-time, and her jewelry all went into a pocket sash. She ducked behind her changing screen and fastened the sash around her waist, settling it underneath her plain blue gown.

Hopefully no one would see the slight lumps it made and take it away. Then she considered the gown itself before lowering it back into place. Light blue was a color that stood out too easily, so she removed and discarded it. She had Tansia bring her a plain brown gown, one that would blend more thoroughly into forest and field, and asked her to pack away the other one. Not that she had many gowns; her uncle had been chary with her needs while she was growing up: Alys had a blue gown, a gray gown, a green gown, and a brown gown.

Adding the plain muslin over-gown, ostensibly to protect her clothing from dirt and soil—though her uncle made her wear the apron-like garment because it made her blend in with the other servants with their own undyed aprons and over-tunics—she exchanged her slippers for boots. She was glad that her uncle had been cheap with her clothing; the hem floated above the floor a few inches instead of dragged, as was more fashionably proper. Dragging clothes would only slow her down if she had to run any distance.

As ready as she could be, she descended to the court-yard. The caravan consisted of ten soldiers on horses, lead-ing pack-mares and her own mount. Alys mounted and perched herself stoically on the sidesaddle, gripped the pommel with her knee and her hands, and did not look back when the lead guard gave the order to head out. She knew her uncle was watching; the last sight she wanted him to see was of a calm, stoic, accepting niece, ever obe-dient to her uncle's whims.

Alys had been scared into obedience at first by his tem-per, then by the hideous versions of entertainment and pleasure he enjoyed too much to do otherwise. She had grown too scared later on that her plans for her freedom and her own, rightful life—achieved with Morganen's help—would fail if she did anything other than obey. At least, on the surface. It was the price she paid for being his kin. Leaving the Corvis courtyard, where she had learned to mock-spar with the eight brothers as a young girl during visits to her by-marriage kin, she let the guards escort her away.

At least they were heading east, which would get her marginally closer to her goal. Alys would wait a few days, until they had ridden out of immediate, close reach of her uncle. She would not escape today. Soon, though. Soon.

It was a good thing one of the guards had her mare by its leading rein; her hands would've trembled, if they hadn't had the solid weight of the pommel to grip.

Her chance came four days later. Docile, submissive, quiet, she had managed to lull the guards' constant watch of her into complaisance. They were trying to be vigilant un-der her uncle's orders to make sure she didn't ruin his bar-gain with the Baron of Glourick. Normally, women across Katan had a choice in who they wed—and usually a very vo-cal one—but Lord Broger had informed her coldly when she had come into his care that she had to earn the right to be clothed and fed, and that the price would be feeding his "pretties," and wedding whomever *he* pleased, once he got the fullest and most useful price for her.

Her only choice at the time had been to make herself indispensable and insinuate with calm logic all of the reasons why she should not be wed. Sitting at the place indicated to her at each campfire, listening to her uncle's soldiers jest about how much she had been worth—a fortune in magical supplies, money, and land—she glanced around her at the night. They were in a forested section, between stretches of farmland and towns. Forest was good; it would allow plenty of cover as she fled.

The light level would also help. Full darkness had fallen, while she had dutifully cooked their meal for them, doing servants' work; the only reason why she even had a tent of her own was that the lecherous baron had insisted she still be a virgin when she came to him. The men her uncle consorted with considered such things valuable, for they found pleasure in inflicting pain and liked the idea of innocence brutally lost. Alys had figured that out early on and had played that card well with her uncle. Mostly it had been to keep Broger from despoiling her himself. Or allowing his son to . . . even though they were blood kin.

. . . *I think it is time I left*, she finally decided, making sure in a quick glance that the guards weren't paying any attention to her. She had her cloak about her shoulders, ostensibly to ward off the cool air of evening, and everything she needed still on her. Two of the ten men were standing watch; the rest were gambling for coin off to one side, exclaiming with each toss, good or poor, of the dice on the ground. *Yes, keep playing with your distractions. Distant Threefold God of Fate, keep them off their guard for me.*

Rubbing her fingertips together where her hands rested demurely in her lap, seated on a rock that had been placed there by other campers using this road over the years, Alys murmured as quietly as she could under her breath. This was not her best form of magic, nor one she had been able to practice often enough to make it easy, since she had been forced to conceal the extent of her powers from her uncle early on. He thought she had only enough to renew the shield-caging for his beasts and a little to protect herself long enough to feed them, when a servant terrorized into doing it would more likely be devoured along with the first butchered bucketful of meat.

Feeding them was one way of keeping her terrified of his anger and retribution, to his mind; if she barely had the power to protect herself from them, she surely didn't have the power to protect herself from him. The deception had worked, too. Alys had never been particularly brave to begin with; she had been gentle, like her father and her mother. There was no urge within her to compete with others, to boast and brag about her abilities.

Of course, playing with the Corvis sons had taught her how to steel her nerve and join them on their more exciting adventures: climbing trees, using sticks in mock sword fights, pretending they were great mages when they were little, and mock-battles filled with the young heroes—and heroine—defeating vast, imagined armies of the same beasts she had later been forced to help her uncle keep. Living under his cruel fist, she had learned how to shut away her fear and do whatever she had to, to think through and past her fear, and present an undisturbed, obedient face to the world.

With her heart pounding in her ears, she finished the long, whispered chant and looked around. The men near the fire were still gambling. She couldn't see the ones who were beyond the firelight, watching the darkness, but she doubted they were all that alert, either. Drawing in a deep, steadying breath, Alys picked up the small eating knife she had used in her meal. Wiping it discreetly on the skirt of her gown to make certain it was at least somewhat clean, Alys nicked her arm and released the spell in a single, barely muttered word.

"*Pookrah.*"

Beasts burst through the trees. Two savaged the guards on watch, as the startled men drew their swords. Several more guards fought to keep the other beasts at bay. The biggest one lunged straight at Alys, who shot to her feet with a scream, the very image of a terrified maid.

It leaped, grabbed her by the throat in its huge, sharp teeth, and shook her body. Blood flung in red drops, and the horse-sized pookrah lunged back into the trees with its prize bouncing all the way, her limp, dangling body still locked in its jaws. A bloodcurdling howl, and the others escaped as well, leaving the bloodied but still-living soldiers behind to gather their wits.

The whole attack had taken less than eight seconds.

The leader of the guards, a mage as well as a warrior, cast lightning bolts into the trees. The counterattack seared bark and leaves, but the wild beasts were gone, and most of his fellows were too injured to give instant chase. Their master would not be pleased . . . but Lord Broger of all people, Alys had known, would understand that recovering his niece was now impossible. Once a pookrah picked a meal for its pack, that meal would be gone long before they could ever catch up with the swift beasts.

The voracious carnivores had been spell-changed from wolves into giant wardogs for some long-ago mage-war. There weren't many of them running around loose, but there were a few small packs that still roamed the mountains just to the north. Alys' uncle would be slightly more upset by his guards' inability to capture more beasts for breeding in his menagerie than he would be at her loss. Though he would also be upset at the loss of land and wealth he had almost gained from her sale.

$\mathbb{A}$rm stinging, still bleeding from the cut she had given it, though it was now shaped like an oversized canine leg, Alys loped in pookrah form through the night. Her best magic lay toward the arts of shapechanging, animal taming, and magical-beast tending; she had long ago planned this form of escape, one among several possibilities that depended on timing and circumstance. In daylight in the woods around the castle, at night on the road to somewhere; it mattered not. She was halfway free. Now she ran hard and fast to evade any possible pursuit.

Scenting rocks with the keen nose of a pookrah, Alys headed that way. Once she leaped up among the rocky scree on the slope, she slowly altered her doggish, cattle-sized feet, shrinking in size to something more natural. She didn't stop until after she had mounted the hill and crossed over to the other side. Only then did she feel safe enough to stop.

Panting, Alys reshaped herself and sat on one of the boulders near the top of the spilled pile. It tilted a little under her weight, then steadied. She fumbled the silk pouch out of her bodice, her eyes still shaped to pierce the night's darkness. Shaking out the pendant, she quickly stuck it to her sternum, just below her throat and pressed the four-point star against her skin.

A sting of heat ripped through her whole body; it made her eyes water and her breath hiss through her teeth . . . but the pendant bonded to her flesh. There was no magic for countering so many spells laid on her that could sever them painlessly . . . though Morg had done his best to find a counter for each and every one of her uncle's spells. It had taken nearly two years of work, with her carefully hunting down and puzzling out the spells her uncle had laid upon her and reporting them to her friend through their intermittent, unpredictable chances at contact. The pain was worth the price, though it made her eyes water and her jaw ache against the tightly clenched urge to scream.

She smelled her own burning flesh, then burning bone, and finally, the tingling cold that cooled the diamond of silver and healed the blackening and blistering of her skin around its edges. Cooled, the amulet sank into her sternum with a tingle of more magic, resting so that it was flush with her skin. The cooling sensation spread through her veins, traveling in her blood until it tingled from scalp to toes and made her tears seem hot on cheeks that felt as cold as death for just a few moments.

The diamond-shaped metal slowly warmed back up to body temperature. It was finally done. Alys shivered, feeling warmth coming back into her body, spreading out gently from the amulet that was now forever a part of her.

*Now Uncle thinks I am truly dead; all of his spells binding me to his knowledge, to his knowing my whereabouts through his damnable kin-tie to me, are severed as surely as if I were dead. All I have to do is make sure no one ever carves this from my chest.*

Alys rubbed the bit of silver centered between her collarbone and breasts. The pain had faded enough to let her know her arm still stung. It had been necessary to spill her own blood by the campfire, both to enforce the illusion and make her snatching and death look real. Some of it still dripped now over these stones, but it was no longer necessary. Certainly it ached and stung, and she had never liked pain of any kind.

*"Sukra medis esthanor; coajis epi demisor,"* she murmured and watched the wound close over and seal itself scarlessly. There wasn't much in the way of color to her night-shaped vision, but she could see details. Peeling off the lightweight, muslin over-gown, Alys scrubbed her arm to get off the remaining blood, then tore the garment and tossed it down the slope, just in case her uncle's soldiers actually tried coming this far to look for her. They wouldn't waste time searching farther, looking for her body, if they came far enough to see that.

Resting only a little bit longer, Alys finally sighed and shifted her shape to that of an owl and launched herself from the stones. Both moons were in the sky, giving her owl-shaped eyes more than enough light to see her way. Sister Moon hung low on the western horizon, just a small sliver of light, but the larger face of Brother Moon was nearly full, rising in the east. The guards would be able to see her spell-shaped tracks for a little while. But she couldn't be certain how thoroughly they would track her down.

It didn't take long to retrace her path from the air. Diving down and settling on a branch within view of the campsite, she watched the men tend to the wounds caused by the complex illusion she had conjured. Some of the less-injured ones were examining the paw prints each illusive pookrah had left on the ground. Their leader was examining the blood she had spilled.

"Should we go after her?" one of the guards asked his commander, eyeing the huge dents in the summer-dry soil.

"No, she is dead." The leader of the group held up a pendant, a silver-clasped sphere of glass. The sphere had blackened, and that made Alys very, very glad—solid proof that the painful severing spells in her breastbone amulet had worked. "This would have led us right to her; it does not flash anymore when I activate it. Therefore, the wench is dead.

"I do not look forward to informing our lord of what has happened."

*No, he won't be happy at all—lost his barter-bride, lost his wealth, supplies, and land, lost it all because I have managed to escape!*—Alys cut off her gloating before it could emerge as a triumphant hoot. She couldn't allow them to see her; a shapeshifting mage could change shape, but not general coloring, and her dark blond hair would remain a golden, light-tan color as feathers, scales, or fur, and her gray eyes would be gray eyes always, whether bulging on eyestalks or slitted like a cat's. Not without applying the kind of illusion-spell that would glow like a lantern to mage-sight.

There was nothing more to keep her there. Alys had the information she wanted, that the pendant under the feathers covering her breastbone had indeed worked. Silently, she launched herself from the limb, oriented herself on the stars, and headed to the east. First she would fly a few hours to get well out of range, then she would find some secure place to sleep until dawn. She had a very long way to go, to get to the eastern coast.

Wolfer paced the ramparts, eyes fixed on the east and the rippling waves of the Eastern Ocean in the distance. Somewhere out there was his next youngest brother, Dominor.

He had been kidnapped by the woman-hating, magicless Mandarites, because Dom was a powerful mage. Dominor had yet to respond to Evanor's calls to him through the magic aether of their world, and his other brothers suspected foul play.

Four days had passed. Four days of no word, four days of impatience, waiting to see if Dominor escaped from the Mandarites' ship somehow, four days of praying to Jinga and Kata that Evanor *didn't* have to tell them through the link the four sets of twins had that Evanor's twin was dead. Wolfer caught himself growling, caught himself imagining shifting his shape and tearing that treacherous Lord Aragol's throat out with claw and fang, and fingered the braided bracelet on his wrist.

*Some people are good people*, he reminded himself, lightly rubbing the braided hairs with their grain. Gently, though the giver, the owner of that hair had painstakingly woven it in front of him with a spell to never loosen or fray. As he usually did when he calmed himself through her braid, he pictured young Alys of Devries, daughter of one of the freeholders near Corvis lands, before she had moved away with her uncle. His uncle, too, by marriage, though something about the man had always raised his hackles and flattened his ears, inside.

He tried imagining her as, what, twenty-four by now? He was twenty-nine, and she was five years younger than him and his twin, Saber. *Probably married with kids clinging to her skirts. A good mother*, he reminded himself. The thought of her married to anyone wouldn't settle in his mind, though. It was hard for him to think of her married to anybody. *Not Alys. She'd kick the man between the legs . . . or perhaps she would just run the other way . . .*

It was the dichotomy between those two reactions that had first puzzled, then irritated, then intrigued him. His Alys had grown progressively bolder, too . . . until she had turned fourteen and a flood had swept her parents away. Her boldness disappeared, after that. Her shyness had become blandness. Her frequent visits turned infrequent, and usually only at her uncle Broger's whim; the man only came to borrow money from Saber, since he had married their mother's sister, Sylvia, providing a tenuous link of kinship-by-marriage between them. *Alys was . . . Broger's younger brother's daughter,* Wolfer recalled, concentrating on his memories of her, because it was more soothing than thinking about Dominor.

A moan wafted faintly through the air. Followed shortly by a shout. Wolfer suppressed a groan, rubbing at his temple. His twin was still honeymooning with his wife, which meant they were making noises like that at any time the mood struck them. *At least they have something to take their minds off the agony and anger of waiting and wondering . . . though I could wish they weren't so gods-be vocal about it . . .*

"Wolfer. Do you see anything?" Trevan asked, joining him on the outer wall between his and their brother Morganen's easternmost tower.

Wolfer shook his head. "No. And don't you try flying after them. You need to wait a couple weeks more, until your blood rebalances itself and your stamina returns."

"Maybe, but by then, they'll be too far away," his younger brother muttered bitterly, rubbing at his scarlessly healed but still sore chest. The bullet-thing had struck near his shoulder, narrowly missing anything important like a lung or a major artery or vein . . . but he needed the muscles and tendons in that area to be healed and whole before he could take to the air for any length of time, and Morganen had run out of the necessary herbs. He studied Wolfer, his green eyes meeting a glance of Wolfer's golden ones. "Have you been practicing your own bird forms?"

Wolfer shrugged. "I hit my head in a fall of three lousy yards, yesterday. Kelly scolded me so hard for hurting myself, she made my ears ring even worse than the blow to my head did."

That made Trevan chuckle. "Poor Saber. Wed to a redheaded virago," the other man mock-commiserated. "If only that had been the true Disaster, and not the Mandarites kidnapping Dom."

Wolfer nodded, his own chest-length brown hair sliding over his shoulders, a few wisps floating in the rampart breeze. He caressed the bracelet braided around his wrist once more and wondered—not for the first time—what had happened to his little Alys, the source of his gift.

# TWO

·❧·

I'm going to have to truth-spell you, young lady, if you want me to purchase this jewelry from you," the goldsmith apologized, eyeing the cloaked woman in front of him warily.

"You may. They *are* mine, rightfully by law to keep or to sell," she added in ritual, as he pulled out a rune-carved length of metal from behind his counter and touched her with it. The crystal glowing at the end of the copper shaft where it touched her wrist remained clear and bright through the whole of her claim.

"So they are," the man murmured, tucking the wand away. He frowned slightly at her. "What sort of trouble could you be in, that you would give so much of it away?"

"I have to get to a friend who is in trouble, to help him," Alys stated truthfully. "I need to be able to afford a Gating to get there in time; he lives on the far side of Katan from here."

"That *is* an expensive enough need to drive you to my door. But I cannot give you overmuch for this small amount of jewelry—some silver, some moonstones, gold with some amethysts . . . none of it magical, I think, which reduces the value. Twenty gilder."

Alys calculated, her face half-shrouded under the curve of her cloak's hood. At least it had been raining earlier, allowing her to use the cloak as a disguise. She wanted no one seeing her face clearly enough to ever have word of her still being alive getting back to her uncle. "Twenty-two."

He shook his head.

"I'll need to hire transportation when I reach the far end of the Gate," she wheedled. "My friend does not live in town."

"Twenty-one, then—but nothing more," he warned her.

"Thank you, then; I think that will be enough."

Nodding, he pulled the jewelry she had set on the counter to his side of the polished wood and pulled out a box. Counting out twenty-one gold coins, he handed them over and shook her hand. "May you reach your friend in time to help him, and may he know the true value of your friendship."

"Oh, I hope so," Alys prayed, taking her coins and escaping.

The Mages' Guild wasn't far away. Ignoring the smell of meat pies from a nearby bakery, the hunger in her stomach, she hurried up the steps and ducked inside, sash pouch gripped tightly in her fist. The clerk at the greeting desk eyed her cloaked figure as she approached.

"Can the Guild help you, miss?"

"I need to Gate to . . . Orovalis City, on the northeast coastline." That was a place just to the north of Nightfall Isle; once she entered the ocean water in a swimming form, the north-to-south current would help sweep her to its shores.

"Orovalis?" the man asked, arching a brow. "That is a long way away."

"I'm in a hurry to help a friend, and I need to get there today."

"You'll need to go to the Gating desk—go up those stairs

over there, turn right, and enter the third door on the left," he ordered her.

Nodding, Alys hurried in the direction he had pointed. The woman at the Gating desk heard Alys' request, opened her book, and checked the list of names and destinations waiting to be Gated, while those waiting to be called sat or paced in the largish room around them.

"You are in luck; there is someone going to Orovalis today—right now, in fact—" The woman tapped the edge of a mirror angled on her desk and spoke. "Roether, please hold the Gate."

*"Acknowledged,"* a voice wafted back from the linked mirror.

"That will be fifteen gilder, since the Gate is already opened, but you have to pay right now, or pay the full twenty for that length of destination later."

Alys fumbled out most of the coins, counted fifteen, snatched back the extra two she had tossed out, and waited impatiently while the woman recounted them.

"Very good; go through that door there, and follow Mage Roether's instructions, please."

"Thank you!"

Clutching the remaining six—six!—coins to her chest, she darted through the door. Six gilder were far more wealth than she had expected to escape with. Six was wealth enough to buy passage on a ship . . . if any ships would dare take a woman to Nightfall Isle.

They wouldn't, of course. The High Council had declared the Nightfall sons banished to the isle and had forbidden any women to set foot on the island, in a vain attempt to thwart the brothers' prophecied Destiny. As it was, Alys knew she would have to swim the distance between the mainland and the island.

The mage in the room, standing before a largish mirror, gave her an impatient look. "Step through the mirror quickly, and don't touch the edges. I can't hold the link for much longer, with today's backlog of travelers!"

Scooping up the hem of her skirt and cloak, Alys hopped through the mirror.

Someone on the other side caught and steadied her as the disorientation hit. "Careful—if you feel sick, there is an urn right over here . . ."

Alys shook her head; she had done this enough with her uncle's mirrors that she recovered after taking just two deep breaths. The other trips had been over an equally long and disorienting distance, but she had done it twice a day for many years now, attending to the morning and evening feedings of her uncle's menagerie. "Thank you—how do I get out of here?"

"That door over there," the woman helping her pointed. "Are you sure you're all right? Most people who come such a long way get very sick."

"Cast-iron stomach," Alys muttered, heading for the door.

Even if she had been sick, there was nothing in her stomach to come back up. She had carefully refrained from hunting mice as an owl; the bones that a bird would cast back up later would have caused her human digestion a great deal of trouble. And now Alys had six solid gold coins to spend on a meal, and a rest, and maybe a bath, and a few supplies to supplement everything she had left behind.

"*Thank* you, Kata," she prayed to the gentle goddess of the two Gods of Katan. Boisterous Jinga had never really drawn her, but serene Kata always had. Not enough to want to go serve in a temple—as if her uncle would have let her—but enough that she felt comforted whenever she had caught sight of a shrine dedicated to the mother-goddess of their people.

Emerging from the magic-cooled depths of the local Guild hall, she immediately felt the sweltering, humid heat of the northeastern coastline. Forced to take off her cloak, she bundled it on her arm and looked around, orienting herself as best she could in a town she had never seen. The architecture was different, with pillared roofs fronting each building, providing shade against the northern-hot sun.

Her wool-and-linen spun gown was too hot, now that she was in a region where everyone was wearing linen or cotton, or thin silk if they could afford it.

Keeping to the shade, sniffing the air, redolent with unfamiliar, northeastern spices, she headed for a food stall to spend one of her precious coins. *No, better yet—an actual meal in an actual tavern.* Spying a carved sign of a winking woman holding a tray of bread and ale, with the Katani characters underneath the wooden shingle for "The Trenching Wench Inn," she hurried across the street. She had to dodge two magic-powered carts, sidestepped horse droppings that hadn't been swept up yet for composting and selling as fertilizer by some enterprising, hardy soul, but finally was free to duck inside.

It wasn't as cool as the Mages' Guild building, but it was cooler than the burning sun outside. She sighed in relief . . . and froze. The only women in the tavern were serving-wenches—low-cut bodices, cleavage-baring corsets, with skirts hiked high enough to bare the knee. That type of wench. The kind Alys instinctively knew served a lot more than bread and mead to the all-male clientele.

Especially since, as if cued by her very thoughts, a woman's moan and a man's shout floated down from the rooms rentable overhead, muffled only somewhat by the wood and plaster of the walls. Some of the men grinned crudely; others ignored the sounds, eating their meals, flirting with the women. There was a mix of women, too, some paler-skinned from the southlands, some darker-skinned from the northlands of Katan, and plenty whose coloring fell between.

Alys bit back a groan. Her first taste of adventure since being cooped up in her uncle's care, and she had to wander into a brothel-tavern! Backing out quickly, she bumped into an entering patron and scrambled to get farther down the street as he gave her a grin, his teeth gleaming white in his suntanned face. Then she gasped and reversed her course, ducking back into the tavern in an effort to hide herself from an even more alarming sight. It was her other uncle,

Donnock of Devries! Seated in a mage-driven carriage heading down the street—coming her way, no less.

*What is* he *doing all the way over here?* Alys thought frantically, hurrying as fast as she could through the scattered tables. Last she had heard—albeit over a month ago—her father's middle brother was taking care of an errand for Broger on the *west* coast, a full two month's journey away, or thirty whole gilders by Gate. She swatted without stopping to aim at a hand that tried to grip her bottom and escaped through the back doorway. *It couldn't have been him! It just* looked *like him, that's all . . .*

"Here, now! What are you doing in here? You're not a part of this tavern!"

Shaking her head and making a hushing noise at the wench who was passing the other way, she peered through the crack in the doorway as soon as it swung shut again—he was coming inside! Heart pounding, she shrank back, then firmed her courage and looked through the crack again. Her uncle, about as black-hearted as his older brother, had grabbed a wench and was squeezing her bottom, feasting on her neck.

Alys could see the woman roll her eyes for just a moment, then muster a smile and a coo for him, nodding her head first at the tray of drinks she was still balancing. Then the wench nodded toward the doorway. As Alys watched, the woman divested her tray of its drinks at a nearby table, collected the coins from the thirsty patrons, handed her tray to another woman, and joined her uncle in heading toward the back door. Straight toward Alys' position.

Turning, Alys fled to the next door down the short hall.

"Hey! Who are you?" the cook called out, looking up from the roasted fowl he was disjointing.

Alys quickly retreated before he could make a further scene and draw her uncle's attention. There was only one other way out of the brief passageway, and that was up the stairs. Scrambling up them, she reached the hall upstairs, breathless from her dash and the fear of discovery.

Blushing at the sounds from behind some of the doors,

she slipped quickly to the end of the hall and cautiously peeked into one whose door stood open. No one was inside. Darting within, she shut the stout panel. The room had a bed, a small table next to it with a pitcher and bowl, some toweling cloths, an armless, unpadded chair to one side by the window, and a largish wardrobe cupboard against the wall. The room smelled of men and women, of musk and sweat and copulation.

She had smelled that scent before. Sometimes it amused her uncle to shock her by ordering her to bring him up one of his tamer "pets" while he was still in bed with one of the household. That was when she had learned what a naked man looked like and learned that her eldest uncle thought about wanting her, about having her.

If she hadn't had so much to live for, if her careful deflections of his interest—*temporary pleasure at best, Uncle, compared to the price you could get for a virgin niece*—hadn't dissuaded him, she probably would have ended up slitting her wrists if he had ever touched her.

She heard footsteps coming down the hall. She tensed, then relaxed as another door creaked open. Then she heard the footsteps again, closer, closer . . . the handle on the door turned! Whirling around, she yanked open one of the wardrobe doors and climbed inside, pulling it almost, but not quite, shut behind her—she didn't dare bang it closed when they were right there!

Trying not to pant too loudly or let her heart pound too hard, Alys heard the murmur of voices, heard the bed-chamber door being shut, and then saw the back of a woman and a man heading to the bed, just within her strip of view.

It wasn't her uncle, Donnock, thankfully—this man had blond hair, not dark brown. As she watched, he grinned and shucked his boots, his tunic, and pants. The woman, a more northern-born one than the blonde she had seen her uncle grab, pulled off her blouse, heeled off her slippers, and started to work on the laces of her skirts. Wide-eyed, Alys held herself very still as the man immediately cupped the woman's light brown breasts together, sucking first on one large, rosy-brown nipple, then on the other, growling something indistinct as he laved them with his tongue. The wench laughed, managed to shimmy out of her skirts, and the man picked her up and tossed her on the bed with a laugh of his own, the rod at his groin twitching and hard.

The angle of the wardrobe gave Alys a fairly clear view as the man spread the woman's thighs, exposing her brown curls and dark-pink, moist core . . . and put his *mouth* there? Shocked, Alys watched as he licked and kissed and nibbled. Even more amazing, the woman not only put up with it, but sighed, then moaned, then squirmed and writhed as if it was something really good. She clasped his head after a few minutes of the odd treatment, her body convulsing, shivering, bucking up into him, as she let out a wailing cry. The man laughed as she panted, sagging limp into the bedding.

He rolled her over after a moment, giving her backside a slap, and pulled her up onto her hands and knees. She wiggled her hips and gave him a laugh, and he gripped his rod, edging closer on his knees. Their position now made Alys have to lean to the side a little to see what he was up to; curiosity and shock compelled her into tipping her head just that little bit more, angling for a better view. He was teasing her glistening-damp slit with the reddened head of his shaft, rubbing the rounded tip against the folds of her cleft. Especially against that little peak toward the front of her core, until the woman begged for more. As Alys watched, amazed at this . . . this *playing*, the man gripped her hips and sank abruptly into her body, slick and swift and deep.

As Alys stared, captivated in shock and fascination, the man swayed back almost all of the way out, then shoved back in so deep, not even the curls of their respective groins could be seen by their amazed, hidden audience. The woman moaned and squirmed, and he pulled back and obliged with more. Alys had never seen *this* position before, since her uncle had always been on top of his wenches, and they had endured it on their backs, not enjoyed it on their hands and knees.

The client groaned and rocked and plunged himself in and out of the wench he was paying for. He reached forward and fondled her swaying breasts, thrusting into her rhythmically, over and over, faster and faster, until he was grunting with each stroke and she was gasping for more. Hairy thighs slapped against the back of her light brown ones as his hands clutched her hips, everything in their straining, animalistic copulating building to a frantic pace.

The man suddenly grimaced and shouted, his back arching as the woman moaned, and they shuddered and bucked together. Drooping over her back, he panted hard through his grin, and the woman struggled for her own breath. Then he slid out of her, his manhood limp, wet, and shriveling. They stayed like that for a few moments, then the man sat up, heaving a sigh of satisfaction.

A moment later, he slapped her hip again and pointed at his groin, stating a crude order that made Alys blush, but the woman obeyed willingly. As the man sank back on his heels, the woman turned around and knelt on the rumpled bedding. She bent low and took him into her mouth, licking and sucking and using her hand, until the capped end of his manhood came out of its little cowl-hood once more, stiff and hard and throbbing visibly in her grip.

The crude things he said as she did that told Alys he liked it a lot, and then he pushed the woman over, his rod stiff and jutting as it had before, and took her the same way Alys had seen her uncle humping over his women. Only, this woman wrapped her legs around her customer's waist and encouraged him with an amazing vocabulary of words, arching herself up into him as if she enjoyed his weight bouncing on her. This time, when the man groaned and arched his back, then slumped in completion, he lay limply insensate for several minutes on top of the whore.

Alys watched in silence as the woman lifted her hands behind his head and checked her nails. The wench cleaned underneath each of them with a thumbnail, relaxed them onto his back again for a few moments more, then finally jiggled the man back to consciousness. He kissed her, climbed off the bed, and used one of the rags and a little water from the pitcher to clean off his no longer rampant groin. Climbing into his clothes, he dug out a couple of coins from his pouch and tossed them at the woman. She caught most of them, hunted in the bedding for the last one while he buckled his belt, and thanked him with a sly admonition to "come again, soon" that made Alys blush three seconds later . . . finally getting the innuendo.

When the man left, the woman got out of the bed, straightened the bedding, threw on her blouse, stepped back into her skirts . . . and walked straight to the wardrobe door. Alys shrank back, but there was nowhere to hide; the clothes hanging on their pegs inside weren't nearly enough to cover her. The woman pulled the door open. And froze, staring at the extra contents of the wardrobe.

"Well, well. What have we here?"

Alys squeaked and got her throat working, her cheeks aflame with shame and embarrassment. She shook her head, her curls wisping free from the braid she usually tried to confine them in, balling her cloak tight against her stomach. "I didn't mean to be in here!"

"I can see that. Usually I'm paid in advance if someone wants a peek at whatever goes on in here . . . and they're invariably men," the woman added frankly. She eyed Alys' flushed cheeks, her wide eyes, and stepped back, flipping her hand. "Come out. If your reason for being in there is a good one, I won't charge you."

Shocked that someone would *pay* to see something like . . . like *that*, Alys crept out. Shaking out her gown, she stared at the bed, then shook her head and closed her eyes.

"You're an innocent, aren't you? Sit down—don't worry, the bed isn't going to bite you," the other woman added, guiding her over to the edge. She sat down next to Alys. "I'm Cari. Who are you?"

"A—" She broke off, and lied about her name. If her Uncle Donnock ever heard of her visit, her Uncle Broger wouldn't stop at anything to hunt her down. "Analia," she lied. "I came in here because I saw my uncle outside on the street, but I couldn't escape through the kitchen because the cook shouted at me, and my uncle was in the tavern room by then, so I ran upstairs, and I came in here, but then you came in, so I had to hide . . . and I . . . and you . . ."

She couldn't finish. The wench cocked a dark brown brow in her light brown forehead and studied her. "Analia, huh? Well, tell me, why were you afraid your uncle might see you? Why were you so afraid that an innocent like you would rather run into a brothel than meet him?"

The gentleness in her tone was the first piece of sympathy Alys had received since the Corvis servants had bid her a regretful farewell. "I'm running away from home," she admitted in a rush. "My uncle's not a very nice man, and if he saw me, he'd drag me home in spellbound chains, and then I'd have to marry a fat, smelly, sixty-eight-year-old lecher, because I'm a virgin and my uncle wants lots of money."

Cari blinked, looked across the room at nothing in particular as she worked that part out, then nodded. "I suppose that makes sense. And of course you had to hide either under the bed or in the wardrobe—but why didn't you shut the cupboard door?"

"I didn't want it to bang and let you know I was there," Alys admitted, glad the woman wasn't hollering or making a fuss. "And I didn't really mean to see anything, but there wasn't enough room to move . . . and I couldn't seem to close my eyes—did you really *like* that?" she asked bluntly. "Was it actually . . . *enjoyable*?"

The wench laughed. "Let me close the door, honey." Getting up, she crossed the room, shut the door, then came back and dragged over a chair. "Have you got a silvara?"

Alys shook her head. "I've got one gilder to my name," she lied, smart enough not to tell this woman or anyone else how much money she *did* have in the sash pouch inside the bundle of her cloak. "But I'm headed to a friend's home, so I don't need much money."

Cari got up again, crossed to the wardrobe, did something to the bottom that lifted the wooden panel up, bent over and did something more, then closed everything up. She came back and held out nine silver coins. "Nine silvaras. Give me the gilder, and I'll answer any questions you've got, for a full hour . . . and if you're as innocent as I think you are, I'll *tell* you what your mother should have told you long ago—you're, what, twenty-two?"

"Twenty-four. My parents died ten years ago. My uncle has been raising me," Alys added, eyeing the coins. Sighing, she unrolled her cloak just far enough to dig her hand in and fetch out a single coin, then exchanged it for the silvaras. "I . . . I suppose I *would* like to know a few things. *Does* it feel good, as good as you made it look?" she asked, tucking the coins away and rolling up her sash and cloak once more.

Cari, Alys guessed about twenty-six or so, turned the chair around and straddled it, bracing her arms across the back. "Honey, I'm a whore. Which means I do it for a living. Now, sometimes it feels good, if the man knows what he's doing . . . or if I'm in the mood . . . but oftentimes for me, it's just work.

"Sometimes I shiver, I sigh, I give a little cry," she added in dramatic rhyme, touching her cleavage-low neckline and batting her eyelashes, making Alys smile a little, "but that's mostly so the guy feels good about what he's doing—I have to please my customers, after all, or they won't come back for more, and they *all* like to think they're Kata's greatest mortal lover. Jinga, on the other hand, knows that most of these guys don't know their rods from a hole in the ground. Unfortunately, a lot of 'em treat women that way—like a hole in the ground.

"Now this is not to scare you off from the pleasures of sex, honey," Cari added, holding out her palm to caution Alys. "The thing is, a lot of guys hate being taught that most 'manly' of arts, which is lovemaking, not just sex. And there *is* a difference. They think they should know how to do it by sheer instinct . . . but not much more than a man in a thousand has that kind of instinct naturally. Now, here's lecture number one: Do you know where babies come from, Analia?"

"A man puts his rod in"—she blushed and stumbled before continuing—"um, in that spot between a woman's legs, and then, if his seed takes root, just over nine months later, she gives birth," Alys recited. "Just like with dogs or cats, horses, sheep, or other creatures. Only their pregnancies take shorter or longer because they're not humans, and it's different for each kind, but it's pretty much the same thing."

"Well, your mother did tell you something, at least. A man's got to put his manhood in there, in a woman's womanhood—I'll use the delicate terms so as to keep your blood flowing through the rest of your flesh and not pooling in your face so much," Cari teased. "Once he's done that, he's got to rub it back and forth, 'til he feels real good, and that makes the seed come out. It sort of looks like thick milk, though it doesn't taste like milk at all," she added in an aside that made Alys choke on the thought of *tasting* it. "But it can plant a baby in your belly if the timing's right, if you haven't got an anticonception amulet.

"*And* you'll need to remember to replace it every year, 'cause the spell does wear off after about a year and a half." Cari stuck out her foot briefly in example, and Alys realized there was a pendant braided by a bit of cord around her ankle. "Do you know all about your monthly flow and the timing of when you can get pregnant?"

Alys nodded. "A woman is more likely to get pregnant in the middle of the month, between flows, and when the flow doesn't come on time, she's probably pregnant."

"Good! Your mother did teach you that much, too."

"I was just beginning my flow, when she died," Alys admitted, feeling a faint pang from missing her mother. It had been a long time, though. "She explained a lot of things to me, but then I had to go live with my uncle . . ."

Cari studied Alys more closely, a look of concern entering her dark brown eyes. "Analia, honey . . . did your uncle do to you what that man just did to me? Did he *try* to?"

Alys flushed; the wench seated in front of her was very perceptive. "He . . . he would have me bring something up to him, when he was in bed with one of his serving girls. And he stated that he wanted to have me, too . . . but I convinced him I was worth more as a virgin. He liked the idea of taking his . . . his brother's daughter . . . but he liked the idea of money and land and other things a lot more."

When the other woman merely gave her a look of sympathy, not of condemnation, Alys felt free to admit a little more.

"Sometimes . . . he would touch my breasts, but I didn't let myself react or push him away, because he would have liked that, and my just standing there, ignoring it bored him. He didn't do anything more. I also held him off from selling me to others that were like him for a long time, too, by telling him that one 'buyer' wouldn't further his ambitions," she explained. "Or I'd say that another wasn't offering a high enough price, that a third wasn't good enough blood-wise to be associated with my uncle through me—"

"Now, *that* was pretty clever of you," Cari praised her. "A lot of bastard men—and I don't mean those born outside the eight altars—have egos much bigger than their p— uh, their manhoods. A smart woman can get around them by playing on their greeds and their weaknesses. So, from what you've said, I take it you're untouched, right? Never did what I just did, with a man?"

Alys nodded, pleased at the other woman's praise. Morganen had thought she was being pretty clever, too, but it was nice to hear it from someone unbiased. It hadn't been easy, after all, keeping her uncle from selling her off too soon.

"How untouched is untouched? If you haven't been breached by a man's rod, have you ever been kissed where that man kissed me, down at my loins? I'll take it from your expression, that's a definite *no*." Cari chuckled as

Alys' eyes widened and her mouth dropped, her escaping curls bouncing with the shaking of her head. "Nor done the other one, where I kissed him at the groin? No? Okay . . . now, have you ever been kissed on the mouth?"

Alys started to shake her head. Then blushed. "There was a boy . . . We tried it. Four times. But we were very young."

"Did he stick his tongue in your mouth? There we go again with that face, young lady," Cari scolded. "You keep gaping like that, and a fly will buzz right in!"

Alys shut her mouth. The other woman shook her dark-curled head and sighed. Not in a disappointed way, but in a "we have a lot ahead of us" sort of way.

"All right, tell me exactly what you saw when you saw your uncle doing things with women, and how it made you feel to see that, and how you felt when he touched you, and we'll see how much damage we have to undo."

With a bit of awkwardness, and many blushes, Alys told Cari in more detail what she had seen and endured. Then added at the end, "—And it *revolted* me! Even with . . . with that boy I kissed, and I liked kissing him, I can't imagine doing anything like . . . *that* . . ."

"I sense a touch of hesitancy in your voice," Cari murmured, leaning her chin on her arms. "Did you see that *I* was enjoying it, and thought a little differently? Just for a moment?"

Blushing, reluctant, Alys nodded slightly.

"Well, what your uncle was doing was sex. What that man in here was doing—and he's one of the good ones, honey—was lovemaking. So yes, I did enjoy it. *This* time around. Lovemaking gives both people pleasure, and I felt a lot of pleasure with that client. *Sex* is messy, uncomfortable, and boring, especially when the fellow doesn't know what he's doing," the prostitute explained to her. "Lovemaking, on the other hand, is incredible; it curls your toes and rolls through you like the good kind of thunderstorm, not the scary kind. It makes your hair want to stand on end, makes you want to jump onto the roof and holler your pleasure to the world, makes you feel like you can fly without even needing magic . . . It's that kind of good when you hit the climax of your pleasure.

"So here's lesson number two: I'm going to tell you everything you need to know about lovemaking," Cari bargained. "That way, when you do find the right man, you'll not only know what to do, I'm going to tell you what you can teach *him* to do, to make sure he's the right kind of lover, as well as the right kind of man for you.

"And just because it's a pleasure to do, as my womanly duty, something your mother never got to finish doing—and because you're the kind of young woman who is supposed to marry a *good* man, not a smelly sixty-eight-year-old kind—if it takes longer than an hour, I won't charge you." Cari winked broadly, resembling the image carved on the signboard outside. "That's 'cause I know a *lot* about lovemaking, honey, and it might take quite some time to explain it all. So, pay attention, and we'll see how quickly you can learn the basics, and the many interesting variations that can 'come' from them."

# THREE

❧

Alys didn't feel very innocent anymore. It took nearly two hours of nonstop instruction, learning, and talking, with a frank discussion of the various intimate female parts and how to make them feel good—blessed Kata!—but that was . . . it was . . . she couldn't—yet it intrigued as well as amazed her—and it ended up requiring a charcoal sketch on a scrap of paper to discuss the various male parts and what to do with them. Plus more discussions on where else on the body were good spots to touch, and how to touch them, and what with . . . and so many *positions*, her head reeled just trying to keep them all straight.

At least she didn't feel revolted just thinking about them in general, anymore. She still felt revolted thinking about her uncle—both of her uncles, but mostly Uncle Donnock—who was probably long gone by the time her "lessons" were over. But Alys *could* think about one person and all of the things she had learned. When she did, she could feel that trembling, nervous but not nervous sensation the professional wench had described to her as the leading edge of desire.

Wolfer of Corvis.

Yes; when Alys pictured Wolfer as the male owning the parts sketched on the piece of paper, she definitely felt a twinge of desire.

Now she was eating a plate of lunch for the price of a few copperas in the back kitchen of The Trenching Wench Inn, seated at a small table next to Cari, who was eating, too. Alys shivered at the thought of seeing what Wolfer's naked body would look like. She had seen him without his shirt, first playing around as a boy, and as a young man on hot days when he had been working at some task . . . but never without trousers. Cari had told her that each man was shaped a little differently, some curved, some straight, some thick, some thin, some long, and some short. Some had a large, tight manly sack, some had a loose-hanging, pendulant one; some loins were very furry, others were more sparse, and if he had dark hair, it would definitely be dark . . .

*Oh, my.*

Just thinking about what Wolfer might look like made her breath grow short and her insides feel funny. She thought that might be what Cari had frankly described as the way desire normally felt. First her stomach flopped inside, then she grew hot, and that place between her legs felt like it was growing moist; it even ached a little. Blinking, Alys firmly returned her attention to her bowl of stew.

"Are you going to be all right, honey?" Cari asked her, as Alys finished the mug of water the cook had poured for her. "Is it far to your friend's house?"

"Not far, thank you. I'm pretty sure my uncle's gone by now," she added.

"Well, go out the back door, just to be sure. And use the refreshing room through that little door there. Sometimes the men in this place just grab a wench and go upstairs without asking first if she actually works here," Cari added with the same straightforward candor that had plowed right through Alys' cherished former ignorance. Cari stood up, then paused, thoughtful. "I don't suppose you know what happened to this boy you kissed a long time ago?"

Alys blushed. "I'm, um . . . going to his family's home, actually."

"Well, maybe you can kiss him and see if you still like it anymore. Just don't forget to get yourself an anklet like mine," Cari added, sticking out her now slippered foot once more. "Glytha's shop. You go left outside in the alley, to the next cross street, turn right, go to the third shop on the right, and go up the outer stairs. Tell her The Trenching Wench sent you, and she'll give you high-quality at a discount—but try not to blush," the other woman added with a wink, "or she won't believe you."

"Thank you."

"No problem, honey. Hope you like kissing that boy when you meet up with him again, and that he likes kissing you. I've got to get back to work, now."

"I, um . . . hope you enjoy your day," Alys offered boldly.

Cari laughed and walked out the door, hips swaying in the same way she had demonstrated to Alys not that long ago, a way she had said that men liked to see a woman's hips sway. Lessons in seducing a man had been part and parcel of the instruction, and that was one of them. "I think I just might, honey . . ."

It didn't take long to find the shop, since it was in the direction of the harbor. Alys looked at the stairs, up at the door at the top, then walked on. Two blocks later, she turned back, stopped again at the bottom of the stairs, stared at them. Finally Alys headed up, firming her expression into the emotionless one she had shown her uncle for so long. The emotional discipline that had saved her for so long in the face of her uncle's perversions and tyranny would keep her from blushing now.

She was in charge of her life now, and a woman couldn't be too responsible about not starting a family until she was absolutely ready to, as her briefly found friend had firmly instructed her during their two hours together. There was also more than one reason to avoid pregnancy just yet . . . and no guarantee that the diamond below her throat could completely thwart the most important one. It had been enspelled against that threat, too, but Alys preferred to err on the side of caution, for now.

The tired young mage almost missed the island entirely.

Then again, she had swum for the rest of the day in otter form, given up trying to find it as night had fallen, and drifted on the current while she slept on her back in a form more used to rivers and lakes than oceans, but still useful enough for her purposes. The distant slapping of waves on a shoreline roused her from her sleep. Flipping over, getting salt water into her mouth and nose, which made her bob and cough, rubbing at her otter-shaped face with otter-shaped paws, she squinted and peered through the predawn gloom.

Curling, fading lines of white. A silhouette of dark ruggedness against the slowly dawning light.

Nightfall Isle.

From the way the current was carrying her past, even at its modest pace, Alys would have to swim hard on an empty stomach to reach its southernmost shore; river otters simply weren't adapted to eating in salty seas, and she wasn't comfortable enough with her magic to try for a sea creature shape, or fly such a long distance when she didn't have a water bird form and would have needed to rest and float at the halfway point, between here and the mainland.

The mere sight of the island did give her energy, though. Diving and flipping her tail and paws, undulating her body, she surfaced and dove, surfaced and dove, checking her heading and cutting across the current, until she was in the lee of the island, out of the current. That helped her to make a lot better headway.

By the time she came within easy swimming distance, the sun was well above the horizon. Squinting against the light, she skirted the rocky, cliff-riddled southern end and swam around to the eastern shore, to one of the sandy beaches there. Alys was looking for any sign of the brothers' home. She knew she had the right island, because there was only the one island out here in this semitropical region of the Eastern Ocean. It was just that it was a rather large island.

The beach she chose looked inviting. Waddling out onto the land, panting, she got herself up above the high-tide line, and flopped in the dry, cool sand to rest, until she had the strength to go look for food. At least her uncle hadn't neglected to feed her, though sometimes he made her go without her food for a day to punish her—never more than one day at a time, though he did often alternate days without food. A starvation-weakened niece was a useless niece to him, after all.

Starvation and beatings had been his two main tools to discipline her, though more the former than the latter, once she had learned how to blank out all expression, all reaction in his presence. Alys had eventually figured out that her eldest uncle only beat her because he enjoyed seeing her cower, seeing her try to cover and protect herself. When he hit her and she simply took it, or went sprawling and did nothing more than just lie there, the pleasure had worn out of it for him. Starvation, however, was a punishment she couldn't ignore as easily. On those few occasions she had dared to actually defy him, even if only just a little, it had been both starvation and a beating.

Obedience had meant survival, so she had forced herself to obey. Alys had learned many things that way, too, keeping her mouth shut and her demeanor subservient, while keeping her eyes and her ears carefully open. *Some-day, what I've learned . . . somehow, it'll put an end to my uncle's evil. Morganen was right, every time he told me that; without my aid, Wolfer and his brothers won't be able to stand up to him and survive, without the things I learned. Though the price I paid was shameful. Helping him do some of his evil deeds . . .*

Guilt and longing fought a longtime war inside of her; living with it was the only way she could deal with it, though it ate away at her heart, deep inside.

When the sun had dried her fur, she finally transformed back into a young woman, stumbled wearily to her feet, and brushed off the last grains of sand. Transforming while still wet only got her clothing wet, she had learned in the trial-and-error of her hidden, mostly self-taught lessons. But by transforming when she was dry, not even the brine-salt lingered behind, save as an easily shaken-off dust.

While she was still shaking off her cloak and skirts, she heard a noise. A growl. Whirling and letting out a gasp, Alys confronted the sound, afraid she might have to fight some wild beast. She was ready to transform and take flight if necessary, though she was very tired and hungry, and fly-ing took a lot of energy.

A large wolf—not pookrah sized, but still very large—crouched on the sand before her, his brownish fur fluffed menacingly around his ruff, his teeth bared intimidatingly, his golden tawny eyes narrowed in a fierce glare.

*Golden eyes. Brown fur. On Nightfall Isle . . . ?*

"Wolfer!" Alys scolded, her fear vanishing in a puff of irritation the instant she made the connection. "You *scared* me!"

The wolf blinked, whined as he stared at her, then backed up in uncertainty. But it was him; now that her fright wasn't clouding her senses, she recognized the shapeshifted magic surrounding him.

"Wolfer, it's me! Alys—remember?"

Wolfer blinked again. The breeze was the wrong direc-tion for him to scent her . . . but she sort of *looked* like Alys. She had more curves than he could recall, based on what he glimpsed through the folds of that scruffy wool cloak, and her hair was braided, not hanging free . . . but it was the same dark gold, escape-artist curls. The same curls that had been woven into the braid forever knotted around his human wrist.

This woman also had the same soft gray eyes, so differ-ent from his twin's steel, set in a delicate, oval face. She

had matured a little more since he had seen her last, but not
by that much. The wind shifted a little, curling her distinc-
tive, feminine scent toward him. He couldn't imagine how
he could remember it so clearly after three years of exile . . .
but he knew it the moment he sniffed the wind.

It *was* her.

With a shrug, he transformed back to his human self. He
had gone down to the beach to stare at the ocean, too restless to sleep, and had seen a shapeshifter changing shape
on the beach.

Alys studied him eagerly, drinking in the sight of his
brown trousers, his gray tunic, and the untamable chest-
length mane of mostly straight but thick, flyaway brown
hair he had to deal with. Just as she had to deal with her
own riot of old-gold curls.

Wolfer blinked, assimilating her presence on the isle.
*"Alys?"*

Smiling, she stepped forward. So did he, as she nodded
and spoke. "Yes, it's me!"

"Alys!" Wolfer broke into a grin. Charging forward, he
caught her up in a bear hug, lifting her up off the ground
and twirling his old playmate around. "Alys! Alys!"

She shrieked and laughed, squirmed for enough room in
his arms to breathe, then hugged him back. "Wolfer, oh
Wolfer—I've missed you!"

"I've missed you, too!" He cradled her body tightly to
his, burying his face in her hair.

Until his body started enjoying more than just their
friendly reunion and started taking note of the breasts, the
thighs, and the hips he held so close. Quickly, before she
could realize he was hardening, he set her down and held
her back from him. Ostensibly to take a look at her . . .
though just looking at those curves, ones he couldn't ever
remember really seeing before, didn't help matters.

"You look—" *Wrong topic!* He dropped his hands from
her shoulders and took a step back to gesture at her, seizing
on her mode of arrival. "I didn't know you had enough
magic to change your shape!"

"I finally settled into my power," she admitted on a slight smile and a shrug. "It's not much, but I can do it."

Wolfer looked around. "Did you have a ship, or come with any others? . . . Where is your uncle?"

Alys was glad she could say what she had to say, at his less-than-happy tone for his last question. "I ran away."

Wolfer snapped his gaze back to hers. "You what?"

She couldn't tell him everything; if she did, she didn't know how he would react—probably very, very badly, the moment he learned all the things she had had to do. They hadn't seen each other in more than three years, and not too often in the years immediately before that. Since she had gone to live with her uncle, in fact. But she did trust him enough to tell him some things; there was no way she could not trust him.

"I've hated every moment I've spent in my uncle's house, Wolfer. He's cruel and mean to a point you would not believe, and I've seen him do things that would shame your family, especially when your Uncle Daron died—"

"Uncle Daron died?" Wolfer interrupted, frowning at her. "Who sits in Corvis, now?"

She didn't want to say it. But she had to. "Uncle Broger. He's been the new Count of Corvis for almost three years, now. Pro tem," she added quickly, as his chest rumbled, increasing in volume. "But he's been acting as if it were the real . . . thing."

Wolfer cut off his reflexive growl, as her voice trailed off with that timidity he remembered so well from her. Gentle Alys. Honest Alys. He reined in his rage, automatically touching the bracelet she had given him years ago. "*We* have been receiving letters from our father's brother, all this time. Daron has been claiming that everything is mostly fine."

Alys closed her eyes and nodded. "He's like that," she confessed under her breath, understating the matter thoroughly. She shook her head. "You don't know what I've been through . . ." Opening her eyes, she looked up at him. "I could only think of one place to go, to escape him. To you—to Nightfall," she added quickly, stepping forward and laying her hand on his folded arm. "Please, Wolfer, please let me stay with you? I have nowhere else to go."

He couldn't resist her soft pleading; he never had been able to. There was something about Alys of Devries that had always softened him toward her, made him look out for her, ever since their first meeting when he had comforted her over a skinned knee. Her request would have been a difficult thing to grant, if this had been nearly two months ago, though Wolfer would have tried.

Before Kelly of Doyle had arrived, Saber would have tossed her off the island, for fear she might be the woman bringing his prophesied Disaster upon him. That Disaster had already come to them, forewarned by the arrival of the outworlder woman Kelly and triggered in the form of the Dominor-kidnapping Mandarites that had visited them just half a dozen days ago.

Newly wed, the eldest of the eight brothers had softened his stance toward women living on the isle. One couldn't escape one's Destiny, after all . . . and thankfully, there was only one Disaster predicted.

"Come," he told her, holding out his hand. "We'll go up to the castle and let everyone know you are here."

"Will there be food up there?" she asked wistfully, as she took his hand and started walking with him, though she didn't see any castle on the green-covered mountainside before them. "And water? I haven't eaten since noon yesterday . . ."

"Plenty of food, but it will take us some time to walk there—"

Alys tugged him to a stop. "Why don't we just change our shapes and fly there? It would be faster."

He flushed with embarrassment. Making her blink and stare. "I'm only just learning how to fly, and I'm not very good at it."

Her brows rose at that. "You've been a shapeshifter in full for, what, ten, eleven years, and you *haven't* got a winged form?"

"I'm afraid of heights," he mumbled. At her skeptical look, he clarified. "*High* heights. Cloud-height. Towers and trees, I can manage—and don't you laugh at me, Alys; it wasn't that long ago I locked your head under my arm and tried to start a fire in your curls with my knuckles!"

"Oh, I'm not laughing at you," she promised, eyes lowered demurely. Though for a moment he almost swore she had started to smile, before an oddly bland expression covered it up. A moment more beyond that, and her features relaxed into their normal expressiveness. "I have a pookrah form that can run really fast, faster than a wolf—"

"*Pookrah?*" Wolfer demanded. "What made you choose such an idiotic form, Alys? Do you *want* an army of mage-warriors on your trail, determined to kill you before they think you'll kill them?"

She shook her head; oddly, his anger gave her the courage to explain, instead of shrink back from him. Probably because she could tell it was out of his caring for her safety. "I had to learn how to make a pookrah shape, to escape my uncle. You don't know what it's been like, Wolfer—I had to create an illusion that a pookrah pack abducted me, then run off in pookrah form to leave a trail of paw prints behind, if multiplied many times by a spell, so that everyone would think I was dead."

"Why in Jinga's Name would you do *that*?" he demanded.

Shaking her head, Alys unclasped her cloak, then tugged down the demurely high neckline of her gown, just enough to reveal the four-point star of metal there. "I had to create *this*. It's a very special amulet; it severed all ties to my uncle. Every spell he placed on me, to obey him, to never run away, every spell set to find me, to tell him where I am, to allow him to scry for me—he could feel through the aether that his blood-kin is alive, though I am ashamed to be of his family.

"I *had* to create the illusion of the pookrah pack so that his soldiers witnessed me being dragged away from our camp, then enspell this pendant to my flesh, so that my uncle would then *believe* me to be dead, killed in the attack."

She lifted her anguished gray eyes to his golden ones, willing him to understand how much she *couldn't* yet say of what her life had been like, through what horrors she could relate. "I did my best to put him off, but he sold me, Wolfer. He sold me in marriage to the Baron of Glourick for land, for spell ingredients, and chests filled with gilder. And he had enough spells wrapped on me to enforce his will and bring me back if I simply ran without planning anything.

"So I planned very, very carefully and made my escape. I have nowhere else to go—I even saw my Uncle Donnock in Orovalis City just a day ago, though he didn't see me, thankfully. You don't know what I've been through. Please, let me stay!"

Wolfer growled softly again, but this time in impatience at her begging. "I've already *told* you that you could. And your uncle should be whipped to the bone for treating you that way. Women are *not* chattel!"

Her face melted into a smile, and she threw herself at him, wrapping her arms around his broad chest. Wolfer hugged her back, until the traitor in his breeches insisted she wasn't just his childhood friend anymore. Easing her away, he was grateful when she ducked her head and stepped back.

"I think I can remember a horse form, though it's been a little while," he rumbled, trying not to let her know how embarrassed he was by being aroused by her mere closeness—it was his blasted twin's fault, after all, taking his wife to bed so often and so vigorously every one of his brothers could hear it more often than not, and thus remember their own state of uncomfortable celibacy.

"I'm not very good at riding anymore, so you'll have to promise not to throw me," Alys warned him. "Uncle never let me go out riding very much, unless I absolutely had to go somewhere."

He started to growl at that, broke off to touch his left wrist . . . and raised it with a faint, sheepish smile as she glanced down in curiosity. "I'm still wearing it, your gift to me. You've probably saved my brothers from a lot of grief over these past three years. I've learned how to control my temper, touching it and thinking of you." His smile shifted to a wolfish one. "At least, I control it a little bit."

She smiled and stroked the braid, first one way, against the grain of her old gift of hair, then with it, trailing her fingertip all the way around. Just that touch, indirect and not even on his skin, made Wolfer want to shiver, to feel more. He lowered his arm, cleared his throat, and concentrated.

A moment later, he stood before her, a brown-coated, golden-eyed stallion. Luckily, she got too busy trying to mount him to look below his hindquarters. *Trying* to get up onto his back. She hopped and squirmed and tugged gingerly on his withers, but never quite made it all the way up, always dropping back into the sand with a thump.

"I can't get up on you!" she finally exclaimed, whapping him lightly in the shoulder. "You're too big, Wolfer!" As he whuffled her hair with his muzzle, she twined her fingers in his mane and tugged him up the beach. There was a rock nearby on the southern spur of the land, where the sand turned to pebbles, then stones, and jutted out into the bay a little ways, dividing it from the next sandy gray white bay with a low finger of somewhat rocky land. Climbing up onto a small boulder, she tugged him a little closer, tried to get on, then blushed and gripped her skirt. "Look away, Wolfer; you're not wearing a sidesaddle, and my skirt isn't exactly sewn wide enough for this."

Snorting, he swung his head away and watched her hike her plain brown skirt up above her knees anyway, with his excellent equine peripheral vision. There was an awkward moment of boot and knee and elbow, of a hand fisted in his mane for balance and control, and then she slid home on his back, settling perfectly in place just behind his withers. Just the thought of his spine being where another part of him wanted to be . . .

He snorted again, glad she was on his back now and couldn't see under his belly. *That's the gods-be-damned problem of being a shapechanging male; most animal forms are* not *designed for physical privacy.* The mage silently berated himself for being unreasonably randy, just

because there was now an unattached female on the island
again. Never mind that he hadn't felt anything for his
brother's wife, Kelly, when she had first arrived, before his
twin had come to his senses and claimed the petite virago.
Shuddering in an equine sigh, Wolfer started toward the
line of trees bordering the beach.

When he stopped and nudged a tree, it took Alys a few
moments to realize he was indicating that the tree they
were under had edible, ripe fruit on it. She had been marveling at the feel of riding bareback for the first time in her
life and what it did to her, knowing on whose back she was
riding, to the various intimate parts Cari had explained to
her. Hungry, she exclaimed her thanks and plucked a trio
of the fruits, trusting him to carry her gently while she
peeled away the rinds with her fingers and bit into the flesh
hidden by the pulpy skin. She was starving, and the fruit
was tangy-sweet, succulent.

While he crested the rise and dropped down to stride on
the damp-firm sand near the waterline in the next bay, Alys
ate her breakfast, rocked gently on his smooth-striding
back. She mmmed and she ahhed, and she moaned and
sucked her fingers, reveling in food, real food, her first
meal since the middle of the day before . . . and stopped
with about half of the third fruit left to go, realizing that
Wolfer wasn't moving anymore.

It slowly dawned on Alys that she had just made many
of the sounds the wench Cari had demonstrated for her, the
ways women often vocally expressed their passion. For a
long, long moment, they were perfectly still together, he
standing as stiff as a statue, she sitting as tight as a sculp-
ture. Their shadow stretched out to the right, away from the
morning sun.

Something about that stretch of gray caught her attention, but when she glanced that way, it took her a few moments to realize exactly what that something was. Horses
only had four legs, and their tail. Since all four of his
hooves were planted firmly on the sand, and his tail was
that shadowy fall at the back, stretched out on the sand by

the morning sun, *that* shadowy bit stretching out perpendicularly between his four legs could only . . . be . . .

*Oh my* . . . She was *not* ignorant of equine anatomy. Male equine anatomy. Alys barely breathed, waiting for revulsion to hit her. Her long and frank discussion with Cari seemed to have worked, though; she felt hot and liquid instead, not sickened and disgusted, especially by how his back spread her thighs wide. Where his spine rubbed against her mound. Her body relaxed, accepting that fact, knowing before she consciously did that she accepted it.

Then her mind caught up, and her heart skipped a beat. He wanted her.

*Well, either it's that, or it's just morning, and Cari said men are more "ready and able" in the morning . . . Oh, but Kata, I hope it's me!* Alys prayed . . . because she had been in love with Wolfer of Corvis, now Wolfer of Nightfall, ever since they had met when he was eight and she was three.

She still clearly remembered their first meeting. She had wobbled across one of the castle's courtyards, while her parents had been visiting to attend to some business affairs with the count and countess, shortly after moving away from her uncle's region of Katan. Toddling about on the flagstones, Alys had fallen and scraped her knee. Wolfer had come along, seen her on her bottom and clutching her knee, bawling at the little scratch that had already stopped bleeding, and had picked her up in his young arms. He had dusted her off, hugged her to make her feel better, and helped the three-year-old Alys onto his small but growing eight-year-old back for a cheer-her-up piggyback ride.

From that point on, Alys was his.

Not normally adventuresome, she had joined in his and his brothers' playing, because *he* had been in those games. She had pestered her parents until they visited often, more often than they had reasons of their own to, all so she could play with Wolfer, her friend. Wolfer, her hero. Wolfer, who had paid attention to her when his brothers didn't always want to play with a little girl, at that girls-are-icky stage young boys often went through. Wolfer, who had taught her how to hold a knife and how to climb a tree ... and who had allowed her to try four kisses on him when she was just beginning to blossom with female curves and everything. Before her parents had died, before her eldest uncle had taken her away, and before everything had changed ... he had been hers, though only she had known about it.

Finally, Wolfer snorted and shook his head and started across the sand again at a walk. A discreet glance at the shadow dancing across the sand showed he wasn't as aroused anymore. Disappointed, she finished the last half of her breakfast fruit in silence and discarded the peel to the tide and sand. Licking her fingers as clean as possible, she shifted the grip of her thighs, sat forward a little, and twined her fingers in his mane.

"I, um ... thanks for breakfast! I haven't eaten since noon yesterday," she avowed in a rush. "You could, uh, try a canter, now. If you wanted to."

What Wolfer wanted was to get her off his back and onto hers in the sand. Snorting, he lunged into a canter, hoping a good run would get the urge out of his system, as exercise often had in his three years of exiled celibacy. She yelped and clutched him with those thighs of hers, her fingers twining in his mane. He smoothed his gait enough for her to get used to his rhythm, which she did fairly quickly. He moved faster when she laughed and leaned forward more, moving with him in the exhilaration of their race over the beach.

"Faster! *Faster!*" Excited by the wild bareback ride, Alys felt no fear as he pounded across the sand, rocking smoothly, swiftly under her; this was her Wolfer, and she trusted him completely. The rhythm of his run rocked her back and forth, forward and back, and just a little from side to side; Alys was glad she was wearing knee-length undertrousers, because of the friction.

The rubbing motion felt wonderful, actually. As he lunged up the next low slope to the next cove, she shrieked and ducked low against his mane to avoid the oversized, overgrown, almost tropical leaves. Thin branches whipped at her body while they dashed through a short stretch of the jungle to get to the next stretch of beach.

The new position increased the pressure against the "pleasure pearl" that Cari had talked about—which looked nothing like a pearl, but was supposed to be as treasured and priceless as one for a woman, according to the wench. At least, Alys was fairly sure it had to be her pleasure pearl. Shivers of silk-like lightning crawled up through her veins, tickling her heart, her spine, and all over that place between her legs, deep inside as well as out on the surface. She shuddered, biting back a cry at the last moment as everything coalesced in a roll of ecstatic, silent thunder. Her eyes closed for a long moment, then snapped wide in shock.

Her first climax of pleasure?

Her toes curled in her boots. Her hair felt like it wanted to stand on end. She wanted to stand on Wolfer's back, beat her chest, and holler her joy to the world, all right! Breathless, trying to still cling to his back with leg muscles that felt like worn-out leather, she pushed herself upright. He slowed to keep her balanced, and she clenched her teeth as another wave of wet, hot lightning swept through her flesh with the shift in position. Another rolled through her, and another; each one arched her back and then relaxed her into straightening . . . and into hitting that point once more.

It wasn't easy, keeping silent in her pleasure. At least the experience was dying down. Wolfer swerved away from the sand and the surf. He trotted up through the shifting, dry part above the high-tide line and clopped onto a flagstone path that wound its way inland, up into the heart of the island between the two small mountain ranges. Blushing as she calmed down, Alys focused on recovering her composure while he carried her up into the forested hills. It wouldn't do for him to notice her reddened cheeks, after all.

He might even ask her why!

# FOUR

❦

Her thighs were feeling rather sore from clinging to Wolfer's equine-shaped back by the time he trotted up the last incline and stopped in front of a high stone wall. The section of wall stood not far from an even taller, broad tower. It was an imposing edifice of pale gray granite, carved along the tops of the crenellated ramparts with eight-point stars. Alys could tell there was a doorway in front of them only because the stones had been cut in a split arch shape. There were no handles, nor even so much as a bellpull.

At a snort from Wolfer, she dismounted—awkwardly, since there was no convenient boulder nearby—and tugged down her skirt. He quickly reverted to his human form, cleared his throat, and stepped forward with an upraised palm, muttering under his breath. The stone-faced doors swung open just far enough for both of them to enter, then swung shut behind them again as she hurried to follow him.

Alys moved forward, gasping in pleasure as she took in the intricately carved palace wing before them and the easternmost courtyard between gate and wing. Wolfer, letting her pass him, found himself sniffing at the air. He turned around, sniffing again . . . and blinked. He recognized that scent. *Aroused female*. He hadn't smelled that since . . . since—well, since last night, but then it had been his sister-in-law, and he had politely ignored it. Before Kelly's arrival, the last time he had smelled that scent had been before the brothers' exile. But this wasn't the scent of his twin's wife. This was . . . this was . . .

This was *her* scent that was so musky-aroused. Alys' scent!

He *hadn't* imagined her shuddering on his back toward the end of his run down on the beach. The way her thighs had clutched him with urgency, then relaxed with satiation. Or the aftershocks of her pleasure, once, twice, thrice, and maybe even more. *Kata, she found her pleasure on my back! Little innocent Alys . . . on my back?*

Not so innocent anymore! Wolfer stared at her, half deeply shocked, half deeply aroused . . . and completely hard. He was very glad she was still too busy taking everything in to look at him, too busy to even walk very far into the courtyard—he couldn't have walked after her if his life depended on it. Not with a normal gait.

By the time she finally faced him, her whole face alight with her delight, he felt halfway back to normal. Except that, smiling like that, she was achingly beautiful to him. The sight of her beaming at him caused his loins to thicken and heat again, even as her joy stole the breath from his lungs.

"It's *beautiful*, Wolfer," Alys praised breathlessly. "I'm so pleased you could stay in such a beautiful home, even if it is an exiled one."

He looked anywhere but at her. "My, ah, sister-in-law insisted on it. It was bad, when she first got here—but it's very nice, now. No weeds, no cobwebs . . ."

Alys nodded, finishing silently what he hadn't said. *No more invasions from forbidden beasts . . . at least not at the moment.* She pushed aside the guilt at that thought with the astonishment of another, eyeing him quickly, uncertainly. "Did you say *sister-in-law*?"

"Yes," he admitted on a rumble. "Saber married eight days ago. And Dominor was kidnapped six days ago, and Trevan was injured trying to rescue him that same day, but he didn't succeed. The Mandarites who visited us still have our brother, too; they've taken him across the sea to the East, beyond our reach."

"Oh!" She gave him an anguished look. "That's awful!"

"That's the Prophesied Disaster," he returned grimly. Then shook his head. "He is still alive; that much we know. Come—everyone will be glad to see you. It'll give us something else to think about, and something pleasant, at that."

Closing the distance between them, he caught her hand and led her into the east wing, at the point where it split into two extra wings. No one was within sight or sound, not even when they reached the great hall. Alys tipped her head back, looking at the arching, plaster-moulded dome of the ceiling far overhead and at the walls with their rippling, slowly changing shades of patterned paint, marveling at what she saw. Wolfer turned around, then called out, his bass voice ringing on a single, sung note.

*"Evanor!"*

*"Yes, O deep-voiced Brother?"*

"Ev, we have a guest," he stated, knowing their "communication" mage would hear him, now that Wolfer had his attention. "I'd like everyone to greet her; we're down in the great hall."

" *'Her'?"* Evanor exclaimed in his ear, via that magic vocal trick of his. Silence followed that single exclamation— silence, to Wolfer's perspective. He could easily imagine the earful his brothers and sister-in-law were receiving, however. Indeed, not half a minute later, the thundering of many sets of running feet converged on them from all directions.

Alys shrank back against Wolfer as she heard people running toward them. He wrapped an arm around her, giving her a little hug of encouragement. It was much the same as he used to do back when they were young and some new adventure of his brothers' had unnerved her. She would hang back in a longish moment of uncertainty before gathering up her courage and joining them, and that little one-armed hug of his always helped make her feel better about joining whatever the activity might be.

She was still taking comfort from his touch when a woman with strawberry gold hair, shoulder-length and lighter than she remembered Trevan's hair to be, skidded up to the balcony one level above on the left, almost flinging herself over the edge as she peered down at them. This must be the sister-in-law. Squinting, Alys could see above and through the carved stone banisters that she was wearing a cheerful green tunic, brighter than the dull green of one of the gowns Alys had left behind . . . and trousers, of all things! *She's wearing trousers, like a man!*

Shocked, intrigued, Alys watched the woman yank herself back from the railing as more came into view. An auburn-haired man she remembered fairly well, if not quite as grown-up looking as he was now, burst into the hall. He skidded on the polished flagstones, eyed her and smiled, his hazel eyes not showing any signs of recognition as he strolled forward.

"Well, hello, lovely lady! Who do we have here?" Koranen enquired warmly, lightheartedly, as he eyed her without a single trace of recognition in his gaze.

The other redhead in the family, the one with the sun-streaked copper-blond curls, came in from yet another archway. "Greetings! Greetings! Welcome to Nightfall, fair maiden; I trust there is something we can do to ensure your stay is a most *pleasurable* one?"

That was Trevan, smooth to the last. From his equally curious look, *he* didn't remember her, either. Wolfer growled under his breath at his brother's flirting, but only for a moment.

Another brother entered the hall, light blond with brown eyes, still wiping his hands on a towel. Evanor, she recalled. He frowned softly at her; Alys struck a chord with this twin, it seemed, but he obviously couldn't quite yet place her.

The woman with the shoulder-length strawberry hair joined them, the eldest of the brothers at her side. His hair was the same old gold shade as Alys', but straight where hers was vigorously curled. Saber, Wolfer's elder twin. He blinked and frowned at her, opened his mouth, and shook his head. And one more arrived, though not the brother she remembered preferring to shun the day. Rydan wouldn't come to greet her until after sunset, she was sure. The youngest of the eight siblings was another matter.

"Alys!" Morganen hurried forward, arms outstretched.

Alys tore herself away from Wolfer's embrace and flung herself into his arms. "Morganen!"

Her throat choked on words, eyes stinging with tears threatening to shed. He hugged her to him and made soothing sounds, letting her know he understood. Letting her hold him, the one person who had helped her all he could by giving her lessons in her magic and giving her support and advice, though he had been literally a thousand miles away, naught but a reflection in pool or mirror for too many years.

Wolfer narrowed his eyes; he didn't like what his youngest brother was doing, not one damned bit! A sharp elbow dug into his side, cutting off the growl forming deep in his throat. Shifting his gaze, he met Kelly's aquamarine one, saw her arched, curiosity-raised brow, and locked it down inside, absently fingering Alys' braid on his wrist. Alys finally drew back from Morganen, wiping at her eyes, as the others moved forward with exclamations of belated recognition. She responded to each of the grown men she had once played with as children.

"It's so good to see you all! Trevan, Wolfer told me about your injury, and I'm glad to see you're well." She gave him a brief hug. "Koranen—you've finally filled out!" An embrace for him, as he blushed; he was the last of them to physically mature, though technically he wasn't the youngest; his twin was, but she had already greeted that brother. She turned to the others. "Evanor, Wolfer told me about Dominor; I'm so sorry."

The blond member of the brothers accepted her consoling embrace, blinking a little at her honest, deep sympathy. Hugging her back, he released her without saying a word. The loss was still fresh for him; even more so than for the others, since it was his twin that was missing.

"Saber! I can't believe you're married!" she exclaimed, embracing the last of the brothers gathered in the hall, equally as brief as the rest, except for Morg. Stepping back, she held out her hands to the last one in the group around her, the only one not familiar. "And you must be Saber's wife; I'm Alys—I used to play with these men when we were all young."

"I'm Kelly, and I think I've already heard of you," Kelly added, glancing at Wolfer and his bracelet. She peered past Alys at the hall. "Did you come alone?"

"I've . . . run away from home," Alys admitted. She glanced anxiously at the others. "I asked Wolfer if I could stay, but this is your home, too. I just . . . I don't have anyone else to go to and nowhere else to stay."

"Her *uncle* was attempting to sell her in marriage to the highest bidder," Wolfer growled, explaining it to the others. They exclaimed at the outrageous statement. "There's more!" he added, cutting through their noise. "She says Broger is the new Count pro tem of Corvis . . . and that our Uncle Daron has been dead since two months after we left Corvis lands. Our letters from Uncle these past three years have been nothing but lies."

"It's true," Alys agreed, informing all of them as they muttered darkly . . . except the one who already knew. The one who had counseled her to be patient, and to wait for the right time. Now it was finally time. Her voice hardened, tightened in a brief surge of courage. "My uncle has a *lot* to answer for."

"Well, your uncle sounds like a horrid, chauvinistic, thoroughly impolite person," Kelly asserted, taking Alys by the shoulders and turning her toward one of the archways. "And you probably have had a long journey and are in need of a bath and a rest and some food and proper

Nightfall hospitality. Now that I've got these bachelors and their home whipped into shape, that is," she added, drawing Alys away from the others. "Did you have any baggage, any belongings?"

"No, just what I'm wearing."

Kelly eyed Alys' clothes and shook her head. "Well, you're in *slightly* better shape than I was when I arrived; I was in my nightclothes. Burned nightclothes, at that, but it's a long story—you're lucky I can communicate now, too. Morganen fixed me up with this nasty-tasting stuff called Ultra Tongue, some sort of potion that thankfully allows me to speak and read Katani and any other language I've encountered so far. Don't you worry; we'll get you fixed up right away: clothes, potions, food to eat, a bed to sleep in. You've got a fuller figure than I do, but I think I have a few things made up that you can fit into. Saber's been fattening me up ever since I arrived."

"You're very kind," Alys murmured in gratitude, liking the woman, even if she was a bit more take-charge than Alys was accustomed to seeing. Her uncle didn't put up with that in his servants, and he hadn't remarried after his wife had died, which was before Alys had had to live with him, so everyone, including Alys, had been a servant to him.

At her comment, though, Alys heard more than one of the brothers snort with suppressed laughter behind her. She craned her neck and looked over her shoulder. Several of them had turned away, covering their mouths, hugging their chests, their shoulders quivering, their cheeks turning red. Only one wasn't laughing. A pair of wolf-gold eyes remained fastened on her, all but devouring her.

The heat in his stare reminded her of the heat in her body, galloping on Wolfer's equine back at the edge of the sea.

ℳmm. Heavenly."

"It is, isn't it?" Kelly agreed, eyeing the somewhat younger woman sunk almost to her nose-tip in steaming bathwater. They were in the west wing, near the split in the Y-shape of the wing, and not that far from Wolfer's chambers. The redhead had finally wormed all of the verses of the "Song of the Sons of Destiny" out of her husband in the past few days; his was more or less completed, and now they had seven more to go through. If order of age was anything to go by, Wolfer was next in line to fall for a woman. And if the looks he had been giving the woman in the bath and the growl he had given at this young woman hugging his youngest brother were anything to go by . . . Wolfer was definitely the next one in line to fall.

*Or perhaps he has already fallen*, Kelly thought with a touch of amusement.

This particular suite of rooms had a small room dedicated to bathing and changing clothes, with shelves lining its walls; another door led into what she liked to think of as a half-bath of sink and water-flushed facilities, or what the Katani of this world liked to delicately call a "refreshing room." It also possessed a bedroom with room for a bed, one of the padded, carved couches all the furnishings seemed to be styled in, a table, dressers, and a few bookshelves. Those were currently cluttered with knickknacks she hadn't found a better place for yet, and which would probably get stuffed into another guest chamber somewhere else in the castle, if the room's new occupant didn't want them.

"So, tell me, Alys; how did you meet the brothers?"

Alys smiled and surfaced far enough to talk. "I was three. My parents had moved away from their family home, because my eldest uncle Broger—the one I was forced to stay with after my parents died almost ten years ago—well, he lived there, and my father didn't like him. So we moved down to a freeholding near Corvis lands, and one day my parents had to do some business with the Count and Countess. I remember being in the courtyard and walking around, looking at everything. At one point, I fell and scraped my knee and started howling. And Wolfer—he was eight or so—came along, picked me up, hugged me, and gave me a piggyback ride to make me feel better. Since we lived so close, about two miles through the woods and meadows the short way, ten miles along the roads, I just . . . kept asking my parents to take me over there so I could play with them, until—"

"Until your parents died and you had to go live with your uncle?" Kelly asked for confirmation. Getting a nod, she handed over a pot of soft soap and a terry cloth scrubbing rag.

Alys eyed the nubbly fabric warily, then exclaimed with delight as she tried it out.

Kelly did a little bit of calculating. "If Saber and Wolfer are twenty-nine . . . that makes you twenty-four?" At Alys's nod, Kelly said, "Ah. I'm twenty-seven . . . and I should warn you, not only do I occasionally have a redhead's temper, I'm also from another universe entirely."

Alys blinked and looked at her, startled by that revelation, and Kelly shrugged.

"On my world, a place called Earth, magic doesn't work very well. And out of ignorance, the less-enlightened masses tend to fear it. Machines do everything for us, not spells, which makes magic scary, you see. I was almost killed by some people who were afraid I might be an evil witch, just because I liked to do different things than they did, things they didn't understand, even though there really aren't any real spells or witches of any kind where I come from. More or less," Kelly amended, thinking of her friend Hope, and Hope's claim to psychic sensitivity. "But I'm here now, and Saber and I fell in love, and I've pretty much completed the first verse—at least, we all pray and hope I have—of the Curse of Eight Prophecy."

"Really? Then you're . . . you're the one who was supposed to bring a Disaster at her heel that would ruin all of Katan?" Alys asked her. "It was all anyone would discuss when the brothers were exiled."

"No," Kelly corrected, tipping her reddish-gold head, "my presence in Saber's bed allowed us to notice an incoming disaster-in-disguise in time to meet and deal with it. Katan *refused* to aid us in dealing with it. The '*And Katan will fail to aid*' part of Saber's verse was grossly misinterpreted by everyone: by the Katani, by the brothers . . .

"Anyway, their interpretation and failure to aid us in handling the problem fulfilled the Prophecy," Kelly enlightened her, "because the mainland exiled the brothers, putting them out here in the right place and time to intercept the Mandarites when they came here looking for land to conquer and loot. Which was a month and a half after Morganen scried me burning in my bed and rescued me by bringing me into this world." She smirked. "That was plenty of time for me to fight with Saber, fall in love, get married, and have the Mandarites show up practically on our doorstep the morning after our wedding."

"Oh. Who are the Mandarites?" Alys asked, scrubbing at her body with the strange, nubbly washing cloth that felt so much better than rough linen or wool did.

Kelly did her best to summarize what had happened. "There's a continent on the far side of the Eastern Ocean, where all or almost all of the women are the only ones born with magical abilities. Apparently, a long time ago the whole culture was like what your uncle tried to do to you— treated women as chattel and little more. But then the women turned the tables, using their magic to make the men subservient instead. Of course, some of the men didn't like that and rebelled. And they carved out a kingdom of their own called Mandare and started working on technological, nonmagical ways to fight back, since their men weren't born with magic very often.

"They came out here looking for land and resources, arrived in the east bay right after our wedding night—Saber did a marvelous job of fulfilling that wonderfully naughty last line of the first verse, 'when sword in sheath is claimed by maid,' " she added drolly, as Alys blushed, "and *very* nicely, too—and that was when we whipped up an impromptu 'Kingdom of Nightfall' with myself as Queen, Saber as my Consort, and the rest acting as courtiers.

We—or should I say, they—even created illusions of people to fill in all of these empty halls; we did everything we could think of to impress the Mandarites and send them on their way. Since the rest of Katan officially wants nothing to do with us, thus 'failing' to aid us as prophesied, we did our best to help ourselves . . . but it wasn't enough, in the end. The Disaster happened anyway."

"Ah." Unable to think of anything else to say, Alys stood up out of the water and balanced on the edge of the bathing tub to finish scrubbing her legs.

"There's more," Kelly informed her. "Dominor was playing the part of Lord Chancellor—I lost my temper at the attitude of their leader, Lord Aragol, and ordered him off the island, you see, which was our intent all along . . . but I digress. Dominor escorted them back to their ship and did his best to soothe any hurt feelings, except that Lord Aragol offered a trade of something called *comsworg* oil. He wanted the salt blocks this island produces as a part of its magical water-filtration system—we have plenty of fresh, pure water, so bathe and drink all you want," she added in an aside. "The Mandarite earl asked Dominor, a mage, to go on board their ship and help seal their hold against leaking; Trevan said this was so that the salt would remain high-quality pure."

Alys nodded in comprehension. Kelly drew in a breath, then let it out. Here came the hard part to admit.

"And then they did something to him so he couldn't escape and couldn't even respond when Evanor called to him, and sailed away. Trevan gave chase, but they injured him with a gun, one of their machine-weapons. A kind of weapon that I'm familiar with in my own world. The weapon is strong enough to injure whomever it hits, even when its target is heavily shielded. Trevan is pretty much healed, but Dominor's still out there somewhere, eastbound on a ship none of us can reach, and there's no way to scry for him until he can contact us somehow, since we don't know his location well enough for his brothers to find him that way. And *all* of us are feeling guilt-ridden over it."

"I'm sorry," Alys murmured, moving on to her hair next, sitting back down in the stone-carved tub.

"Hey, it's not your fault. It's just my Disaster. And Saber's," Kelly said. She waited until Alys finished dunking and rinsing her hair, then eyed her thoughtfully. "You realize, of course, that there are seven bachelors left on this island, and seven more women-inspired verses to go . . ."

Alys blushed again. She knew the verses by heart. She had learned them as soon as the rumors had started in earnest, regarding the Corvis brothers. In fact, she had clung to the rules of the lines with hope in her heart, all this time.

"Do I detect a little blush?" Kelly teased her. "Hmm. Maybe I should test a theory here: . . . *Wolfer?*"

Alys tried not to blush again. She certainly didn't look Kelly's way.

"Wolfer . . . *naked.*"

The younger woman ducked immediately underwater, where the heat of her blazing cheeks made the warmth of the bathwater feel cool in comparison and heard the out-worlder laugh.

"Come out of there! I won't say a word, I promise! Unless you do something stupid," Kelly added, as Alys came back up and wiped at her face, grateful to be able to breathe. "I have a low tolerance threshold for stupidity in adults who are old enough to know better."

"I'll try not to be stupid," Alys said.

"Sorry; I tend to 'open mouth and insert foot' sometimes," Kelly apologized. "I didn't actually mean *you.* After all, you haven't really done anything stupid yet. I don't think you will anytime soon, either. You don't strike me as that kind of woman."

The odd expression made Alys' mouth quirk up, relaxing her. She glanced at the aquamarine-eyed woman. " 'Open mouth and insert foot'—I like it."

"Good. Because I've been dying for female companionship for almost two months, now, and you're it for the time being. Not that I'll be pestering you too much right away;

Saber and I *are* newly married, you know," the older woman added, smiling.

Alys, thinking of all that Cari had told her, bucked up her courage. "Do you like it?"

Kelly eyed her. "Like what? Marriage? Or the newly married, going at it like rabbits part?"

Alys blushed. "The . . . second part."

"Oh, yeah! I get hot just *thinking* about it." Kelly fanned herself with a hand, then stilled and eyed Alys, where she was scrubbing herself in the tub. "Do you know anything about . . . the marriage bed?"

Grateful for the delicate question, Alys allowed herself to be bold and confessed. "I had a two-hour lecture from a . . . a tavern wench on the whole subject yesterday, before heading out here."

"A tavern wench?" One of Kelly's strawberry blond brows arched up at that. "As in . . . ?"

Alys blushed once more. "A whore. I saw my Uncle Donnock coming down the street, panicked, and ran into this . . . brothel-tavern in Orovalis City, out on the eastern shore. Only he came inside, so I fled upstairs, and the next thing I knew—I—I was hiding in a wardrobe, and Cari and this other man were—right *there*! In the room with me! She discovered me in the cupboard after he had left, and she was really nice, and told me all sorts of things, but I'd seen my Uncle Broger doing it to his serving wenches, and they didn't seem to like it at all . . ."

"Wait a minute; you saw your *uncle*?"

Alys flushed and looked down at the water.

Kelly narrowed her eyes. "Was this deliberate on his part?"

"Yes."

"Did he rape you?"

Somehow, the blunt words didn't shock her, not coming from this particular woman. "No. But he wanted to. I convinced him I was worth more as a virgin . . . so he didn't." When Kelly stayed silent, Alys looked up. The aquamarine-eyed, strawberry-haired woman was glaring out the narrow quartet of windows illuminating the room, her expression rather fierce. "Kelly? Is something wrong?"

"He should not only be *made* to eat dirt, he *is* dirt! And I'd hoped I'd left that kind of sick perversion behind on my *own* world!" the redhead hissed.

"*Your* uncle treated you that way, too?" Alys asked, shocked.

"No. No, nothing like that," Kelly said, shaking her head and looking at Alys again. "But those sorts of atrocities were beginning to be discussed openly by my culture, to help the victims and punish the perpetrators and hopefully make others think twice about doing anything like that themselves.

"*Real* love isn't sick like that—and Alys, *it is not your fault*," Kelly said slowly and clearly, holding Alys' gray gaze firmly. "You didn't do anything to deserve that kind of treatment. I can tell just by being around you, and for less than half an hour, that you're not a woman who teases men mercilessly. *You* didn't do anything to cause it. This is entirely your uncle's shame. In fact, you are to be commended for redirecting his attention so well. You're very brave."

"Thank you—Cari thought it was smart of me, too. That's the wench I talked to."

"She sounds like a nice woman. I wish I could meet her," Kelly said. "But I'm kind of stuck on the isle, at the moment."

"You would actually want to meet a whore?" Alys asked, surprised.

"I try to judge people on their actions and their motivations. If she's happy doing that kind of work, then I'm glad she likes her job, and I hope she makes lots of money and never catches a social disease from it," Kelly stated firmly. She eyed the younger woman in the tub. "Hold up your fingers."

Alys drew them out of the water. They were pruny and wrinkled. Kelly grinned.

"Okay, we know you haven't been bitten by a water-snake. Time to get out, young lady, and dry off while I run over to the sewing hall and fetch back some clothes."

"Watersnake?" Alys asked with a sinking feeling in the pit of her stomach. About a month ago, her uncle had forced her to help him teleport a clutch of his watersnakes to Nightfall, scry-linked through the eyes of one of his wyverns. She hadn't actually sent them, but she'd been forced to fetch and hold the spellbound cage until he was ready for them.

Kelly chuckled, holding out one of the nubbly terry cloth towels she had shown the brothers how to make on her arrival. "My very first night here, we were attacked by mekhadadaks—and mind you, it took me a month to learn how to say that name. Then, several weeks later, wyverns and watersnakes. And demonling-things in another wing in the same attack, though I didn't see them, myself. I was in the room the snakes were teleported into. Saber got bitten, though he got most of the poison out, and I soaked a pair of slippers to the skin stomping on them. I'll tell you, I can laugh about it now, but at the time . . .

"It also forced the two of us into, how shall I say . . . ? *Intimate* contact, when he'd been stomping around, glaring at me, and resisting his Destiny very vigorously until then." She shook her head wistfully. "We must have talked for eighteen hours straight, stuck in that tub together . . . well, between soaking and drinking and running to the refreshing room, while the poison worked its way through our systems.

"They tell me they used to be attacked once every week or two, until I cleaned up the castle and made everything look different. Then Morganen came up with this color-changing paint," the talkative outworlder added, gesturing at the walls that had looked like a pattern of green-on-green tropical leaves before Alys had begun her bath, and which now looked like a gentle, star-studded, dark blue night sky.

Alys blinked at the slowly shifting designs, amazed; the changes had been so subtle, she hadn't even realized they were happening! "This . . . this stuff changes the appearance of the rooms and the halls enough so that it's hard for . . . for anyone to teleport anything in here, doesn't it?"

Kelly nodded. "Yep."

"It foils the mage or mages who have been sending these creatures, for they cannot scry by mirror over the distance; their memory or painting or whatever of the room is too different to succeed, anymore," Alys figured out, rubbing herself with the stimulating, odd, nubbly textured drying cloth as she stared at the slowly changing walls around them. "From hour to hour, the room subtly changes, and that means it is never consistent!"

It was amazing, really; a genius-level piece of self-defense against scrying. *This* was the reason why her uncle had been thwarted of late! She was glad of it, too, though Lord Broger hated being thwarted in anything and usually took it out on whomever was near at hand.

"Kata . . . mages and nobles would pay a fortune for the secret to this paint!" Alys exclaimed, eyeing the walls.

Kelly nodded her strawberry-copper head.

"Exactly. But I don't think the boys are going to sell the secret of it any time soon. So . . . we haven't been attacked, lately—though that could change at any time—and we've only suffered the Mandarites of late. But that was more than bad enough," Kelly muttered. She sighed and smiled. "I'll go fetch some clothes, and we'll see what fits you; I've been cutting my own clothes loose, since I've been gaining back the weight I lost. I was in bad shape before I came here; the people who tried to burn me down in my own house ruined my sewing business to the point where I could barely afford food, so I was slowly starving to death. But now I'm getting it all back . . . so long as I avoid Saber's cooking."

Alys frowned at that. "What's wrong with Saber's cooking? I didn't even know he *could* cook."

"He does. As they all can, more or less . . . but his

brothers don't let him do it often." Kelly tucked her hands on her waist, cocking one hip slightly. "Let me put it this way. You know how Koranen's associated with fire?"

Alys nodded. She'd seen him burn down a henhouse accidentally, when his magic had started developing years ago. "I know he is the Son that is Flame, yes."

"Well, so is Saber's spicy cooking."

Alys grinned. "I take it you don't like it?"

"Once in a while, maybe, when I get a craving for *chili*, but I'd rather have *him* hot and spicy in my bed." And with a wicked grin, Kelly took herself out of the bathing chamber.

# FIVE

### ❧

**T**rousers. She was wearing trousers. Loose-legged, gathered at the ankle, with a thigh-length tunic over them. Alys had also been given fresh under-trousers and a half-length corset that was wonderfully cool in the heat of this summer climate. It was distinctly warmer than the one she had known back around the Corvis and Devries lands.

The outfit had been stitched from cool, cheerfully dyed cotton in shades of green and blue. With her hair still damp, but detangled with hair lotion and combed out, then pulled back into the braid she had grown used to wearing—to keep it out of the cages of her uncle's "pretties" while she was feeding them, lest they yank her in for a different meal—and wearing trousers of all things, Alys felt . . .

"They give you a real sense of freedom, don't they?" Kelly sighed, eyeing her new female companion.

"Yes. Yes, they do!" Alys agreed, looking up from her clothes at the other woman. She stepped forward and then strode forward, then jumped a little, spread her feet on landing, and bent her knees. That was the exact word for it: *freedom*. "I *like* this!"

"Where I come from, women get to wear just about anything they want," the other woman confessed as Alys spun around, delighted in the freedom of movement. "Of course, I get away with it here because I'm from another universe, but if you like, I'll formally decree that everyone can wear whatever they want—within certain general bounds of decency—whenever they want to wear it."

"Decree?" Alys asked, stopping mid-spin.

Kelly shrugged mock-modestly. "I *am* the Queen of Nightfall, after all. Well, on weekends, holidays, and when visitors are here."

Alys raised a puzzled brow at that, then shook her head. "If you say so . . ."

"So, what do you like to do?" Kelly asked her.

"Do?" Alys repeated, confused.

"I do sewing, and embroidery, knitting, crocheting. Evanor, who's the most domesticated of the brothers— he'll make a fantastic househusband for some lucky woman someday—is showing me how to weave on one of the looms in the sewing hall. That's what *I* do. I embroider and sew and make clothes. Quilts. Pillows," the woman stated with a shrug. "I used to make rag dolls, though since we're isolated here, and since the guys don't want to advertise the fact that there are women here in case someone comes hunting for us, I haven't got any reason to make rag dolls for sale anymore, and I have no kids yet to make them for." Kelly eyed her, tucking a stray lock of her straight, strawberry blond hair behind her ear. "So what do you like to do?"

"I . . . can feed things. Different types of animals. I could probably hunt, though I'm much more of a caretaker. So long as they're not vicious," she added firmly, thinking once again of her uncle's "pretties." "I don't want *anything* to do with vicious creatures, ever again."

"Well, in that case, feeding the chickens is out," the other woman muttered wryly. "I had that chore once. *Once*," Saber's wife added in emphasis, mock-shuddering. "They not only pecked me to death around the knees, half of them got out of the coop, and it took over an hour for the others to catch them—they're *vicious*, trust me."

Alys shook her head. "Oh, no, that's not vicious. I could feed the chickens and anything else you have; I'm not going to stay here and do nothing to recompense you. I do know how to spin, weave and sew, and crochet, though I'm not very good at embroidery. And I can cook, and clean—oh, and garden. I'm good at helping things grow and keeping chattel-animals healthy."

"Well, we only have the chickens, and that's mostly for fresh eggs. But I *would* like some milk, if we could get a handful of dairy cows and a bull to keep them in calves," Kelly mused aloud. "We get cheese and butter on the trading ships, but it's not the same thing as milk and cream."

"I could take care of the cows," Alys offered. "And milk them, and even make cheese." Her uncle had taken delight in making her do servant's work all day long. She hadn't minded, because it limited how much time she had to spend with him. If not necessarily with his vicious pets, which had to be fed twice daily.

"I'll speak to Saber. The traders are due here tomorrow—not that they're going to be very happy, after tomorrow," she added with a little shrug. "We get the fresh water from the ocean, through some sort of water-purifying thing in some buildings down by the west shore that extract the algae and the salt. The algae's apparently great for fertilizer, once it's composted a little while, and the salt's been just taken for free by the traders, in these big, coffin-sized blocks," Kelly explained, stretching out her arms to indicate the huge size. "But I've declared all of the resources of Nightfall to belong to its citizens, which means they belong to the eight brothers and me—and now you—so we're going to fight to keep the salt and start trading it for profit."

"That might be difficult," Alys agreed. "No man likes having to pay for something when he's used to getting it for free. Cari told me that."

"A smart woman. Saber's still cautious about advertising

my—our—existence here, but the way I see it, Katan threw them away and this island with them; they don't have any right to anything on or immediately around this island anymore. Not the fish in its reefs, not the fruit on its shores, and not the salt blocks its water system makes." She braced her hands against her hips. "So I'm going to fight for it. This is my home now, and *I* say what goes on in my home."

"You're . . . rather fierce, aren't you?" Alys ventured hesitantly. And watched as the other woman blushed.

"Yeah, I guess I am." She eyed Alys, then smiled. "*I* know what we can do . . ."

Eyeing her hesitantly, Alys wondered what that could be. "What?"

"I'm going to do you a favor and introduce you to the art of *kung fu*. You're going to love it—and if you ever encounter your uncle again, and he's nasty to you, he's going to hate it. Trust me."

"My uncle only cares about art if it's worth a lot of money; he neither hates it nor likes it," Alys stated.

Kelly laughed. "It's not really *art*, like a painting on a wall. Just trust me, you'll love it. But the first thing we have to do is pick a room, get it cleared of furniture, make some practice mats to pad the floor—well, actually, I think for you a tour of the castle would be the *first* thing to do, right?"

"I suppose so," Alys agreed. "I've never been here before, and it looks large enough to get thoroughly lost in."

"You'll get used to it," Kelly promised. "I learned where everything was by bullying the brothers into cleaning the place, and it was a disgusting mess at the time. I am very glad *they* did the vast majority of it, using their magic and their muscles; I tried my hand at doing it the hard, non-magical way, and I'd *much* rather bully them any day. Come on; I'll show you all around."

Hips. Hips that swayed. Hips that sashayed. Arms that hovered in a bent, almost clasped position at the base of her ribs, just above her waist, so that the hands were close together. Emphasizing the dip of that waist just below them, the flare of those hips . . . the breasts mounding soft and full above by the lacing of her undergarment, underneath her somewhat tight tunic.

"Wolfer?" Alys repeated, leaning in a little closer with a concerned look. "Are you all right? I just asked you a question."

Wolfer blinked and tore his mind—or rather, a part of him that had nothing to do with his mind—away from her body. *When had she grown up? When did she become a woman? Why the hell didn't I notice all those years ago?* He looked at her eyes, just over half a foot lower than his; at the same height as Kelly. That made her seven inches shorter than his six-foot-one. Still within reasonable kissing height. "What was the question?"

Alys liked the depth of his voice, the way it rumbled from some deep, secret place in his chest. It made her own chest expand in pleasure . . . and his gaze slipped down again for just a moment. "I said, could you come and help Kelly and me move some furniture?"

"Furniture?" he repeated, then blinked and shook his head, frowning. "What *is* it with that woman, anyway?" Wolfer demanded. "We just *moved* the Gods-be-damned furniture, last month!"

"Kelly needs to empty your twin's old suite of all the furniture, so we can have a . . . 'kungfoo' room, whatever that means." Alys frowned herself, looking up at him. "Do *you* know what that means?"

"How should I know?" he growled irritably. "Saber's the one who married her! It's probably some strange, other-worldly thing of hers—and why are you wearing trousers?"

Alys straightened and gave him a look that bordered somewhere near brave and unbudging. "I *like* trousers. Kelly convinced me to try them, and they fit, and I like the way they feel on me. So I'm not taking them off!"

His golden eyes darkened slightly, his lips parting on an

indrawn breath as he thought of her without any covering on her legs at all. The way he had glimpsed them out of the corner of his equine-shaped eye for just a brief moment on the beach that very morning. He licked his dry lips; her gray eyes caught the movement and stared in fascination, almost as if she had never seen a man lick his lips before. Wolfer instinctively did it again. More slowly. Her own lips parted; her tongue came out, touching her own rose-pink softness, which he longed to lick himself—

"There you are!" The moment was ruined, shattered by Kelly's cheerful call. She came over and clasped her hands around one of Wolfer's biceps. Well, as much as the red-head could, considering the size of his arm. "So, are you going to flex these muscles and help us clear out Saber's old room?"

Alys didn't like how at ease the other woman was with touching Wolfer. Especially when she longed to do just that herself. "Did you find your husband and ask him to help us?"

"Saber's already clearing out the last of his personal stuff," Kelly said. She frowned slightly, eyed Alys, arched a brow . . . then smiled, just a little. A sly, secret-holding, feminine smile. She patted Wolfer's arm then let go of him. "Since Saber's under my command, you can command his twin, here, to your heart's content. Wolfer, you *will* promise to obey her every whim, won't you?"

He eyed his sister-in-law suspiciously. "What do you mean by that?"

Kelly gave him an innocent look as Alys blushed. "Exactly that. She and I are moving that furniture, but we need your muscles, so if she asks you to move a chest or move the bed, you'll move it, right?"

Remembering what Cari had told her about men, ego, and flattery, Alys nudged her shyness into boldness and stepped forward, touching his other arm. She half-caressed it with her palm, her fingertips, making him glance down at her. "That is what men have muscles for, isn't it? To make them big, and hard, and to use them to make a woman happy by . . . by moving the bed, when asked nicely?"

*She couldn't . . . she didn't just . . .* Wolfer choked inside, colored outside. His bicep twitched under the stroke of her fingers, the resting of her palm, bulging into her touch.

"You're so much bigger than I am," Alys added, blushing a little, rubbing his impressively sized muscles with her thumb, unwilling to stop touching him. "I can't make the bed move without your help."

*Jinga's Balls, I want to make that bed move!* he swore silently. But not across the floor—not unless it was from the sheer strength of him thrusting into her. His blood pounded in his ears, pooled in his groin. Certain parts of him were certainly willing to try.

"Bring him along, Alys," Kelly ordered, turning on her heel and walking away. "*Now*, Alys," she added over her shoulder, as neither of the other two moved.

Alys stroked her fingers over his skin again. He caught her hand as her fingertips trailed down toward the sensitive skin on the inside of his elbow. Wolfer growled softly at her. "Don't play with me."

Golden brown lashes lifted, and soft gray eyes looked up at him. Her lips pursed, forming half-whispered words. "But we've always played with each other."

He wanted to curse—she *sounded* innocent, now. He forced himself to gently remove her hand. "We're adults, now. We cannot play with each other as we used to do as children."

*I know*, Alys wanted to say, but he stepped around her and strode down the hall before she could. She watched him walk away . . . and found herself admiring the strength of his shoulders, the flexing of his muscles, his easy, graceful, masculine gait. Sighing, she followed him. She was always following him. She needed to take the lead sometime soon.

If she could find the bravery to do it in full, instead of just in little snatches, that was. Alys feared it would take full-time bravery to snare the Wolf, and she wasn't a full-time-bravery kind of woman.

An hour later, she didn't care about being brave. Wolfer had taken his shirt off. Instantly, the intensity of her beach ride came back to her. She felt the trembling heat return, the ache she had felt while staring at his blatantly aroused shadow.

With the noon heat radiating through the open windows, even on the southern side of the northwestern wing at the split end of the western spoke of the palace, it was hot in the room. Longing to strip off her own clothes, she wiped at the sweat on her face, which was beading from the effort of carrying the smaller items—stools, cushions, pillows, and bedding—from Saber's old room to another of the guest chambers in that end of the wing. Now that he apparently lived in that fancy chamber on top of the great hall's dome, the eldest of the eight brothers had no need for the room. His wife did, however.

Not all of the rooms were completely furnished, though the larger items had been left behind by successive generations of exiled families. Alys and Kelly both learned from stray comments of the two men that others who had been exiled had usually lived on Nightfall until they died and the isle was abandoned again. The heirs and those servants allowed to accompany them—none in the brothers' case, and especially no women—were allowed to leave at any time. They usually removed themselves when the exiled persons died, to go take up the estates held in pro-tem trust until the death or return of the exiled members.

In all of the wings, the practical rooms were in the straight sections closest to the donjon at the heart of the palace. Those included the herb room, kitchen, dining hall, sewing room, and ale room in the north wing—though technically the kegs were kept in the basement of the donjon—along with other storage rooms and even a dungeon, replete with cells, keys, and chains. Kelly and Alys had both wrinkled their noses at that particular part of the tour, though at least the brothers hadn't needed to do much work to scour everything clean. Whatever horrific use the chamber had been built for, it had been a long time ago.

The armory and indoor weapons salle lay in the west wing, along with rooms filled with crumbling maps and charts of the island, the waters around it, and the minor continent of Katan. The ballroom, the grand solar, and the painting gallery lay in the east wing. The audience hall, library, and light-globe storage room were found in the south wing, with small sitting rooms and salons scattered all around the four main wings. The bedrooms, most of the refreshing rooms, and bathing chambers were usually in the long, split ends angling out from each wing.

There had to be more than a hundred bedchambers, Alys decided, some with attached sitting rooms, private bathing chambers, and refreshing rooms. Some held just private refreshing rooms, though most of those without the extra suite-like chambers were up in the attic, where there were communal refreshing and bathing chambers for the servants who would have lived here long ago. Plus there were the larger bathing chambers, with several soaking tubs, the stairwells, the refreshing rooms every so often—the straight sections of the wings ran on for roughly a hundred yards, the wings two-thirds of that length.

Even taking into account the stout thickness of the outer stone walls and the thick stone separating and defining each chamber with the privacy of insulated quiet from its neighbors, the castle was huge. And that wasn't even counting the eight huge towers guarding the slightly curved, eight-sided outer wall; each had several levels, and most of them, workrooms and storage rooms for each of the eight mage-gifted brothers. Add to that a few outbuildings, stables, a barn, woodwright shop, smithy-forge—chicken coop included—and several gardens. Plus the four courtyards nestled between the four Y-endings of each wing. It was an echoingly huge home for the eight brothers to have lived in alone for three long years. Nine people, with the arrival of the strange but nice woman Kelly, and now ten with Alys staying among them.

Alys watched Saber remove his shirt as well, his own tanned flesh about as sweat-slick as his broader-chested twin's. She tried not to stare at him as he whispered to Kelly, moving over to the other woman's side as the two men worked on dismantling the bed. Alys waited patiently until Saber kissed his strawberry-haired wife and moved back to the bed, their murmuring apparently a moment of shared endearments before the elder of the twins went back to work.

Only then did she whisper to the other woman, "Kelly . . . why are we clearing out *this* room, when there are plenty of sitting rooms we could be using?"

"One, it gets Saber completely out of this room and into mine, making him feel more like it's his room, too, at the top of the great hall—men like to feel important, in their wives' lives," Kelly added in an aside. "And two, this room has its own bathing chamber and refreshing room. The bathing chamber is like yours, big enough to change in, as well as use the facilities. That makes it perfect for changing into something fit to work out in, do our exercises, getting all sweaty, bathing afterward, and changing back into something clean again."

"Oh." Alys still didn't quite understand what Kelly was talking about. But she certainly didn't mind that all of this effort was making Wolfer's smooth, lightly haired chest ripple with flexing muscles. He looked very manly. He smelled manly, too; her shapeshifter's nose could smell the musk of his sweat. It was more . . . more *earthy*, a scent more masculine, yet more pleasant than his brother's. Alys supposed from the way Kelly would inhale and smile at her husband now and again that Saber's scent had its own special attractions for the other woman, but Saber didn't draw Alys like Wolfer did.

The bed was the last piece of large furniture to go. The men took down the railings of the stripped canopy supports, and the two ladies dutifully moved forward to carry these lighter parts into one of the bedchambers in the attic that lacked a bed, no doubt inhabited by some servant long ago, one that could at least fit a bed of this size. When they came back, both men were straining at the side rails, the mattress already moved aside. They were trying to remove the rails from their slots in the headboard, with the foot-board already removed. The tongue-in-slot joints, however, had swollen and split with age. Saber's finally came out with a mutter of magic and a jolt; the boot he had braced against the headboard thrust him back with the release of the sideboard, dumping him on his backside.

Kelly immediately hurried over and fussed over him, while his slightly younger brother cursed and struggled to support the headboard and its remaining sideboard. Alys quickly leaped over the downed footboard and threw her-self at the headboard, helping Wolfer support it.

"Thanks, Alys," he managed tightly, shoulders and arms bulging, abdominal muscles tight above the waistline of his breeches. His side wasn't budging, though.

Saber let his wife help him to his feet and moved to sup-port the large headboard. Kelly shifted closer to Wolfer, wrapped her hands as best she could around the board next to Wolfer's, braced a leg blessedly not encumbered by a skirt on the panel, and added her own pull to the second eldest brother's. Leaving the eldest to push against the headboard.

Saber tried using a subtle touch of magic on it again, the same as he had for the other side. It didn't move. None of them made any headway. The problem with using rougher magic was that Saber didn't want to destroy the bed frame, in case it was ever needed again. That meant finding some other, less damaging way. Trevan was the brother who had the touch with wood, but Trevan's chore was fixing their lunch today.

"Enough! It's not going to budge," Wolfer said, as the other two relaxed their efforts.

"We can't take it up the stairs like this," Saber reminded him. He looked over at his wife, who was coiling the rope that had been strung tightly under the feather mattress and the thickly stuffed wool-and-cotton tick that had lain between mattress and ropes. "Kelly, fetch the dagger from my waist and see if you can shave either piece of wood."

Nodding, she plucked the knife from its belt sheath, inserted herself in front of Alys and Wolfer as the two of them shifted back, Alys quickly moving around to Wolfer's side of the board. Kelly poked and scraped at the opening. It took a while, but finally she finished and moved herself out of the way, carefully wiping the sharp-edged blade of dust shavings before resheathing it at her husband's waist. "Try it now."

It took effort; Alys wrapped her arms around Wolfer's waist to give him more leverage, and with the other two both pushing away the headboard while they pulled on the side—it finally popped free. Only because Alys was ready for it did she manage to keep herself and Wolfer on their feet, while Saber and Kelly bumped with the headboard into the wall behind it.

"Thanks," Wolfer murmured as Saber braced the thick, carved headboard so it wouldn't fall and injure anyone. He wished Alys would let go of his waist a little faster, a little more circumspectly. Instead, she released him by stepping back, her hands sliding briefly across his skin above the waistband of his breeches. He also perversely wished her arms would linger on his bare flesh a little longer, that her soft breasts were still pressed into the hard muscles of his back.

Alys didn't say anything. She couldn't. Not with her throat tight, with her lips pressed together against the urge to find out what Wolfer's sweat-slick skin tasted like. Taking the side panel from him so he could manage the heavy head- and footboards with his brother, she headed for the attic. As she walked, breathing deeply as she managed the awkward piece of timber, Alys discovered that her clothing

now carried his scent. It made sense; her clothing was
slightly damp from embracing his sweating skin.

*Yes, he's definitely nicer to smell than Saber.*

Wolfer winced as Alys sniffed deeply yet again; somehow, he didn't think she was sniffing the meal that Trevan
had prepared. She was seated on an extra chair settled at
the dining table between his and Morganen's.

The dining table had been placed in one of the salons
above the kitchen in the north wing, moved there to clear
the donjon hall and make it into an impromptu audience
chamber to impress the Mandarites. The same foreign bastards who had ended up stealing Dominor from them. No
one had moved it back down into the great hall. Nor would
they likely bother in the future; the room chosen had once
been a small dining hall and comfortably fit the large,
eight-sided table with a bit of room to spare.

Since clearing out his twin's old room had taken up the
whole morning until just before lunch, he had only had
enough time to wipe himself down hastily with a damp
cloth in his room. Not enough time to bathe away the smell
of his sweat, or even to change his clothes. She inhaled
deeply again. Wolfer hoped it was the scent of the seafood
salad and herb-buttered bread they were having that she
seemed to be enjoying. Trevan had cooked shrimp until it
was tender-pink, then chilled it with a spell and mixed it
with some kind of savory-sweet sauce over a bed of
greens, carrot slivers, slices of boiled egg, and cheese.

Another sniff made him self-conscious. He could still
smell his exertions. She probably couldn't smell Saber's
lingering sweat, since his twin sat on Wolfer's other side
from her, but she was right at Wolfer's elbow. Wolfer was
afraid to raise that elbow more than a bare inch or two, in
case the smell should cause her to pass out. He really
hoped all that sniffing was for the food. It didn't help him
that most of the time whenever she closed her mouth
around her fork, she closed her eyes and slowly opened

them, *mmm*ing under her breath as she savored each morsel of food.

*When did she turn so . . . so sensual?* he asked himself, watching her chew out of the corner of his eye. Watched her fingers grasp her mug of spell-chilled water, ignoring the handle in favor of picking it up directly by its side. It was as if the cup represented the way she sometimes grasped life directly, a contrast to the daintily graceful way she wielded her fork and the corresponding way she usually let her gentleness show through in timidity.

*Every contrast about her is still fascinating to me . . . but now it's more, somehow.* She *is* more, he admitted to himself, absently taking another bite of his bread. *More curves, more curls . . . more woman than the girl I last knew.*

He would have mourned the loss of his old childhood playmate a bit more, Wolfer instinctively knew, if the woman sitting beside him hadn't developed new qualities to fascinate him in their place. Koranen was busy telling the others something funny that had happened to him while picking the fresh fruit that now sat on the table, available for anyone who wanted more to eat than just the summer salad their brother had made. Wolfer didn't hear a word of the punch line, for a pair of gray eyes slanted up toward him. He watched Alys as she lifted a slice of fruit to her lips—the very same type she had eaten while riding on his back that morning.

This time, he saw the perfect pucker of her lips enclosing the juicy wedge of tangy-sweet citrus. He could almost hear the moans of pleasure she had made the last time. He wanted to bend his head down, take the other half of that wedge in his own teeth, and mate his mouth to hers, to share fruit and kiss in a sensual expression of hunger. He wanted to taste the juice on her lips, her tongue, then lick the sticky liquid from her fingertips.

When she firmed her lips a little and bit through the fruit—so gently, so sweetly—his breath escaped through parted lips. Dragging his attention back to his food, Wolfer drank from his mug of beer, his current choice of drink, though there was water, juice, and ale also available. The spell-chilled carafes sat on a sideboard his sister-in-law had unearthed from somewhere and had a couple of his brothers drag in, making the former sitting room into a real dining chamber. *Women and their furniture*, he thought, distracting himself from the more dangerous thought, *Women and their mouths . . .*

"So, will you need us to put furniture into the room after the meal is over?" Saber asked his wife.

"Nope. Alys and I can haul in one of the wooden benches I saw outside."

Wolfer thought about the size of the wooden benches outside and their weathered splinters, and winced. "I'll bring it in, after it's been sanded."

"That would be very nice of you," the woman at his right murmured demurely. "It would have been a struggle for us to move ourselves."

His muscles swelled slightly under her praise of him for being strong and thoughtful and manly. Wolfer promised himself he would attend to the bench right away. She inhaled again, her head still slightly turned in his direction.

As soon as he bathed.

"If you're only going to put a single bench in there, why did we clear out the room?" his twin was arguing with his wife. "I thought you were just changing furniture, for some bizarre female reasoning."

"None of your business—and that kind of flattery won't get you anywhere. Evanor, do you know if there is any thick wool or cotton batting to be had?" Kelly asked the light blond man across the table from her. "Not as thick as an under-mattress, but not thinner than two fingers in width when compressed—even if it has to be layered."

"Not that I'm aware of, not unless you want to use actual quilts. Why do you need it?"

"How about felt?" she asked, avoiding the question neatly.

"We have plenty of that," he agreed. "It's in the east wing attic, near the Y-split, in one of the servants' chambers. It's left over from a previous occupant but it's still in fairly good shape, for felt. A bit nibbled on by bugs and things, but only in smallish holes here and there."

"Excellent. I'll take a look at it right after lunch, then."

"*What* do you need it for?" Saber demanded, wary of his wife's evasiveness.

His wife patted his thigh, seated next to him on the same kind of double-seated bench Alys remembered her parents sharing their meals on. The kind her uncle had sat on alone, and occasionally allowed one of his favored serving wenches to sit on with him, if she was serving him his food particularly well.

"It's women-stuff. Now that there's another woman in the hall, I intend to teach her a few otherworldly things that you don't need to know about."

"Perhaps I can change your mind?" the eldest of them murmured, eyeing his wife speculatively.

As the other woman smiled smugly, Alys wondered who would win the contest of wills between the two of them. Kelly was a lot more forward and assertive than she was, that was certain.

Alys inhaled deeply yet again. Cari had said that some men smelled a little better than others, but the helpful wench hadn't said anything about some men smelling simply fantastic—as delicious as a dessert served straight to her senses, skipping right over the main meal. If a dessert could be male, wolfish, and spicy-musky-earthy, that was. It was pure Wolfer. The scent of a mate.

She simply couldn't inhale enough of his smell.

# SIX

·❧·

**N**o, no, place your foot a little more like this—do you feel the difference in your stance?" Kelly asked, getting down on the felt matting, quick-stitched together into large strips of "quilts" five layers deep.

Alys let the other woman slide her foot into position, then tested it. "Yes . . . yes, I think I do. And then I . . . do *this*, right?"

As Kelly quickly got out of the way, Alys swept her arms in front of her: punch, sweep, punch-punch-sweep, swivel, and kick. Dropping down into a similar stance from the one she had started with, she eyed her instructor.

"Did I do it right?"

"More or less. Your wrists are bending up slightly—the back of your hand needs to be level with your forearm. And your blocks are still a little high. And you need to pull your toes up and thrust with your heel on your kicks, so you don't stub or break anything . . . but you're a lot better than when we started," Kelly added frankly. "These are the little things you correct once you start getting the feel of the overall moves. Now, practice that combination again."

Alys did it again. Then again. And again. She did it

slowly. She did it a little faster. She did it very fast at her instructor's sharp order—and flubbed it, throwing off her balance with a too-fast sweep of her arms that, when she tried to snap the kick, toppled her onto her backside. Five layers of felt saved her from a bad bruising, at least. But not from a light bruising; it was only a few moth-eaten layers of felt underneath her rump, after all.

"Ow."

Biting her lip on a grin, Kelly crossed over and helped Alys up. "Well, I think your backside just thoroughly trounced the floor. We'll work at this slowly for a few weeks and increase your speed only gradually, I think. Perfect the form, first; speed will come in its own time."

"This . . . kung fu . . ." Alys dusted off her backside, then blotted her forehead with her forearm. It had taken them most of the afternoon to find and piece the felt together for matting in simple anchor-stitches every hand-length or so. Even close to sunset, it was still warm, though. "Why am I learning it, again?"

"So that the next time you encounter anyone like your uncle, you can make him eat dirt. Here, take your stance again, and I'll show you," she added, backing off a step and dropping into a stance of her own. "Now, go through the move."

She blocked Alys' punch, threw one of her own that Alys, startled, managed to block, parried the two Alys gave back, attacked and got blocked again—and *oofed*, staggering back as Alys' foot connected solidly, following the pattern combination the younger woman had just learned. Alys dropped her foot, her hands going to her mouth. "Oh! Kelly—I'm so sorry!"

Kelly, rubbing her stomach, one hand braced on her knee, grinned up at the other woman. She straightened and pointed at Alys, catching her breath. "Whoo—don't you *dare* apologize! You did *exactly* what you were supposed to do! Good job!"

Alys blinked. "You're not mad at me?"

"I'm *pleased* with you," Kelly corrected firmly, smiling.

"Of course, I did deliberately let you in through my guard, especially at the slow speed we were going, but the move, at full speed, looks like *this*—" A sudden whirl of arms, a spinning twist and kick of Kelly's body, and Alys saw exactly how powerfully that bare heel could strike when properly applied.

She stared at the freckled woman, amazed. "By Kata, you could probably *kill* someone doing that!"

"Only if you somehow managed to break their neck, by kicking up *this* high." Kelly demonstrated, tipping over a little more sideways with the side kick they were using, thrusting her heel at head height before dropping it back down. "Or by somehow crushing a vital organ in the abdomen, but that's not very likely at the strength level you and I can use. At Wolfer's or Saber's strength, maybe; you and I are in this more for disabling an enemy, not for killing one. Mind you, there are other things we could do to take out an enemy, and not just take him down. But you don't yet know enough about kung fu to try. Basics first. Bloodbath later."

"I . . . I'm not sure if I can do that," Alys murmured, shocked at the other woman's matter-of-fact approach to such things. The only person she wished she was brave enough to kill was her Uncle Broger . . . but he had bragged more than once of certain spells set to backlash on anyone who dared to try. Her fingers touched the diamond-shaped star embedded in her skin, rubbing it through the front of her blouse. Not even that piece of carefully enchanted metal could save her from such a thing.

"It's a weapon no one can take from you," Kelly pointed out reasonably, not privy to Alys' internal turmoil and doubt. "And the next time you encounter your uncle and he tries to do something you don't like—gods of this world forbid you should ever actually have to—you can do *this* to him." She swept her arms out, slashing, whirling, and dropped to her knees with a hard-fisted punch at a height that would devastate any man, right at the apex of their thighs. Bouncing back up to her feet as she yanked her arm back, Kelly relaxed her stance and grinned at Alys. "See?"

Alys thought about doing that to her uncle. For a moment, anger swelled up in her, and she thought she *would* do it when she saw Broger again, or maybe Donnock, since he was physically closer to the island. But it didn't last long within her. Both of her uncles were more powerful mages than she was, and the thought of what they would do to her if she attacked them filled her with nerve-racking dread. "I . . . I don't know if I can do that."

"I see we've still got to work on your self-confidence, young lady," Kelly stated. "Now, let's go over that first pattern again. Don't think of it as fighting," she added as Alys hesitated. "Think of it as exercising, for now." When that didn't move the maiden, Kelly smiled slowly, slyly. "Or think of it as a way to attack Wolfer."

"A-attack *Wolfer*?" Alys stammered. "I couldn't—I wouldn't ever—I mean . . ."

"Oh, yeah," the other woman agreed, wriggling her eyebrows, her fingers flexing like claws. "Attack him, fling him to the floor, pin him down, rip off his clothes, and have your *very* wicked way with him!"

Alys' eyes widened. Then she giggled. A shocked giggle, but still a giggle.

*Aha,* Kelly thought, eyeing the other woman. *This is how I can motivate her.*

*Poor Wolfer—not!*


Morganen ducked the vicious swipe of Wolfer's sword. He scrambled back, tried meeting the next swing of his brother's blunt practice blade, and almost lost his own.

"By Jinga! What's gotten *into* you?" he demanded, ducking around one of the practice pells in the weapon salle. It was cooler to practice in than outside in the northern courtyard where the brothers usually battled when the weather was good and the temperature was not overly hot or cold. He winced as Wolfer slashed at him in earnest, though the other man's blade got intercepted by the nicked wooden arm of the pell, as Morganen ducked behind it again. Yet one more gouge-mark had just been carved into the poor thing; it would have to be replaced soon. "I thought you asked me to spar with you because you wanted to *practice* with me, not *kill* me!"

Those golden eyes narrowed. Wolfer stalked around the pell. His youngest brother stayed on the far side of it from him. "Since when have *you* been best friends with *her*?"

The youngest brother straightened, blinking his aquamarine eyes. "Is *that* what this is about? The way we greeted each other?"

*"Yes,"* Wolfer snarled, lunging around the pell as his brother stood still. Morganen defended himself, but he lost ground to his more massive, muscular, second-eldest brother.

Morganen couldn't admit that he'd kept in scrying contact with her—not yet; it was too soon for Wolfer to know the truths he himself had known all along. But there was something he *could* admit, more or less. "Wolfer, I was her magic teacher! Remember?"

Wolfer eased up his attack a little, and Morganen got in a solid blow to his brother's shoulder-guard, making it clang as the practice blade met the protective curve of metal. He narrowed his golden eyes. "When did *you* give her lessons?"

"We used to talk by mirror—I *am* the best mage in the family," his youngest brother added pointedly, as his brother switched sword hands and tucked his "injured" arm behind his back, honoring the blow. "Even back then, she knew that. And it doesn't take—ow, dammit!" Morganen snatched his gauntleted hand away, as he backed up quickly to put a little space between them, switching sword hands himself and hiding his hard-rapped knuckles behind his back. "It doesn't take even an idiot that long to see that she had to escape by magical means and was probably grateful I taught her enough to know how to escape! You know what a stingy bastard Broger of Devries is. He probably didn't pay for any formal mage schooling for her, let alone any private tutoring beyond a few tricks here and there to make her more useful to him."

"You may be right," Wolfer allowed, flicking his head to get the wisp of brown hair escaping its headband out of his face. He attacked his brother again, hard. "But you will *not* hug her so closely again!"

"Hey, I'm not the one who's in love with her!" the mage shot back, defending himself as best he could verbally and physically, though mostly physically, since that was taking most of his attention as his brother swung his longsword.

A beat later, Morganen's aquamarine eyes widened, and Wolfer's golden ones narrowed. No fool, Morganen yelped and fled, dashing out of the salle, his long, light brown hair streaming behind him. The Wolf gave chase, as was his nature.

They raced up through the eastern wing, raced through the broad great hall, and kept going into the west wing. Someone stepped out of the archway to one of the stairwells just as they passed, making Morganen curse and swerve, barely avoiding the two women emerging from the doorway. Wolfer wasn't so lucky. He skidded to a stop, but his momentum was too great. As his sister-in-law gasped and threw herself quickly toward the far wall, getting clear of his unstoppable charge, Wolfer skidded into Alys, armor and all. The only good thing was that he quickly lifted his sword high, moving it out of the way to keep from harming her. The bad thing was that they thoroughly collided.

She *oofed!* and grabbed onto him as the impact spun them around. Tumbling, Wolfer smacked his helmless head on the stone-paved floor, even as his armor clanged and his childhood friend thumped on top of him with another little grunt. They stayed like that for a stunned moment, then she recovered first, much more rapidly than him.

"Oh! Wolfer!" Alarmed, Alys' first thought was for his safety. Her bruises from his armor were nothing compared to his, surely. Alys squirmed, found herself straddling him, and gingerly touched the armor covering his chest and his shoulders, then reached for the unprotected back of his head. "Are you injured? Please tell me you aren't hurt!"

Morganen came back, grabbed the intrigued, voyeuristic Kelly, and dragged her into the stairwell. That moved both of them out of view, giving the two on the floor some privacy. Of course, Kelly and Morganen were grinning all the way at such fortuitous, Destiny-inspiring luck. There was nothing quite like an injured warrior and a concerned maiden willing to fuss over him to cement a romance, after all.

Wolfer, stunned from the blow to his head, blinked and looked up at the curly haired woman bent so tenderly over him. A woman who was straddling his armored waist like a sexy hallucination. His wits were elsewhere, surely; that was the only possible explanation for what he did next. Dropping his sword, he reached up, cupped that dark golden head, and dragged her mouth down to his. Boldly claiming those sweet lips with his own.

Sucking in a startled breath, Alys stilled and resisted for a moment as his mouth claimed hers without any gentle preliminaries in a hungry, hot, devouring kiss. He seemed to sense her hesitation and gentled his mouth against hers accordingly. Instead of pressuring them into yielding, his lips coaxed hers to soften. Instead of invading, his tongue licked at her lips, teasing her into parting them on her own.

"Alys? Wolfer!" Evanor's voice cut through their kiss, jerking both of them apart. Alys scrambled off of the armored brother and bolted to her feet, blushing. The other Nightfall brother stalked up to them and glared down at the armored man on the floor. "*What* were you doing to her, just now?"

Wolfer flushed at the demand, too flustered to reply with the truth under Evanor's disapproving glare. He slumped back against the floor, closing his eyes and going completely limp, the picture of a man slumped insensate on the floor.

"Wolfer?" he heard Alys ask with a touch of concern.

Feeling her crouch and nudge his shoulder, he slowly "roused" when she nudged him again.

"Unh . . . Alys?" Cracking open his eyes, he looked up at the ceiling, then around him, sitting up gingerly, lifting his hand to the back of his head. "I don't remember . . . how did I get here? Why am I on the floor?"

Alys flushed, her gray eyes widening. But not in concern. They narrowed a moment later—she *knew* when a man was faking! He had just kissed her for the first time since she was a curious twelve years old and he an obliging seventeen, and that had only been a single, quick peck of their lips—and he *pretended* not to know what he had been doing just now? "You—you—*ooh!*"

Shoving at him hard, thrusting him back onto the floor, Alys stood up again. Literally stomping on his breastplate, she stalked off in a huff, her curls bouncing where they had escaped from the braid Wolfer had disheveled during their interlude.

"*That* was smart," Evanor drawled. In just three words, he managed to make Wolfer feel even more like a fool. "No woman likes being insulted that way, Wolfer—you don't know a thing about courting, do you?"

His face heated as he sat up again. "I'm not courting her!"

Evanor crouched next to him and hooked his finger under the braid of hair just visible between armguard and gauntlet. "Then why have you been wearing *this* all along . . . which might be interpreted as a 'chain of silk'?"

Wolfer growled, baring his teeth. Evanor, no fool, removed his touch. He didn't back off, though. Cradling his wrist and its bracelet, Wolfer glared down at it. "There is no silk in it! No chain. It's just a bit of braided hair she cut from her head and gave to me. As a *friend.*"

"She wasn't kissing you back as a *friend,*" his blond-haired brother pointed out, crouching by him with his forearms on his knees. "She doesn't look at you the way she looks at the rest of us . . . and you don't look at her like I've ever seen a friend look at another friend." Evanor stood and looked down at him. "She looks at you and you look at her like a woman and a man who are interested in each other.

"Destiny is Destiny, Brother. And you're next in line for the fall. *Don't* screw it up."

*I hate it when he's right.* Groaning, Wolfer dropped back to the floor, eyes squeezing shut. In doing so, he missed the little smile curving Evanor's mouth, the first real smile he had given since his twin had been captured. Wolfer stayed there while his brother stepped over him and continued down the hall, wondering to Jinga and back how his life could have gotten so complicated.

A lys was still mad at him at the evening meal and didn't once look his way. She even smiled a few times at Rydan, who grunted and did his best to ignore her, though the rest of Wolfer's brothers responded to her shy charm. But she didn't once acknowledge *his* presence. And because he had scullery duty, Wolfer couldn't follow her when she left immediately after the meal was over.

Banging the pots and pans, dunking the dishes with force into the soapy, quick-cleaning enspelled water that filled the largest scullery sink, Wolfer growled under his breath. Koranen, whose turn it also was to help, kept himself strictly in the kitchen, cleaning it up and only bringing his elder brother dirty dishes and utensils when he absolutely had to enter the scullery next door. Wolfer wasn't in a mood to be sociable, so it was just as well the second youngest was being cautious around him.

The glass water pitcher broke when he thoughtlessly banged it about. Cursing, Wolfer closed his eyes, calmed his mind, focused his will, and muttered the glass-mending spell their mother had insisted all of them learn as soon as they developed their magic. Broken pieces leaped up out of the water, realigning themselves as the spell worked.

Lady Annia had possessed a small amount of magic herself, mostly household oriented . . . but she had refused to use it to repair yet another object her sons had broken in and about Corvis Castle, training the boys from the moment the two eldest twins had developed their very first speck of magic inside. That had essentially made each brother responsible for what they had *all* done, all the way to the flowering of Koranen and Morganen's own magics. She had insisted on responsibility being shared among all eight of them. When the glass pitcher was whole again, Wolfer washed it much more carefully, and the rest of the dishes, too.

There was a reason why he was so mad. Alys. And her behavior toward him at dinner. She had fumed and been silent toward him, when all he wanted was for her to smile at him, to lift those soft gray eyes to his. To lift those sweet, pink lips for him to taste, and only him.

Lifting the last dish out of the rinsing water, he set it very gently on the drying rack with the others, pulled the cork from the drain, and wiped down his hands and arms. Patting the braid of her hair a little drier with the drying cloth, he slowed his movements and looked down at it, really looked at it.

*It can't possibly be the "chain of silk" . . . can it?* And yet, when he thought about it . . .

*"When claw would strike and cut to bone/A chain of silk shall bind his hand . . ." My hand. I didn't see her put any silken chain in the braid—I saw her braid it from a lock of hair she separated out from behind her ear. Watched her select and braid that lock with my own eyes, and cut it on the spot! She couldn't have bound me by anything . . . except . . . Except I have stayed my hand in anger many a time from cutting into someone, literally or figuratively, by the thought of her and this braided bracelet, remembering how kind she was, and how gentle she made me feel . . .*

It kinked, as it always wanted to do when it started to dry, legacy of the thumb-sized curls it was made from. He smoothed it automatically. " . . . *So Wolf is caught in marriage-band." Marriage . . . Alys, married . . . to me?*

He thought about it. It didn't feel very odd—no more so than the realization that she was a fully sensual adult woman felt odd, compared with his long-standing memories of her as a half-shy, half-bold playmate, then later as a withdrawn, half-grown girl . . . who had always played most of all with *him*, when she played with him and his brothers. Who had always followed *him* with little sneaking peeks of her eyes, some soft, puzzling emotion in her gaze that had made him uncomfortable, because he didn't know what it was.

It hadn't been the same sort of pleasure a couple of the Corvis castle servants had introduced him to when he was old enough, the kind that could be found in a bed. Pleasures he had felt uncomfortable associating *her* with . . . *because* of that admiring look in her eyes, Wolfer now realized. He hadn't been ready to accept her admiration of him.

*She was always mine, wasn't she?* The realization first painfully tightened, then released something within his chest. That brought him an almost giddy sense of freedom, of anticipation. *Everything she did—when she was brave and adventuresome, was to be with* me. *Not my brothers. Not for anything else. She always wanted to be with* me. *She escaped her horrible uncle, and she came here to Nightfall, where she would feel safe with* me.

The revelation turned him away from the dish-draining rack without bothering to wipe and put the dishes away.

"Hey! Aren't you going to put those away?" Koranen called out.

Wolfer shook his head. He had to find her. He would find her, and they would . . . they would . . .

"I'm an idiot," he muttered under his breath, turning back to the dishes in their drying rack. He couldn't just go up to her and tell her he was ready to marry her. Especially not after his "performance" in the west hall, when he had been too embarrassed to admit kissing her.

"I already knew that," his second youngest brother quipped, as Wolfer mulled over what he was going to do.

"But would you care to explain why *you* think that, at least?"

Wolfer reversed course once more, heading out of the kitchen again. He leveled a finger at Kor and growled. "Just for that, *you* can finish the dishes!"

*"Hey!"* His auburn-haired brother glared at him.

But Wolfer was already striding out the kitchen door. He had some strategic planning to do.

# SEVEN

·❍·

Alys awoke instantly. There had always been the fear that her uncle would come to her room and catch her asleep, so she had forced herself to be a light sleeper. He had never caught her unaware, and she had disappointed his lust several times by sitting up just as he reached her bed and asking him blandly if he had given up his dreams of wealth and alliance with whomever bid the highest to have his *virgin* niece as their bride.

Except . . . except she wasn't in her old rooms, either at Devries Hall or in Corvis Castle. She was in her new room on Nightfall Isle. Still, the faint sound of the door easing open on near-silent hinges woke her, disorienting her for a few moments. She remained lying in the bed, straining with her ears, seeking to feel out the identity of the intruder with her meager mage senses.

It wasn't her Uncle Broger or her other uncle, Donnock.

It was Wolfer.

She almost pushed herself up onto her elbows and demanded to know what he was doing in there. Peeking with the one eye not half-buried in her pillow where she lay on her side, she saw him enter the room and close the door. A large basket hung from his hand. It was filled with *flowers*, of all things. Helped by the early morning sunlight filtering faintly through the curtains in her room, she recognized the flowers. They were from the gardens outside their wing of the castle, most of them barely beginning to bud.

She shut her eyelid quickly, as he glanced warily her way.

Ears straining for each sound, she heard his feet creep quietly across the floor. The scent of dew and pollen increased as he moved near her bed. His personal odor accompanied them, cleaner and fainter than he had smelled at the midday meal the day before, overlain with an aroma of soap and lingering moisture that said he had bathed not too long ago. The scent of flowers increased as she sensed him moving to stand right beside her, where she lay on one side of a bed much larger and softer than her previous ones had ever been. Then his feet padded quietly away, the door creaked softly, and quietly bumped shut . . . and the flower scent lingered, making her nose twitch.

Opening her eye cautiously, Alys found herself staring at a rose. It was in that delicately graceful state she loved, between still-closed bud and full-opened bloom. The red petals were still lightly beaded with dew. Sitting up, Alys blinked in surprise when she dislodged a shower of stems and blossoms; he had laid them over her and the bedding, covering her so gently, she hadn't even felt a thing.

She didn't know what to make of the silent offering. Alys didn't think he knew she had been awake, not from his stealthy giving . . . which left her wondering why he had done it so secretively at all. *Unless he was embarrassed to let his brothers know he was doing it . . .*

*As he must have been as embarrassed as I was to have his brother catch us yesterday in the hall.* She could see why he had pretended not to know what he had been doing now, as an excuse to explain away his actions at the fourth-born brother's demands. Her lips firmed for a moment, wishing he'd had enough bravery to kiss her openly and not care who knew about it . . . and then her mouth curved.

*That's the bowl calling the plate a dish! You're about as much a coward as anyone, Alys of Devries, so you have little business calling* him *one.*

The flowers made her feel bold, though. Edging them gently aside, for she didn't want to crush them, she got up, dressed in the trousers and tunic Kelly had given her, then gathered all of the flowers up again, except for the one rose. The roses, she noticed, all had their thorns removed; they had been mixed in with bluebells and *tanzitas,* marigolds and *orchidaria* sprays, which had no thorns. It was a considerate touch that made her smile. Bundling them into the crook of her arm, since he had taken his basket with him, she poked her head out into the hall then snuck down the corridor to his room.

She knocked tentatively but received no answer.

Feeling very bold, Alys opened his door and slipped inside. His was a suite with a sitting room, though Wolfer was not inside the front room. Tiptoeing to the next chamber, she peered past the edge of the door. No one was in the bedroom, either. Hurrying over to the bed, she started scattering the blossoms on the haphazardly straightened covers.

A watery sound behind the other door in the room made her gasp and toss the remaining flowers on the bed in a lump, glancing about her quickly for a place to hide. She dove under the bed as the flushing of water in the refreshing room eased and stopped, grateful there was very little dust underneath the huge piece of furniture. A glance at the door showed it swinging open. A pair of boots strode into the room, the door closing behind them . . . and those boots abruptly stilled.

Their owner was noticing the flowers on the bed! She squeezed her eyes shut, holding her breath, mortified and no longer brave. Not at the thought of being caught.

Wolfer stared at the flowers on his bed, his fingers freezing in the act of tying his trouser laces. The very same flowers that he recognized as the ones he had picked and laid all around the sleeping Alys not minutes before now lay on *his* bed, just as he had placed them on hers.

*Almost* as he had placed them on hers, rather; these were scattered over about half of his bed, and then just . . . dumped in a bundle. As if interrupted by his return from the refreshing room.

His eyes shifted to the bedroom door. He was supposed to go down to the kitchen and help make breakfast, since that was his household chore this morning. But the door stood partly open, barely wide enough for someone slender to have slipped out through . . . maybe quickly enough for them to have escaped through before he had emerged from the refreshing room, and maybe not.

Narrowing his eyes, he looked around the bedroom for any clues. Nothing. There really was no place for her to hide . . . except under the bed. Dropping in a quiet crouch by the refreshing room door, bracing his hands on the floor, he peered under the edge of his bed a couple yards away.

Alys lay underneath it at an angle to him, her eyes squeezed tightly shut. She looked like she was holding her breath, afraid of being caught. Acting as if putting flowers on his bed was a naughty child's prank. Grinning, Wolfer crept closer across the floor on hands and feet, kneeling absolutely silently by the side of the bed. When he was ready, he reached under its edge—and grabbed her ankles with a yank.

She yelped and scrabbled, kicking futilely. Wolfer laughed and slid her easily out from beneath his bed in spite of her struggles. Attempting to cling to the taut ropes holding his wool-stuffed pallet and its feather mattress up, even though her belly-down angle was awkward, she tried to stay under the bed. And failed. As he grinned, tugging on her a hand-length at a time, Alys kicked and squirmed even harder, shrieking as his hands deliberately groped up past her knees . . .

"Wolfer!"

He growled playfully, hauled her out completely, and flipped her over, pinning her writhing body with his own to the floor. Unable to suppress the mischief roused in him by her very presence, he did what he had once done to her as a young boy. Grinning, growling, nipping with his lips sheathing his teeth from her skin, he pretended to be a big wolf and "eat" her, lunging at her cheeks, her forehead, her ears, and her throat as she shrieked and threw up her arms to protect her face, then her torso.

Wolfer stopped only when he got to her chest, which was no longer a flat, childish chest lying underneath the soft cotton of her clothes. No, his Alys had grown delectable, unmistakably womanly curves, ones that inspired a low, soft, hungry growl from deep within his chest. Alys gasped and stilled under his touch as soon as she felt his mouth stop there.

He felt her nipple bead right through the material of tunic and under-corset support. Against the corner of his lips. Gray eyes met gold, in the quiet of early morning. Gazes locking, Wolfer shifted his head just a little, and took that cloth-wrapped bud in his mouth. With the cloth cushioning his grip, he rolled her nipple gently with a side-to-side twitch of his lower jaw.

Her eyes closed, and her head arched back against the floor. Pushing her breast closer. He closed his lips around the full peak and suckled through the layers of cloth. Then growled at the ineffective, bland taste of cotton. A shift of his weight, and he pushed her tunic up. He growled softly again when she struggled, but it wasn't to impede him; rather, she helped him pull the garment over her head. That bared her underlying corset bodice. It also bared a strange, finely edged diamond of metal embedded in her skin, melded with the flesh of her sternum.

She had mentioned it before, but Wolfer decided it could wait. He had more important things to investigate. A dip and an impatient tug of his fingers, and her breast came free of its confining cup. She gasped as he claimed her breast once more, this time in warm, wet, full intensity, his mouth feasting on her flesh. It pleased him that he had such an immediate, devastating effect on her.

Alys cried out, wrapping her arms around his head. This wasn't her uncle bouncing revoltingly on a serving wench.

This wasn't Cari and that client of hers doing shocking things in that brothel. This was her Wolfer doing an incredibly exciting thing to her! The way she responded, clasping him to her, seemed to go straight to his head. As his soft brown hair feathered against her skin, he pulled her other breast free and lavished it with his attention as well, growling in that way that said *big, hungry wolf*. Licking, nipping, he devoured her with his sensuality on his hard bedchamber floor.

Each tug of his lips, each scrape of his teeth, each laving swirl of his tongue shot silken lightning down to her belly, to that place between her legs that was her core. Her knees squirmed wider, propelled by that lightning-writhing need, making his hips slip down between her thighs. The way they parted for him made him groan and growl hungrily, pressing his groin into her.

Once, twice, and a lingering, rotating third time, he pressed in just the right spot, that same spot he had rubbed while she had ridden him in stallion form . . .

Her head thudded against the floor as she cried out, hips thrusting up into his. Wolfer gasped, releasing her flesh from his mouth, his whole body tightening with the pleasure of having her buck convulsively against him in the depths of her pleasure—he had to be inside her! *Now*. As she slowly sagged and relaxed under him, his hand dove for his half-tied laces, eager to unknot them once more—

*Knock knock knock!* "Wolfer? Have you seen Alys?"

"*Jinga's—*" Biting back the rest of the curse, Wolfer stopped undressing and braced himself over her with both arms. Breathing hard, struggling with desire, he fought with his baser instincts. It didn't help that he was staring into a dazed, uncertain but blissful look on Alys' face, a look *he* had put there, to her almost bewildered satisfaction.

"Wolfer, is Alys in there?" Kelly's voice demanded again from beyond his sitting room door. She banged on his door again. "I heard you swearing in there! I better have interrupted you *before* you got very far!"

Wolfer scrambled off of Alys and charged the outer

door, growling with masculine rage. Yanking open the only entrance to the corridor, he snarled at his twin's wife, exactly like an enraged wolf.

Typical of the odd, extra-dimensional woman, Kelly didn't react with fear. She snapped her hand up and pinched his ear. *Hard*. And then yanked him down to growl herself in his ear.

"Alys is a *sweet* young woman who is very shy about sex, because she was almost molested by her uncle—*do you understand?*" the strawberry-haired woman holding him so painfully asserted under her breath, her near-whispered words pitched for his ears alone.

Wolfer started to snarl back for her to mind her own business. Until her meaning made it through to his brain. Dread froze him in place. *Molested*. Her own *uncle*? His anger drained right out of him with shock and dismay.

"I said *almost*," Kelly asserted, reading his reaction with remarkable accuracy. "She was very smart and held him off, by reminding him he would get more by selling her to the highest marriage-bidder if she were still a virgin. So she's not only hesitant about sex, she's also a virgin. Now, I don't want to have to chaperone the two of you, if you can't keep your pants closed," she added with a pointed look down at his half undone laces.

They were visible below the hem of his tunic, which was still rucked up from where he had shoved it out of the way to undo them once again. Thankfully nothing showed; he wouldn't have cared to explain to his twin why he'd given his sister-in-law an eyeful. Kelly released his ear, as he quickly tugged his shirt back down.

"I do believe you had breakfast to make for today's chore? I, for one, am getting hungry," she stated pointedly.

Wolfer bit back several choice replies. He chose the most diplomatic his whirling mind could think of. *"Suffer."*

Slamming the door shut between them before she could grab his ear again, he leaned his forehead against the panel. *Almost molested! Jinga, I swear I'll kill Broger of Devries! He's not fit to exist anymore!*

Her breasts tucked back into her corset, her tunic held over her chest, but not yet donned again, Alys peeked around his bedroom door. She had been too caught up in the shudders of her second taste of pleasure ever to have heard what had been said at his suite door. Not in such low-spoken words. Still, even though the timing had been awkward, she was curious about what the interruption had been for.

"Wolfer? Who was that? What did they want?"

Guilt slammed through Wolfer, warring with the lust roused by her voice alone. "I, uh—I'm sorry."

Of all the things she had hoped to hear . . . that was not one of them. Alys blinked. "You're sorry?"

He nodded, his head still resting against the door.

"You're *sorry*?" Anger rose up in her, fueled by humiliation. "You had me *on the floor*, sucking on my . . . my—and you're *sorry*?!"

Wolfer frowned. That didn't sound like a timid, scared maiden. Come to think of it, she hadn't *reacted* like a timid, scared maiden—he was experienced enough to know a cry of pleasure from a cry of fear after all, even if it had been a number of years. He rolled his head a little and peeked at her. She certainly looked like an insulted woman, not a timid maiden. Her hands had planted themselves on her hips in an unconsciously Kelly-like motion, and those gray eyes were glaring at him. The only defense he could think of was the truth. Sort of. "I . . . um, I thought I was scaring you."

"*Scaring* me?" Alys raised her brows, then lowered them and stomped over. "I'll scare *you*, you—you—*ooh*!" Dropping her tunic to the floor, she fisted her fingers in his own clothes, hauling him away from the door and down to her level. Her mouth mashed into his, forcing Wolfer to grab her to balance the two of them. That mouth was more than willing . . . but she moved it with very little imagination or experience as she mashed it against his own. Proving that at least some of Kelly's claim was true, regarding her inexperience.

Wolfer cupped her head, gentling the kiss. He showed her how by leading her with his own experience. Perhaps not as much as Trevan had managed to learn before their exile, but he did have more than his Alys did. This time, when he licked her lips, she responded with a sigh and a lick of her own. Her fists flattened, smoothing against his chest; her touch made his heart pound harder with the need to reach her. His hands slipped down to her shoulders and arms, around to her back, then down to her trouser-clad backside as her hands slid up to clutch at his shoulders. Pulling her intimately against him.

*"Wolfer, where are you? I am* not *making breakfast on my own, dammit!"*

Evanor's magic-projected voice in his ear made him jerk.

Alys pulled back, her bravery losing ground to uncertainty. "Wolfer? Is something . . . ?"

Wolfer rested his forehead against hers, closing his wolf-gold eyes for a moment. Opening them, he met her gaze. "Evanor's calling me. I have to go make breakfast."

"Oh."

It was a tiny, disappointed sound. Wolfer leaned in and kissed her gently on the lips, then on the tip of her nose. "We will do this later, and we will go as slowly as you like. *If* you want us to continue . . ."

"Oh." Alys swallowed, cleared her throat, and firmed her courage once more, staring at his chest and the rumpled lines of his tunic where she had fisted it. Her fingers smoothed the material, tracing the muscles underneath with unconscious seduction. "I, ah . . . yes. I want us to . . . to continue."

Wolfer groaned. This was not helping him to let go of her.

*"Wolfer! Get your backside down to the kitchen right now!"*

"I have to go." With one last brush of his lips against hers, he reached behind him, opened the door, and backed out, shutting it between them.

Leaving her in his room. Alys touched her lips, licked

them, blinked . . . and slowly smiled. Then grinned, and spun around in the morning light spilling in through the sitting room windows, arms spread out, uncaring that her tunic was still discarded on the floor, leaving her only in her under-bodice and trousers.

*He wanted her!*

It was a conspiracy of silence at the breakfast table. Everyone slanted looks at Wolfer and Alys, but no one said anything, beyond, "Pass the pancakes, please," "More honey, anyone?" "Let me pour that for you," and similar, ordinary, casually murmured words.

Saber finally wiped his mouth with his napkin and spoke, mentioning something besides food. "The traders are due today."

"Who gets to break the bad news to them about the salt?" Kelly asked. "I'd love to do it myself"

"You are staying *here*," her husband asserted firmly. The freckled woman opened her mouth to argue. Saber cut her off quickly. "They'll probably try to kill you the moment they so much as see you, so you'll stay up here. For now. I'll handle the salt," Saber added. "But I'll need some help. I did it all on my own once, shortly after you arrived, and it was *not* something I'd care to repeat. Not while it's still technically our honeymoon. Some of the wagons also need their propulsion spells renewed. Morganen?"

"I can't help you right away," the youngest of them pointed out, wiping his own mouth, smothering a yawn behind his napkin. There were faint, dark circles under his eyes, hinting at a restless night. "Kor, Ev, and I were working late in the forge last night with Rydan, trying to make a mirror that would focus exclusively on Dominor, and so extend our scrying range for finding him. We didn't get very far, though we tried all night. What we really need is some of his blood . . . and naturally we can't get any, since he's not here. So we're still tired. We'll join you in a few hours, though, after we've napped."

"Fine. Trevan and Wolfer, then. You'll have to come down to the beach with me," Saber said, flicking a glance at his twin, then at the woman on his twin's other side. "Stay here with Kelly, Alys; it's safer for both of you to be inside the castle walls. At least, for now."

Alys glanced at Kelly and ventured to speak. "Your wife and I were talking about getting some cows. For fresh milk and cream? I could tend the cows and the chickens, to earn my keep."

"I doubt the traders will be happy to pay for salt blocks with a small herd of cattle," Saber muttered. He shook his head. "We'd need to clear out a pasture for them to graze in for the first step, anyway, and get enough grass to grow high and long enough for grazing and for harvesting against the cold season. Not that it gets nearly as cold here as it used to back down in Corvis Lands."

"Well, I can do that, too," she offered. As the others looked at her, Alys shrugged. "I'm good with animals, and good with plants. Magic-wise, I mean. Not *great*, but at least a little good."

Kelly smiled. "Alys has also generously suggested she take over the feeding of the chickens, to make herself useful. I, for one, would be happy to have *anyone* else tending them besides me."

"My poor, henpecked wife," Saber sighed.

His brothers choked on their laughter. His wife pinched him. Not hard, Alys noted, but she did nip him lightly on the earlobe with her fingertips. Saber caught Kelly's wayward hand and kissed it, then kissed her on the nose when she mock-narrowed her eyes.

Wolfer spoke up, his bass rumble cutting through the suppressed merriment. "How soon do I have to be down on the beach?"

"Right after breakfast, same as usual, just in case they come early on the incoming tide," Saber pointed out.

Wolfer glanced at Alys, who blushed and dropped her gaze. *Dammit. You'd think Destiny would arrange things so I could* be *with her, if she's my fated bride.*

A horrid thought crossed his mind at that moment.

*What if she* isn't *my bride-by-Destiny? What if it's supposed to be someone else and not her?* The thought was not a pleasant one. It *couldn't* be, after all—the very thought repelled him, thinking of her walking the eight altars with someone else. In such a short, short time, his childhood friend had come to mean so much more to him than just a youthful companion. She *had* to be the one, his Destiny. Wolfer was not going to let someone else come into his life and take her away from him!

Unfortunately, there was nothing he could do about it right away; he had to go to the beach today.

But he still needed to talk to her. When breakfast ended, as those assigned to the chore cleared the table and the rest left, Wolfer managed to catch Alys' hand and tugged her into the nearest room, a chamber now crowded with its own furniture plus what had been in the dining room before it was restored.

"What is it?" she whispered, curious to know why he needed to talk to her alone, even though he was due to leave immediately.

"Will you . . ." Wolfer's palms were feeling sweaty; he wiped them on his thighs. He wasn't sure if he should kneel or not, but didn't dare take the time to do so, just in case they were interrupted by the others. "Uh, that is, would you do me the great hon—"

The door opened behind him, and his twin stuck his head inside. "Beach, Wolfer. *Now*."

*"Jinga's Balls!"* Wolfer swore, making Alys widen her eyes as he whirled on Saber. "What do we have to do to get some *privacy* around here?!"

His twin blinked, his dark gold brows rising at Wolfer's outburst. Those bemused steel gray eyes shifted to the mist-gray eyes of the other occupant in the room. Saber sighed and shook his head. "You'll have plenty of time for that, Wolfer. *After* the traders have come and gone."

His twin growled hard in frustration, directing it straight at the source of this latest interruption.

"Oh, shut up, Wolfer!" Saber snapped, scowling at his brother. "*I* have to abandon my wife to see to my duty in dealing with the traders! *You* can suffer, too." Saber opened the door wider, the picture of impatience as he waited for Wolfer to join him.

Snarling under his breath, Wolfer stalked out. He stopped long enough to glance back at Alys as he passed through the doorway, then growled some more. The second born of the brothers snarled all the way to the western courtyard, climbed up on the cart next to Trevan, rumbled his anger at his twin as Saber joined them in the cart, and growled as they left the castle and started down the hill.

Halfway down, on a flat, level spot on the western road, Saber tapped the fifth born of them. Trevan lifted his foot from the speed lever and pushed on the brake lever, stopping the cart the brothers had enchanted for transportation on the horseless isle.

Morning noises from the jungle surrounded them: leaves rustling in the breeze, insects chirruping, birds twittering . . . Wolfer growling.

Saber stared heavily at his twin. "Do you *mind*?"

"*Yes,* dammit!" Wolfer snapped, losing his temper. "I was going to *propose* to her! And *you* had better stay well away from her, and keep your rod in your trousers, or by the Gods, Trevan, I'll rip it out by the *roots*!"

Trevan pulled back his light auburn head at the tirade; he studied his elder brother a long, silent moment, then turned and eyed Saber, who was riding in the back of the cart. He was sitting next to the few magic items the brothers had managed to make for sale in the past two weeks, distracted by the prophesied Disaster and its aftermath. The redhead sighed and shook his head. "It's just sexual frustration. It'll go away as soon as they have some privacy."

Wolfer tipped his head back and howled out his frustration. He snarled and glared at his brothers, lowering his head as his cry echoed and faded through the forest. He bared his teeth at them, the veins on his muscular neck standing out in the morning light filtering through the trees, as he roared at his blood kin. "That. Is. The. *Point!*"

Trevan eyed him askance. "My. Aren't *we* grumpy to-day?"

Whirling, Wolfer leaped out of the cart. He was in wolf form even before his paws touched the ground. Diving into the underbrush, he loped into the forest, determined to exorcise his frustration with a bit of exercise. Instead of tearing literally as well as figuratively into his blood kin.

Seated on the cart, Trevan and Saber glanced at each other. Shrugging sublimely, Trevan gripped the steering reins and pressed down on the acceleration lever with his toe, sending the cart forward once more.

"Sexual frustration," the copper-haired man confirmed sagely.

Saber didn't know whether to grin or feel pity for his twin. He settled for both, glad Wolfer was no longer within view. It wasn't fair of him to find amusement in his twin's suffering, but from the moment of her arrival, even Saber could see exactly who was the next agent of Destiny in the family.

Little Alys of Devries. All grown up into a woman now. A woman who had her sights just as set on Wolfer of Nightfall, as Wolfer had his sights on her.

Who would've thought it?

Deep in the jungle, Wolfer leaped over a fallen tree and loped through the clearing it had made. He startled a trio of summer deer from one of the two wild herds that grazed Nightfall Isle, one sticking to the western side of the elongated island, one to the eastern, only coming close enough to intermingle every now and then at the far northern and southern ends and avoiding the swayback pass that the castle was perched on between the two mountain ranges. A covey of *plinka* birds took flight, their red, black, and yellow plumage contrasting starkly with the forest greenery.

They were swift, too, darting up among the branches as he drew near.

His fangs snapped at a leaf that whacked his muzzle in passing. Bounding up a hill, he had to pick his way down the steep slope on the far side carefully. One of the harmless tree snakes slithered quickly out of Wolfer's way as he used a log fallen at an angle against the hill to descend more quickly. His toenails clicked as he trotted across a section of the curving, flagstone-laid road, then crunched softly over fallen leaves on the forest floor. A *pipka*, looking much like an oversized mouse, flashed across the earth in front of him, but he wasn't hungry enough to give chase, though for a moment, his wolfish instincts were tempted. The crunching of bones in his jaws might have been some form of physical outlet for his frustration, but it wasn't the outlet he wanted to use.

Naturally, he made it down to the beach before his brothers did. And naturally the ship wasn't there. Growling, Wolfer trotted to the north, toward the road on a low ridge of land that led out to the spur containing the one remaining, functional stone jetty and another leading to the water processing building. That road led past a large, rectangular, stone-lined lake and up a switchback road, which was connected to the road that led to beach and castle, forming a loop.

The western beach differed from the eastern one in that its north side had water deep enough to harbor a ship close enough to shore to offload goods directly onto a dock. The south end of the western cove had a stretch of shallow sand that turned into tide pools at the far, southern spur of the bay, suitable for shipyards. Once upon a time, there had been wooden docks and lots of buildings, as this had been a bustling port city. Now, there were only jungle-claimed remnants of stone foundations, their wooden walls and roofs long since decimated by the inexorable march of time.

*Building* wasn't really the right word for it, since it was more than one structure, and was still very ornately carved . . . though *temple complex* had too many religious connotations. It was a large, octagonal compound holding eight octagonal buildings around the edge and one large warehouse in the center, each with columns all around the outside, eight on each side.

Most things of Katan were represented in twos, fours, and especially eights, to represent the four seasonal faces of each of their two gods: Jinga and Kata in the spring as compassionate Lover and Maiden; in the summer as protective Lord and Lady; in the autumn as nurturing Father and Mother; and in the winter as wise Sage and Crone. The great mage who had made this place long, long ago—a place of rare, permanent magic—had clearly tapped into the potent power that was the number eight in the Katani corner of the world. In other regions, it might be different, but here, eight ruled.

Shifting shape as he reached the entrance, Wolfer stepped inside the tree-surrounded compound and entered the first huge, domed building. With more water being processed with the extra people in the castle and all of the fountains opened up once more, more algae was being produced, and more salt was being compressed into purified blocks. That meant they were piling up faster.

Not nearly at the volume the original inhabitants had used, of course—that had been a whole island's worth of water needing to be constantly purified for use. In fact, there were eight huge sluice gates in this chamber alone, where the purifying process began . . . and only one of them was open, and only by a fraction. Thankfully, the permanent magic imbued in the thousand-year-old structure guaranteed that those thick steel sluice gates were not rusted shut in any of the buildings and kept the stones of those buildings strong and solid.

The whole thing was a work of beauty. Wolfer walked around the fringe of the building to check the sluice, which his brothers had widened slightly to accommodate the water needs of the castle fountains. The constantly swirling saltwater pool was at or maybe even below sea level, depending on the tide. That was only because the processing

pool was so big and deep, as big around as the building itself, minus room for a broad catwalk. The catwalk had
metal ladders leading up from the water, to be used to rescue anyone who might fall into the pool while fishing for
smaller sea-creatures that sometimes made it beyond the
outer grille.

Those ladders and the railings bordering the holding
pool were wrought with metal that occasionally echoed the
ripple and scroll of a wave. Even the tiles lining the inside
of the building undulated in their patterning, reminding
one of the sea. As much care and detail had been crafted
into the processing plant as would normally go into a
Katani temple, but the feel of the place was just a little too
secular and practical to be reverent.

Everything looked all right. The brothers liked to check
the system regularly, even though it was spelled to keep
working without much in the way of maintenance. Sometimes seaweed and driftwood got tangled in the intake
grille, especially after a storm, but not this time.

Wolfer left that building and made the circuit of the
other three saltwater chambers. The inspection was giving
him time to calm down. There were four saltwater pools all
told, though the unused three were dry as bones. They were
interspersed with the other three empty buildings, where
the water, after passing through a magic-laced grid built
into transfer pipes running between the tanks, was separated into slightly smaller pools of fresh, desalinated water.
Which wasn't saying much, since they were still huge
basins. Occupying the extra space in those chambers were
two sets of ramps that came up from that enspelled, hidden
latticework underground.

The water, he knew, first entered into the saltwater tanks
through a grid that screened out all but the smallest forms
of life—usually anything from a shrimp on up, but which
sometimes missed small fish. Then it passed through one
more filter to catch the life-forms that might have slipped
through, just to be sure, and passed through the separator.
All of the algae-plankton and excess minerals were ex-

tracted, dried, and pressed into blocks that came up one of
the two sloped, polished, smooth ramps, one block simply
pushing the next up without any need for extra magical or
mechanical conveyance.

All of the salt came up on a second ramp, dried and
compressed into huge, purified white blocks at the same
time as the algae ones did. Entering the fourth of the de-
salination buildings, the one that was still active, Wolfer
noted that Trevan and Saber were finally there. They were
using spells to lift and levitate the blocks of algae, carrying
out the huge green slabs to the cart.

Normally the traders took the algae, too. When it was
crumbled and mixed into the soil, it made an excellent fertilizer, since the salt had already been extracted and
couldn't harm the soil. But if the brothers were going to
make the traders pay for salt, they were going to make them
pay for the greenish fertilizer, too. Satisfied everything
looked all right, Wolfer turned and headed for the innermost
building.

In the ancient days, according to the history books in the
library of the island, ships used to come every single day to
pick up salt and carry it away for trade, because that much
salt could be processed when all four pairs of processing
tanks were going. In the past three years, they had usually
made somewhere between one and two blocks each of salt
and algae every day. Lately, with the fountains running and
the sluice opened a little more to compensate, they were
making about three of each a day, from the looks of the
amount that had stacked up on the roller-lined ramps.

Entering the warehouse, Wolfer hopped up onto one of
the large, flatbed, magic-propelled wagons they had made
shortly into their stay, to use solely for hauling the green
and white blocks around. The eight-sided warehouse in the
center, with its eight-and-four sets of pillars supporting the
roof, used to be filled with blocks and blocks of salt and algae, plus other warehouses elsewhere in the ancient city-
port of Nightfall. Now it held dust and a couple of horseless
wagons.

Pressing the pedal did nothing. Wolfer frowned down at the contraption, then extended his senses into it. All mages could sense anything that had magic, including other mages. Nothing met his questing probe.

*Great. The spell has to be renewed on this one. I'll remind Morganen to take care of it when he comes down to help. Or if not, I'll throw him out of his tower and tell him to come down here and do it anyway.* Hopping down, he crossed to the next one, and pushed down on its pedal. It lurched forward, freshly enspelled, and he quickly steered with the reins before he ran into a support column.

Even with twenty blocks of salt—and Dominor, unwittingly—traded to the Mandarites, there was still more than enough to sell to the traders. If they were willing to buy. *And if they don't buy it, we'll send out word in the mirrors that Nightfall has salt cheaper than what the traders have been selling it for . . . and there* will *be some people willing to ignore the by-permission-only trading allowed by the Mage Council at the new and full of Brother Moon.*

Personally, Wolfer liked the idea of throwing out the rulings of King and Council about their exile. He had liked it when Kelly had summarily declared Nightfall a freehold by Katani-authorized admission and had then declared herself Queen of Nightfall, though Wolfer had pretended otherwise. With his newfound frustration over Alys, he was itching and ready to pick a fight with someone. Maybe, if he was lucky, the traders would get ugly about suddenly having to pay for what they had previously taken for free . . .

# EIGHT

·❄·

"Cousins! How glad I am to see you! You remember your Uncle Donnock, don't you?"

Wolfer blinked and looked up. He knew that name. He also knew that face. Broger of Devries' middle brother, he recalled. He hadn't seen as much of the man as Alys' father, Tangor, or Broger himself, but Wolfer had met him in the past. The second-born mage had never really liked this man, though to be fair, he didn't know him well. Still, even before his magic had manifested itself strongest in the shapechanging area, Wolfer had always felt as if his fur fluffed along his spine and his ears flattened whenever he was around this particular man.

Of course, he had always felt that way around Broger, too; only Tangor had been pleasant company, of his three uncles-in-law.

Now the dark-haired man strode down the gangplank of the trader's docked ship, letting the Katani sailors carry down a traveling trunk for him. They set it on the dock among the chests, barrels, and crates they normally brought. Donnock's arms were open, and a smile curved his somewhat handsome face, the sea breeze ruffling his finger-length, cropped brown hair. "I've come for a visit!"

Wolfer narrowed his eyes, suspicious. He might have accepted that fact, even though it was the first "visit" ever from one of their kin, by marriage or by blood, except he knew the man was liked by the eldest Devries brother . . . and that Broger of Devries had treated Alys very badly. That last part alone was enough to make Wolfer growl.

Saber was no fool, either. He found the sudden visit suspicious as well. After the "trade salt for valuable oil, and come and help enspell our holds to keep it clean" too-good-to-be-true deal of the Mandarites, he was feeling very suspicious of anything out of the ordinary. He also knew that Broger liked this living middle-born brother of his, and that Broger had not only treated Alys badly enough to make her finally run away . . . he had lied about their blood-uncle Daron being alive and holding Corvis for them pro tem.

Saber lifted his chin with a glance toward Koranen, directing the second-youngest as the most friendly of them all to greet the man, and stepped back, singing under his breath. *"Evanor . . ."*

*I hear and am curious, O Eldest Brother,"* the missing brother sang back. He was sitting with Alys and Kelly up at the castle, to give them some extra magical protection while the traders were here, as well as to help work on one of the endless household tasks the lightest-haired of them enjoyed taking care of.

*"Evanor, Alys' Uncle Donnock has come to pay us a visit. Ask her what she thinks of this."*

Evanor frowned. The three of them were in the sewing hall, working together on a larger wardrobe for their latest member; he was doing most of the cutting work, standing at the table, while the two of women were doing the stitching, Kelly at a smaller worktable, Alys at a chair half tucked into one of the window alcoves. "Alys?"

"Mm?" She looked up, a needle tucked between her lips while she measured out a length of thread and snipped it from its spool.

"Saber says your Uncle Donnock is here, on the island."

Alys lost all of the color in her face. Evanor feared she was going to faint in her chair and took a step forward. She removed the needle from her mouth with an unsteady hand, inhaled and exhaled slowly a few times, and spoke. Tightly. "Get him off the island. *Now.*"

Both Evanor and Kelly blinked. The latter spoke first, her confusion evident in both voice and face. "Why do we need to kick him off the island, Alys? I've never even met the guy!"

Alys opened her mouth to explain, then flushed. She couldn't, not for the largest reason. They would kick *her* off, too. Of any of them, she owed Wolfer the first explanation. She picked a lesser reason instead. "He's close to Uncle Broger—the moment he realizes I'm on the island, he'll tell Broger, and *he'll* come after me.

"Please," she added, looking at Evanor. "Don't let him anywhere near the castle, or the water-thingy you were telling me about, where the traders go to get their salt and make their trade. Get him off this island as quickly as you can. *Please.*"

Evanor studied her thoughtfully, his brown eyes narrowing a moment, then nodded his blond head. He projected his voice all the way to Saber's ears. *"Brother, Alys is terrified of Donnock; she fears he will tell her Uncle Broger she is here, and maybe do worse. She asks that you don't even let him get off the boat."*

𝕸iles away, down on the quay, Saber grimaced. Of all of them, the young woman Alys knew her kinsman the best . . . and her reply only supported his instincts that there was something distinctly hooked, netted, and landed about this "visit." Stepping forward, he addressed his kin-in-law. "I'm afraid we cannot allow you to stay, Donnock."

The dark brown-haired man blinked, paused as a second cart bearing a couple of the other brothers rattled onto the quay, then returned his gaze to Saber. Dannock frowned at the younger mage. "Why not?"

"It would be violating the conditions of our exile."

The middle-aged man gave a rude noise. "I do not fear the Council! Besides, I am kin, and kin are allowed to visit."

"*Blood* kin," Wolfer growled, hearing and joining his twin in the debate. "You are not related to us by blood!"

Donnock narrowed his hazel eyes for just a moment. Then smoothed his expression into a more charming one as the youngest set of twins joined them. "I've come all this way; surely I can spend one night in comfort? I don't have to stay until the traders come again in a fortnight, but I simply cannot abide staying on that ship overnight.

"Even if your castle is a falling-down ruin, I'd far rather stay there. Anything to get away from the stench of rotting fish." He moved down the dock a little farther and peered at the eastern horizon, defined by the two ranges of mountain peaks on the fifty-mile-long island and the green saddleback due east of the bay. "I thought it was located right over there, and that it was visible from the water, but I haven't spotted it yet."

Saber shifted, getting himself between the man and the beach. "You cannot stay. You will have to sleep on board the ship."

"That's a rather hard stance, Saber," Koranen asserted, glancing at his twin for support. As the two youngest, they hadn't had much exposure to the man now on the dock, so he didn't see any reason why he couldn't stay; neither had they heard Saber's muted, far-distant conversation with Evanor. Koranen eyed his twin. "Right, Morg?"

Morganen did not meet his twin's gaze. Or anyone else's.

Saber opened his mouth to explain, noted the curiosity on the older man's face . . . and carefully spoke in Mandarite, which all of the brothers spoke, because they had drunk the rare, powerful Ultra Tongue potion. It was a tongue Donnock could not comprehend. All that was required was speaking in the lilting "accent" that the Mandarites used, and the enchanted potion did the rest.

"Our newest inhabitant is terrified he'll tell her uncle Broger she's here, or worse, that maybe he might do something to her himself. So he will *not* be allowed to stay," Saber emphasized quietly. "I myself don't like the way he's insisting on seeing the castle; it makes me glad Dom created that illusion-cloaking sphere to 'camouflage' it, as Kelly's people say."

"Alys is afraid of him?" Wolfer asked his twin in a low, suspicious growl. Saber shrugged, so Wolfer sang low under his breath. *"Evanor . . ."*

*"You howled?"*

*"Is our newest guest afraid of Donnock?"*

*"She turned ash white the moment I mentioned his name—she's all but terrified out of her wits where he's concerned, I'd say,"* the unseen brother recited in Wolfer's ears alone, boiling his blood with the confession.

"Well?" Donnock asserted at the same time that Wolfer listened to his distant brother. "I'm not standing here all day! This is very poor hospitality you show to a kinsm—"

*Smack!* Wolfer's fist connected with Donnock's face, cutting off the man mid-complaint. The other man staggered back with a grunt of pain, and Wolfer closed in with another hard-struck blow. Donnock staggered back once more, throwing up his arms to protect his now-bleeding face.

"Wolfer!" Saber was shocked by his twin's abrupt attack.

"You bastard!" the older man shouted, staggering and shoving at Wolfer's hands, trying to get out of the range of his blows. "*Croesoth*—ow!—*minorokh*—dammit!"

Wolfer replied in Mandarite, so that his cursing, dodging, spell-attempting target wouldn't know Alys was on the isle. "She's terrified of him, Saber. That's good enough for me!"

*"Wolfer!"* his twin snapped.

Donnock was trying to simultaneously block Wolfer's

hard, fast blows and chant some piece of protective or maybe offensive magic—but it was hard for him to get even half of the words out. His heel reached the edge of the dock, and he started to go over. Wolfer snatched out and yanked him back by a fistful of the older man's tunic . . . and held him conveniently in place, punching him over and over with thumping jabs of his other, muscle-driven fist.

The older man slugged Wolfer in his rock-hard stomach, drawing his knife with his other hand, while Wolfer's brothers surged forward to pry them apart. Wolfer bared his teeth with a feral snarl and grabbed Donnock's wrist, snapping it and forcing the knife to drop to the planks underfoot. *Anyone* who scared his Alys had to answer to *him* and his righteous vengeance in his beloved's name.

Determined sibling arms pried them apart. Donnock, bleeding from mouth and nose, his eyes puffy and blackening already, snarled at him, almost like a wolf himself. "You piece of *trakk*! I'm going to cut out your heart and feed it to a *grodak*, you—!"

Wolfer lunged out of Saber's and Trevan's arms and got in a powerhouse of a left cross, just as the other man jerked forward out of Koranen's and Morganen's grip, unwittingly meeting the blow. It whipped the older mage around and dropped him like a rock, knocking him out. Wolfer immediately shook out his throbbing knuckles and straightened his tunic, feeling proud of his warrior prowess in this blatantly successful protection of his Alys. The sailors who had been carrying the man's trunk and the other, more normal bundles eyed him askance, giving him, his brothers, and the man stretched out on the planks a wide berth on the broad, wooden dock. His brothers looked at Wolfer's victim and winced.

"Great," Saber muttered, running one hand through his dark gold locks, then gesturing roughly at the man crumpled on the weather-beaten boards that formed their one functional quay. He continued in Mandarite to keep the debate hidden from the trader-sailors edging warily around them. "*Now* what are we going to do with him?"

"Morganen, enspell him so that he sleeps long enough to reach the mainland—and then spellbind him so that he cannot ever come here again," Wolfer ordered the youngest of them.

"That's going too far, Wolfer!" Saber snapped, losing his temper. "We could have just kept him down here on the beach and sent him on his way with the tide tomorrow! Even if Alys is afraid of him, leaving him on the beach wouldn't . . ." He broke off and looked down at the youngest of them, who was kneeling next to the unconscious man and chanting over him. "What are you doing, Morg?"

Morganen didn't stop until the first spell was complete. Just as the older man was starting to rouse with a groan, he slumped unconscious again under a final syllable and a pass of the youngest brother's hand. "Wolfer is right, Saber. It's too risky to allow him even onto the beach.

"If Broger has been lying to us about Father's brother Daron being dead all this time, then it makes Donnock's visit and insistence on seeing the castle very suspicious in my mind as well. And there is his comment about feeding Wolfer's heart to a *grodak,* which I remind you is one of the monsters our unknown assailant has sent to us a couple times in the past three years," he added dryly, flexing his fingers in a new incantation. "I will add a spell to make him forget he ever came here and a spell to make him go elsewhere and perform some other task, to make sure his mind does not naturally wear off the forgetfulness spell all that quickly . . . though how long he will stay forgetful and away from here even with the extra spells compelling his mind, I cannot say."

"Wait—you think Broger and his brother here might have had something to do with our troubles these past three years?" Koranen asked his twin.

Saber mulled it over. "Alys said Daron died only two months into our exile. Not long after that, we started being plagued with teleported beasts."

"It *could* be just coincidence," Trevan pointed out. Then shook his head. "But my instincts aren't telling me that."

"We have no proof," Koranen reminded them, as Morganen began the second, longer, and more complex chant, geas-binding the man so that, no matter how he tried, he would circumvent his own efforts to get back to Nightfall Isle.

Morganen, being one of the supporters of sending their uncle-in-law far away—and one of the few who knew the truth of Alys' story—wasn't paying much attention to what they were doing, leaving them to handle the discussion on their own. Then again, Kor knew his twin held many secrets, even from him. Wolfer's suggestion was a good one, however, and he had the power and the knowledge to keep Donnock of Devries from ever returning to Nightfall.

"And no way to prove it, stuck on this island as we are," Saber concurred with his seventh-born sibling.

"Evanor says Alys turned white the moment he mentioned Donnock's name," Wolfer pointed out. And then he paled, too. "Jinga . . ." He breathed the god's name, golden eyes widening. "She couldn't possibly be involved in this, too! Not *her*!"

"Wolfer!" his twin called out, but the moment the horrible thought crossed his mind, Wolfer took off, first sprinting on two feet, then impatiently switching to four hooves in his fastest form. The sailors carrying their cargo across the flagstone road between dock and jungle cursed, dodging the brown stallion as Wolfer raced for the hills in a clatter of hooves.

Saber says they have enspelled Donnock so he cannot visit again, probably by a geas, and ordered the sailors to put him back on their ship," Evanor related. "Apparently he's unconscious at the moment, thanks to Wolfer's unpredictable temper."

Alys relaxed. Slightly. Bending over her sewing again, she avoided looking at the other two. She knew that both of her uncles would react badly to Donnock being enspelled and geas-bound to keep himself away from the island. Once they figured out what had been done to her uncle, things would go rapidly downhill. Pushing it out of her mind, she focused on her sewing chore, desperately clinging to the moment while that moment was still peaceful, not terrifying.

War was coming to the island, whether the brothers wanted it or not . . . and it was in part her fault.

She had all of one sleeve stitched up when the sewing hall door banged open, startling her into a yelp of fear and a jerk that jabbed the needle into her finger. It was only Wolfer, though. Tears in her eyes, Alys pulled the needle from her flesh and stuck her finger in her mouth.

Wolfer saw her nursing her finger from where he stood in the doorway and cursed himself silently. "Forgive me— I didn't mean . . . I'm sorry I frightened you, Alys."

Alys glared at him over her hand, mumbling past her throbbing, pricked finger. "An well you foulb be! Tha *hur*, Wuffer!"

The other two in the room eyed the pair of them in curiosity; Evanor and Kelly didn't appear to exist anymore, even though they weren't more than a couple yards away in the longish sewing chamber. Completely ignoring the most domestic of his brothers and their sister-in-law, Wolfer strode to where Alys sat on a stool. It had been placed just out of direct reach of the sunlight in one of the window alcoves, taking advantage of both the light for her sewing and the cooling breeze coming in through the window without placing her in direct line of the midsummer heat. He dropped to one knee, held out his hands to touch her, and hesitated.

He couldn't believe, now that he faced her, that she, gentle, sweet Alys, could ever have anything to do with the troubles that had plagued him and his brothers since their arrival on Nightfall. *No, I know she's innocent; her uncle may not be . . . but Alys is. I have no doubt in my heart of that.* Looking into her soft gray eyes—currently narrowed at him in a halfhearted, pouting glower—he knew she wouldn't, couldn't ever harm him or his brothers. Not willingly. Not deliberately.

Reaching for her injured hand, he pulled the finger out of her mouth. A brief inspection showed it had stopped bleeding, though there was still a little red dot where the needle had gone in. Lifting it to his mouth, he kissed it gently. "Alys . . . will you marry me?"

Forgotten but still present, Kelly felt her jaw drop. Her mouth slowly curved up in delight. A glance at Evanor showed his own blond brows had risen, with a mixture of delight and an amused, resigned, "it was inevitable!" look on his face as well. They shared identically astounded, pleased grins, as the blushing, curly haired recipient struggled to reply.

Alys stammered. "Wolfer—I—you—ah—you—I"

Wolfer kissed her finger again, this time on its tip, not the side where the needle had pricked her. He kissed each of the other fingertips one by one between words. "I believe . . . that you are . . . my Destiny, Alys." He turned her hand over and kissed her palm. "Marry me." He kissed her wrist. "Marry me." He lifted and kissed the knuckles of her other hand. "Marry me." And turned it over and kissed her other palm. Each deep-voiced request vibrated straight from the depths of his soul. "Marry me."

"Oh, Wolfer . . ." She gently freed her hands and cupped his face. He burrowed his cheeks in her palms, enjoying the feel of her flesh. Alys lifted his head, making him lift his eyes and look at her. Fear warred for a moment within her. She reminded herself to trust in Morganen's advice to her over the past few years, and drew in a deep breath. "Wolfer . . . you must know I would never willingly do anything to hurt you . . ."

"I know," he murmured into her palms, turning his head and kissing them again, oblivious to their delighted, avidly witnessing audience. "I *know*."

That made her feel worse for a moment, plagued with guilt. "Not willingly, Wolfer—never, ever if I could have helped it." She lifted his smooth-shaven jaw again. "I've always loved you."

His golden eyes widened, then darkened with growing heat. "Marry me, Alys."

She closed her gray eyes, bowing her head. "I am afraid of so many things, Wolfer . . ."

"Shh," he admonished her, shifting closer and enfolding her in his large, muscular arms. "I will not let anything harm you; not from this moment on—you *will* marry me, won't you?" he added in prompting, since technically she hadn't said either yes or no. "I'm not going to let you go until you say yes. Everywhere you go, I will go, too. Even into the refreshing room if need be . . ."

"*Yes*, I will marry you!" she half-sobbed, half-laughed, clinging to him.

Wolfer groaned and gathered her closer. "Jinga, how I love you! I always have; I just didn't really know it until now." She burrowed in closer, half sliding off her stool in the effort to get closer to him . . . and Wolfer winced from a sharp prick of pain in his leg. "Ow!"

Alys pulled back slightly, concern in her gray eyes. "What is it?"

Wincing, he gently released her, one hand going to his thigh. "I think your needle bit me!"

That made her smile, and she wiped at her emotion-damp eyes. "Well, you deserved it, making it bite me first with your noisy, door-banging entrance!"

Plucking the needle free and rubbing his thigh, Wolfer mock-glared at her. "Don't you dare turn into another ter-magant like my sister-in-law."

"Hey!" Kelly protested, breaking up the illusion of privacy between them. When they both glanced at her, she mock-frowned at them. "I *resemble* that remark!"

It took all three of the non-Earth humans a few moments to get the joke buried in her retort, but when they did, Evanor groaned, Wolfer grinned, and Alys winced then smiled.

Kelly sighed and shook her head, looking over at Evanor.

"Looks like we'll have to set this stuff aside and see what we can come up with in matching wedding clothes."

Evanor agreed. "I believe we have some gray silk somewhere that would look flattering on both."

Wolfer raised his brows at that. "Wedding clothes? Do you know how long it will take you to sew us some wedding clothes? I plan on walking the eight altars with her tomorrow night, as soon as the traders have gone!"

"Absolutely not—in fact, I forbid it!" Kelly added flatly, cutting her hand through the air over her own sewing. "As Queen of Nightfall, I *insist* on a two-week waiting period for all marriages."

"Two weeks?" Alys repeated, dismayed.

Kelly gave her a pointed look. "You *do* want enough time to come up with a suitable wedding gift for him, don't you?"

Alys looked between the other woman and Wolfer, unsure what to do or say.

Wolfer narrowed his eyes thoughtfully, then grinned a wolfish grin. "Two weeks is fine by me."

"It is?" Alys asked him, confused.

"Of course. Two weeks is enough time for me to get you gently accustomed to the eventual physical expression of our love," he informed her gently.

*Eventual physical expression of . . .* Alys raised one dark blond brow, eyeing him in puzzlement, until she finally figured out what he was trying to say. "You think I'm afraid of . . . of copulating with you? Wolfer, that's the *last* thing I'm afraid of with you!"

She blushed furiously as she said it, but she did say it, and did it with that boldness that occasionally peeked out from deep within her soul. Wolfer eyed her, then glanced at his sister-in-law. "I thought you said she had almost . . . that she wouldn't be interested . . ."

"I didn't say or suggest in any way that she wouldn't be interested," Kelly asserted. "I simply suggested—and rather strongly—that you take things slow and easy, so you don't frighten her with your lust."

Alys blushed a decided shade of red. So did Wolfer, but his was more of a flush of anger than a blush of embarrassment. He jabbed a finger at her. "I should have given your husband a *gag* for your wedding gift!"

"And maybe I should get *you* a muzzle!" Kelly shot back mock-sweetly, since it was said through clenched teeth, hands on her hips, even still seated as she was.

Alys scowled at her. "Don't talk to my Wolfer that way!"

Wolfer blinked and eyed his brave, defending bride-to-be. He felt a rising delight that she would defend him so fiercely.

She lifted her chin and continued firmly, "That's *my* job."

Kelly gasped with laughter, switching moods abruptly. "Oh, I have so *missed* having a woman around this place!"

Alys giggled, too. The two men in the room frowned and eyed each other, seeking to see if either Evanor or Wolfer understood what the two women meant. It was a complete mystery to both men, though. Shaking his head, Wolfer tossed Alys' lapful of sewing at the bench seat by the window and pulled her up from her stool. "Do not mock me. *Either* of you."

He swept Alys up in his arms, making her draw in a quick breath and wrap her arms around his neck. Kelly stood also, frowning at them.

"Just where do you think you're going with her?" his sister-in-law demanded as he started for the door.

Wolfer paused. And gave a wolfish smile. "Where do you *think* we're going, and for what purpose?"

"*I* had to wait for *my* wedding night," Kelly pointed out. She looked at Evanor for support. "Don't your people wait until your wedding night?"

He shook his blond head as Wolfer continued out of the sewing hall, a blushing Alys clinging to him. "Of course not," Evanor enlightened her. "So long as the proper precautions are taken against unwanted conception and that both parties are over the age of sixteen and are fully and freely consenting adults, there is no impediment to making love. One simply has to be very respectful of another person's right to say no, in Katan."

"But then why did *I* have to wait?" Kelly demanded, frowning at both men.

"*You* making love with Saber was associated irrevocably with Disaster," Evanor pointed out in his smooth, silken tenor, returning to his cutting work. Looking inescapably masculine, as all of the brothers did, even in the middle of what many in her own universe would have called "sissy" work. "We all chose to have you two wait until the timing was convenient for us to handle the advent of the Prophesied Disaster, which was fated to come right on the heels of . . . well, *you* know. Not just for planning a proper feast, presents, and wedding clothes."

"Well, then I should get to have *twice* as much fun—or *more*—for having to wait for so long!" she asserted.

Evanor grinned. "Would you like me to pass that remark along to your husband?"

Kelly considered that for a full three seconds. Then nodded regally. "Yes, please. And ask him to look for more gray silk, if you would be so kind. I'm not certain if what we have on hand is going to be enough. Waiting or not for their own wedding night, you and I are going to have them *properly* attired for the ceremony, two weeks from now."

# NINE

❦

Alys could feel Wolfer's heart pounding in his chest. It thumped against her arm where it was caught against his body; he felt snug and warm and, blessed Kata, she was touching him. It wasn't far at all from the sewing hall to his chambers, both being in the western wing. Taking the southern of the two branches, he carried her to his sitting room door and tried to get both of them inside with an awkward nudge at the handle.

His efforts made her take pity on him and reach for it herself, since his arms were so wonderfully occupied at the moment, holding her so carefully, so closely. A thump of his boot heel shut the door firmly behind him, and then they were alone. More or less.

Wolfer drew in a breath where he stood . . . but not to speak to the woman in his arms. *"Evanor."*

As Alys arched a brow, the family communicator responded in his ears. *"Yes, Wolfer?"*

"Two things. One, refrain from relaying any messages save dire emergency—and I mean it had *better* be a life-or-death emergency—for the next . . . three hours," Wolfer calculated. "And two, stop eavesdropping right *now*."

"*I hear nothing, I say nothing . . . and I'd better not hear from either of you, too, for three hours,*" his brother responded. And fell politely silent.

"I *think* we're alone now," Wolfer managed to say, drawing in a deep breath of hope and satisfaction. He found himself enjoying the feel of her flesh pressing against his with the motion, as well as the feminine scent of her, flowery from soaps and slightly musky from sweat. He breathed deeply again just to keep enjoying it.

Alys blushed, then gathered her courage and peered around his sitting room. It was a masculine room, with the minimum in embroidery, coordinated colors, and excessive cushions. In fact, most of the cushioning on the furniture was done in leather, not in cloth. But it was still only the outer sitting room. "This doesn't look like your bedchamber."

He grinned. "And how would you know what that looks like, since you spent more time under my bed than looking around my room? Unless you plan to crawl under my bed again?"

"*Into* it, not under it," she asserted firmly. "When we're finally *in* there . . ." And she felt his heart actually skip a beat. He cradled her closer and strode into the bedroom, kicking that door shut as well. She jumped a little in his arms when the door banged sharply. The windows were open to any stray breeze that might take the summer heat from the room.

"Shh," Wolfer soothed her. "You can say *no* at any time." He didn't want to think of what she might have endured in the "almost molested" category and closed his eyes for a moment. *Jinga, give me strength to keep my next few words . . .* "No matter at what point we reach, if you say 'no,' I *will* stop. Whatever we are doing at that time. I promise you that."

He was so sweet. Even if she hadn't been biased already by loving him, Alys decided he was definitely what the wench Cari would have called "one of the good ones." Then again, just thinking about what they had been doing in this very room earlier that morning made her flush with embarrassment, longing, and pleasure. "Aren't you going to put me down now?"

"I like holding you," Wolfer confessed roughly, meeting her soft gray eyes with his golden ones.

Her heart skipped a beat, then pounded. When he crossed to the bed and sat down on its edge, shifting her onto his lap, she squirmed close. Making him draw a quick breath.

"Easy!" This time it was an admonition, not a reassurance. Her hip had half-rubbed, half-dug into his groin. But it wasn't easy to caution her when she seemed to want to abandon caution, with that same mix of hesitancy and bravery that had driven him crazy in his youth . . . and that still fascinated him every bit as much now as it had back then.

Her mouth peppered him with kisses, from his jaw to his brow and back again. She squirmed even closer, and her lips caught his ear. Wolfer shivered at the pleasure arcing between ear and groin at her unpracticed but powerful touch. His breath caught in his throat with another shiver; her tongue traced the soft curve of his lobe, then up around the edge—and he quickly pulled her back by her shoulders when she started to graze her teeth against his flesh.

"Whoa! Maybe I should be the one having *you* promise to stop, should *I* say 'no,'" Wolfer teased.

Alys instantly doubted herself, her bravery deserting her once more. "You didn't . . . like it?"

Wolfer quickly cupped her cheeks. "I liked it *too* much—I'm trying to go slowly, remember?"

Her gray eyes searched his gold, inexperienced and maybe a little uncertain, but unafraid.

Groaning, Wolfer leaned in close and kissed her. He enjoyed the way she instantly kissed him back, no timidity, no hesitancy. *This is how to do it*, he thought hazily, letting his hands roam in gentle sweeps over her body, from arms to shoulders to back. *Keep her kissing, keep her mind—Jinga! . . .*

Her hands had started doing the same with him, touching his arms, bared thanks to the sleeveless edges of his tunic. Only hers slid inside the larger armholes of his tunic, where his hands couldn't go in her clothes. The feel of her palms smoothing the skin of his back was heady and thrilling. They hadn't even done more than kiss, yet, and she had wrapped herself around his senses.

Wolfer eased back out of their kiss, easing her back as well with his hands on her shoulders, then down her arms to get those hands—those hands!—off of his flesh. He mustered a smile as she gave him a questioning, uncertain look, and managed a coherent question. "Would you like me to take off my tunic?"

Alys blinked. Her lips parted, shut, parted again, and those gray eyes stared at his gray, cotton-covered chest as if trapped there by a spell. Wolfer decided the intensity and desire of her gaze would qualify as a "yes," even if she couldn't quite verbalize it.

Leaning back just a little to put some room between them, he unfastened his belt. Dropping it to the floor by the bed, he eyed her for signs of fear. When she didn't show any, but instead glanced between his face and his chest, he reached down and eased the hem of the tunic up. Which wasn't easy, because he was sitting on the thigh-length material. It finally came free, and he quickly lifted it up over his head, then tossed it beyond her back somewhere. The way those soft gray eyes widened and flicked everywhere over his bared flesh was gratifying. His Alys looked as if she couldn't stop gawking at him, couldn't help but be fascinated by him.

Alys indeed stared at him; he was so different from anyone else she had seen. There was a fine dusting of brown hairs, barely noticeable but for the way they clustered around his flat, small, male nipples, and the way they collected in a thin line down by his navel, at the waistline of his pants. Alys was grateful he didn't touch her yet, letting her grow used to the sight of him shirtless, so different from the days when he had been shirtless as a child, and then as a youth. His full size had only developed at around twenty or so; by then, she had already been under the repressive thumb of her uncle for about a year and wasn't allowed near men who took their shirts off so casually. She certainly hadn't been allowed to spend more than a few minutes here and there in his and his brothers' company.

Hesitantly, she raised her hand. Laid her palm flat against his sternum. The muscles to either side of it instantly flexed, mounds of strength to match the beat of his heart against her fingertips. His hand shifted up over hers, holding her flesh to his. A moment later, he lifted her hand to his mouth and kissed her palm, just as he had when he asked her to marry him. Warmth ran through her, spreading from her palm and her heart; oddly, it made her shiver. So did the intense look in his gold eyes as he lifted them to her gray ones. And when he returned her hand to his chest, she felt her skin growing goose bumps with pure awareness of him. Wolfer. Male. His hand slid down her arm, leaving her palm against his heart. Leaving the next move up to her.

Her mouth curved up a little on one side, then on the other. She blushed as she recalled something Cari had said. Easing her hand back until just her fingertips brushed his chest, she glided them to the right. His chest hairs tickled her fingertips as she gently touched the soft-satin flesh of his nipple.

Gold blazed at her as his breath hitched, his body tensed. Resting her fingertips where they were, she lifted her other hand. Alys touched his other breast, tracing the contours of the muscle . . . the faint ring of hairs, and the tiny, soft-hardening peak they guarded. A sound rumbled in his chest that wasn't quite a growl, and wasn't quite a groan. It resolved into her name as she touched him with both hands now, learning and experimenting shyly with the texture of his male flesh.

"Alys," Wolfer half-warned, half-encouraged her. His hands lifted to her wrists, because being touched that way was torturously exciting. She removed her hands of her own volition, slipping them free of his light grip, and he wanted to bring them back. Where they went next made him do nothing at all.

They went to her own belt. Unfastening it, she dropped it on the floor with a soft *clank* of the buckle. A hesitation, then she quickly pulled off her own tunic, baring her corset. His hands instantly went to her cotton-covered ribs, steadying her on his lap. His fingertips dug in a little as she shifted her hands next to the laces of the corset.

"Alys," Wolfer rumbled again, this time in something closer to a full warning.

Her boldness came back. Albeit with a shy little smile. "I'm going to let you do to me . . . whatever I do to you. So you have to pay attention . . . okay?"

One of his brown brows arched. Something came out of his throat. It might have been a "yes," if he had been capable of forming any words. She was doing it again, driving him crazy with her mixture of boldness and reserve. Not that he minded.

He shifted his hands down to her hips as she pulled the laces apart, then pulled the corset over her head instead of bothering to unlace it all the way. Her full breasts bobbed free; rather than see them bounce uncomfortably without support, he quickly shifted his hands up to cup their falling curves. They were full, warm, soft, and heavy. The way his body immediately agreed a woman's breasts should feel. A sigh rumbled out of him as he gently cupped them and even more gently squeezed.

"Mmm . . ." Her own matching sound of pleasure was lighter, higher than his deep voice, but it blended well with his as she arched her throat and closed her eyes, her hands coming up to cover and encourage his own.

"Anything you do . . . I get to do to you?" Wolfer asked, looking from her breasts to her eyes. They fastened on his muscles, and she nodded, shifting her hands to touch his chest. Touching his male nipples with exploring little caresses.

Wolfer slid his fingers up just enough to touch her areolas in unison with the movements of her own hands on his flesh. He traced their softness, spiraling in to the larger pebbles of her own female nipples. In symmetry, they fondled and explored; in gentle rhythm they touched and rubbed, nipped and rolled . . . until it wasn't nearly enough for Alys. It wasn't a matter of gathered bravery, but of heated desire that ducked her head, that brushed her nose against his chest for an inhale of his heady scent. Pleased with her impending lover, Alys pressed her lips to his tensing muscles. Then darted her tongue out for a lick at the contrast of small, soft male areola, and even smaller, hard male nipple.

Wolfer tipped his head back with a grimace of control as she licked, then nipped softly, experimentally with her lips. He couldn't take much more of this sweet torture! When she took the tiny bud in her teeth, he couldn't help himself—

*"Oh-hoooooooooohhh!!"*

Alys jerked upright, shocked by the sudden burst of sound. *"Wolfer!"*

He broke off the howl and looked at her, golden eyes gleaming ferally. Another sound came from deep inside his chest, a deep, rich growl of desire. He grinned and licked his lips, holding her gaze.

Amazed, flustered, and yet encouraged, Alys slipped off his lap, because the angle she wanted was too uncomfortable to reach, seated sideways on his thighs as she had been. He tried to stop her, but she pushed his hands aside, half-knelt by the bed . . . and tasted his other nipple. A low keen rose up toward another howl. Wolfer choked it back and jerked her up, hauling her onto his lap. This time, she was perched straddling his thighs, not seated sideways as before, her knees folded onto the bed to either side of his hips.

Again, he lowered his head and gave her a hot, golden look that should have given *him* the nickname of "Flame," and not his second-youngest brother. The blush in her cheeks let him know she definitely felt his heat. It pleased him deeply to know that he could affect her with just a look.

"Why . . . why are you howling?" Alys demanded, when she could catch a breath, when he blinked in the middle of that intense stare.

He grinned. A wolf-tasting-lamb kind of grin; he even licked his lips. His voice was rough with desire, and very, very low, vibrating straight to her body through every point his body touched hers and places deep inside as well. "Let me *show* you . . ."

One arm caught her low around the back, tugging on the ends of her waist-length, loosely braided curls, making her head drop and her back arch. That bared her throat. The other hand plumped up one of her full breasts for his mouth. He lowered his head when she leaned back, exposed by the position yet still trusting him to keep her from falling off his lap, and parted his lips just above that proffered nipple. Anticipation built in his prey . . . and the predator descended that last distance for his first, loving, potentially lethal taste.

It was a full, deep suckle that swirled his tongue around her turgid, rosy tip. Fire shot from breast to groin and back again within her, filling her lungs with a gasp and a deeper arch of her back. Giving him more of what he was already taking. He growled, vibrating the sound against her flesh, and hauled her abruptly closer with the arm around her lower back. Snuggling her core against his groin, he rubbed the lump of his arousal against the throbbing of her desire, teasing where both of them desperately needed to be.

Alys knew *exactly* why he had howled! Sound and feeling ripped through her in a shuddering spasm of unbelievable pleasure. She was riding her stallion all over again, half naked on his lap, and by Kata, it was *great*! "Wolferrrrrr!"

Wolfer buried his face against her breasts and tried, tried very hard, not to climax right with her as she cried out his name. Tried not to rip the lower barrier of their remaining garments out of the way and bury himself in her in the very position they held at that moment. But it was no good. Even as he reached for the waistband to give in and tear off her trousers, to get inside of her before he embarrassed himself like an untried youth, she writhed in just the wrong—or rather, the right—way against him.

*Something* made Wolfer jerk and thrust against her with a groan that rose into a shout of her name. The friction re-triggered her pleasure, and she groaned with him, shuddering a second, longer time. Alys clutched at his shoulders as he used both of his hands to pull her in hard and rotate her against him. It eased, resurged a little, slowed down, came back some more, then eventually ebbed, much in the same way a tide came and went.

Alys' arms didn't want to hold on much longer; she felt so limp and sated from what had just happened. So it was with relief that Wolfer drew in a breath against her chest, let it out on a groan, and slumped backward with her still in his arms, sprawling onto the bed. Burying her face in the curve of his throat and shoulder, she nuzzled him, inhaled his sweaty, musky, wonderful scent, and enjoyed the feeling of her bare breasts mashed against his equally bare chest. Enjoyed the way her thighs straddled his waist, too.

Embarrassment flooded through him as Wolfer came back to his senses. He had *not* meant for that to happen—was there nothing under Jinga's sun that was more embarrassing for a full-grown man than *that*? It was even more embarrassing in its own way than admitting openly that he was afraid of heights!

And yet, Wolfer couldn't regret it. *Who knew my little Alys could be so hot, and make me do . . . that?* He was still grinning like a sated idiot when she finally lifted her head from his shoulder, wisps of curls tumbled around her still somewhat flushed face.

"Wow." Alys blinked down at him. She felt a little shy, now that the rush of desire was over, and didn't dare lift her chest from his, lest she bare her breasts. "You, ah . . ."

"Yes, I did," he confessed uncomfortably. He was about to reassure her that he would still be able to do more in a few minutes, when she frowned down at him in confusion.

"You did . . . what?"

*She doesn't know?* Wolfer closed his eyes. *Thank you, Jinga!*

"Wolfer? What did you do? I was going to say I, uh—that is, *you* . . . Wow—I think Cari would call you one of the '*really* good ones' . . ."

He opened his eyes to golden slits, curious. "Who is Cari?"

"She's a whore I met in Orovalis," Alys admitted candidly. Then widened her eyes, blushed, and sat up, clapping her hands over her mouth.

His groin stirred as she sat on it, rousing more quickly than the bone-deep lethargy of his half-clothed, incredible, involuntary sating would have led him to believe. Her admission, however, made him ignore it in favor of sitting up. Thankfully, that dislodged her somewhat more onto his lap than his groin. ". . . A *whore*? When and *why* did you talk to a whore?"

Alys fluttered her hands down over her bare breasts, then gave up and crossed her arms, half-defensively, half-protectively over her chest. Blushing as she confessed. "I Gated to Orovalis with the money I earned from selling my jewels—not that I had many, but I got a discount, because someone was going through the Gate to Orovalis at the very moment I showed up to register for it, so they slipped me through. Then I was hungry, so I looked for a place to eat. Only I saw my uncle coming down the street, and the only place to duck into was . . . well, a wenching inn."

"A wenching inn. *You* went into a *wenching inn*?" he growled.

She whacked him in the chest with the back of her hand. "*You've* been in wenching inns!"

"No, I haven't!" Wolfer shot back. "I seduced the castle staff!"

"Really?" Alys asked, breaking off with a sidetracked blink. She ran the list of wench-like servants she knew through her mind and frowned at him. "Who?"

He was *not* walking into *that* particular trap. "It was over and done with years ago—and don't change the subject! What happened when you went into this . . . this . . . ?"

"The Trenching Wench," she supplied, with a little lift of her chin. "Uncle Donnock came in and grabbed a wench, while I hid behind the back hall door—only I already knew he was supposed to be on the *west* coast barely a month ago, so he must have taken a mirror-Gate eastward, too. When he headed for the door, I ran upstairs, because I couldn't escape through the back without raising a fuss from the cook, and I hid in one of the rooms.

"Only a man and a woman came in—not my uncle, but another pair—and they . . . *right there*," she hedged, blushing, "while I was hiding in the wardrobe cupboard. And then Cari found me after the man left, and I asked a few questions, and she ended up offering to teach me several things so that I could eventually teach you, if you weren't any good. But you are, and I probably will only have to teach you the, um . . . unusual stuff. If I can ever get up my courage to try it, that is—and I will!"

Wolfer stared at her as she finished, flipping her hand at him before folding it across her bare breasts protectively once more. He tried to absorb the implication. Alys—who was still a virgin—had learned sexual secrets from a tavern whore? Enough to *teach* him things? Only one thing about her confession worried him. "Does this mean you're not a virgin anymore?"

She blushed and whacked him with the back of her hand. "Yes, I still am! You don't have to rub it in—I *can* be very inventive, once I get past my timidity, so don't look so stricken about it. It only takes one time, and then I'm not a virgin for the rest of my life, so you can just suffer!"

He caught her hand when she would have hit him again. Lifted it to his mouth. Suckled her palm like he had her breast. When her breath caught and her soft gray eyes went a little softer, borderline dazed in just a few bare seconds, he released her skin. "I'm not upset. In fact, I'd say you learned your, ah, lessons a little *too* well. But it's just as well we did what we did, because now I can take my time with your first time."

Alys frowned in confusion at him. He was talking in the doublespeak of innuendos, and she wasn't even really getting the first half of their conversation, let alone the second half. There was only so much Cari's lessons could do for her until she figured them out in full for herself, after all.

Sighing at her confused look, Wolfer shifted his hands to his waist, unlaced his trousers, and caught her wrist. Before she had time to protest, he was sliding her fingers down inside. Against his half-aroused, wet shaft.

"What . . . ?" Pulling her hand back when he released it, she looked at the milky white fluid on her fingers. *Milky? Oh, my!* Blushing bright red, she looked down where she hadn't dared to look moments before. "You . . . um . . . ?"

"*You* blew my self-control right off the island," he confessed, gently catching and returning her hand to the loosened front of his breeches. She touched him tentatively and Wolfer groaned. Her timid exploration turned him on far more than any touch of his own would have done. Blood pooled in his groin, stiffening the flesh she was caressing with feather-light fingertips. Finally she gripped him fully, and a shudder of painfully hot pleasure passed through him.

Alys jerked her hand away. "Oh! Did I hurt you?"

"Do it again," was all he could manage verbally. His hands fumbled at his trousers, pushing them down farther and baring him to the tops of his thighs. Wolfer closed his eyes and tipped his head back slightly. "Please, Alys."

Returning her hand, she gripped him. He was hot, and silken-soft, hardening, lengthening, and throbbing with each beat of his heart. What Cari had said to her about it not tasting at all like milk made her curious suddenly. His eyes popped open in confusion as she slipped once again to her knees on the floor, this time bending over a little as she gripped him, bringing her head close to the head of his shaft. Cari had also told her that it was common for the elder-born of male twins to be "cut," and the younger-born to be "uncut"; in other words, that their foreskins had either been removed or left intact as soon as they were born, to be able to differentiate between the two, especially for purposes of determining the heir. Wolfer was definitely the younger twin.

"*Alys!*" he squeaked, actually squeaked, shocked by her bold, suggestive position.

The sound of his voice breaking made her laugh and made her very brave. "*You* sound like a virgin, now!"

"I—you—I—*oh, Jinga!*" Dead—he was *dead*—no, he was gloriously *alive*, except he flopped back onto the bed like a dead man as those lips—*Alys' lips!*—touched him. Tasted him with an inquisitive flick of her tongue. Enveloped and suckled him as he had suckled her breast, while her fingers played with the loose skin beneath the head of his shaft.

She liked the salty taste of his flesh more than the bitterish taste of his seed, but it was his seed, a part of him; it wasn't all that bad, she supposed. Gently cupping the egg-like spheres in his soft, manly sack, she used her lips to play with the loose cowl of skin near the tip of his shaft, then ran her tongue around the exposed rim. Experimenting with the things her briefly met friend had told her about just a few days ago, she enjoyed the way he shuddered and groaned. Alys definitely liked doing these things with her Wolfer; she even thought briefly that she should send a letter of thanks to Cari at some point in the future, before returning her full attention to savoring her Wolfer intimately.

"Enough! Alys, *enough*," he added firmly, pulling her away from him, though his body certainly demanded more. He couldn't let her continue, though. Her disappointed uncertainty made him explain his reasoning. "Much more of that, love, and I'll release all over again. Next time, I want to be inside you . . . so no more. For right now," he added, since he wasn't about to deny himself that particular pleasure in the future. "Later, *definitely*. I . . . ah, I think we should get our boots off, and everything else. While we're both still capable of thinking."

"Oh."

The suggestion turned her shy again. While he lifted his foot to unlace his boot, she clutched the bedcovers, which were hanging over the side of the bed, protectively to her breasts, and worked one-handed at removing her own footwear. Wolfer saw what she was doing and wanted to laugh and bang his head against the bedpost at the same time. She was doing it again, driving him crazy with her vacillating, timidity-bravery thing.

Alys looked up in time to meet his bemused, pained expression. "What?"

He smiled wryly. "I love you, Alys."

# TEN

The whole world stilled around her while she absorbed his words. She soaked in the warmth of them, the tenderness in them. Alys didn't think she would ever get tired of hearing him say that. It gave her enough courage to release the bedding and simply pull off her boots.

Wolfer groaned as she turned brave and bare-breasted once again.

Alys stilled at that sound. "What now?"

"Never mind." Standing up, he peeled off his breeches. Then caught her staring up at him. It only stiffened him even further. As he was now naked, his physical interest was quite blatant.

Wolfer held out his hand to her. When she took it, he felt like howling again. This time in the cry of a wolf accepted by his mate. Not yet in the eyes of the law—such as it was, on the Isle—but soon. Very soon. Pulling her up, he surprised her by dropping to his knees in front of her and helping her remove her own loose-cut trousers and undertrousers. As soon as he helped her to step out of them, he tossed the last garment aside and wrapped his arms around the backs of her thighs, burying his face against her soft, feminine belly.

"Wolfer! That tickles!" Alys added, a little unnerved by the intimate position, with so much of her bare skin pressed against so much of his own. She shivered as his tongue came out and tasted her navel. "Wolfer . . ."

He tipped his head back and looked up past her breasts. "You said I could do anything to you that you've done to me." Reaching out with one hand, he muttered and enchanted the bedcovers, sliding them to the foot of the mattress. Keeping one arm around her thighs, he slid the other around her back, then stood, picking her up. As she looked up at him, he smiled slowly. A wolf-dining-on-lamb kind of smile. "I intend to do just that. Right now."

She had only a moment to guess his meaning before he was laying her in the middle of his bed. Parting her thighs gently but ruthlessly, he settled himself between her knees and dipped his head. A moment later, as her memories of that client-man and Cari flicked through her head, Wolfer did the exact same thing. To *her*.

Soft, firm, warm-hot wetness caressed the folds of her femininity. The incredible intimacy made her gasp as he probed the entrance of her core with his tongue, then ran the tip of that tongue up around the sentinel that was her pleasure pearl and back down again. His lips nibbled, his teeth nipped, deliciously, delicately, and his tongue—his *tongue!*

Within a very short time, she was panting, then moaning, then writhing, because it *was* something very good— hot and wet and soft and excruciatingly good! And frustrating, as he paused to rearrange his position, moving his hand into the fray. Something nudged her, pushed into her, stroked a little, and made her pant and lift her hips instinctively, even as she clutched at the sheets from uncertainty at the unfamiliar, probing invasion.

Having never deflowered anyone before, Wolfer was expecting some tightness. And he'd once overheard his brother Trevan talking about virgins needing "gentle widening" with fingers first, to become "accustomed" to a man. He'd never heard his younger brother mention how those inner muscles would tighten around his finger, how her flesh would contract and quiver, making his own tremble in enflamed sympathy.

Sweat beading on his brow, he eased a second finger in with the first, and did his damnedest to remind his body it had already achieved release outside of her once. He wasn't going to allow it to happen a second time. Not this time around. Her breath hitched when he tried a third finger; she was too tight for that. So he went back to easing two fingers in and out, and suckled on that little sentinel near the gate his fingers were playing in.

When she tightened all over, he stopped, leaving her quivering on the edge of another pleasure-peak. Her pants matched his own heavy breathing, but hers just escaped into the air. His puffed against her nether curls and the slick, pleasure-swollen flesh they sheltered. She whimpered as he leaned in and licked her. A slow, full lick of his tongue that caressed every part of her down there. A rapid flick of his tongue against the little peak of her pleasure, and her breath hitched again; the blatantly sensual act kept her balanced right on the edge of aching bliss.

"Wolfer!"

"Alys," he rumbled in breathless acknowledgment, pushing himself up onto hands and knees as he moved into position over her. His manhood slid up the inside of her thigh, hot and throbbing. It met and pressed against her slick core as she parted her thighs to accommodate him over her. Wolfer closed his eyes, focusing on breathing, just breathing for a few moments. She squirmed against him, and his eyes snapped open. "Hold still! All right? Just . . . hold still. This is, uh, going to hurt a little—but I swear I'll make it feel good afterward. Trust me?"

"I do," she sighed. And squirmed against him again. "Wolfer, I want you. *Inside* me."

"So do I," he breathed, and balanced on one elbow just long enough to make absolutely certain he was in the right spot. Shifting his hand to her hip, he pressed into her a lit-tle, then a little more. He wasn't even really inside of her, but she was already wincing and stiffening with pain. He backed off, tried to go slower, but there was no way he could do that. He was simply too large, and she was too small. Lowering his forehead to her chin, he let her kiss him, let her clutch at his shoulders and try to hitch his hips closer, while he thought desperately for some nonpainful solution. There was none; not a single one his highly dis-tracted mind and body could come up with and agree upon. "Alys . . ."

"Make love to me, Wolfer!" Alys demanded. She tugged on his shoulders. The feel of him, despite the way he made her feel tight and painful with pressure, was driv-ing her crazy with the need for much, much more. She needed to be irrevocably a part of him, to join with him. It was pure instinct, and it was driving her past her discom-fort.

Wolfer managed a shaky laugh. "I'm trying! But this is . . . I can't . . . Put your legs around my waist, sweet."

She complied, parting her thighs even wider and hook-ing her knees over his hips, curling up into him. It pressed him even more against her . . . and it hurt. She winced a lit-tle.

He lifted his head, saw her flinching expression clearly in the sunlight coming in through the northern-facing win-dows of his room, and kissed her. "I'm sorry, Alys. Quick and fast, all right?" he added against her lips, gold eyes meeting gray with regret for the hurt he had to inflict on her. "Do you remember that time back when we were kids, back in the spring when you were eight or nine, and you jumped into the Pawna River, when it was so cold it was a shock?"

Distracted by his words, Alys frowned slightly, then nodded as the memory came back. She had been nine, back when he and his twin were fourteen. Saber had dared Wolfer, Wolfer had dared her, and she had been the first one to jump into the freezing water on the first "warm" day of that spring. Just to prove she was brave enough for Wolfer to admire.

"Do you remember the feel of the water?" Wolfer asked, tightly reining in the need to plunge straight into the slick flesh he could feel against the head of his manhood. "How it swirled around us and caressed us right through our clothes. If you did it right now, your nipples would get all tight and cold, but this time . . . this time, I'd heat them with my mouth, and you'd heat my body inside of yours to keep it safe from the cold."

Alys shivered.

"We're going to jump into that river together," Wolfer warned her, bracing his weight on his knees and one elbow, his other arm holding her lower back and hips firmly so there would be no escape. He kissed her again, then pulled back and looked into her trusting gray eyes. "Right *now.*"

His thrust was hard, direct, and relentless. Her face scrunched, and her mouth opened—but only the tiniest sound escaped from a throat locked tight with pain. Not a scream of agony, which he had expected, flinching in anticipation.

A bare heartbeat later, her features smoothed and went oddly bland, completely expressionless, for all that her body was still tightly stiff, under and around him. She breathed smoothly, steadily, each deep breath flowing into and out of her nose. Her gaze wasn't even focused on him, but past him, on some indefinable point behind his ear. Wolfer panted and tried not to let his body explode before the rest of him—namely, his heart and mind—knew she was ready to enjoy the feel of him buried deep in her hot, wet, blessedly tight womanhood like this. Her pleasure was far more important than his own was to him, however imminent his was.

The pain ebbed slowly, as Alys controlled it in the way she had learned to control it after years of living under her uncle's temper. She stopped resisting his presence. Her lover shifted slightly, sinking farther in, as her thighs slowly relaxed and opened wider under the weight of his flesh. There was a little stinging, stretching, sharp pain . . . but not as much as his initial thrust had caused.

Tender lips brushed at her own, at her cheeks and chin, her forehead and eyelids. She could feel Wolfer's heart pounding in his chest, thumping where it was pressed to her breasts. Sweat slicked the shoulders under her fingers as he held himself as still as possible inside of her. He was full and hard; it felt like he was trying to meld into her . . . and as more of the pain faded, the pleasure returned. The feel of him pressed into her was what she still wanted. Everything her body had craved seeped slowly back into place, now that the pain was almost completely gone; the gentle salutes of his kisses added their reassurance, while she finished assimilating the aching change wrought in her flesh.

After a few more moments, her body decided it would tentatively agree with his reassuring kisses, and Alys relaxed. Then lifted her knees a little, relieving the pressure on the small of her back. He let loose a soft sound, too loud to be a breath, too soft and quiet to be a groan. Releasing his tight grip on her hips, Wolfer shifted that arm up past her shoulders, trying not to move inside of her—it was sweet of him to be so careful, she thought—and cupped her head with both hands, bracing his larger body over hers with his elbows. Trying not to squish her with his greater weight. Alys opened her eyes to see what was keeping him so carefully still.

"Are you all right?" Wolfer asked tightly. He could barely breathe, he wanted to thrust so much. At her brief, thoughtful pause, then a tiny nod of her head, he kissed her lips and rested his forehead against hers, closing his eyes. "Do you forgive me, Alys?"

"I love you, Wolfer."

Her whisper was his absolution. It was exoneration, vindication, everything a man in his position could want, and doubled at that . . . for it was not only forgiveness in four little words, it was the whole world in those four, seemingly meager words. Incredibly erotic words, given that he was buried inside her tight body. He felt himself swell a little more and moved involuntarily, pushing into her even more, needing to be fully within her, as far as he could go. Her lips parted on a soft sound, and he quickly stilled, opening his eyes, afraid that he had hurt her. Soft gray eyes focused on his concerned, golden gaze.

"Why did you stop?" Alys asked, confused. He was so thick and hard inside of her, his brief movement so natural, she wanted to know why he wasn't doing anything.

She *wanted* him to . . . ? "Thank Kata!"

His heartfelt groan made her smile; Wolfer was normally one to swear by Jinga, as she remembered things. It pleased her that he knew exactly which aspect of Divinity—the female one—was providing him so much pleasure this day in his bed. He pulled out a little and pushed back in, slow and gentle out of consideration for her sore flesh; his gentleness provided more intriguing pleasure than lingering, stinging pain. Alys shifted her arms and trailed a finger down his spell-shaved cheek, then covered his lips with the pad of her fingertip.

Still smiling as he rocked smoothly, slowly into her body, she murmured, "They say that, once each generation . . . Kata and Jinga come down to the world and possess two lovers: one soft and gentle, one strong and fierce."

She snuck a look up at him, her fingertip resting against his lower lip. He nipped her digit, suckling on its tip as he had the peak of her breast. The rhythmic pull matched each surge of his turgid flesh into her softening body, igniting desire between the two places. Her knees lifted and hips tipped into his thrusts. That made him growl and gently take her finger between his teeth. Alys managed another smile and continued breathlessly.

"So . . . on behalf of the goddess . . . should She choose to drop by . . . you're welcome."

Releasing her finger, grinning fiercely, Wolfer surged more strongly into her. Giving her a taste of what he really wanted to do. Desire rose through her in a surge as sure as his thrusts, making Alys groan and twist and writhe under him, wanting what he was doing to her and growing desperate to let him know it with her increasingly eager body. It hurt; it still stung a bit, but the rest of it felt so good. Exactly what she needed.

He caught her hips with one hand, showed her how to meet him with encouraging tugs even as he devoured her mouth with teeth and tongue and lips. Greedy for everything he had, everything he could give, Alys returned his kisses, letting him hitch her knees higher on his hips, letting him thrust into her deeply, fully, over and over, until her head arched back with a wild, groaning cry that was almost, almost like a howl. Her fingernails dug into his back, then her fingers slipped instinctively to his buttocks to clasp him closer and closer with each burial of his flesh in hers.

Wolfer gasped, his head arching back, and convulsed in her, pressing hard and close and full. His seed spurted inside even as he convulsed and pounded into her. Somewhere in there, he hit something inside of her, something that triggered a flash flood of her own pleasure in a series of deep shudders that seemed to go on and on and on as they bucked together, rumpling the bedding beneath them. When Alys could think again, he was still pushing into her—slowly, but still going, still shaking in little shudders that made her flesh quiver with pleasure. Finally, Wolfer ceased all motion, save for his unsteady breathing. Still buried inside her, he sighed heavily, letting his sweat-slick forehead droop against the curve of her shoulder.

She couldn't breathe very well. He was bigger and heavier, made of solid muscle mass, and she needed to breathe. But contradictorily, she liked the feeling of being squished under him. Thankfully, just before she absolutely had to ask him to, he moved. With a soft moan, Wolfer pulled out of her and shifted to the side. His right arm draped across her ribs, just under her breasts, and his left one propped up his head. Golden eyes regarded her from under sleepy, half-closed lids as he made that sound again. The deep one that made her ache to curl up against his broad, muscular chest and feel it vibrating all around her.

"Mmm . . ." His large palm cupped her breast; his thumb rubbed her satisfaction-softened nipple. It pebbled under his touch. The sleepy look changed slowly, picking up an unnerving, rather predatory gleam. "I can see it will take a lot more than this to satisfy you. First while riding my back, then on the floor of my bedroom, now in my bed itself—"

Alys buried her blushing face in his chest, making him laugh. "You *knew*?"

Wolfer knew what she was referring to. "I have the nose of a wolf, remember?"

He slid his hand down over her ribs, her stomach, to the curls at the apex of her thighs. As she twitched, he dipped his finger down along the edge of her folds. Scooping up a little trickle of moisture, he brought it back up again, glistening with what they had done together. There hadn't been much in the way of blood spilled, for all that she had been a maiden; at least, there didn't seem to be much on his finger. No doubt he would find a stain later.

It pleased him to see her nostrils flare, her chest expand, drinking in the scent of their pleasure. The whole room smelled of sex, musky and sweaty and pungent-sweet. "We smell even better together, don't we?"

She blushed again, but his direct statement made her bold. Catching his wrist, Alys leaned closer and licked at the moisture on his fingertip. It was very daring; not only were her juices on his finger, but some of her maiden's blood, too. She wanted him to know she didn't regret what he had done for her, not even the pain of it. Not when it had been so enjoyable in the other moments.

"Whoa!" Wolfer stared wide-eyed at the woman lying on her side with him. He didn't need to glance down to know what the amazing, daringly erotic gesture did to him. A moment later, when his engorging rod brushed her thigh, she glanced down to see what had happened. Wolfer slowly grinned. "Well, it seems I've picked a mate as adventurous and insatiable as I am."

Alys reached down, hesitated a moment, then gripped

him gently. She felt as well as saw him shudder. The groan dragging from deep in his throat made him tip his head back, telling her without words that he liked her fingers on him. She looked back down at his erect flesh. This thing of his, this manhood, had given her much more pleasure than she could have imagined any man could give a woman with such a funny-looking thing.

Even she knew that the pain of a maiden's first time would fade within a day or two, and Cari had reassured her it would then be nothing but pleasure. If the man knew what he was doing. Luckily, she now had plenty of faith in Wolfer knowing what he was doing. Experimentally, Alys tested the softness of the sliding cowl of skin at the tip of his shaft; her thumb traced the hardness of the little ridge defining the head, and brushed over the damp dimple at the very top, as he had brushed his thumb over her nipple.

"Jinga! And I used to think you were innocent!" Wolfer muttered, catching her wrist as her explorations excited him faster than he wanted to go. His own words reminded him of her lost innocence. Of the incredible moment when he had sunk into her—of the blood still staining his shaft, down at the base. That was where it had gone. The thought of the pain she had suffered deflected his arousal with his concern. "Alys, I didn't . . . I'm sorry. Let me check you and make sure you're not badly hurt, all right?"

He was already moving as he said it, pushing her back into the bedding. Making Alys nervous as he settled between her thighs. Very nervous, when he parted her feminine folds and examined her intimately but not sexually in the clear light of day. "Wolfer!"

"Jinga, you're still bleeding!" Feeling like a brute, Wolfer breathed the words of a minor healing spell over her most intimate core. The seeping of her blood ended as her rose-pink flesh mended. Grateful, he pressed a tender kiss to her flesh. He noticed that made her squirm and sigh. Licking his lips, Wolfer moved back up over her. Resting on his side, he pulled her back up against him, into his arms. "It won't hurt nearly as bad next time—it wouldn't have hurt nearly this much, if you weren't so tiny in comparison."

"I'm bigger than Kelly," Alys pointed out, her voice half-muffled by his shoulder.

"I hadn't noticed," he admitted honestly. When she tipped her head back to look at him, he shrugged. "I simply do not notice anyone else when you're in a room with me."

"Oh, Wolfer . . ." The look she gave him would have melted anything right along with it. Her fingers lifted, tracing the contours of his face. She could feel the slight rasp of stubble along the underside of his jaw and around the edges of his mouth. "I feel like I'm in a dream."

Wolfer leaned in and kissed the slight pinch of her brow. "Then why are you frowning?"

"Because I'm afraid it's a nightmare," she confessed quietly, studying his chest.

That piece of feminine logic puzzled him. "Making love with me is a nightmare?"

"Waking up to *find* it was a dream would be the nightmare."

"Rest assured, this is not a dream," Wolfer told her, lifting her chin so that she had to look up at him. That made the silver diamond just below her collarbone flash with light, drawing his attention to it. Reminding him that her uncle had not only stolen the County of Corvis, but quite probably had laid spells on the woman in his arms so that she could be found and brought back . . . and resold to the highest bidder. "Alys . . . do you like your Uncle Broger?"

Gray eyes flew up to golden, wide with shock. "You must be joking!"

Wolfer grunted in satisfaction. "Good. Then you wouldn't mind it if I killed him."

He might have just been jesting, but Alys lost all color in her face. She caught the hand still lifting her chin by his knuckle, held his fist tightly in her own. "Promise me you won't do that, Wolfer. *Promise* me!"

Her seriousness made him frown. "Why should I promise that? If he treated you badly, then he doesn't deserve to live," he stated seriously, soberly. "The moment he gives me an excuse, I won't hesitate to retaliate. He is a poisonous snake, and you don't allow a poisonous snake to live when it threatens you, or someone you love."

Alys shook her head, closing her eyes. "He has spells that are set to release powerful magics in spellbound revenge against whoever kills him. I overheard him discussing it with Uncle Donnock one day. I might have killed him myself, but for hearing that. But, I'm not . . . I'm not brave enough to die."

"You are one of the bravest people I know—" Wolfer returned, trying to soothe her, but she shook her head, burying her face against his chest once again, this time to hide her fears as she wrapped her arms around him.

"No, I'm not! I'm *weak*," she said, clinging to his warmth for comfort, breathing in his scent.

She was driving him crazy again, this time with her protestations. Sighing, Wolfer gathered her closer and rolled onto his back, nudging her torso and limbs into place over his body. He stroked her springy hair, escaping its braid haphazardly.

"I don't care what you think you are, Alys. You can be anything you want to be—I've *seen* you become anything you wanted to be, remember? You were brave for me when we were children . . . but you've also been brave for yourself. And even if it drives me crazy sometimes, I love you whether you're timid or fearless, frightened or brave." He kissed the top of her head and slid his hands down her bare back. Cupping her buttocks, he held her against his half-aroused flesh. She probably needed a distraction from her current line of thought; luckily, he had one in mind. "What was the name of that wench you spoke with?"

Alys dredged it up, answering his question and its change of topic. "Cari . . ."

"Mm. Cari. Did this Cari ever mention anything about a woman being on top of a man when they make love? Because Saber was telling me that's his favorite way when he and Kelly make love, and I figure whatever's good enough for my twin should be good enough for me."

She couldn't help the short laugh that escaped her at the thought that crossed her mind. "Does Kelly know your twin has talked to you about him and her like that?"

Wolfer stilled. "You aren't thinking of blackmailing me, are you?"

"You? No," she admitted truthfully, lifting her head and propping herself up on his chest with an elbow. "Now, *Saber . . .*"

Wolfer caught her and rolled them over, pinning her under him with at least some of his weight carefully on his knees and elbows as he mock-glared down at her. "You will *not* attempt to blackmail my twin for anything! You will come to *me* with everything you need."

He leaned down and nipped at her lips with his own, punctuating his words.

"*I* will provide you with every opportunity to be timid and brave, to explore the world and be sensually satisfied. I will protect you and help provide for you. And for our children when we have them. I will teach you how to be a wolf in both body and spirit, so you can run fearless and free at my side." His golden eyes met her gray ones. "You are mine, Alys, and I am yours. You don't need anyone else. *Especially* not Morganen!"

"Morganen?" Alys asked, uncertain what he meant.

"I saw the way you greeted him—you are in love with *me*, not him," he growled. As if he could make it so just by saying so, the bite of jealousy nipping at his heel.

"*Morganen?*" she repeated, this time incredulously. "I love him like a brother! Like a dear *friend*," Alys added honestly. "But I don't love him like I love you, Wolfer, and that's the truth. *He* knows this, *I* know this—*you* are the only one who apparently doesn't! You have no reason to be jealous of him!

"He is simply my *friend*," she repeated, seeking to convince him so that he didn't try to kill his youngest brother with the fierce, protective jealousy of a wolf. She touched her silver-studded chest with one hand, and touched his un-ornamented breastbone with the other. "*You* are my heart. You always have been." Slipping her hands up to his face, she stroked back the curtain of his soft brown hair. "I think I loved you even before I was three, and skinned my knee."

Her tenderness enthralled him as surely as any spell. More surely. It warmed his heart, which heated his loins, and a sound of pleasure rumbled from his chest. "Remind me to kiss your knee, later."

"Why later?" she asked, puzzled.

Wolfer smiled slowly and used his own knee to nudge her thighs apart. They parted readily enough for him, proof she was willing to ride with him once again. "I think that healing spell I used has made you all better . . . but there's only one real way to find out. So it'll have to be *much* later."

"Wolfer!" Blushing, Alys hid her embarrassed pleasure by tugging his mouth down to hers. If they were kissing, he wouldn't see her skin turning pink. He had other ideas, and barely brushed her lips before moving down. He kissed the metal diamond embedded in her skin, then the curves of her breasts, shifting down her body a little to reach them.

"I love the way even *these* turn pink when you blush . . ." He took a beading nipple in his mouth and gave it a long, slow, lascivious lick.

"Wolfer!"

He just loved the way she said his name in the rising tide of her desire, a protest that was no protest at all. Wolfer decided he would make love to her until she had said it a hundred times more. And then make love to her all over again, just to be sure.

# ELEVEN

❦

**B**efore we begin trading," Melkin, the captain of the trader ship stated, "I want to know what that fracas was about and why you insisted my men put that man back on board my ship again."

Saber wished he could strangle his twin, just for a moment. Mainly for leaving him to somehow explain this mess. "He is neither kin nor friend. You and the other traders who come here know we've been plagued by mage-sent beasts; sometimes you sleep in the Chapel so that its protective spells shelter you when the trading goes late, though we do everything we can to clear out the invasions before your visits. We . . . well, we believe he was here to get a scrying-fix on this island."

The trader-captain was no fool; unlike other Katani, who might feel glad to see the brothers dead, he knew his trade visits were very profitable. Nightfall products, crafted by the powers of the exiled mage-brothers, had a reputation for high quality. That high quality meant better profit than anything else that might be similar in make and purpose elsewhere, but of lesser duration, power, and construction. The shorter man spat to one side, expressing his opinion on the matter. "He won't get on my ship again, then. I'll see to it that the word is spread among the others. No visitors without your clearance. I'd hate to lose my best suppliers to someone's asinine fears."

Saber nodded. He glanced at his brothers; there was no better time to relay the change in their trading policy to the sailors. Though there probably wasn't any good time to do so. "There's another thing that has happened since the last visit by a trading ship."

Captain Melkin raised a brow. "What would that be?"

"Nightfall has been disavowed from the protection of Katan," Morganen offered in explanation. "By a member of the Council of Mages, no less, which means ourselves and everything on or around this island is officially disavowed."

"Disavowed?" one of the sailors with Melkin asked.

"They told us we were on our own from here on out," Koranen informed the other man and his fellows. "Which technically makes us no longer a part of Katan."

Saber finished the rest of the news. "There's more. There is a new authority laying claim to the island, now, and all that is Nightfall. You'll have to deal with that fact, now."

"What could it be, if not Katan?" another sailor-trader asked, puzzled.

"Nightfall is now an independent kingdom. Which means you won't be getting the salt and seaweed blocks for free anymore," Saber explained as blandly as he could.

That caused an immediate uproar among the sailor-traders. Melkin's voice cut through the others as he jabbed a finger at them. "Now see here! We come here 'cause the salt is free and cheap, and the green stuff is good to sell, too! What makes you think we'll be cutting into our profits by having to pay you for what we've always gotten for free?"

Arms folded across his chest, Saber didn't move. He happened to agree with his wife about this point; the salt *was* theirs to sell, and they should by their rights as the island's inhabitants profit from it. "Because it is *ours* to sell.

To you or to others; the choice is yours. Until someone is willing to buy them from us, the blocks will remain ours."

"No one will go for that!" Melkin warned him. "*Buy* the blocks? Not by Jinga!"

Trevan looked at his fingers idly. "Perhaps not for a few weeks, but as the demand for high-quality salt goes up while no one brings any in, it'll just be piling up here. And I remind you that autumn is coming. Preserving-season. A lot of people will be looking to buy a lot of salt.

"Eventually, even with our new policy of selling the blocks, whoever comes along will find that the net profit they will make, turning around and selling it on the mainland again . . . well, it will be just too tempting to resist. And when some lucky trader *does* decide buying it is worthwhile," he added, glancing up at the men across from him and his brothers, "they'll have a huge stockpile of salt to buy from us at a bulk rate, and thus sell at a monstrous profit on the mainland."

"We don't have to buy it from you—we can just *take* it!" one of the sailors asserted, snapping his fingers at the Nightfall brothers.

Morganen arched a light brown brow, looking very much the righteously arrogant Mage of Prophecy as he folded his arms lightly across his chest. "*Take?* When the Council of Mages greatly preferred exiling us over attempting to kill us? And I do mean *only* attempting!"

Saber cut his hand through the air. "Enough arguing! The price of the salt per block is two gilders."

"Outrageous! We only sell it for three! That's a full two-thirds of our profit," the trader-captain asserted, scowling.

"The price for the algae-blocks is also two gilders apiece," Saber continued smoothly. "Of course, you do not have to decide right away if you want to purchase any. The blocks are enspelled to remain here until we allow them to go, so there will be no chance for you to steal anything, should you not wish to pay. I suggest you think about what you want to do. In the meantime, we can move on to the rest of the trading; that part has not changed in any way, and you are too much of a businessman to let the salt-trade dispute disrupt the rest of this session." At the sea-trader's reluctant, scowled nod, Saber started the bargaining. "Now, I have five accuracy-enhanced, enspelled throwing daggers for sale . . ."

Wolfer! Wolfer! Wolfer! Wolfer!"

*Jinga, I love that voice!* Especially chanting his name in rhythm like this, matching the thrusts of his body into hers, sobbing with the power of their passion. Wolfer wanted it to go on forever, but he was made only of weak, male flesh, not fervid wishes and erotic dreams. "Alyyyysss . . ."

The groan ended on a shout that drove him into her one last, hard-shuddered time, making her groan out his name. "Wol-ferrr! Oh, sweet *Jinga*!"

Even in the midst of blinding pleasure, that made Wolfer laugh. He pushed into her again, then nipped at her mouth, reveling in the ebbing pleasure coursing through him. "You're welcome!"

Alys blinked, coming back from her dive over the precipice. It took her a moment to actually register his words, and then another few moments puzzling out what he meant. The moment she realized he was twitting her about her "Kata says you're welcome" jest, she bapped his shoulder and mock-glared at him. "Wolfer!"

"I much prefer the *other* way you say my name, Alys," he teased her, kissing her quickly as he pulled out. Then frowned. "Are you all right? Are you sore?"

She blushed, but smiled. "A little. Are *you* sore?"

"Not yet, but if it makes you feel better, I'll try to be," he murmured with a wicked grin. And got bapped again lightly with the edge of her hand. Grinning fiercely, he nipped and nuzzled and growled at her throat, making her giggle and struggle to get free of his attack. Though it was in general much like the playful way he used to attack her when they were kids, this time around it was a sensual, erotic act. One that ended with her panting and arching her back, pressing her breasts up into his face, pushing them into his mouth as he alternated suckling on each tip. Wolfer obliged her by mouthing as much of her flesh as he could, laving her budded peaks with his tongue.

She couldn't take much more of it, and finally struggled in earnest. He fell back after she shoved hard at his shoulders a third time, slumping onto his back as she panted next to him.

"You don't want . . . ?"

With a feminine growl of her own, Alys flipped over from her back to her stomach. Or rather, onto his stomach. Her hair, released in full from the futile containment of its braid at some point during their joinings, cascaded down around her shoulders. It pooled on his chest in a tangle of dark gold ringlets. Her smile made his heart thump under her forearms.

"Oh, I *want*," she agreed, drawling the words with the occasional bout of self-assurance that always got to him, contrasted with her hesitancies. "But *I* want, this time around."

He thought of her mouth on his chest, her hand on his rod, and knew Jinga was rewarding him for every single piece of good he had ever done in his life. *Or maybe it's Kata rewarding me* . . . Golden eyes, already hot, heated even more. He closed them with a little smile and relaxed back into the bedding. "Mmm . . . Have your wicked way with me, woman!"

Already, Alys felt as if she knew his body well. And not nearly well enough. As she hesitated, wondering where to start first, he cracked open one wolf-gold eye.

"You can start anywhere you like, you know." Closing his eye again, he let out a martyr's sigh. "I'll just lie here and suffer the horrible devastation of your wicked, feminine wiles . . ."

Slipping her legs to either side of his hips, she sat up. Right on top of his semi-limp groin. Which responded by heating and thickening once again as his eyes snapped open.

On seeing the triumphant little smile she wore, Wolfer decided challenging her was both a good and bad idea. Or maybe handing over the reins wasn't such a good idea after all. That smile suggested he was in for a lot of sensual torture.

Alys, on the other hand, had just discovered how powerful it felt to be on top. Cari had mentioned it might be fun—not for her very first time, but later, when she was accustomed to lovemaking—but the insightful wench had failed to mention how heady it would be to be the one on top and in control of the lovemaking. She stayed right where she was, savoring the feel of him throbbing against that place between her thighs, feeling herself growing moist and hot and insatiable for another round.

It got to her, this position. With a lift of her thighs, she freed him from the pressure of her groin. Which allowed him to spring up and finish engorging, until the tip of him emerged from its cowl of foreskin and brushed her intimate folds, which were thoroughly slick with their lovemaking. The reddened shaft jerked slightly with each beat of his heart. His eyes closed as his manhood touched her, his features strained a little with control whenever he brushed her . . . but he didn't take over. Apparently Wolfer was determined to let her have her way with him. So long as she didn't take too long about it.

It was a little awkward, but she gripped him, positioned him just right . . . and sank down, removing her hand. Brown lashes flicked open, and gold, pleasure-dilated eyes met her gray, pleasure-shuttered gaze.

He had to clear his throat to speak. "*This* is what you . . . ?"

Alys smiled. A slow, wolfish—or rather, she-wolfish—smile as she finished sheathing him. He was thick and full and filled her like nothing ever had before. It was exactly where she wanted to be, and what she wanted to do with him. She stayed like that for several long, appreciative moments. Then tried tightening the inner muscles Cari had told her about.

"*Sweet Kata!*" The shout bucked his hips up into hers, then levered him up, his knees and torso pulling straight up. Grabbing her hips, Wolfer stared wide-eyed at Alys—his not-so-sweet, no-way-by-Jinga-was-she-*innocent* Alys!

Smiling, she did it again. The ecstatic constriction dropped him back on the feather-stuffed mattress with a thump . . . where he dangled right on the edge of an orgasm.

Alys giggled at his hilarious reaction. She did it a third time, squeezing internally . . . and lost all urge to laugh, for he grasped her hips, straining up into her with rolling thrusts of his groin. Alys felt each distinct eruption from his manhood buried deep and tight within her flesh. Felt each pulsing ejaculation as he groaned in pleasure, grinding her against him.

The sudden intensity in her lover struck a sympathetic, almost empathetic fire inside of her, tilting Alys' head back on a satisfied moan of her own. Enhancing it was the way he pressed against that spot inside of her, the blissful one she hadn't known existed until now. Of course, the way he rubbed his pubic bone up into her didn't hurt, either.

When the pleasure faded, his hands helped her slump down onto his chest, both of them wrung out by this third mutual expression of their desire. Panting, Alys closed her eyes and breathed in more of the heady scent the two of them had just created. From the rising and falling of the chest playing mattress under her, she could tell he was content to just lie there and breathe deeply as well.

Finally, Wolfer found enough energy to speak, though he had to drag his voice out of his chest in a bass rumble before coalescing into actual words. "Nnnhhh . . . next time you want to play with me, woman . . . please, go ahead and do that again!"

She laughed at that, a short set of exhausted chuckles that puffed against the hairs on his sparsely dusted chest. "You're welcome, Jinga."

Wolfer's shout of laughter filled the room.

No, this isn't going to be enough silk," Kelly murmured, measuring out the gray material by the old sewer's trick she had learned: At her height, by pinching the cloth in one hand and extending her arm, where her bra strap would be located on her far shoulder was exactly one yard. To make two sets of clothing, they needed at least another five yards. "Tell Saber to pick up that silk if he can get it; if they didn't bring any gray, we can dye a lighter shade for contrast. Or maybe use white, or black."

Evanor sang the request under his breath, as she checked the next chest, just to see if there was anything in there worth salvaging. There *would* have been enough of the gray, if bugs hadn't had a small feast here and there in the lengths of silk. After a moment, the blond-haired, brown-eyed man shook his head. "No silk at all."

Kelly held up lengths of creamy, undyed silk. "Maybe this'll work? Redyed a lighter shade of gray, for the tunics and the overskirt?"

"You have strange taste in clothing, 'Queen' Kelly," Evanor teased her. "What makes you think Alys will want to wear your strange styles?"

"Because she likes trousers, and the overskirt is a good compromise for someone who's used to wearing a skirt, but still wants the freedom to move." She dabbed at the sweat on her face with the back of her wrist. "Though with the increasing heat of summer, I'm tempted to make shorts and start wearing those instead."

" 'Shorts'?" the fourth brother asked her.

She tapped the edge of her hand on the middle of her thighs. "Pants that reach only to here—you would call them under-trousers, and use them for undergarments—well, only if they don't have the gusset seam down the center—but we put in a seam and use them as a logical and highly practical summer garment for both men and women."

"I think my eldest brother would have something rather strident to say, if you tried that," Evanor replied lightly in his smooth, fluid tenor.

Kelly snorted as she rose, bundling and taking the cream silk with her. "Just wait until I make myself a bikini to wear down on the beach—*that'll* give him an outright heart attack!"

Evanor swept up the gray silk and followed her out of the storage room. They reached the stairwell and started down. Through one of the open windows drifted a masculine shout from another of the wings, followed by a feminine cry. There was no need to guess the reason why. Not with *that* tone in both distant but vocal throats.

Evanor blushed a little. "Well. At least *two* of us are getting lucky, these days . . ."

Kelly gaped at him. Then burst into a hearty laugh that ended with her wiping at the edges of her eyes. "Oh, my . . . I really *should* be a little more sympathetic toward you and the others," she finally apologized as they reached the next floor down and headed for the sewing hall, "but all I feel is the urge to laugh!"

"Saber's verse did come true with the disaster of the Mandarites and the stealing of my twin," Evanor agreed, his smile wavering a little on that last part. "But Wolfer's verse seems a lot easier to bear."

"Yeah, I noticed," Kelly agreed as they entered the sewing hall and carried their burdens to one of the worktables. She shook her head. "Alys only showed up yesterday— how could he have made up his mind so quickly? I mean, Saber took *forever* to come around to me, by comparison!"

"Wolfer's always been like that. Quick to anger, quick to decision." Ev smiled with the memories of a younger brother. "Of course, that always got him into plenty of trouble when we were young, but he did pick up a knack for controlling his temper and making better decisions. Eventually."

Kelly picked up the embroidery-marked ribbon that she had made for a measuring tape, measuring in the inches she was used to instead of the smaller measurements the Katani-style measuring ribbon used, which was somewhere between an inch and a centimeter. She fetched the charcoal-sketched measurements she had taken only that morning and started measuring out the yards that Alys' clothing would need. "Then again, I guess they did know each other for a long time before you all were exiled. I think Alys has always been in love with him. Some women are like that: One look, one moment, and they know forever."

"Or in your case, one growl, and you knew forever . . ."

"Oh, ha, ha, very funny. Besides," Kelly added coyly, dropping her sarcasm, "Saber *grunts*; he doesn't really growl. Not like Wolfer does, but then my husband hasn't got that 'James Earl Jones' deep voice going."

" 'James, Earl of Jones'?" Evanor repeated. "I do not remember an earldom ruled by any Jones family—"

Kelly burst out laughing again. "No, no . . . I see I still have a few things to explain to you, Ev! James Earl Jones, Barry White, Brian Blessed . . . Maybe, if Morganen's up to it, we can try and find someone listening to or watching any of those three on a CD or a videotape somewhere in my old realm through his scrying mirror, so you'll know exactly what I mean. But let's get these wedding clothes started; I'll start work on the trousers; you measure out ten yards of the cream and start the dyeing."

"As Your Majesty commands me," Evanor jested, sweeping her a mock-gallant bow.

Ah, so you *do* exist!" Trevan teased as Wolfer and Alys entered the dining chamber together.

Alys blushed. Wolfer sent his younger brother a warning look. He escorted her over to her seat, placed to the right of his chair. When they were both seated, Wolfer's twin shook his dark blond head and sighed.

"Evanor has informed me that you have asked Alys to wed you, Wolfer," Saber stated. "I just wish you'd stayed long enough to help the rest of us with the trading."

"How did that go, anyway?" Kelly asked her husband from his other side. "Did you sell the salt?"

"No. We did sell the algae-blocks, though," Saber admitted. "Fertilizer is in high demand in the far north, and the green blocks make some of the best fertilizer available. The northlands aren't as lush as the mid and southern regions, since it doesn't rain as much in the warmer climates," Saber added. "The locals up there have to be careful about over-farming the soil."

"Two hundred years ago," Morganen added, "they farmed too much and turned the soil to barren dust. It took them years of careful enspelling and fertilizing to restore the soil to fertility once more, if you can imagine."

"Not only can I imagine it, *my* world did the same thing, though less than a hundred years ago," Kelly added candidly. "Some of those areas are still rather bad, ecologically. You didn't have any trouble keeping the salt, did you?"

"None." Saber glanced at his twin. "Thanks to you, Wolfer, they weren't going to get any of us mad. You created a problem with your attack on Donnock of Devries, of course . . . but you did solve one at the same time, making the sailors wary of turning us into enemies.

"Just . . . try to think ahead a little about the consequences of your actions next time, though. Morganen's forget-it spell *will* eventually wear off, and he'll probably still be mad when he does remember what happened. We can only guess how he'd react, then," Saber stated, sighing roughly. "I say we change the look of the cove and the quay immediately, just in case he thinks of teleporting in a little revenge for you breaking his wrist like that."

Alys, listening to this piece of logical truth, sent Morganen a nervous, questioning look. At the slight shake of his head, she relaxed; she trusted the youngest of the brothers to know when the best time for her many confessions should be. He had helped counsel her during her years with Broger, after all, and she had survived those years by following his advice. Now was not the time to inform the others that she could guess with great accuracy what probable courses of action her two uncles might take.

Next to her, Wolfer saw the tiny exchange between his youngest sibling and his mate, and frowned slightly. *I know she's in love with me,* he thought as the conversation moved on to the items traded and bought. *But what hold does Morganen dare to have on her? Why does she look at him, instead of at me?*

He didn't think he had anything to be jealous of—Alys had fled to *him*, after all—but still, she had exchanged a tiny look of communication with his youngest sibling, something that said they knew what each other was thinking at that moment. Suggesting a tie of some kind between them. *Jinga, what could it be?*

He didn't want to feel jealous of his youngest brother, but Wolfer did, just a little. He didn't like the feeling, and he didn't like whatever it was that caused this instinctive feeling within him. One that said something deeper was going on than what he could see on the surface of things.

"I think the demand for salt will go up as autumn approaches," Koranen pointed out. "People without enough magic to preserve their food with spells will need it for their meat and their fish. I think we should leave all the fountains running, stack up the salt, and send out word at the end of summer that Nightfall is willing to sell its high-quality salt to anyone interested in coming to the island to pick it up and pay our price."

"And the algae?" Morganen asked his slightly older twin. "You want to leave it in the storage shed *all* winter long, until spring arrives? That stuff starts to reek after a few months, you know. It only stops smelling when it's been mixed into the soil."

"We sell that now, while we still can, to places like the northlands," his twin returned reasonably. "*Then* we store it. There aren't any permanent spells in the warehouse that we know of to keep it from smelling, but that's an easy enough spell to maintain on a temporary cycle."

Rydan entered the hall. He came late to the table, but with a fresh keg of stout hefted on his black-clad shoulder, their evening drink of choice. A simple arch of his black brow asked his younger, strawberry-haired twin to explain the tag end of the statement he had just heard.

"We were just talking about how to store the algae blocks

over the winter without them smelling, so we could sell them come the spring for fertilizer," Trevan summarized.

A slight dip of the other man's head was all the answer he gave, acknowledging the current topic of conversation.

Alys eyed him a little uncertainly, for the sixth brother had turned even stranger in the handful of intervening years than she last remembered. She focused on the conversation at hand, venturing a tentative suggestion. "I think you could break up the blocks and mix them with vegetation, say the bushes from the pastureland we'd need to create for cattle. There's lots of dead brown leaves coating the jungle floor, I've noticed. I've done something similar with green and brown vegetation back home, and the resulting compost was good. With the algae-blocks, I think it will be even better."

"You know, I think she's right," Kelly agreed, backing her up quickly. "I saw this show—well, never mind how I learned it; that would take too long to explain—but I heard that if you mix green stuff with brown stuff, you know, grass clippings with dead leaves, plus a little leftover food, like fruit peels and the like, you get a perfect compost mixture for fertilizing your garden.

"We'd need some open-slatted boxes and a bunch of earthworms, but with all the salt extracted from the algae stuff, it's got both green from the algae and brown from the plankton. Add land plants to that, and it's bound to create a superior-grade fertilizer, increasing the value of it in sale to others. Not to mention the smell would turn more palatable in time, or at least not so dead-fishy. It wouldn't be as easy to transport, no longer being in a nice, convenient block form, but it would be worth the cost of shoveling it, I think."

Trevan sighed, shaking his head as he glanced at Evanor. "What is it with ladies, these days, Ev? All these two want to talk about is manure, manure, manure—where has all the *romance* gone?"

"You want me to bean you with a bun?" Kelly asked, lifting one of the rolls left over from breakfast in mock-threat.

"Don't even think of it, Kel," Saber warned his wife, while Rydan started pouring stout ale from the keg he had brought for everyone. She arched one of her brows at that, not much of one to take orders very well, and he gave her a stern behave-or-else look.

Surprisingly, it was Rydan who answered her silent rebellion, handing her the first mug. "That's a perfectly good, fresh roll, Sister. Month-old stale ones bruise better."

"You traitor!" his strawberry-haired brother cried out, clutching at his heart as if mortally wounded by the betrayal. "My own twin, giving the enemy advice on how to do me in! See if I ever bake *you* another batch of rolls again!"

Kelly eyed the bun in her hand and shook her head, sighing as she set it back down. "If it were lumpy and unleavened, I might actually do it . . . but I can't kill a man whose buns are better than mine." She sent a sly glance to the dark blond man on her right, with the matching wedding torc at his throat. "Which means *you're* safe, too, Saber, baby."

As Saber frowned in confusion at his otherworldly wife's odd quip, Alys' eyes widened. *Cari said . . . she said one of the many names for a man's backside is . . . buns! Oh, my!* She blinked for a moment, then smiled, unable to *not* share this fact with her future sister-in-law. "Well. I, ah, guess that means my Wolfer's quite safe, too."

Now all of the men at the table were giving the two women puzzled, uncertain looks. Kelly and Alys glanced at them, looked at each other, and quickly smothered identical giggles.

"*Women*," Rydan groused, thumping Alys' mug on the table in front of her. Making the two of them giggle all over again, in a room full of perplexed men. He had started it, after all.

# TWELVE

❦

As they reentered his suite, Wolfer realized it wasn't exactly the kind of chamber that welcomed a female presence. Everything was solid, plain, and, well . . . masculine, in his rooms. Leather, wood, some minor effort at cushions on some of the furnishings, but none of the fussy little throw-pillows women seemed to like. There were curtains on the windows, but they were a heavy-woven muslin dyed a plain golden shade, complementing the tan of the leather and the various browns of the wood in his furniture.

The only uniqueness in his suite was the paint on the walls, and that was simply because they were enspelled with the same color-changing paint as the rest of the palace. Currently, the enchanted pigments were chasing rainbow shadows from corner to corner across a pale golden background, if at a slow pace. The rest of the room was just . . . masculine-looking. *Not exactly a woman-welcoming chamber, by any means.* He cleared his throat, catching Alys' attention.

"You can change a few things in here, if you like. The curtains, maybe bring in some cushions . . ."

Alys, halfway to the bedroom, stopped and looked back

at him. Then looked around the sitting room. She couldn't find much fault with the way the chamber looked; her own room had been spartan, with just her bed, a half-empty wardrobe for her small amount of clothing, a table and chair, and little else in it. He had far more lightglobes in this room than she had possessed oil lamps, but that was because her uncle had considered magic illumination too fancy to waste on his niece. And that was accounting for the fact that lightglobes gave off a lot more light than mere oil lamps ever did, and didn't need to constantly be refilled with oil, which eventually grew expensive to purchase. No, this room had more luxuries than she was used to having.

"I don't see what's wrong with it," she offered hesitantly, taking another look to be sure.

"Well, you will be living in here with me," Wolfer pointed out. Then hesitated himself. "Unless you'd rather move to another set of rooms?"

She took pity on him with a shy but teasing little smile. "And make you rearrange *more* furniture?" At his open grin, she shook her head and looked around the room again. "You'd really let me change things?"

Moving over to her, Wolfer wrapped his arms around her from behind, resting his chin on the top of her head, since her five and a half feet were shorter than his six feet plus. "This is your home now. My bed is your bed; my rooms are your rooms. If you want to put up velvet and lace curtains, or toss around a bunch of embroidered pillows to cover up all the leather in here . . . I can put up with that. So long as I can toss you around in my bed."

His grudging avowal to suffer for her sake made her smile. "I *like* leather . . . but I think I'd like to see just a little more color. If you don't mind. I haven't had much color in my life."

"If you call that dress you arrived in an example, I'd say not," Wolfer agreed. He nuzzled the top of her head with his cheek, enjoying the springy-soft feel of her curls. He wondered for a moment if their children would have straight hair, or tightly curly, or perhaps something loose and soft between the two extremes. "I was going to get more leather today, when the traders arrived. But since I got distracted—rather nicely," he added, squeezing her gently, "I'll have to make do with what I have on hand. Or maybe go hunting for it in the morning. Would you like a lesson in how to make yourself into a wolf, tomorrow morning? It's not that much different than a pookrah, and it's a lot safer."

"True. If I turned into a pookrah, your brothers might accidentally shoot me," Alys pointed out. "A wolf-shape would be nice to learn. But I have to warn you," she added shyly, "it kind of takes me a little while to get the hang of a new shape. That's why I was a river otter when swimming through the ocean, instead of a sea otter. It would have taken me a week to learn the new shape, unless I was really lucky and could get it right quickly enough. But I didn't want to wait that long."

"I take it your uncle didn't do much to teach you anything about your magic?" Wolfer inquired, remembering Morganen's comment on the matter.

"He taught me a few spells, but only those that would make me more useful as a servant for him," Alys admitted, carefully skirting around what kind of spells they were. Namely, the kind to corral and command his "pets," so that the beasts wouldn't tear her to shreds while she was feeding and exercising them for him. "Morganen did what he could to help me, of course . . ."

"Before we left for our exile here?" Wolfer asked in confirmation.

"He taught me what he could, when he could," Alys evaded, hating that she had to keep silent about certain aspects of her past . . . and afraid of revealing the truth.

She was afraid of how the man holding her might react. She might have loved him ever since she was three, but Alys wasn't blind to his faults. Sometimes her Wolfer leaped before he looked—and usually leaped for the throat, if something angered him. She returned the subject to his rooms. It was safer.

"I'm glad your room is on the second floor. Kelly showed me the chamber she shares with Saber, up at the top of the central dome."

"At the top of the donjon, yes," Wolfer agreed.

"Well, I'm not too keen on living that high off the ground. I'm not afraid of heights," she added quickly, daring to tease him just a little about his childhood fear, and getting a squeeze in return, "but I'm not interested in having to mount so many steps each night, when I'm tired and just want to fall into my bed."

"*Our* bed," Wolfer reminded her, and turned both of them toward the inner door, steering them in that direction. "So. A little more color out here, maybe some extra cushions . . . but nothing too frilly, right?"

"Right." She opened the door for them, since his arms were still around her as they shuffled forward in paired, rocking steps. It was a silly embrace, but then he'd always been willing to be a little bit silly for her. Just for her. It was one of the reasons why Alys had been so willing to be brave for him in return. She smiled as they entered the bedchamber. "And in here . . ."

Both of them looked around the bedchamber once the door was open, taking in the similar decor. The only thing different was the fact that the walls in the bedchamber were currently patterned like a forest canopy, with white birds flying in slow motion across the view. Though she had been on Nightfall only a few short days, Alys was already beginning to ignore the effect of the walls. Instead, she studied the actual furnishings, and the way they were laid out across the room.

Only one thing was wrong with the room in her opinion, but she didn't know if Wolfer would care to hear it, so she hesitated over expressing one of her oldest desires.

"What?" Wolfer prompted as the woman in his arms remained quiet for too long. He wanted to make her comfortable in his chambers, so comfortable, she would never want to leave him. "Anything you want, Alys, you can have. *Anything.*"

"I want . . . I want a rug," she confided hesitantly.

"A rug?" Wolfer raised his brown brows. *That* was what she was so reluctant to confess?

"A *thick* rug," the woman in his arms stated when he didn't say anything more . . . and most importantly didn't scorn her request. Her long-held dream. "A *big* rug. So big I could lie down on it and stretch out my hands and my toes, and never feel the floor," Alys added, remembering too many winters with cold stone underfoot at the castle at the center of Corvis County. "So thick, I could sleep on it. And blankets. Lots of blankets when winter comes—enough to drown under."

"It doesn't get that cold, here on the island," Wolfer pointed out pragmatically. "We're farther north than Corvis. Only in the worst of our coldest winter storms do we get a little snow, and usually only on the tops of the two mountain ranges. Usually on the southern range at that, since it has the higher peaks. But even that much usually vanishes by midmorning."

Alys shook her head. "There were too many nights I was afraid to go to sleep, for fear I would be too cold to wake up in the morning," she confessed quietly. "Devries land was a lot farther south than Corvis, once I had to go live with my uncle. Even at Corvis Castle, the winters were still too cold, and my bedding too thin."

"Spells or no spells, remind me to kill your uncle the next time I see him," Wolfer rumbled darkly. He lifted Alys by the sweet curve of her rump before she could protest his bloodthirsty intentions, carrying her closer to his bed.

Holding her against his chest with one muscular arm hooked under her backside, he stripped back the blankets with a sweep of his powers . . . and spotted the brown-dried stain on the bedding, proof of her innocence only so many hours before. Proof she was really here, and really his. He kissed her temple, muscles trembling a little. Not from holding her, but from being gifted with her. Setting her down on the mattress, Wolfer shed his clothing, speaking as he removed his tunic.

"I will *always* be here, in this bed, waiting and ready to keep you warm, Alys." Hands going to the lacings on his breeches, he kissed her lightly, quickly on the mouth, then grinned. "I think I even know how to make you very hot each and every night, if you want . . ."

A small, shy smile curved her mouth. The look in her gray eyes when she lifted her gaze to his was anything but shy, however. After less than one day's taste of pleasure and desire, she seemed ready enough to play innocent-and-bold with real finesse. Wolfer knew he was going to love being driven crazy by her when she was this way in bed with him, too. He loved her, and that was more than enough for him.

Alys jerked awake, her heart pounding from a nightmare, her surroundings unfamiliar and frightening. Her eyes adjusted immediately to the darkness around her, but her other senses weren't yet ready to focus. She didn't know why there should be a warm, male-smelling body in the same bed as her, nor why that bed should be so soft and lump-free, nor why someone should be knocking on a door somewhere in the distance.

Memories dragged themselves into her waking mind, allowing her heart to beat normally again. She was in Wolfer's room on Nightfall Isle. *Thank Kata I'm not still at my uncle's "mercy"!* she thought, closing her eyes in relief.

Then flinched awake again as the knocking increased to a thumping. The man next to her mumbled something in his sleep, but didn't move, and certainly didn't get up to answer it. Of course, she had sort of worn him out last night, Alys decided. He had worn her out, too, but the adrenaline rush from her unfamiliar surroundings, the fear of being back under Uncle Broger's control, had chased away most of her urge to sleep.

Slipping out of the bed, she groped around for something to wear. Finding Wolfer's larger tunic as the first piece of clothing she could locate, Alys tugged it on. It covered her to the knees but no further, so she grabbed the fur blanket draped over a nearby chair and wrapped it around her waist to hide her legs. It was still dark as she shuffled her way out into the sitting room; light from distant parts of the castle illuminated the chamber through the windows just enough for her to see. Without tripping or bumping into anything, she made it to the door. Her fears on waking were still unnerving her, though.

Alys jumped in fear as the intermittent thumping changed to outright pounding just as she reached the door. But there wasn't any reason for any of Wolfer's nice brothers or sister-in-law to pound . . . not unless . . . Heart in her throat, Alys readied one of her few offensive spells, the one she used to smite the nastiest beasts in her uncle's menagerie into dazed obedience, and yanked open the door. One hand holding the blanket at her waist to hide her bare legs, she flicked the other hand off the door handle and high into the air, glowing and ready to lash her power down on—

—Rydan. Who flinched reflexively and threw up his own hand, his palm glowing with the beginnings of a protective shield. Alys froze, mortified. She had been so afraid; between the nightmare of her disorientation and the impatience of his knocking, she hadn't stopped to *really* think about who could possibly be on the other side of the door, not calmly or logically. She managed to lower her arm, relaxing her grip on her power, and worked her throat. It squeaked at her first attempt to speak, then came out in an unsteady, ashamed whisper.

"I—I'm sorry . . ."

Black eyes, shadowed slightly by the lightglobes dimly illuminating the corridor, flicked past her into the chamber behind her, then back to her face expressionlessly. "Did I interrupt you?"

It took her a long moment to catch his meaning. Alys blushed furiously when she did. Her throat locked again, this time from a whole new level of embarrassment. She shook her head quickly, her waist-long, sleep-tangled curls shifting with the motion. A couple locks slid free of her shoulders to dangle in front of her face, hiding some of her embarrassment.

"It is Wolfer's turn to help prepare breakfast," the night-dwelling sixth born of the eight brothers informed her calmly. He started to turn away, then eyed her for a brief moment. "Until you are in the chore-roster, you should help him. Sister."

He turned and padded away without another word, as silent as a shadow, before Alys could unlock her throat again. She wanted to thank him for . . . well, for acknowledging her impending position in this household, but she really couldn't. Alys knew she didn't deserve anyone's thanks, gratitude, or appreciation. Not until the time was right, and she had confessed all to these people who had accepted her. Which she would have to do before she married Wolfer. It was only fair. Only then would she know that they truly accepted her among them.

*If* they could accept her, afterward.

When she turned around to return to the bed, shutting the door behind her, she squeaked and jumped back against the panel in fright. Wolfer stood right behind her, naked save for a second blanket loosely wrapped around his waist. He had approached as silently as his black-clad, black-haired, black-eyed younger brother had left. He didn't look nearly as unnerving as Rydan did, with his chest-length brown hair rumpled and tufted awkwardly from sleep, his golden gaze bemused by her less than steely nerves. A glance at the closed door, then at her, and he cocked one brown brow.

"Chores?" he asked in that deep voice of his.

The one she had felt rumbling against her flesh every time he had murmured endearments and encouragements during their lovemaking. Alys could feel it as clearly as if he were standing chest-to-breast with her, and blushed. Nodding, she clutched her blanket a little tighter, feeling shy with the sexual longing stirred up by the mere sound of his voice this morning.

Wolfer quirked his brow again when she blushed and wouldn't quite look at him. She was doing it again, vacillating between bold and shy. Smiling, he padded up to her, cupped her jaw, kissed her sweetly on the lips, and let go. If he didn't, he'd never get down to the kitchens. Rydan would be upset with him . . . and his sweet Alys would be too sore to walk.

So, instead of taking her in his arms, discarding blankets and tunic, and making love to her right then and there, he merely cupped his arm around her shoulders and drew her back into his bedchamber. "Let's find our clothes and get dressed. Or we'll *never* get dressed."

She blushed again, making him grin.

For a moment, Alys couldn't do anything but stare. Wolfer had suggested he take her outside the castle walls after breakfast and teach her how to transform her shape into a she-wolf . . . but she had expected to walk. No sooner had they entered the eastern courtyard than Wolfer transformed into the same stallion that had given her that incredible . . . ride.

From the way one golden equine eye surveyed her, then winked slowly and deliberately, *he* was remembering the last time the two of them had been together like this, too. For a long, shocked moment, Alys couldn't have moved even if both of her uncles had suddenly appeared behind her. Considerations of modesty were swept away, though, as the memory of the pleasure she had found in riding him bareback rose within her like an incoming tide. Breathless, warm under her bodice vest, blouse, and Kelly-style trousers, she wiped damp palms on her hips and eyed him speculatively.

Just as he shifted his weight impatiently, she made up her mind and lunged at him. With a yank on his mane and a thrust of her legs, she managed to leap up just enough to hook one leg over his back, then hauled herself, grunting and puffing, up onto his back all the way. Squirming a little, grinning, and blushing, she got herself settled in just the right spot.

Strangely enough, the position didn't remind her of the previous horseback trip. Instead, it recalled a time from ages and ages ago, when she would climb onto his back and he'd trot around, his elbows hooked under her knees, pretending to snort and whinny like a horse to entertain her as a little girl. So she thumped him lightly with her boot-clad heels.

"Okay, horsie! Let's go!"

From the equine snort he gave, he wasn't expecting her playful reaction to being up on his back. But he seemed willing enough to play the game. Swishing his tail, he pranced toward the eastern gate. Trevan was already there, in the act of swinging open the doors to attend to some chore.

With a cheerful wave, Alys passed him, mounted on his brother's back. She clung as Wolfer headed down the sloping, zig-zagging road that led eventually to the eastern beaches. A few minutes later, a golden-copper eagle soared into the sky over their heads, veering off to the left, flying toward the northern half of the island. Wolfer veered to the right, venturing into the forest along a deer trail that led to the south.

Her childhood joy in riding didn't linger long. The uneven way he picked through the jungle floor, over fallen trees, around thick stretches of bushes, up little ridges, and down into small valleys, rocked her body over his brown-hided spine. The awareness she had of the last time added to her stimulation, until within half an hour of beginning their ride, Alys was impatient for him to find a spot to stop. She didn't want to experience her pleasure riding his back this time; she wanted to experience it riding *him*.

Wolfer, however, had a specific destination in mind. When they finally reached it, he stopped at the edge of a little swale in the forest. It was carpeted with moss so thick, one could dig for half a foot before reaching actual dirt. If it had been a rug, it would have fitted his bride-to-be's requirements, for it carpeted the forest floor in an area roughly twelve feet by twenty, forming a sort of oval next to a trickle of a stream. A snort and a twist of his head made her blink.

"You want me to dismount?" Alys asked. The nod of his long, brown, equine head had her slithering reluctantly off his back. Instantly, her right hand had a hold of, not his mane down by his withers, but the hair growing at the nape of his neck as he transformed back to his natural shape.

His musky male odor mingling with the scent of moss and water, tree and earth, Wolfer quickly divested her of every scrap of her clothing. Letting her hands roam over his body, he enjoyed the impatient way she removed his garments. But when she started to tug him down toward the mossy bed he had located for them, he shook his head.

"No . . . let's go for that ride again," Wolfer murmured, running his fingers through the inevitable tangle of curls he had helped her brush out when they had dressed earlier in the morning.

Alys lifted her eyes to his, wide and uncertain. "Like . . . like this? Naked? But . . . your brothers . . ."

A smile curved his lips. Leaning in close, Wolfer dipped his head and nuzzled her ear. "Saber is either busy with his own bride or working in his smithy, Kelly is no doubt sewing if she isn't with my twin, Dominor is missing, Evanor is moping inside the castle over his brother's absence, Trevan roams the northern half of the isle for his territory, while I claim the south, Rydan is asleep at this hour, Koranen is most likely in his own forge, and Morganen was due to go down to the salt-block warehouses to replenish the spells on the wagons this morning.

"If any but Trevan and Morganen stir outside the walls, it will be toward the western cove. The trading ship that is still out there will be leaving with the morning tide and will have no reason save the purchase of our salt to come up to the castle . . . and less than no reason to come all the way out here. Even if they could find us in this part of the island." His teeth nipped her earlobe quickly, gently, making her breath catch. "Besides, after our first morning ride, I longed more than you can know to have you naked on my back, wet with your pleasure, and so ready for me all I had to do was transform, twist, and fill you.

"I would take you on the beach, but I do not think sand would feel all that nice if it clung to certain intimate places on either of us," he added with a grin, pulling back slightly to show her he was teasing her. "This moss will be a wonderful bed for both of us . . . and a good place for you to get in touch with the wild that lies within you. A good shapechanger cannot transform into a new animal shape all that easily without getting in touch with her animal side, after all . . ."

Nuzzling her throat as she absorbed his words with a shudder, Wolfer nipped at her soft skin with his teeth. The bite was a sting that didn't come anywhere close to harming her, but it did make her suck in a sharp breath. It also made her sway into him, her bare breasts touching his bare chest, her belly brushing against his erection; their thighs slid together, bodies rubbing in satiny warmth.

Alys clutched at his shoulders; Wolfer's hands cupped the curves of her buttocks. He lifted his mouth from the curve of her neck and smiled down at her. Smiling back, she started to lean close enough for another kiss, then sighed, thinking.

"We should do the shapechanging first."

"Oh, we should, should we?" Wolfer returned, arching a brow at her.

She nodded reluctantly. "I need to be fresh and strong, when I try this. And you . . . make me all weak inside. During and, um, afterward," she added, cheeks warming with the topic. "It's *nice*. I like it, but . . . I think I should concentrate on the lesson. You know. First."

Sighing, Wolfer nodded his head. A squeeze of her rump and he stepped back, releasing her. "All right. We'll start with your pookrah shape. It's dog-like. It has the same general bone structure and musculature, the same internal organs. Now, can you do partial transformations?"

Alys nodded, trying not to look at his naked form directly. All those muscles were rather distracting. Her intermittent lessons with Morganen had certainly involved far less interaction than this. "Yes. They're, um, easier for me in some ways."

"They can be difficult for some," he agreed. "Can you do a partial transformation between shapes?"

"Um . . . a little. It's easier for me to go back and forth from human."

"Well, we'll try anyway. Transform," he instructed her. The sooner the better, too; her body was dappled here and there with sunlight, highlighting a patch of breast, a bit of bicep, and shining in golden highlights through her dark blond curls.

Nodding, Alys took a deep breath. "Um . . . don't hurt me. I'm not *really* a pookrah, remember."

Wolfer rolled his eyes. She really was silly, sometimes—and in the span it took him to glance skyward and back, she had reshaped herself into a brindled-gold, horse-sized wardog. Elongated canines protruded past the lips of a narrow snout. Gray eyes narrowed warily, and triangular ears flattened slightly in uncertainty. She now stood as tall as Wolfer on long, lean legs that connected to narrow hips and chest.

Claws the length of a little finger tipped each toe on her paws, digging into the moss cushioning the floor of the glade. They were strong and sharp, designed to rend and tear more readily than a normal dog's claws. There were more muscles on her frame than there would be on a coursing hound; pookrahs were designed to be strong as well as fast. Fierce and cunning, too. Their minds had been magically altered to be smarter than the average canine's, and hardwired to chase down and rend anything that looked like prey or that they had been trained to consider an enemy.

A string of saliva dripped off one of her canines, and she licked her lips, panting a little.

"That's a . . . a very realistic transformation." *And an*

*unnervingly accurate one,* Wolfer thought. There had been only a few pookrah attacks in the three years that he and his brothers had been exiled here . . . but there had been some. Careful to move slowly, in case the instincts of her current shape were strong, Wolfer lifted his hands, making a shrinking motion. "Can you make yourself smaller? Wolves aren't the size of horses."

The pookrah licked her lips again. The ears flattened a little; the tail and hind legs trembled. She shrank a little, but not far, by a finger-length or so in height. Craning her head, she looked at herself and tried again. A thumb-length, this time. A whine of frustration rose from her throat, an odd sound for a species Wolfer had only ever heard baying for his siblings' blood.

"Come on," he encouraged her. "A lot more than that. Shrink down. Make yourself smaller!"

She strained again, and again . . . and rippled back into her normal flesh. Bracing her hands on her knees, she panted for a few moments. A shake of her head, and she looked up at him. "I'm used to doing this in a mirror . . . I just don't have a good enough body-sense to do it without looking at myself."

Wolfer's brows rose at that. "That's strange; most shapechangers I know have a harder time transforming while they watch themselves. They'll use a mirror to check their progress, but the visual disorientation during the actual attempts usually throws them off their stride."

"It doesn't throw me, but we don't have a mirror out here. Maybe if we went back to your rooms?" Alys offered, folding her arms across her breasts. She wasn't too comfortable, being naked in front of him. Not because she was naked, exactly; it was more because she was using her magic openly in front of him. On top of being naked in front of him.

Shaking his head, Wolfer lifted his hand toward the stream. *"Nucsolk!"*

A bubble the size of his chest rose up out of the trickling water. It flattened and elongated into an oval, shimmering as he directed it with his will. Angling and spreading horizontally as well as vertically, it hung in the air next to her. Another muttered word and the doubled surface hardened. It was a little misty, not like a good glass mirror, but it did display both of them with enough clarity to be useful.

Alys blushed at their reflections, surrounded by semi-tropical foliage. "We look like temple images of Jinga and Kata, as lover and maiden at the Dawn of Time . . ."

Moving up behind her, Wolfer wrapped his arms around her. He pressed his lips to the crown of her head and smiled. "You're welcome."

"Wolfer!" She tried to elbow him, but he held her still until she stopped struggling. Another kiss dropped onto her curls, then he released her. Stepping back, he gave her room to transform.

"Again. Pookrah, and make it small."

A swirling ripple of flesh, and the horse-sized wardog stood in her place. She studied her reflection, narrowed her eyes a little . . . and shrank. A finger-length at a time, but she shrank all the same. Ears pricked forward with concentration, tail-tip twitching, the lean, short-haired canine reduced itself to the size of a hound over the span of a minute or so.

"Good . . . good," Wolfer praised her. "Now, hold that size. Feel it from your bones to your skin, and *hold* it . . . Good," he repeated as she stood there, studying herself. "Now, come back to yourself . . . and then transform to *that* size of a pookrah."

A breath, and Alys resumed her natural form. Another lungful, and she shrank and shifted shape, getting it in one go. Wolfer caught himself before he could shout with pleasure; she was still a pookrah, however small, and he was essentially defenseless. Not to mention naked. He did have his magic, but she might be fast enough to chew on certain parts of his anatomy before he could cast a protective spell, if he startled her badly.

"Very good," he murmured quietly instead. "Now come

back to yourself. I'm going to shift my own shape into a wolf, and I want you to examine me all over. Touch, smell, sight, all of me. You'll need to feel the fur to know how to grow it, and feel as well as see how much more stocky and muscular a wolf is, compared to a wardog."

Transforming, Alys nodded. The mirror was really helping. So was his gentle tone of voice. She knew she had a lot of work ahead of her, though. Shrinking her size was just one of dozens of adjustments she would have to make.

It was nice to have a teacher in the same place as her, for once.

# THIRTEEN

⋅✠⋅

**M**organen stared down into the mirror resting on his workbench. The soft chime had interrupted one of his experiments, but the alerting spell let him know a certain someone was about to communicate. The oval looking glass misted for a long moment, then two patches cleared. On the left appeared the face of Donnock of Devries, bruised in-law to the Corvis bloodline. On the right was the face of Broger of Devries . . . in-law and usurper of the bloodline.

*How easy it would be to reach through and smash both of them . . .*

All it would take would be a subtle alteration of his spying spell, a casting of a powder very similar in composition and enchantment to the one he'd used on his main mirror to bring Kelly from her world to his . . . and the reach of his will, extended into the hearts of both men. A simple matter, were it not for the fact that Morganen simply didn't like to kill. Alas, the youngest of the eight mage-brothers wasn't a murderer by nature. He much preferred to fix things, rather than smash them. Any fool could smash and destroy; it took someone with far greater skill to create and mend.

*Definitely more of a lover than a fighter,* he thought with a sigh, reaching for his mug of stout. Not that he had much of an opportunity to *be* a lover either, right now. His gaze slid to the cheval mirror in the corner, but it was quiescent. *Mind back on your work,* he chided himself into paying attention as Broger and Donnock spoke.

"What do you mean, 'what trip to Nightfall'?" Broger demanded of his younger brother. "You're on the gods-be-damned boat! Didn't it go there?"

"I don't . . ." Donnock's face, peering up through the surface of the looking glass, blinked in a somewhat stupid, confused fashion. "I don't remember. Why am I here, again?"

Broger wasn't slow-witted. Unfortunately. "Damn and blast! They've probably cast a forgetfulness spell on you. I'd love to know who colored your face with all those bruises, too. Get back here immediately. Hire a mirror-Gate and come straight back to the castle."

"Why?" Donnock asked, still looking a bit dazed and lost.

"I'm going to have to crack open your memories, that's why."

Donnock shook his head, as if trying to rid it of some internal pain. Or more accurately, trying to think clearly through the fog Morganen had imposed upon him. "But . . . won't that risk damaging my mind?"

Eyes squinted shut in his bewilderment, the younger Devries brother missed the sardonic look of his eldest sibling. "That's a risk we'll have to take. I need a clear scrying of the island. I'll assume that you've been there, since you cannot remember a thing about your visit. They must have some reason to suspect a visit from you is not as friendly as it seems. Yet they do not *know* anything. Otherwise they would have ordered you bound in enspelled chains.

"Well. It matters not what sort of suspicions they might have regarding me," the older man dismissed. "The news I just bought is all the excuse I need for a full assault. So long as there are no witnesses, their deaths will be blamed on the Disaster of Prophecy." Broger smirked up at Morganen's face, though he didn't know it, thinking his scrying link with his brother was secure. "Come back quickly. Your life is valuable to me, now. As are the contents of your mind. I need a clear visual of that island."

The communication ended with a flick of his hand. The mirror on the table misted and turned gray for a moment, then cleared. When it showed only his own reflection, Morganen sat back, thinking. *What news could he have "bought" that gives him leave to think he could kill us with . . . impunity. Of course! Kelly talked with that Council mage. They know there's at least one woman on the Isle, and that means they expect a Disaster any day, now.*

*Which means I should keep a closer eye on the Council. They might not believe Dom's kidnapping is sufficient to mark a Disaster large enough to be prophesied . . .*

*But what does he mean by his brother's life being valuable to him, now? Wouldn't it be valuable to begin with?* It was a conundrum to ponder. Of course, Broger wasn't Morganen; the man's mind worked in twisted ways that Morganen didn't necessarily want to follow. *Perhaps a consultation with Alys; she knows him well enough to guess what he might have in mind. Certainly she'll know what he last had in his menagerie, what he would inundate us with in his "full assault."*

The corner of his mouth curved up as he contemplated finding a moment to have a private chat with his soon-to-be next sister-in-law. *Presuming Wolfer doesn't try to eviscerate me just for looking at her, of course . . .*

**O**h!" Alys squeaked, hands releasing her victim and flying up to cover her mouth. "Oh!—I *did* it!"

Kelly twisted from her sprawled flop, shifting onto her side. Planting her hand under her cheek, she arched a strawberry blond brow at her student. "Yeah, you certainly did. You did it very well, too. With actual power and oomph behind that throw. But you also did something wrong, at the very end."

Alys cringed. "I did?"

*"That."* Kelly pointed at her, confusing Alys. "First, you were startled that you succeeded at all, and now you flinch at the thought of doing wrong. You have *got* to learn to have confidence in yourself!" Curling onto her knees, Kelly stood and dusted off her practice clothes. Alys moved to help her up, hovering a little in concern.

Both of them were clad in simple trousers and sleeveless tunics. Alys had cast a cooling charm on the walls of the room, which meant the windows and door had to stay shut to keep the air comfortable, but it helped keep them from sweating too much as they exercised. Crossing to the table in the corner, Kelly finished the juice in her mug and poured herself more from the pitcher she had brought up from the kitchen. She saluted the younger woman, as Alys joined her, equally thirsty.

"You're doing really well. But you have to work on your follow-through. You *cannot* let down your guard, young lady," the outworlder chided Alys, giving her a pointed look. Her aquamarine gaze was wry. "What if I'd retaliated while you were still busy being amazed by the fact that you managed to throw me to the ground? Tossing someone to the ground *isn't* going to end the fight, you know."

"But . . . you said it would. Didn't you?" Alys asked, confused. This *kung fu* stuff was rather strange. Useful; she couldn't deny that . . . but strange.

"I said it would give you an *opportunity* to end the fight," Kelly corrected. "Once he's down and vulnerable, you attack your foe to disable him, and you do it while he's still trying to get back into a defensive position. *Before* he can defend himself adequately. Kick him in the ribs, or the kneecap. Stomp on his hand, then on his groin. Kick him in the butt, woman! Do *something* that follows through on your attack, something that keeps him down and stops him from trying to hurt you again!"

Alys nodded. She *knew* her soon-to-be sister-in-law was right . . . but it was hard to go against so many years of learning how *not* to react. Of learning to just take punishments stoically. Not to resist, or rebel. Sipping at her juice, she nodded again and cleared her throat. "It's just so . . . so *hard*. I had to just take what my uncle was doing to me, and not show any reactions so that he'd get bored quickly and stop hurting me."

Her unsteady admission made Kelly's heart twist with pain. The older woman kept forgetting that Alys' background and history weren't like her own. *Self-sufficiency made you strong in the way of the Doyles,* she thought. *But the Devries way is apparently one of stoic, fearful survival, for Alys. Hmm . . .*

"Okay, how about we look at this from a different angle. You learned how to endure, and then . . . what, continue on with whatever you had to do?" Kelly asked her.

Again, Alys nodded.

"Well, then we'll build on that as our foundation. Did you have to go back to doing chores or whatever?"

"Yes, of course," Alys agreed, unsure where Kelly was trying to lead her. "If he didn't like something that happened in his work, he'd come out and strike me on the face with the back of his hand. When I just righted myself and continued with my chore, he'd say something vulgar, threaten me, and stalk off again to find someone else to hit. Someone who would cringe more satisfactorily. And I'd go back to feeding the chickens or whatever."

"Then that is how you must view kung fu. As a chore you need to get back to doing, whatever happens in a fight," Kelly asserted. Taking the mug from the younger woman, she set it next to her own on the table and tugged her back onto the center of the layers of felting they'd put down for practice mats. "Okay. I'm going to slap you in the face, and just like we practiced, you're going to take advantage of the moment right after I slap you to throw me. Okay?"

That earned her a dubious look from the younger woman. "You're going to *slap* me?"

"Don't worry; I'm not going to hit you hard, and it'll all be slow . . . but I want you to recover from the blow, grab my arm, twist and duck, and roll me over your hip just like we've been practicing. And then, while I'm down, you're going to aim a gentle kick at my thigh. That is your chore. Got it?" Kelly asked.

Alys blinked, thought it through to try and settle it in her mind, then drew a deep breath and nodded. "Got it."

"Good." Her hand lifted and swung inward in a somewhat leisurely swipe.

It smacked lightly into Alys' cheek and continued past her shoulder. Alys reached forward, caught Kelly's arm, twisted under it, moved into Kelly's body, and heaved, thrusting with her hip and shoulder. Obligingly, Kelly didn't resist, flopping onto the padding. Alys almost forgot the next step, but shifted her weight and thrust her heel against the downed woman's leg.

"Good!" Rolling away, Kelly rose to her feet, came back, and smacked Alys with her other hand. And then froze in place, giving her a pointed look. "Well?"

"Oh!" Alys grabbed her arm, and fumbled her way through an opposite-side throw, then stomped downward again.

"Good. Again!" Slap, throw, stomp. Slap, throw, stomp. "Now try stomping on some other body part of mine—still slow, and don't actually try to hurt me just yet . . ."

Slap, throw, stomp at her shoulder; slap, throw, stomp at her foot—this went on for several more rounds. Until Kelly threw Alys for a loop by shoving her shoulder hard, rather than slapping her cheek slowly. Alys reacted even as she swayed back, affronted by the unexpected attack. She surged forward, shoving Kelly back. The redhead slapped her, *cracking* her fingers in a loud, stinging blow against her cheek.

A whirl, a body check, and a thump landed Kelly on the felt matting. A slam of her foot . . . landed it on the matting between the other woman's abruptly spread thighs. Those legs snapped shut, tripping her and sending her to the padded floor as well. Scrambling free, Alys surged to her feet, panting and wary.

"Hold! *Excellent!*" her teacher praised her, rising as

well. "Very good! You took to the lesson like a duckling to a pond, there. You didn't let either my surprise attack or your *own* surprise at a successful defense stop you from fighting back. Good job, Alys!"

Relaxing a little, Alys accepted the praise. Her limbs started to tremble. "I . . . I didn't understand for a moment why you shoved me, but when I shoved you back and you slapped me . . . it was just like you said. I suddenly knew what chore I had to do, to follow through."

Kelly hugged her. "Excellent! You have the idea in your head, now! Come, we'll do this a few more times, then we can call it a night, all right?"

Her fingers touched the warm spot on her cheek where Kelly had struck her. The blow was really light, compared to the clouts her uncle would deliver. It stung, but it wouldn't even leave a bruise. "You . . . um, you can hit me harder, if you need to; I can take it."

The look Kelly gave Alys was a grim, tight one. "I'm sorry you had to suffer so much abuse, Alys. I *won't* hit you like that. But . . . in order to keep you from freezing up with shock, I do have to hit you at least a little bit. I'm not happy about it."

"But you can't train me to react properly without it," Alys agreed. "It does help, thinking of it like just another chore I have to do, in between dealing with my uncle's anger. It helps a lot."

That earned her a smile from the other woman. "Then we'll keep thinking of it that way, and just put you down for kung fu lessons as one of your daily chores."

Alys giggled. "*If* you can tear me away from Wolfer's side. He seems to think one of my own daily chores is sharing hours of pleasure with him!"

"He's *very* much like his twin, in that respect," Kelly confided, her tone lascivious, and both women laughed. Grinning, the outworlder shook her head. "You can't blame them. Three years without a woman on the isle? Poor things. Ah, well. From the looks of things, six more women will be showing up here sooner or later."

"And will you teach all of them this kung fu thing?" Alys asked her, gesturing at their makeshift salle.

"Of course! Just the ladies; the gentlemen have magic on their side," Kelly dismissed with a flip of her hand.

"Well, so do I," Alys reminded her. "Not as much as the twins do, but some."

Kelly arched one of her reddish brows. "Does *everyone* on this world have some magic?"

"Oh, no." Alys shook her head. "Not everyone. It's mostly been concentrated into the upper classes through interbreeding; the higher your noble standing, the more magic you are likely to be born with. Of course, the gods do favor the common classes with magic once in a while. I'm not completely sure about other lands, of course, but that's how it works in Katan. And in Aiar-that-was. Before it was destroyed."

"I've heard of that place," Kelly admitted, fetching their mugs of juice. "Where is it, again? Is it close enough to visit?"

"It's a continent far to the north, about as far above the Sun's Belt as Katan is below it," Alys explained. "Aiar also lies beyond the Great Reef. No ship with a deep draft can cross it safely, though," the younger woman informed her. "And because of the shattering, the great Portals were closed. There aren't very many mirror-Gates that can reach that far. So only shallow barges dare travel north or south to do any trading, and only in the calmest times of the year, because they're barges, not proper ocean ships. The traders take mages with them to calm the waves, but there's only so much you can do when a really big storm comes along. It's very risky, though the profits are correspondingly high."

"Well, I'm not all that fond of boats and ships and travel-ing on the water," Kelly shrugged, "so it's not like I'm plan-ning on taking a trip northward that way." She let out a short, dry laugh. "Not like I could go west, either, since the Mage Council would throw a fit at a visit from not only the woman who triggered the brothers' curse-thing, but a woman who went and claimed all of Nightfall for herself."

"Why did you do that, anyway?" Alys asked. She blushed right after saying it. "I'm sorry, Kelly . . . That was rude of me to ask."

Kelly laughed. "Not really . . . I think for several reasons. To give the brothers a sense of home instead of a sense of exile, for one. And to assert my authority over them for another. Magicless as I am," she admitted with a shrug, "I need *something* to keep the boys in line."

"But all they have to do is say 'no,' and they won't have to obey you," the younger woman reasoned. "There's no way you can make them do what they don't want to do."

"Not unless I want to use kung fu on them, and even then, they could use their magic on me," Kelly admitted. "But then, that's why I made the claim 'only on weekends, holidays'—they're sort of like holy days, only they're for secular reasons, too," she explained as Alys gave her a confused look. "And then 'whenever we have visitors.' You see, by giving it a limit based on a specific time or situation, it allows them to believe that they're still in control the rest of the time.

"Eventually, we'll have more visitors," the redhead stated confidently. Then added ruefully, wrinkling her freckled nose, "At least, I'm *hoping* we'll have more visitors, and not just the other six prophesied wives. There might even be enough people living here one day to need some sort of government . . . and by then it'll already be in place. All we'll have to do is bring it up to full speed at that point in time."

"Maybe," Alys conceded. The other woman's logic was subtle, but strong. "But why you?"

"Why not me? I do have some experience in organizing people, back in the other world," Kelly stated. "And in organizing activities. That's what a leader does." She flashed Alys a smile, her aquamarine eyes gleaming with mirth. "Besides, I insist on living in a civilized land. Why shouldn't I take charge? It guarantees that the civilization I run will be one that I find acceptable. Including the living conditions. You're lucky, Alys, that you came here *after* I insisted the boys scrub this place from attic to basement, shortly after my arrival."

Alys found herself chuckling at Kelly's mock-shudder. "Well, better for you to be a queen than me. I haven't got what it takes. I know my limitations."

"Hmm. Well, feel free to stretch your boundaries once in a while," Kelly told her. "It builds character, or some sort of philosophical manure like that."

Kelly's comment made Alys laugh and think, *This outworlder woman is certainly different . . .* But not in a bad way. The younger woman wondered what her home universe was like, to produce such witty irreverence. And so much self-confidence.

"Okay," Kelly said, setting their mugs aside. The sun was just beginning to touch the western horizon, and supper would be served soon. "One more time, this time as close to full speed as you can, but still keeping it under your control. Remember, at this point, form is more important than speed, but go for speed, too."

Adjusting her stance on the matting, Alys prepared herself. The two women faced off, Kelly arched her brow, Alys nodded, and Kelly lifted her arm. The backhanded swing was already in motion when they heard a *click*. Startled, Kelly didn't pull enough of the blow; the force of her hand striking Alys' face spun the younger woman partway around. A roar followed the blow, as did a large, charging body.

Kelly reacted instinctively, grabbing and twisting and flinging Wolfer by one of the arms reaching for her. She flung him toward Alys, who reacted better than the older woman hoped, grabbing and whirling and flipping her beloved over her hip. Dumping him on the felt matting with an audible *oof* and *thud* from the impact, and a yelping flinch as she started to stomp on his upper thigh. Alys gasped, checking the instinctual move to follow through . . . and fell on top of him as she stumbled, trying to recover her balance.

For an awkward moment, the pair were nothing more

than a tangle of limbs and torsos. Wolfer growled something about killing Kelly and tried to set Alys aside, but she
was babbling an apology for hurting him and trying to
make sure by touch as well as sight that he wasn't hurt.
Watching the pair of them, Kelly bit her lower lip to keep
from laughing, then cleared her throat.

"Enough—*enough!* Alys, you did exactly as you were
supposed to do, and no, he's probably not damaged for life.
Bruised and shocked, but that's about it. Wolfer, stop
growling at me. I was *teaching* her how to defend herself!"
Kelly informed him tartly. "If you hadn't distracted me by
barging in here uninvited, I wouldn't have accidentally hit
her so hard!"

"Dammit, Kelly—you don't *hit* a woman like that!"
Wolfer snapped, finally untangling himself from Alys long
enough to shove himself to his feet. She followed him as he
growled protectively, "Especially not *this* woman!"

Kelly glanced at Alys, arching a skeptical brow. The
younger woman's gray eyes widened a moment in puzzlement, then narrowed in comprehension. Grabbing Wolfer's
elbow, she tugged him around to face her. "Wolfer, that's
enough! I *am* going to learn how to defend myself, and
Kelly *is* going to teach me!"

"But, Alys—"

"I took *you* down, didn't I?" Alys pointed out breathlessly. She was still a bit amazed that she had managed to
do so, but was ready to take pride in the accomplishment.
Wolfer probably weighed half again what she did and had
the muscles to match . . . yet she had dumped him onto the
padded floor with astonishing ease. Poking him in the
chest, she added bravely, "And don't you dare tell me for
one instant that you don't get hurt when you learn how to
fight! I remember very clearly the day Dominor broke your
arm in sword practice, and you telling me that *bruises and
breaks happen in practice!* Don't you *dare* apply a double
standard to me, now that I'm learning how to stand up for
myself in a fight!"

She poked him again as she spoke, then a third time for

good measure. He frowned down at her, but in a sort of thoughtful way. Not an upset one, though his hand did rise to rub at the muscles she had bruised. "That was just . . . practice?"

"Yes! Like you trying to beat the stuffing out of your littlest brother the other day!" Alys reminded him. And then poked him a fourth time. "And no more beating on Morganen, just because he and I like to chat with each other! I didn't come here to marry him; I came here to marry *you*!"

Something clicked behind those golden eyes. They narrowed. "You *planned* this, all along?"

Alys flushed and started to stammer some sort of disclaimer. That wasn't *quite* what she'd meant . . . though it wasn't quite a lie, either. Kelly came to her rescue, tapping the mage on his elbow. He glanced her way, and she folded her freckled arms as she gave him a quelling look.

"Don't even think of being angry at her, Wolfer. It's not like she's holding a gun to your head to get you to marry her!"

Wolfer paled a little. He had seen from a distance the demonstration the Mandarites had made of their gun-weapons, and the demonstration Kelly had made with one of her own world's versions. He had also seen the wreck of Trevan's shoulder, and the blood his younger sibling had lost. "Don't even joke about that, Kelly!"

She rolled her eyes, but kept her mouth shut.

Alys touched his other elbow. "I didn't mean it like *that*, Wolfer. I meant . . . well, I *hoped* we would still feel for each other like we used to . . . and more. And we do! I never felt that way for Morganen, and I never will. So he's perfectly safe for me to talk to . . . you big, overgrown, jealous pookrah!"

"There's no cause to insult me like that!" he protested, mock-frowning at her. "I'm a wolf, not a wardog!"

"If the two of you are going to keep flirting with each other like this, I'm going to have to ask you to take it elsewhere. This is a dojo, not a brothel," Kelly interrupted dryly. "Besides, we're not quite done for the day. Out you go, Wolfer."

"But I came here to—"

*"Out!"* Tugging firmly on his sleeve, Kelly dragged him out of the chamber. "You can have her after we've done our cooling-down exercises and stretches!" Closing the door in his face, she turned to her pupil, sighing. "Sorry about that, but if we don't go back to work, we'll stiffen up. And you did really well, defending yourself against him."

She grinned, but Alys looked down at the floor, catching her lower lip between her teeth.

"Hey, what's wrong?" Kelly asked her, softening her tone.

"It's . . . it's one thing to go up against Wolfer. It's another thing entirely to go up against my uncle."

"Don't start thinking like that," the outworlder woman ordered her. "An attack is an attack, and you have every right to defend yourself. Your attacker is nothing more than a target to be disarmed or disabled. And you did well. But now we have to stretch. Come on."

Nodding, Alys started copying the other woman's movements. Her mind was still split in two; she'd trained herself *not* to attack, so she felt uncomfortable in doing so. But she had also tossed Wolfer to the floor. He was larger, stronger, and more skilled as a warrior than either of her uncles, who had focused more on wielding spells than swords. Even her cousin Barol preferred the subtlety of magic to the bluntness of might. Thankfully, he had not been around much in the last three years, having gone off to manage his father's estate shortly after Broger had taken over the Corvis lands.

*I should get the brothers to teach me more offensive magics,* she thought. *And defensive ones, too. It won't do any good to know how to throw my uncle to the floor, if I can't protect myself long enough to get close enough to try.*

*May Kata and Jinga keep him far from here, for a very, very long time . . .*

# FOURTEEN

A lys," Morganen addressed her, as Trevan passed around the last of the bowls of food.

"Yes, Morg?"

"I would like two or three hours of your time every morning, after you've completed your chores."

"Why do you need three hours of her time?" Wolfer asked his youngest sibling, suspicious. He still felt a little edge of jealousy whenever he thought of Alys' relationship with Morganen. They said they weren't attracted to each other, and they didn't seem to be, but he still felt like Morganen was stealing some of her affection away from him.

"Because I am her primary instructor," Morganen returned calmly, carefully phrasing it that way. He didn't want his second-eldest sibling to feel left out or indignant. "And now that she's had the chance to settle into a routine among us, it's time I finally gave her the testing and intensive training I couldn't give her when I first started teaching her."

"I am perfectly capable of teaching her—" Wolfer protested.

"And you can teach her all that you know," Morganen agreed, as Alys stopped eating, uncomfortable with the rivalry between the two of them. "I certainly wouldn't even begin to teach her how to be a shapeshifter. But I know what she knows, or what she should know, based on what I could teach her. I will examine what she does actually know and fill in the gaps in her education." He lifted his hand as Wolfer started to protest again, waving away his brother's objections. "Once I have evaluated her skills and compensated for anything that's missing, I'd also like her to spend some time with each one of us, learning what she can from each brother."

Rydan snorted.

Morganen glanced at his black-haired brother. "We all have different styles and areas of expertise, Rydan. Even you could possibly teach her a thing or two. At least, that is the assumption until we know how much would be useful for her to learn from you."

"Is this really necessary?" Koranen asked his twin, passing a bowl of greens to the other redhead in the family. "Not that I object to teaching her . . ."

"Alys never had a formal education in magic. She doesn't know what she can or cannot do. Not as thoroughly as the rest of us," Morganen pointed out.

"I think he means the two-to-three-hours a day," Evanor said. "That will take a fair amount of your time. What about the mirror to scry on my twin? Aren't you supposed to be working on that?"

"The silicate we used was too impure," Koranen answered for his twin, shaking his auburn head. "The glass cracked before we could finish enchanting it during the firing, today. Unless Rydan can find us a purer source, we're going to have to import a ton of the highest grade we can get out of the Glazier's Guild."

"Several tons," Saber corrected. "Kelly told me about this thing her world has, a way of watching areas like a permanent scrying spell. Now that we're a sovereign nation"—his mouth quirked on one side as he said that, glancing at his wife—"we need to watch our borders, as it were. And I think I'd like a Hall of Mirrors like the one the

Council maintains. Somewhere that we can go to look all across the isle and see what is happening."

Wolfer and Alys both blushed. The second eldest of the twins cleared his throat. "Uh . . . *all* of the island? Under close surveillance?"

It took Saber only a moment to catch on and flush as well. He cleared his throat. "Not in *that* close of detail. I'm thinking more of . . . of panoramic views. And mostly the coastline and the two roads. I don't want to be caught by surprise from the east by the Mandarites if another ship comes this way again, and I don't want the traders sneaking up from the west, either, if they think they can steal away the salt blocks without paying for them."

"Short-range mirrors, with semi-fixed focal points," Trevan murmured, setting down his fork long enough to rub at his chin. His other arm was still in a sling, supporting his injured shoulder, but he was healing quickly. "They'll be quick to enchant, at least, and easy to make, compared to a mirror set to scry for Dom an ocean plus who knows how much farther away. But that mirror needs to come first."

"They can wait until after we make the new mirror for him," Saber asserted. "We'll also need silver and quicksilver for the mirroring, lime and ash for the glazing—we're going to need to produce a few more items to be able to get what we want in trade. Some of what we'll need won't be cheap, especially since we're not going to be turning around and selling it to others."

"Well, I've got that *comsworg* oil we traded for when we lost Dom," Koranen pointed out. "While we're waiting for the sand, I can focus on making more lightglobes. Unless you think you can find us a pure source nearby, Brother?" he asked Rydan. "You deal with stone better than the rest of us."

"There's none here," Rydan answered in his usual terse style. "Under the sea . . . maybe. No guarantees."

"I'll contact the Guild by mirror and contract with them for a shipment," Saber stated, settling the matter. "Go ahead and look for sand under the sea, Rydan. I'm not going to wait for you to find scrying-grade silicate, of course; importing it will be worth the cost to guarantee the quality. But even if we have to purify it ourselves, it would be good to have a high-grade source nearby."

Rydan nodded, but didn't say anything.

"We also need to discuss what we're going to do about Uncle Broger." Saber stopped and grimaced. " 'Uncle' . . . I don't want to call the man that. If he disposed of Uncle Daron just to get his hands on our family's estates, he's no one I want to claim as kin. Even if it's only by marriage."

"If I remember right, he's mage enough to control and breed illegal creatures," Trevan offered. His brow pinched in a frown. "But all the different things that have been sent . . . he couldn't have cared for them on his own. Not without someone noting his absences."

"Donnock could be working with him," Koranen offered. "Not just to get a scrying fix for the island, but taking care of the animals."

Saber shook his head. "Donnock is Broger's man of business; he does all the traveling. He'd never be around to take care of the beasts. My bet would be his son—what was your cousin's name, Alys? I can't remember it."

Setting down her fork, Alys answered him quietly. "Barol."

"Barol, that's it. Broger's son Barol could have been doing it," Saber offered. "Did you see him disappearing frequently at around the same time every day?"

Now she felt miserable, a knot of guilt twisting in her stomach. Unable to eat, barely able to swallow, Alys answered as truthfully as she dared. "He, uh . . . went to take care of Uncle Broger's estates, when Uncle took over your family home."

"That was almost three years ago," Evanor pointed out. "So it couldn't have been him. One of the servants, maybe?"

Acutely uncomfortable, Alys stared at the surface of the table and tried to find the courage to confess as the others debated the matter. They were going to figure it out any moment, now . . . any moment. A shy, wary peek upward showed one set of eyes fixed on her face. A set of eyes that, though as dark and intimidating as midnight, were still clear with comprehension.

"You didn't have any choice . . . did you, Alys?" Rydan asked her quietly. Not condemningly, just factually. His words still stunned the rest.

A glance at the other brothers around the table showed them staring at her in horrified silence. Well, not Morganen, who was giving her a sympathetic, supportive look. Saber had narrowed his eyes in a calculative sort of way, and Evanor was more blinking from disbelief than horror . . . but Wolfer's reaction was the important one. His nostrils flared with several deep breaths.

A slight lift of Morganen's chin told her to go ahead and confirm Rydan's guess. The man at her side made her uncomfortable, but the time had come for the truth. She couldn't lie about this, anyway, not after having been given their hospitality.

"No, I . . . I didn't have any real choice." She bit her lower lip, wincing in anticipation.

Muscular hands slammed on the edge of the table, rocking it. The chair next to hers scraped backward, as Wolfer shoved to his feet, whirling away from the table. He stalked through the door, yanking the panel wide enough that it banged against the wall, making her flinch and hunch her shoulders. In doing so, she bit her lip, hard enough to draw blood. Wincing, Alys tongued the wound gingerly in an attempt to soothe it.

"Well." Saber's voice filled the quiet following the furor of his twin's exit. "I don't suppose you'd care to explain exactly what you did, and more importantly, *why* you did it?"

"Don't be an ass, Saber!" Kelly snapped. "She's not a big, strong, strapping brute with muscles like a mountain, or a highly powerful mage-brother! It's quite obvious to me that her uncle bullied, and threatened, and probably even beat her into doing whatever he wanted. The fact that she escaped and came *here* and isn't serving him anymore is proof enough that she wasn't interested in serving him willingly."

"If she wasn't interested in serving him willingly, why didn't she escape a lot sooner?" Koranen argued. His gaze slid to Alys' face, a slightly guilty edge to his expression, but he pressed the point as he looked back to Kelly again. 'It's been three years, after all!"

"And why didn't she tell us sooner?" Trevan asked. His words were directed at Kelly, but his green eyes rested on Alys as he spoke.                          .

"I didn't want you to hate me," Alys mumbled, wishing she had some courage. Even the self-assurance that earlier had helped her to dump Wolfer on his back would've helped. "I didn't . . . I just fed the animals. And . . . brought the cages to the mirror . . . I'm sorry."

"Sorry? You came here to us for *shelter*, and you didn't tell us you'd been helping our enemy all along?" Saber asked her. Kelly thwapped him on the chest with the back of her hand, but he ignored her. "Is this how you repay our friendship and our hospitality?"

"Saber!" Kelly protested.

"How could you do it?" Trevan demanded. "Why didn't you run away as soon as you knew what he was trying to do to us? How could you stay there and help him?"

"*I* would've run away!" Koranen agreed heatedly. "I would've done anything to escape, rather than betray my friends!"

Alys shoved to her feet, tears blurring her view of the others. "I *couldn't* run away!"

"A likely story!" Saber scoffed. "Anyone can run away!"

Angry, she grabbed the edges of the tunic Kelly had loaned her and yanked the neckline down, baring the silver diamond embedded in her sternum. "Do you see this? Do you *see* it?"

The eldest brother blushed a little, since revealing it had also exposed some of the curves of her breasts. Even Trevan looked uncomfortable, and Alys remembered well how he'd ogle anything with curves. Including her when they had been younger, though not openly.

"Do you know what this is? This is the *only* thing that is

keeping my uncle from tracking me down! It is the *only* thing that is keeping him from tapping into my very life-force and draining it to use in his spells! He could've killed me with a single word, raping my magics from my body in the process, if I hadn't scraped and bowed and *kissed his ass to stay alive!*" Jerking her clothes back into place, she glared at the lot of them, excepting only Morganen and Kelly. "You know what? You can kiss my ass, too!"

Whirling, she ran from the dining hall.

Kelly stuffed a knuckle into her mouth and bit it, her shoulders shaking as she struggled to suppress her laughter. The other woman's anguish and suffering wasn't amusing, not even in the slightest . . . but the way the Ultra Tongue translated Alys' complaint was very funny. It was such an American thing to hear, very otherworldly sounding in this land of magic and fantasy. Catching Morganen's disapproving frown, she mastered the urge to laugh and cleared her throat.

"Well . . . There you have it. There's more to her story than meets the eye. A lot more than she's revealed so far." A sidelong look at her husband showed him brooding. Kelly arched her brow. "What, you don't believe her?"

"I don't think I can," he returned grimly. "I have never heard of a spell that can strip the magic from a mage and funnel it into another mage's enchantments . . . and the only use of a life-force I've ever heard of is in a blood-sacrifice by the darkest of sorcerers. The more I learn about our uncle-in-law, the more I'm inclined to believe he could sacrifice someone's life to fuel his spells . . . but she makes it sound as if he wouldn't need any wards or runes or a consecrated blade to perform the sacrifice.

"*I* think she was overreacting," Saber finished. "Which makes me wonder how much of her story is pure exaggeration."

A heavy sigh from the far side of the table stopped the others from commenting. Morganen's forefinger tapped against the sanded surface of the table, his expression pensively unhappy. "Actually . . . that's not true."

"It isn't?" Trevan frowned.

"To the far northeast is a land called Mekhana. It is the land of the so-called Dead God," Morganen explained. "It is rumored . . . only a rumor, but a disturbing one . . . that His priests drain the magic from their mage-born citizens to sustain His existence. And from any enemy mages they catch. If I have heard of this thing, it is possible that Broger has heard of it . . . and unlike me, he is unscrupulous enough to want to either beg, borrow, steal, or somehow recreate the process just to gain himself a little more power."

That made the others study him. Saber arched a brow at Morganen. "He *is* unscrupulous enough . . . ?"

A pause, and the youngest among them continued. "Yes, well . . . While we're on the subject of deep, dark confessions . . ."

Saber quirked one of his brows. To the right, Evanor and Koranen eyed the youngest of them. To the left, Trevan folded his arms across his chest, unconsciously echoing the pose of his black-haired twin, though Trevan's expression was skeptical and Rydan's was thoughtful. With similar poses, Kelly could definitely see how closely related the two brothers were in their facial features, for all that their coloring didn't quite match.

"Well?" she prodded her youngest brother-in-law.

"Well, you're going to be angry with me, my brothers," Morganen began his explanation. "But . . . I've known all along about dear Uncle Broger, *and* all that he's been forcing Alys to do. Even before we were exiled, I knew what she had to endure. And I've been coaching her in what to do and say all along."

Saber's brows rose. Trevan sat up in his chair. But it was the youngest brother's twin, Koranen, that found his voice first. "You *what?*"

Morganen met his brothers' and sister-in-law's shocked looks with a calm expression matched only by Rydan's still rather thoughtful regard. "I coached her. I helped her, trained her, covered for her, and instructed her for the last eight years. Though for the last six years, it was more or less entirely from a distance."

"You *knew* all along that she was helping her uncle send those beasts to us?" Saber demanded, sitting forward and scowling at his youngest sibling. "You *knew* that Broger was our hidden enemy?"

The frown Morganen returned to him wasn't as fierce, but it was just as firm. His forefinger tapped the table. "These things *must* unfold in their own time, Brother. I knew early on that Alys was the woman predestined to bind Wolfer's hand, and with it, his heart. When I knew what sort of life she was being forced to lead under the fist of her uncle, I knew that one day she would be coming back to us, and I tried my best to give her what she needed to survive in his care."

Evanor eyed the youngest of them. "That thing on her chest, that she says blocks her uncle's spells . . . did you have a hand in it?"

"Of course. She researched all the spells her uncle had laid into her, while I did the research on their countermeasures. I then designed the amulet, and she crafted it. But our method of communication was . . . erratic, at best," Morganen confessed quietly, his voice tinged with a touch of grimness. "I wouldn't have let it drag out nearly so long as it did, but for that. We didn't dare communicate in such a way or for such a length of time that her uncle would have noticed. What would have taken six months at most stretched into roughly two and a half years. After that . . . well, it was just a matter of encouraging her to survive until the time was right for her to join us."

Gray eyes narrowed in accusation. "You manipulative bastard!" His other brothers gave him inquisitive looks, but Saber's attention was focused on the youngest figure seated across from him. "You *deliberately* manipulated Kelly's presence into this world, you manipulated Alys' arrival—did you have a hand in Dominor's kidnapping, too?"

"Hardly! I had nothing to do with that!" Morganen

snorted. It was only when Evanor glared at him—a harsh look that normally did not grace the kindly brother's face, Kelly noted as she silently observed—that the youngest mage-brother relented. "But . . . I do admit I could have fetched him back. It would not have been easy, but I could have done it."

"Dammit, Morganen!" Evanor swore harshly. The short-lived outburst seemed to drain most of his rage out of him, leaving him with a frustrated, pleading look. "Why *didn't* you bring him back?"

"Because when I heard about the women-hating land of Mandare, and the women-as-mages land of Natallia, their enemy . . . I figured that *somewhere* overseas," Morganen explained calmly, filling his goblet with a little more wine, "he'd find a woman who could be his match. As Prophecy demands of him. He certainly wouldn't find one around here. The timing of it is a delicate process, you see: I knew that, with Kelly and Saber married, Alys would be free to come here and ensnare Wolfer's heart. Or rather, re-ensnare it. She won it long ago, after all."

He lifted his cup in a mock-salute as the other brothers fumed. Kelly eyed him warily, herself. Morg had seemed such a young, affable, harmless sort of fellow when she'd first met him. Well, after she'd gotten over her shock at him being a living, breathing mage of course. Now he was revealing how he'd tricked and arranged and plotted. It was a bit unnerving to hear, even if she had benefited from his manipulations.

"And me?" Evanor asked him in a voice somewhere between bottled annoyance and sardonic resignation. "Have you someone lined up for me?"

"I haven't the slightest clue as to who would make a good wife for you," Morganen returned calmly. "I don't even know who would make a good wife for your twin. All any of us can do is monitor the situation."

"But we cannot do that without a functional mirror. A mirror we could use to bring him home," Koranen stated, studying his twin as he folded his arms across his blue-clad chest. "Tell me, Morg, did you have anything to do with the cracking of the first one?"

Morganen sipped at his wine. "No. That was a flaw in the materials being used. I had nothing to do with it; I was as surprised as the rest of you."

"Can you scry for him by some other means?" Trevan asked, pinning his youngest brother with a hard look worthy of an irritated feline.

A hesitation, and the mage replied, "Yes."

"You *can*?" Evanor demanded, his brown eyes widening. "Jinga's Sacred Ass! Why haven't you told us this before now?"

"Because it's not for you to interfere with his Destiny!" Morganen retorted crisply. Setting his goblet down, he glared pointedly at the others. "*Each* of us has a role to play—a role that the Gods predetermined for us! I may not be a Seer, but I have been giving our 'Song of Destiny' a *lot* of thought over the years! As is *my* foretold place to do so!"

Despite the youthful lines of his face, framed by wisps of his light brown hair, Morganen looked more mature than Saber at that moment, as Kelly observed his mannerisms. Looked, sounded, and acted more mature. *Well, maybe only as mature,* she amended to herself as she silently looked on. She had suspected for a long time that Morganen knew a lot more about what was happening than he let the others know. Now he was letting them know, and they weren't very happy about it. She couldn't blame them, but it was fascinating to watch. *Sort of like a controlled nuclear meltdown, or being shown the world is round instead of flat . . .*

"But my brother could be in danger!" Evanor protested. "Even if the Mandarites don't do anything to harm him, he could drown from a storm, or something!"

"Relax, Ev. I'm keeping an eye on him," Morganen dismissed, picking up his goblet again. "I have set a number of spells on him to protect him from complete disaster, should the need arise."

"Jinga, you're arrogant!" Trevan snorted. Morganen sipped at his drink with an air that Kelly thought was probably equal parts affected and genuine unconcern . . . proving he was too arrogant to even argue the point, let alone confirm it. Either that, or he just wanted to irritate his brothers; she couldn't be sure.

Saber narrowed his eyes thoughtfully. "Just how powerful *are* you, Morg, that you can do these things and maintain them from such a distance?"

"Does it matter?" Morganen asked his eldest, lighter-haired brother rhetorically, arching one of his brows. "Either you won't believe me, and will pester me for the truth . . . or you will start expecting things of me that maybe—just maybe—I'm not strong enough to do. It should be enough for the rest of you to know that I'm keeping an eye on our missing brother, and that I'll do what I can to make sure he's relatively safe."

"He'd be safest *here*," Evanor argued heatedly. "Let his prophesied woman come to him! I don't want my twin in the hands of those mechanically obsessed, misogynistic brutes!"

"Have you considered the fact that the Mandarites will most likely return?" Morganen countered calmly, unsettling the others. "They tried to claim Nightfall Isle for their own. They stole our brother out from under us, and if they give it some thought, they will subsequently wonder why we didn't follow them with a whole fleet of the ships we supposedly have. Dom was our 'Lord Chancellor' after all," he reminded them, dipping his head toward Kelly, their self-styled Queen. "They'll eventually come to think that we're too weak for pursuit. And so there is another reason for letting him travel to Mandare, not just a search for his pre-Destined wife."

"What reason?" Saber challenged him skeptically.

"Reconnaissance. We need information. This is a nation Katan knows nothing about," Morganen reminded them. "I've consulted with some of my contacts on the continent. Katan knows something about the Natallians; we've even had some sporadic trade with them in the past. But then there was a civil war about sixty years ago; many of our own ships were attacked, and trade tapered off within a dozen years, because the waters of their coastline were too strife-riddled. They still are, by all accounts."

"All the more reason to get him out of there!" Evanor protested.

Morganen shook his head. "I have spells to guard against that. Besides, this land of Mandare is relatively new. They probably don't have the industry or the resources that their enemy does. Dominor has been kidnapped because he is a powerful male mage; they'll most likely want him to serve them willingly, since that would be the most beneficial situation for them."

"Which means they'll be trying to seduce him into working for them," Kelly concluded for him. The other brothers glanced at her as she expanded on her comment. For a moment, it looked like half of them had forgotten her presence. "It would be beneficial in terms of reconnaissance, for him. They'll be telling him all about their strengths in order to impress him and convince him to follow along with their plans for him, and in the meantime, Dominor is smart enough to figure out their weaknesses based on what they're *not* going to tell him, combined with his own observations."

"Exactly. He's really the best man for the job," Morganen observed, pausing to drain the last of the wine from his blue-glazed goblet. "He's sophisticated enough to lure them into believing he's interested in whatever they have to say—once the offense of being kidnapped has been smoothed over—and subtle enough to hide his true feelings on the matter until he's in a position of advantage and power over them."

"And once he comes back, we can use that information to smooth over diplomatic relations with Katan, as well as protect ourselves," Kelly continued, surprising even Morganen with her offer. She shrugged. "What? I'm fully aware that your former homeland doesn't like the thought of women coming to the isle. I'm also aware they'll throw up a fuss over my claiming it as a sovereignty after they

tossed it along with the lot of you in the proverbial waste-
basket. By sharing information about a potential enemy,
we might make them think more kindly about us. It's called
diplomacy."

"Let's hold that as an option for later," Saber replied.
"Such as *after* we get our brother back."

"I still don't agree with your *allowing* him to be kidnapped, Morganen," Evanor grumbled, visibly unhappy.
"If you can keep an eye on Dominor from this far away,
then you could've just scryed and spied on the Mandarites
directly, yourself!"

"Evanor, your twin's segment of the 'Song of the Sons
of Destiny' suggests *very* strongly that his fated future wife
will come to him as a sort of battle of wills. A battle of
the *sexes*," Morganen added, emphasizing that last word.
"Surely even you can agree that the most obvious place for
him to start looking for her is in a pair of lands where the
genders are at war with each other?"

That made the fourth-born brother subside. Unhappily,
but quietly. Fingering his own goblet, Evanor didn't come
up with a reply. Kelly, on the other hand, found herself biting her knuckle against the urge to snort. She didn't quite
succeed.

Her husband eyed her askance. "What?"

Extracting her knuckle, she smirked at him. "And you
thought *our* courtship was a battle royale . . ."

It was Evanor who laughed the hardest at that, breaking
the tension around the room. With the meal more or less
over, the others rose and began departing. Only Morganen
noticed how the darkest-haired brother slipped silently out
of the dining room, though it was Rydan's turn to clear the
dishes as his evening chore. Saying nothing—the youngest
of them could only guess at their oddest sibling's motives—
Morganen cleared the table in his stead. He could always
ask the taciturn mage later where he'd gone and what he'd
done.

And, if nothing else, Rydan would at the very least owe
him a future chore.

# FIFTEEN

·ͽϾ·

He found her on the dock, legs dangling over the edge of the jetty, several yards above the waves of a low tide.

She'd thought about attempting to fly due west toward the mainland in the owl shape that had brought her down here, and then transforming into her river-otter shape for the remainder of the swim, but she wasn't too sure about the currents. They had been stronger than anticipated during her arrival, and she knew they curled back out to sea again at some point after sweeping past Nightfall in their journey south.

Besides, there really wasn't anywhere for her to go. The only friend she had outside of the brothers and a handful of her uncle's servants was Cari of The Trenching Wench. As much as she enjoyed lovemaking with Wolfer, she didn't think she'd enjoy it nearly enough with anyone else. Not enough to enjoy making a living at it, at least.

Still, when the tall figure padded quietly up to her, paused, then lowered himself to dangle his own booted feet over the waves, Alys knew that the man beside her had forgiven her for her role in her uncle's atrocities; if he hadn't, she didn't think he would have done something so friendly as seat himself beside her.

That it was Rydan, however—and not Wolfer—was a little startling. Even unnerving. Alys didn't quite understand him, and frankly never had. A sidelong glance at his pale skin, lit only by scattered starlight and the slightly thickened sliver of Sister Moon peeking out through the clouds off to the west, showed he wasn't angry. Enigmatic, but not angry.

As a young boy, he'd been energetic like his brothers, yet a tad moody. Not sullen—not always—but moody in the sense that his emotions flitted more strongly and rapidly through him than they had through his siblings. As he'd grown into puberty, she recalled him becoming more and more moody in the sullen sense, and then becoming withdrawn. Gradually, he had ceased being enthusiastic about joining the others in their activities, withdrawing even from his twin, Trevan, at times.

Now he was a night-dwelling enigma. She couldn't tell what was going through his mind as he sat next to her on the edge of the stone-and-wood pier. The only thing Alys knew for certain was that somehow he understood the choices she'd been forced to make, and the fact that her regrets were honest ones. All this, without a word being spoken between them.

His presence was oddly calming. Even when Sister Moon disappeared behind a thicker bank of clouds near the horizon, leaving them in near-darkness, she didn't feel threatened by him. There was no doubt in her mind that he could be quite scary if he put his mind to it. Possibly even more terrifying than her uncle; he just had that sort of air about him. But . . . he was gentle toward her. The corner of her mouth quirked up. *If you can count ignoring me most of the time as part of being "gentle"* . . .

"Give him time."

Alys jumped a little. She hadn't expected Rydan to speak. "Erm . . . Wolfer?"

A soft sound escaped him. It could've been a snort, with a little more effort behind it. "Who else?"

"O-Okay . . ." she agreed. They sat there for a little while, and she kicked her feet, trying to figure out what that meant. "How much time?"

"Another hour, maybe two. I'll talk to him, if you like." At her startled look, he glanced over at her. Alys silently wished the moon would come back, because it was hard to tell if that really was a smile curving his mouth; the night was that dark around them. "Knock some sense into him."

"I didn't *want* to help my uncle," she asserted quickly. "I just didn't have much choice . . ."

"I know."

They sat for a little while more, listening to the waves lapping at the dock and the beach around them. Alys cleared her throat, kicking her feet again. "He scares me, you know."

"Wolfer?"

"Broger," she clarified. Then amended quickly, "Well, Wolfer does, too. But more because I'm afraid of disappointing him to the point where he'll just hate me, and . . . and won't love me anymore. Uncle . . . terrifies me. And I don't know how to stop him. I don't know how anyone can."

"We're strong enough to destroy him," he reassured her quietly, shifting as if to get up.

Alys reached out and touched his arm, stopping him. "No, you're not."

His arm shifted out from under her fingers, reminding her that, as Rydan had grown older, he had liked less and less being touched by anyone. She lowered her hand. He didn't seem to take offense, despite the subtle removal. Indeed, the moon peeked out from the clouds just enough to show that one side of his mouth had curved up. "I could've destroyed him when I was sixteen, little one. I've only grown stronger . . . and I have several brothers to back me up."

"Are you strong enough to stop his magics from flinging a Death Curse back upon you?" she challenged him sharply as he started to rise again. He paused and frowned at her, crouching next to her on the edge of the pier.

"A Death Curse?" Rydan asked, staring at her. The

moonlight brightened further, allowing her to see his frown of confusion.

"He wove spells around himself. Anyone who kills him, or even attempts to kill him, will have a Death Curse flung back upon them. Especially if they use magic," Alys told him. "He bragged about it to me when one of his rivals sent an assassin. The man tried to knife him in the back . . . and found himself torn to shreds by the magic protecting my uncle. He said that 'neither spell nor sword from an enemy's hand can cut me down without destroying the source of my harm.'" She shivered, crossing her forearms over her chest. "I fear what would happen in a direct confrontation with him.

"I even thought about siccing his own beasts upon him, thinking the magic would retaliate against them, not me . . . but they're enchanted against that. And he . . . he drew upon my energies while he was recovering from the knife wound. Not just me, but from Uncle Donnock and Cousin Barol, too—his own son—though mostly from me." Her left arm twisted behind her back, pressing against the spot where her uncle had been stabbed. "I suffered phantom pains for almost a month, though his wound seemed to heal in a matter of days."

Rydan pushed upright, then looked down at her, studying her in the moonlight. "If this is true . . ."

Her fingers rubbed the silver diamond embedded in her sternum through the fabric of her tunic. "I wish it weren't. I don't dare get . . . get pregnant while he still lives. I fear he might have some spells laid upon me to draw power from the flesh of my flesh, as it were, as well as my own flesh directly. The protective spells Morganen and I came up with protect *me* from the effects of his magic." Glumly, she stared out at the glimmering surface of the sea. "I despair sometimes of *ever* being free . . . Truly free, I mean."

"I know."

They stayed like that in the moonlight, Alys sitting on the edge of the dock, Rydan standing next to her like a dark sentinel, both of them quiet. A short while later, as Sister

Moon descended closer to the horizon, he turned and padded away. After a moment, Alys craned her head over her shoulder to watch him go . . . but when she looked, he was gone. Not even his footsteps could be heard anymore.

Nothing disturbed the dark quiet of the shore behind her. She was alone. *And somehow, I'm not surprised he can disappear into darkness, as if he were a shadow himself . . .*

Facing forward, she stared across the sea again, lost in her less-than-happy thoughts.

ℒou're an ass."

Wolfer jumped and whirled around, fingers slipping off the braided hair tied around his wrist. His eyes sought the source of the insult, finding it in the pale hands and face of the sixth-born Corvis son. Once again, his younger brother had managed to sneak up on him. "I *hate* it when you do that."

Rydan's mouth curved in one of his rare smiles. "I know. And you're still an ass."

"I know." He *did* know it. Wolfer had retreated to the jungle while he was trying to deal with his rage, but the jungle reminded him of her, of his lessons in teaching her how to change her shape . . . and how to enjoy their bodies together. So he had retreated farther still, to the chapel where his twin had been wed not that long ago. The garlands of flowers had long since been stripped from the columns, leaving the polished granite and inlaid marble bare. Half of the chamber lay in deep shadows; the rest was lit by the pallid silvery-blue light of Brother Moon, which was peeking over the edge of the mountain range to the east, and the last wisps of Sister Moon's equally pale light off to the west. He had hoped to redecorate the modest temple for his own wedding, but now he wasn't sure when that might be.

It wasn't that he wouldn't marry Alys, exactly. It was that he would first have to apologize to her for storming out like that, and the apology would have to be accompanied by an explanation. Wolfer had come to the conclusion that he could forgive her for doing whatever it took for her to survive in her uncle's so-called care, that he still loved her and wanted her in his life . . . but his anger came in two parts: a twinge of betrayal that she would help her uncle against them, even if it had been a necessity of her survival, and a far greater fury at her uncle. He wanted to rend the man's flesh from his bones, to snap his teeth around the older mage's throat. And yet she was terrified of anyone killing her uncle.

She would also have some explaining to do, Wolfer knew. Such as what spells, exactly, he had cast to protect himself. What magics he would be most likely to use against them. What beasts he had available to send. Where those beasts were kept, too, in case they could somehow destroy his menagerie while his attention was elsewhere. *Or, more likely, alert the Mage Council as to their whereabouts, and let* them *destroy the monsters' lair for us.*

Provided they could get the Council to cooperate, of course. An anonymous tip might be best. But that only took care of the plague of magical beasts. It didn't cure the root of the problem: Broger of Devries.

"Are you going to go to her?" Rydan prodded, drawing his attention back to the reason his darkest-haired sibling had snuck up on him like that.

"Why? Do you know where she is?" Wolfer retorted dryly.

"Yes."

His sibling's answer surprised him. Not that Rydan knew where Alys could be found, but that he'd added a lilt to the answer, making it sound conditional. Wolfer leaned back against the altar of Jinga's aspect as Lover and folded his arms across his muscular chest. "And?"

"And are you going to ask, or yell?" Rydan countered calmly.

*Oh, so that's how you're going to play it, Brother,* Wolfer thought. He settled his arms a little more comfortably and crossed his ankles. He didn't think Jinga would mind him sitting on the edge of one of His altars too much. Kata might, being a civilized Goddess, but Jinga was a bit more casual. "What makes you think I'd do either?"

The last, pallid rays of Sister Moon vanished from the chapel; the crescent of light had slipped below the horizon. The crisscrossing of the shadows vanished, leaving only the glow of Brother Moon shining down through the glazed central dome of the roof. "She said her life-force was in her uncle's grasp. That he could steal it from her with a word, before she forged an amulet to counter his magics."

"I know." The corner of Wolfer's mouth twitched up as—for one moment—Rydan was caught off-guard by his admission. Of course, Wolfer hadn't *known* it in that exact detail, but he had known about the amulet, and her uncle's ability to track her without it.

The younger man's puzzled look smoothed over. It was replaced by a sardonic look and an arched brow as Rydan folded his arms across his own chest, echoing his older brother's stance. "So why are you still here?"

"I want to talk to her when I'm not angry."

The pale moonlight faded as a cloud drifted across their sole source of illumination. "But you're not angry at her."

Wolfer didn't bother to ask where Rydan got his insight. The other mage's instincts were better than his own sometimes, for all that Wolfer was more in touch with his inner animal nature. He shook his head. "No, I'm not angry with her. I'm angry with the situation. I'm . . . upset that she did help him, but furious that *he* made it necessary. That he coerced her. That she still fears him. She shouldn't have to fear anyone."

A pale hand, looking almost disembodied as its sleeve blended into the darkness around them, shoved him on the shoulder. "Then *go* to her and tell *her* all of this."

"Yes," Wolfer grumbled, since his brother's words had an unspoken "idiot" appended somewhere in his tone. "I know; I'm an *ass*. Where is she?"

"Western docks." Rydan stepped back into the shadows, vanishing from sight. Wolfer called out to him as he retreated.

"You'll be next, you know. Well, maybe not *next* . . . but you're destined to fall in love, too."

A soft sound wafted from the shadows. It could've been a snort, with more effort. Wolfer touched the braid on his wrist, letting the corner of his mouth curl up.

"It's not so bad, you know. Being in love," the second eldest added. "In fact, I rather like it. I think you will, too."

There was no reply. He did hear the padding of footsteps as his brother retreated . . . and something in the distance, a faint rumbling that could've been thunder. If there had been the right sort of clouds in the sky for it.

Wolfer didn't question Rydan's wordless retreat, or the source of that subtle, distant commentary; the most reclusive of them hadn't been labeled the Storm on a whim, after all.

This time, it was a different set of footsteps that approached. Or rather, that trotted up to her. Alys glanced over her shoulder at the sound of claws clicking softly against the wooden planks of the pier. The wolf noted her movement and stopped for a moment, backlit by the rising light of Brother Moon. She couldn't see the expression in his eyes, but he padded forward after a moment more, his head and ears lowered. In canine terms, it was an almost apologetic approach, though his tail was raised halfway and wagging a little.

Apparently he expected her to forgive him, or at least had strong hopes for a reconciliation. Alys knew he had a temper; she had winced from it often enough as a child. But as an adult, he had clearly mastered most of his emotional outbursts. Removing himself from the dining chamber as he had done was just a part of ensuring that he didn't stay exposed to the source of his anger; even the most placid-tempered man would grow increasingly upset if the source of his irritation remained to abrade his nerves, after all. Her father had been that way, once. A placid-tempered man for the most part, but he had lost his temper a few times.

Wolfer had managed to temper his emotions, too, it seemed. So, as the shapechanged mage approached, Alys twisted a little farther to face him, opening her arms. The wolf pushed up against her, leaning into her with a sigh as she embraced him. The whuff of relieved breath comforted her. Burying her face in his fur, she squeezed him until he pulled back, then she loosened her grip. A ripple of fur and flesh, of bone and cloth, and her arms now looped around his ribs. Alys leaned into him this time. Wolfer wrapped his arms around her, his legs dangling over the edge of the dock next to hers.

"I'm sorry I left like that," he rumbled quietly. "I was just . . . I know you didn't want to help your uncle. I'm a little upset that you did help him send all those things to plague us, but I do understand. You just did what you had to do to survive because that was the situation you were stuck in at the time. I'm still angry, but it's almost entirely at him. Which is as it should be. Your uncle is the source of all our troubles, after all, and he shouldn't be allowed to keep doing these things. He must be stopped."

"If you try to kill him, even if it's a physical attack . . . his magics will punish you," Alys whispered, gripping his torso a little tighter. "I don't want him to hurt you."

"Every defense has a weakness," Wolfer reassured her. "We'll find a way to defeat him. We'll just have to get together with the others, ask you a lot of questions about your uncle, and toss out ideas until we find a couple of solutions to the problem."

"*If* they'll let me come back to their home," Alys whispered. Rydan forgave her, and Wolfer had, too, but that didn't mean Saber and the others would. *Well, Morganen knows, and forgave me long ago for all I had to do . . . and I think Kelly's on my side, too . . .*

"I think Kelly will keep my twin in line. Between her

and me . . . and Morg," he allowed, doing his best to banish the specter of jealousy over his youngest sibling's ties to *his* woman, "I think we can keep the rest of them in line, too."

A soft laugh escaped her. Snuggling closer, Alys breathed in the warm, musky scent of his flesh. Both of them had grown and changed in the intervening years since their childhood friendship, but she still loved him. "I missed you."

Wolfer knew what she meant. "I missed you, too. Will you . . . will you still walk the eight altars with me?"

Heat rose in her cheeks. Lifting her face from his chest, Alys stared up at him. Most of his face was in shadow, but enough moonlight shone behind them to gild the edge of his cheek and catch at the corner of his eye. She could see his anticipation of her answer. "I will, but . . . I think I would like to wait until after, um . . . after my uncle is taken care of. You see, he said some things that makes me think he could . . . that he could tap into the life-force and potential magics of any child I might have, and . . . oh, stop growling!"

Her hand lightly smacked his chest. Wolfer cut off the sound with a rueful twist of his lips. Rewarding him with a stroke of her hand down the front of his tunic, she continued.

"I don't know if it's true or not, but I do want to be very cautious about that sort of thing. That's one of the reasons I got myself the birth-control amulet I'm wearing," she reminded him, sticking out her ankle. It was hidden by her boot. "I don't want to take any chances."

Disappointed at the thought of delaying a family, Wolfer had to concede her point. "If your uncle is evil enough to use the lives of his own kin to augment his powers, without their freely consented permission . . . I could see him doing something like that. I suppose we could put off having any children. But why should we put off our marriage?"

"I don't know if he could sink his magical claws into

my husband's powers or not, as well," she murmured unhappily, looking away from him. "I wouldn't put it past
him."

"Then we'll consider that a possibility, too. Come,"
Wolfer told her, shifting out of her arms and rising to his
feet. He offered her his hand. "We should go back and
round up the others for a discussion of what you know. And
if they're being as stubborn as mules, well, the sooner we
know they're being stubborn, the sooner I can growl at
them and get away with it. Since you don't like me growling without a good reason."

Again, she felt her face grow warm as she rose with his
help. "Actually, I like you growling when we're in our bedchamber. It, um . . . makes me think of all the things we do."

"Oh." He processed that for a moment, then grinned
down at her. "I'll take that as permission to growl at you all
the more, then!"

"Wolfer!" She bapped him again with the back of her
fingers. He chuckled and shapechanged himself into his
stallion form, to give her a ride back to their home.

It was Kelly who had the wisdom to send someone to
fetch pen, ink, and paper to write down everything Alys answered to the questions posed by the brothers. By default,
it was Kelly who ended up writing down those answers, to
free up the others to ask questions about literally arcane
matters that she still didn't quite comprehend. Having had
some time to calm down, the seven brothers had accepted
Alys back among them with little reservation, and a few
had even apologized to her for any rudeness earlier . . . and
then grilled her thoroughly on her uncle's monsters, magics, and most likely methods of defense and attack, in an
interrogation session that lasted until almost midnight.

It was Kelly who slowed things down a little. Occasionally, she had to ask questions in her ignorance, and though
her first few interruptions had been answered impatiently,
the mage brothers gave up being irritated and just an-

swered them factually. They even inserted explanations as they continued to ask Alys—and Morganen—questions, but their answers didn't make the brothers very happy. There weren't many avenues by which they could get around Broger of Devries' defenses, and almost all of them wound up with one or more of the brothers either being mortally injured, or killed outright. Capturing him wouldn't be much of an option; with such active defenses as he possessed, Broger's captors wouldn't be able to enforce his captivity. Which left them with the unhappy prospect of finding a way to end their enemy's life.

It was also Kelly—and her ignorant outworlder questions—that found their solution. She directed this question at Alys, not at the others. "Well, what about his *own* magics, Alys? You're saying that no one else could harm him, but what if one of his own offensive spells was . . . was *reflected* back at him? Like redirecting a bright ray of sunshine with a hand-mirror to blind an enemy's eyes? Only in this case, the enemy is the original source of the sunlight."

Eight pairs of puzzled eyes gazed at the outworlder in their midst. Three sets of brows drew down in matching, puzzled frowns, four more sets rose in surprise . . . and one set of lashes blinked. Morganen, who had been sitting with his boot heels propped on the edge of the dining table despite Evanor's glare, dropped his legs and sat forward. "That's *it*! It would be his *own* energies, so the spells would backlash upon *him*!"

"I don't think the wardings would attack *him*," Alys interjected quickly. "I mean, I've seen him cast spells on himself without any harm. But . . . if it were a *lethal* attack on his part, or at least something serious enough to wound him mortally, and we just . . . if we just . . . I can't believe I'm suggesting this," she muttered, unhappy with the thought but forcing herself to express it. "But if we just keep him from healing himself, and he, um . . . dies on his own . . ."

"I think the Gods would forgive us, if we were to finish

him in such a manner," Wolfer agreed, eyeing his curly-haired future bride.

Evanor nodded, agreeing. "And though we might be punished somehow for not helping to heal him . . . since we cannot harm him directly, it *would* be by his own doing that he would be killed."

"Defeating him in this way would only work if he were to cast a lethal offensive spell at one of us," Trevan confirmed, tapping the table with his fingertip. "Which would not invoke the Gods' Law of Harm against anyone but himself. Unless he were to have a lingering sort of demise. Or maybe just a maiming . . . sorry, Alys, but I'm feeling a bit more bloodthirsty than you. I, too, have been bitten by a watersnake, clawed by a tremor-fiend, and narrowly escaped being the meal for a dozen other things over the past three years, the same as the rest of us. I am not feeling that charitable toward him, even if he is your blood-kin."

"I think we all feel a mix of anger, discomfort, and indignation. But . . . if that were the case, if he were only maimed or badly wounded, not mortally so . . ." Koranen shrugged. "Well, it would pin him down long enough for us to hopefully find a way to strip away his protections, and then we could turn him over to the Council. Who *would* execute him for harboring all those illegal beasts."

"Hang on," Kelly interjected. "He may have harbored these beasties on Katani soil, but he's been *sending* them to Nightfall. Which means he falls under *my* jurisdiction."

The others frowned at her. Saber lifted one of his sand-colored brows. "*Your* jurisdiction?"

"Hello? Queen of Nightfall, here," the freckled redhead reminded him, touching her chest with the hand not holding the nib-pen. "I've claimed this island, and all who live upon it. His crimes have been committed on Our soil, against Our subjects. If you'll pardon my use of the Royal 'We,'" Kelly amended, tipping her head slightly. "As the sovereign, it is my duty to declare what the laws are . . . and I say that anyone who sends beasts to attack and harm us is breaking the law. Ergo, if he's breaking the law, and

trying to kill us by it . . . then I say let him die as his punishment, if his own magics don't do the job for us right
away."

"Kelly, you cannot—" Saber started to argue.

*"Actually,"* a voice stated sharply, cutting him off.
Saber allowed it out of surprise, for it was Rydan who
spoke; he tended to interrupt even less than he spoke,
which of course meant that his brothers tended to listen all
the more to the black-haired mage when he did so. "Broger
did *not* commit any crimes on sovereign Nightfall soil."
The sixth-born mage smiled slightly, sardonically at his
puzzled sister-in-law. "We were technically still a part of
Katan during his last infestation."

Kelly had to acknowledge his point with a nod and a
sigh. Her husband looked like he would have said more,
but Trevan spoke first. His tone was thoughtful.

"You know . . . if he comes here again to attack us—
which is the most likely course of action, since we're not
exactly free to go and seek him out—then he *would* be
committing crimes against the populace of Nightfall. At
which point he *would* fall under Her Majesty's laws, and
Her Majesty's judgment," the other strawberry blond asserted carefully.

"Kelly, please don't tell me you're still going through
with this . . . this *game* of pretending to be our queen?"
Saber asked his wife.

*"I* don't think it's a game," Alys stated, drawing attention away from the other woman in the chamber. The
males seated around the table eyed her askance, prompting
her to defend her position. "Well, I don't! If the Curse of
Eight Prophecy comes true, then there are going to be six
more women coming here. And with all of those women,
there will be children born. And since they'll all be
cousins, you'll have to bring in *more* people, so they can
wed outside of their own bloodline . . . and *their* children
will need husbands and wives, and theirs, and theirs . . .

"And there will be people who will want to come here
and settle just because they can. There's miles and miles of

room on this island, waiting to be populated by farmers and herders, craftsmen and fishermen!" Alys reminded them. "If we don't settle how the government will be run right now, when there's still only a small number of people to govern, then it'll be all the harder to establish law and order when the others start coming here."

"Alys, nobody's going to be coming here!" Koranen protested, waving the notion away with a sweep of his arm that made his twin duck to the side a little. "This is Nightfall, land of the exiled! It's been that way since Aiar fell, and it will continue to be that way for centuries more!"

"Not unless the conditions of the Island Curse are fulfilled," Morganen pointed out, correcting his twin as he straightened up again. "Isn't one of the conditional lines 'When royalty has reigned'? And has that not just occurred with Kelly's claiming of this land?"

"I need to find a copy of this new 'Curse,'" Kelly muttered as the older brothers stared at their youngest sibling.

"When you do, mind sharing it with me?" Alys returned equally under her breath, leaning past the eldest pair of the Corvis twins. Kelly nodded.

Saber sighed and rapped his knuckles on the table. "Before we get that far . . . do we *want* to have a sovereign ruler, whether or not he or she is a mage, like some lands have? Or a mage-king who heads the Council of Mages, like Katan has?"

"I don't think you'd want a mage-king," Morganen retorted dryly. "I would rule over all of you, as the strongest mage on the island, and I would far rather *not* be a ruler."

"Anyone coming here to live would be expecting a mage-king or mage-queen," Evanor pointed out. "They would also be expecting the most powerful of the island's Council to be that ruler."

"And again, I don't want the position!" Morg repeated, lifting his hands to absolve himself of that option.

"Neither do I," Rydan offered bluntly, reminding the others once again of his presence. Slanting his gaze around the table, he added, "I would not care to live under Dominor's rule, either."

"Excuse me, but what if the people we invite here don't *want* a magocracy?" Kelly interjected. "If they want that, they can stay on Katan, because that's not the sort of government I'm thinking of for this land."

Saber started to say something, paused, then licked his lips and asked his wife, "What *do* you envision? You come from a world where magic doesn't exist, so how do your people choose their leaders? By birthright?"

"By dozens of different ways, actually; there are well over a hundred different nations, where I come from," Kelly enlightened them. "Now, I come from a *democratic republic*—"

"A what?" Koranen asked her. He wasn't the only one frowning in puzzlement. Just because Ultra Tongue translated the spoken and the written word for its drinkers didn't mean that it completely translated the culturally unique terms. Kelly was speaking in Katani, as far as they were concerned . . . but she was still an outworlder.

"Representational government," the redhead explained, keeping it short and simple. "Every adult of the age of eighteen or older has the right to vote for a local government official, who then represents their region in the greater government. A democracy is where everyone gets a vote, and a republic is where people are governed by representatives. A democratic republic is where the people vote to select their representatives."

From the skeptical, dubious, and downright disturbed looks on the faces around her, Kelly knew she wasn't going to succeed with that one. *Which only figures,* she knew, *since only those governments where the people* themselves *want democracy actually succeed as democratic republics. You have to have the will to make it work, to make it work successfully.* Changing mental gears, she made a slight change in what she had in mind.

"Now, I realize from the looks on your faces that this is

a really radical idea. And it only works well when everyone involved is interested in the idea. But . . . what I'm thinking about is a variation on that idea, and a variation on what you already know: a constitutional monarchy."

"A what monarchy?" Trevan asked.

"Constitutional monarchy," Kelly explained. "Certain inviolate rights for all citizens are spelled out in a constitution—a charter with a simple set of rules and laws that even the king or queen must obey—and then you have regional representatives who bring their people's concerns before the king or queen. The monarch usually has the final say over what happens, unless a very high percentage of the representatives choose otherwise, and that percentage is spelled out in the constitution. It has all the stability of a sovereign monarchy, but with the added reassurance to the people that they can have a say in their government.

"After all, a leader only leads by the will of the people," she reminded them. "And best of all . . . it can be implemented right now as a democracy, with all island inhabitants having a voice in the government—you being my advisors—but with the monarch having final say. You know that I'll be relying on all of you to give me good advice anyway, so it's basically not much different than what we have right now," Kelly reminded them. "And when we have enough people, they can divide themselves up, vote for town mayors or district representatives, and they can advise whomever is the sovereign at that point in time in the form an elected cabinet of advisors."

"Does this actually work?" Morganen asked her, his tone more curious than challenging.

"Back in my old world, there is an island, the Isle of Man. It's less than half the size of this one, and it has been ruled successfully in this very manner for over a thousand years. And right next to it is an island many times the size of this one, Great Britain, that has been ruled in this way for almost as long, about eight hundred years. It's a very stable form of leadership, as I said. In fact," Kelly added, "Great Britain at one point had so many colonies around the world—much like the Mandarites were seeking to form—and various other protectorates, lands that had accepted their protection against others, that it was said that the sun never set on the British Empire."

Saber studied his wife. "Remind me to ask your friend, Hope, for a book of your world's history."

"I'm already doing that," Morganen agreed. The others glanced sharply at him, and he shrugged. "What? I already said I'd keep an eye on her, for Kelly's sake."

Saber snorted. "Her name is *Hope*. I think you're keeping an eye on her for your *own* sake."

"I remind you, I have to see the lot of you safely wedded before I can even think about myself," Morganen returned flippantly, sitting back in his seat. Alys, knowing Morganen somewhat from their years of clandestine conversations, guessed that part of that flippancy was defensiveness in disguise. "She is Kelly's friend, and I am keeping an eye on her for that reason. Make of that whatever you will."

"Can we get back to the subject of how to destroy Broger of Devries?" Wolfer asked the others. He stifled a yawn and added, "Government can wait. Especially if it's a version of what we already have. We need a way to reflect Broger's spells back onto himself. It's rather late; we shouldn't waste more time on something we can talk about later."

"The idea of reflecting his spells back on himself . . . that suggests a literal mirror to me," Evanor told the others. "I have song-spells that can reflect magics back at their caster, but I'd rather use a mirror than my own voice. The less we counter his powers directly, the less likely we are to be affected by his countering words."

Morganen nodded. "I think I might know a spell for enchanting a mirror to reflect back any magic cast in its direction. And I think the quality of sand we already have on hand might be good enough to craft them. Certainly, we should have more than one mirror; there's no telling from which direction we might have to defend from an attack."

A hand raised, and the others looked at Kelly. "Could I

have one of these mirrors? All of the rest of you have magic to protect yourselves. I can probably fight off any of his beasties physically, but I can't deflect any spells back on their owner."

"*She* gets the very first one," Saber stated, poking his thumb at his wife. His brothers and Alys nodded their agreement. "How soon do you think you can find that spell and figure out how long it will take to enchant the mirrors, Morg?"

"I'll start looking after breakfast tomorrow morning. Wolfer is right," Morganen added as he lifted his hand to hide a yawn. "It *is* rather late."

A soft laugh made the brothers look at Rydan, whose lips had curved up a little as he sat there, arms folded across his chest.

His twin whapped him on the shoulder. "Stop being so smug, you night-lover!"

# SIXTEEN

❧

**W**olfer stifled a yawn as he closed the door behind Alys and himself. His quarters weren't lit until she reached up and tapped one of the lightglobes in its stand; soft light illuminated first the sitting room, then the bed-chamber as she tapped one of the globes in there as well. Wolfer left the light in the other room lit; they had plenty of *comsworg* oil from which to make new ones, if these should burn out anytime soon. They had traded several blocks of salt and his next-youngest brother, Dominor, for several gallons of the stuff after all, even if the trade had supposedly been for the salt alone.

*Wherever he is*, Wolfer thought as he followed Alys into his bedroom, *I hope his . . . well, knowing him, I can't hope that his own path to love and happiness is gentler than mine has been.* The thought curved the corner of his mouth in merriment. *That's just not his way. He's too intense for "gentle." But I hope it isn't too much more interesting than mine and Alys' courtship has been. Which culture has the saying, "May you live in interesting times"? The distant land of Threefold Fate?*

It didn't really matter. Alys was plucking tiredly at her

clothes, wanting to get undressed but looking worn out from the emotional end to her day. A whispered phrase allowed Wolfer's magic to finish unfastening her clothes, drawing them from her limbs. She gave him a smile for the help, but had to cover it with her hand as she yawned.

"Oh! I'm sorry. I'm just out of energy, I think."

"Why don't you use the refreshing room first?" Wolfer offered as he worked to remove his own tunic. She nodded and padded to the door, almost tripping as the disrobing charm removed the last of her underclothes. Suppressing the urge to snicker, Wolfer stripped himself down to his skin. When she came out again, he pulled her against him, warm flesh to warm flesh, and kissed her.

Alys sighed happily . . . and then yawned. "Dammit!" A blush stole over her face as she realized what she'd done. It was the second time that evening she'd sworn; the first time, she had vulgarly ordered Wolfer's brothers to pucker up and kiss an indelicate part of her anatomy. Ducking her head now, she muttered into his chest, "I want to . . . to have some fun with you, but I'm too tired to even try."

Kissing the top of her curly dark blond head, Wolfer released his mate. "There's always the morning. I don't have any chores until noon, which means you don't have any, either. Though I suppose I should offer to help the others with their mirror-spells."

"I should help, too." She nodded. "Not that I know much about creating magical mirrors, but I do know some of my uncle's spells. But for that, we both need our sleep."

He closed the door between them. Alys climbed into the bed. It was a warm evening, so she climbed out again, stripped off the thicker of the two blankets, then returned herself to the bed, muttering a mouth-scrubbing spell to get the film off her teeth. She had left her uncle's care with a teeth-scrubber in the bags and bundles of her belongings, but that had been left behind when she manufactured her "death scene" at the hands of illusionary pookrahs. The charm left her mouth a little tender after each use, compared to a scrubber, but it would do until she could get a replacement. Wolfer had one sitting on the sink counter in his refreshing room, but she hadn't felt right about borrowing it without his permission.

There were a lot of things she didn't have with her anymore that she would like. Little things, like a hairbrush, a teeth-scrubber, ribbons for her hair, a pair of indoor slippers other than the old pair Kelly had found for her among the palace's discarded belongings, a new pair of outdoor boots for when she had to feed the chickens. Her monthlies were due in another quarter-turning of Brother Moon, too; she'd need supplies for that. *And if Morganen is going to quiz me on what I've learned and give me new spells to master, I'll need pen, ink, and paper . . .*

All of those things would take money, and someone to purchase them for her, since she couldn't barter directly with the sea-merchants the brothers traded with twice a month. She didn't have many coins left, and Alys wasn't quite sure how to earn more on an island with only nine other people in residence. Wolfer came out of the refreshing room, looking muscular and handsome and wonderfully naked. Wondering if she was really all that tired, Alys scooted back across the bed, making room for him so he could join her.

She was studying him speculatively. Wolfer arched his brow at her. "Yes?"

Shivering at the sexy, deep-voiced rumble, Alys scooted closer. It was a warm night, but she liked the heat of his body. "I was just wondering . . ."

"I thought you were too tired," he half-purred, half-growled, tugging her until she faced away from him, allowing their bodies to spoon together.

"What? Oh . . . well, not quite as much as I thought . . . but I was thinking about something else."

"Oh?"

"Well . . . I need employment. I sold what little jewelry I had smuggled inside my clothes in order to pay for my mirror-passage to this side of Katan, but it took most of my money to come here. And I need . . . things," she explained.

Wolfer smoothed the tickling feel of her curls away from his nose. "Well, there's lots of . . . things," he teased her gently, "in the palace, left over from previous visitors. But if we don't have it, just tell me and I'll buy it for you. We can order almost anything from the merchants who visit us."

"I know you want to buy things for me, and it's very nice of you, but . . . it's not the same thing as *me* earning the money. It's not the same thing as me contributing to . . . to the economy of Nightfall Isle," she stated, figuring out how to put it into words. "I want a job. I want to be paid for my work, even if it's just washing dishes and feeding the chickens."

"You mean the citizen-chickens," Wolfer rumbled, chuckling.

"The what?" Alys asked, craning her head to look back at him.

He smoothed her hair back down and explained. "Oh, it was something Kelly said when she laid claim to the island, back when the Mandarites first arrived. We were setting up the illusion of a kingdom, and she had laid claim to all of us twins as her 'citizens,' as inhabitants of the island. And then pointed out the only other inhabitants were the chickens, though she wasn't sure if they should be counted as fellow citizens. And so the joke just sort of . . . stuck." Wolfer shrugged.

"Citizen-chickens." Alys thought about it. The idea was an amusing one. She laughed softly and squeezed the arm he had wrapped around her waist. "Fine, then. I want to be paid for dealing with the ornery, cantankerous, pecking-mad citizen-chickens. As the official Nightfall Isle citizen-chicken feeder."

"Considering how much 'Her Majesty' loathes said chickens, I think she'd be willing to bestow a handsome salary upon you, in exchange for never having to do that particular task again," he chuckled. "Hmm . . . that does beg the question of who should be our Exchequer. Proba-bly Saber. He's used his position as the eldest-born to appropriate funds from the rest of us for large purchases. Of course, he's also the Royal Consort and Lord Protector. Dominor has a good handle on finances . . . but he's the Lord Chancellor."

"Do all of you have titles?"

"Oh, yes. Saber is Consort, Protector of the Queen, and General of the Armies," Wolfer explained to her. "I'm Master of the Hunt, and Captain of the Armies. Dominor is Lord Chancellor, a title well-suited to him since he loves formality and bossing others around. Evanor is Lord Chamberlain . . . which I suppose could include Exchequer, since he's in charge of the household, which would include managing its accounts."

"And Trevan?"

Wolfer laughed again. "Kelly asked what he 'did' around here, and Trev was rather insulted by the question. We called him sneaky, so she named him her Lord Vizier, her 'Chief of Intelligence' . . . which I think is basically a Spymaster. Koranen is her Lord Secretary, and Morganen is her Court Mage."

"And Rydan?" Alys asked, curious.

"Lord of the Night, Protector of Nightfall."

"I thought you said Saber was the Protector," she pointed out, confused.

"He's the protector of Kelly. Rydan gets to protect the whole island. But only at night," Wolfer rumbled, teasing his absent brother. "He's not allowed to protect it during the day."

"He is an odd one, isn't he?" Alys murmured, yawning at the end of her question.

"Yes. I can only imagine what sort of woman would be able to tolerate him and his odd ways." Wolfer yawned himself after a moment, then pulled her closer. "We'll have to come up with a title for you."

"Maybe I could be the Exchequer?" Alys offered. "I do know how to balance accounts; my uncle had me keep the records for the supplies spent in feeding his menagerie, and keeping his collection of spell ingredients well stocked.

Of course, I'm not the exchequer he had hiding those amounts in the set of tax books the king's collectors got to see; I'm not good enough to hide dubious sums . . . but I can keep an honest set of records."

That made him chuckle again. "I think that's a better qualification than your tone of voice would suggest. I don't think 'Queen' Kelly would appreciate an embezzler in the family."

"Mm. Probably not. But if some other wife-to-be comes along, and she's better at managing accounts than I am, I wouldn't object to stepping aside. So long as I can be Lady of the Herds or something . . ." she mumbled, as sleep started to claim her. "Because I really do . . . want . . . dairy cows . . ."

Wolfer yawned again as he felt her body relaxing limply against his. He himself missed fresher forms of milk than the aged cheeses they bought from the traders. But like so many other things, right now that was a discussion for another day. Especially given dawn wasn't all that far away.

Morganen frowned, peering into the elongated, oval mirror lying flat on his workbench. He wiped the grit of sleep from his eyes as he studied the two figures revealed in the silvered glass. The one on the left was Donnock of Devries, the one on the right, his older brother Broger. He'd used this mirror to spy upon them before; what was odd was the hour. The youngest mage-brother had only been asleep for a few hours before being summoned from his bed by the subtle chiming of his warning spells.

"Won't be able to get a connection for another week," Donnock was explaining. "The aether isn't right over the Faraday Valley, according to the scheduler."

Morg smiled as he wiped at his tired eyes again. He'd arranged the aether between the east coast of Katan and the lands of Corvis to be less than ideal for mirror-Gating, to slow them down.

"I don't want you to take that long," Broger countermanded. "Find an alternate route. Angle north or south, around the problem. Come via Castrin, or Idella City."

"That'll take most of my coins—" Donnock started to argue.

"Burn the expense!" Broger shot back. His jowls jiggled slightly as he spoke, revealing signs of his gradual aging to the silently watching Morganen. "Get back here within forty-seven hours! And eat nothing but meat from now until you arrive!"

The mirror misted on the right, then the left, signaling the end of their communication. Morganen sat back, frowning softly. Why was dear Uncle Broger so determined to have his brother return within two days' time? And more oddly, why would he demand Donnock eat nothing but meat?

*It almost sounds like he's preparing his brother for some sort of ritual magic. There are a few rare spells that require the mage's body to be "aligned" with his energies . . . but in all other cases I've heard about, the mage had to re*frain *from eating meat . . .* Morganen shook his head, letting the plait of his chest-length, ash blond hair slide over his back. It was all very strange.

His brothers might accuse him of knowing everything, but he didn't. He only knew some things. Definitely, he didn't know whatever Broger of Devries, usurper Count of Corvis, apparently knew.

*That's something else I'll have to ask Alys about, in the morning . . . or rather, in a few more hours*, he thought wryly. As much as he knew he had to get back to sleep, he needed to research what sort of rituals required their mage to eat nothing but meat, rather than fruits and vegetables. Letting the mirror on the table relax back into a normal reflection, he crossed to the wall and touched one of the stones. They dissolved, recognizing his aura.

The shelf-lined chamber beyond wasn't actually a part of his workroom tower, but rather existed in a level dug deep beneath it. Through a very clever series of enchantments, he had figured out a way to copy tomes encountered through a scrying mirror. This was his private library, secretly duplicated from the archives of hundreds of other mages across Katan, mages whom he had scryed upon clandestinely.

It helped that he could read very quickly. In fact, Morganen had read every single one of these books, though his memory wasn't page-perfect. Enough general information was retained, along with some of the more interesting spells, that he could usually remember which book or group of books contained what he was looking for. The shelving system he used seemed eclectic, maybe even eccentric, but it worked for him. All he had to do was walk down to the end of the row, turn left for seven stacks of shelves, and turn right; in that corner, he should find what he was looking for.

The contents of the books weren't quite what one would call Light reading; the spells that required eating nothing but fruits and nuts were Light-based magics. It made sense, therefore, that meat-eating spells would be of the Dark. Padding through the hidden library, Morg headed for the alcove with the most restricted of his books. No knowledge was wasted; he might not want to cast such spells himself, but if he knew what they were, he'd have a chance at finding a counter for them.

His brothers needed to survive their biggest confrontation with Broger of Devries and his horde of beasts; the Song of the Sons demanded it, and he was the one who had to ensure it.

Alys was lying naked on the beach. Strangely enough, this fact didn't bother her. In fact, it felt nice; her whole backside from nape to calves felt the warmth of the sun-baked sand, while her front was tickled by errant gusts of wind. Except she was also lying on her side, on something soft and comfortable, and there was something lumpy about the sand that was prodding the small of her back. Her mind, fuzzy with how comfortable she felt, reasoned she was probably lying on a blanket, and the lump was probably just a piece of driftwood.

The breeze tickled over her skin again. It tweaked her nipple, then skimmed over her stomach and tugged at her thigh, lifting her right leg up and back, hooking it over something. Alys woke abruptly, holding herself still as she scrambled mentally to make sense of her surroundings.

She was lying on her left side in a soft, feather-stuffed bed. A warm body had snuggled itself against her . . . a warm, masculine body. The lump that in her fading dream had been a bit of wood nudging the tail end of her spine wasn't wood at all, but a different sort of stiffened material. And the breeze wasn't a breeze; it was a largish hand that, content with the drape of her thigh over a set of much more muscular legs, drifted up the inside of her limb, where it feathered lightly over the curls of her groin. The arousal-dampened curls of her groin.

Wolfer was being sneaky. Gentle rocking motions slicked his fingers, allowing them to slide between her folds, until with a curling motion, he dipped them into her flesh. Stroking them in and out, he made her want to rock her hips into each surge of his digits. The edge of his thumb brushed against the sentinel of nerves guarding her secrets; Alys shivered, feeling the pleasure of it ache all the way up through her breasts.

Somehow, she found her voice. "Good morning . . ."

"Mmm," he rumbled, nuzzling close enough to tickle her ear with his breath through her curls. A slight wriggle downward of his body, a shift of his hips, and the lump prodding the small of her back slipped instead between her splayed thighs. "A *very* good morning."

That made her laugh. Alys wasn't sure why; they had the threat of her uncle looming over their heads, with all of his spells and all of his beasts. Plus there was the disapproval of the Council of Mages, over on the mainland, who would not be happy to learn that *two* women now lived on the isle, never mind the prophecy-driven threat of just one. And, thanks to her uncle, she didn't feel comfortable planning to

have a family with the handsome man . . . who was now re-
placing his fingers with his manhood, filling her with an
achingly sweet slowness.

Until he nudged up against the front wall of her
body . . . and the rather full flesh that lay on the other side
of that wall. Stiffening, Alys tried to ignore it. Really, it felt
very, very good when he withdrew slowly and wonderfully,
stimulating her flesh, and when he pushed back inside
again, that felt good, too—until he hit that spot again. Reminding her she had been asleep for several hours.

Squirming forward, Alys pushed at the hands trying to
hold her in place. "Let go, Wolfer—please!"

"What's wrong?" he asked, lifting his head from the pillow as she scooted out from under the lightweight bedding.
"Alys?"

"Refreshing room!" she blurted as the change in position to upright made the urgency worse.

He sagged back onto the bedding with a rough sigh,
closing his eyes in disbelief as she scrambled around the
foot of his bed and hurried into the other room. His body
ached for release. The dampness on his flesh should've
cooled his ardor as it slowly evaporated, but he just stayed
hard. Leaning forward, Wolfer buried his face in her pillow, inhaling the sweet, feminine musk of her scent. Now
that she was up and out of his bed, she would likely want to
stay up, since it looked close to the right hour for breakfast.

He heard the gurgle and splash of water as she cleaned
herself, and then the patter of her feet. The bed dipped in
front of him. Lifting his face from her pillow, he found
himself confronted by a mass of brown curls as she . . . as
she scooted backward across the mattress, squirming under the light blanket and sheet that had covered them during the night. A bit more of squirming, and she managed
to drape her leg over his thigh, and then reached down between their bodies to awkwardly grab him.

"I've got it!" he quickly asserted, freeing her fingers
from bending him at an awkward angle. Or worse, causing

a premature moment of embarrassment. Once he had control, he slotted himself back into her, pressing up and in like he had before. "Feeling better?"

"Lots," Alys muttered, feeling her cheeks warm in return. "Um . . . thanks. For waiting, I mean."

His irritation left him in a soft laugh. "Thank *you* for coming back to the point where we left."

A giggle escaped her. "My pleasure."

"Mm, and mine, too," he growled, nipping playfully at her ear. She squeaked and squirmed, and he thrust firmly, making her gasp. Wolfer growled again in pleasure as she wriggled back into his next stroke. She cried out softly as he slid his hand around her hip, delving his fingers into her folds. "Do you like that?" he panted, playing with her flesh as his buttocks clenched rhythmically. "Do you?"

"Oh, gods yes—Wolfer!" Back arching, Alys clutched at the bedding with her left hand. She still felt the urge to use the refreshing room, a little bit, but she knew it wasn't an actual need. And without the actual need adding to it and turning it into a highly uncomfortable pressure . . . it was a pleasure. Whatever he was stroking inside of her, combined with the stroking of his fingers outside of her . . . it was incredible.

Making love to her like this was good, but his left arm was tucked uselessly under the pillows. Pausing while deep inside of her—which made her whimper and squirm gratifyingly against him, wanting more—Wolfer worked his arm under her ribs. Embracing her firmly around her hips and her ribs, he planted one foot on the bed and levered both of them over. He managed not to slip out of her as he rolled to his back, a minor miracle.

Breathing heavily, Wolfer eased his grip on her torso. His hands slid down to her pelvis. With her legs drooping to either side of his, he was in danger of slipping out of her. Arching her back, Alys dug her heels into the bedding to make sure she had enough leverage to prevent that. It pressed him a little deeper into her, eliciting a pleased grunt.

His own knees lifted, giving him leverage, too; the leverage to thrust gently into her. The hands on her hips pulled at the same time, rocking her into his movements.

Their coupling was shallow. Wolfer wanted more. Pausing her, he shifted his hands to her shoulder blades, pushing her upright. She struggled to help him, finally sitting up with her buttocks pressed to his abdomen, facing his bent knees.

"Wolfer?" Alys asked, a little unsure. The position they were now in held a different set of pressures, unfamiliar ones. Not unpleasant, just unfamiliar.

"Ride me," he coaxed her, sliding his fingers back down to her hips.

Squirming a little, Alys adjusted her legs so that she would have the right sort of leverage. Rising a little, she sank down onto him. The new angle was nice. Very nice. She rose a little higher and slid down again, then rose more—and he slipped out. Embarrassed, she fumbled for his flesh, blushing. Clearing her throat, she accepted his help in repositioning him, and eased back onto his erection.

Resuming her strokes, she started to enjoy herself again . . . and nearly lost him again. Sighing, Alys sank down as far as she could go, then rocked backward a little, and snapped her hips forward experimentally. He grunted and clutched her hips with his hands, caressing her curves with his fingertips to encourage her. Doing it again elicited another grunt.

"That's . . . that's very good," Wolfer rasped. Sitting up and facing his feet, she felt very tight to him like this. Pressure in different ways from the usual. She snapped her hips again, tightening his abdomen with pleasure . . . and on the rebound, he slipped out again. Sighing, she groped for his shaft. He helped guide her into place, she started to sink down . . . and he popped free, sliding the wrong way through the folds of her femininity.

Alys squeaked, then growled in frustration. The noise made Wolfer laugh and catch her hands as she grabbed for him again. Embarrassed but understanding that he wasn't laughing at *her*, she chuckled with him. "Can we try something else, now?"

"Of course," Wolfer agreed. He, too, had been on the verge of rumbling his displeasure at the inadvertent interruptions. He helped guide her off of him, letting her settle at his side on the bedding. "What would you like?"

She parted her lips to say something, and Evanor's voice rang in their ears. *"Breakfast! Time to rise and eat something, you lazy lovebirds! You cannot fly very far if you don't have any energy!"*

Wolfer muttered something unpleasant under his breath in regard to his brother's cheerful interruption. Alys blinked in shock. "You can't . . . you can't do that! It's not . . ."

"Oh, it's anatomically possible . . . if someone else does it to him."

She wrinkled her nose. "I didn't mean *that*. Cari told me some men and women like to do that, and that it can be quite pleasant, if the proper care and time are taken . . . I meant, he's your *brother*."

"Then he can do it to himself. I'll ask Morganen if he knows of any lengthening charms. Later," he added as she opened her mouth to argue. "You were going to pick a position for *us* to enjoy."

"Um . . ." Her gray eyes gleamed after a moment. "Like we did before? To start with?"

"All right." Helping her to turn around, Wolfer snuggled up close to her again. Lifting her leg, he let her upper body shift forward a little so that she could reach down and help guide him into place. The feel of her hand pulling back his foreskin revived his interrupted interest, too. It wasn't that he had softened, just that some of his momentum toward the peak of his pleasure had diminished. Feeling her guide him into her body, the wet heat of her femininity enfolding him in her depths, definitely revived his body's attention.

She shifted back at the wrong moment, however, and he almost slid out. Alys reached down again, making sure he didn't slip . . . and felt the movement of his flesh under her fingertips as he pushed into her again. It was weird, kind of messy from the moisture of her body, and yet erotic all at the same time. And good-feeling. Alys petted him as he stroked into her. Wolfer choked and curled over her back. His hand left her hip, shifting down to tangle with her fingers. They delved under hers, touching and stroking her clitoris.

That aroused her even further. Not just the touch of his fingers, circling in counterpoint to everything, but how their hands bumped and mingled, giving each other additional pleasure. It aroused him, too. Awkward as it was, it didn't take long for her to gasp his name and shudder, which gave him permission to thrust a little deeper, a little faster. She tightened around him further, enjoying the depth and pressure on that spot inside of her. With a choked growl, Wolfer released himself, wrapping her in his arms as much as he could, given how they lay on their sides. Shivering, he clung to her as his heartbeat subsided, loosening his grip just enough so that she didn't have to struggle quite so much to catch her breath.

*"You know,"* Evanor's voice sang into their ears, *"your breakfast is definitely growing cold. I don't want to know what the two of you are doing, but whatever it is, you're going to have to reheat your food all on your own. And if you don't get down here soon, it'll be stored in the pantry cupboards under a stasis charm!"*

Alys giggled. "I'm actually rather good at food-heating spells . . ."

Wolfer hugged her closer. "I knew there was a reason why I wanted to marry you."

"Wolfer!" she mock-protested.

"Alys!" he mocked back, and received a pinch on his forearm for his troubles. They mock-tussled for a moment, until Evanor interrupted them from a distance one more time.

*". . . Assuming, that is, if the rest of us don't just eat it all."*

*"Evanor!"* Wolfer sang back. *"We're coming!"*

That made Alys giggle madly. She giggled so hard, his softened shaft slipped out of her . . . which only made her laugh even harder. It was only after Wolfer moved away and sat up on the side of the bed, finally feeling his own urge to use the refreshing room, that she calmed down enough to gasp, "I thought we already had!"

To his surprise, Wolfer felt his cheeks heating in a blush at her words; he hadn't expected such a frank joke from his shy little Alys!

# SEVENTEEN

❧

**A**bout time you made it," Evanor observed dryly as Wolfer and Alys entered the dining chamber. "We're running low on provisions. I've a list of things for you to do, if you'll attend to it. Both of you."

Wolfer sighed, accepting the slip of paper as soon as he was finished holding the back of Alys' seat for her. Settling into the chair beside her, he eyed the writing on it. "Let's see . . . most of this is in the forest. We have . . . vira-peppers, finger-fruit, kiwi nuts, wild greens, naquah roots, earth apples . . . lovely, you're making me dig."

"You're the one with the dog's paws," Evanor quipped, as he enchanted a rag to wipe the far end of the octagonal table.

"Funny. And I see you're making me swim, too," he added. "Two barrels' worth of fish?"

"Fresh, by preference. And shellfish," Evanor added. "We're getting rather low."

"What, no deer for me to hunt down as well?" Wolfer quipped dryly.

"We're getting cattle, remember?" The lightest-haired brother winked at Alys. "Do you still sing, Sister-to-Be? I missed the way the dairy maids at Corvis would sing in the mornings and evenings as they walked the cattle to and from pasture."

"A little bit," she demurred. "Not like you."

"*No one* sings like he does," the second-eldest muttered.

"And I'll take that as a compliment," Evanor retorted. "Go fetch the food, will you? Or we'll starve to death, waiting for the next attack."

"I wasn't scheduled for any chores until lunch," Wolfer reminded him. "This will take up most of the day!"

"*I'll* take your cooking chore," Evanor bartered. "You're better at fishing than I am."

"What about the others?" Wolfer asked. "And Alys' morning lesson with Morganen?"

"He said it's been put on hold until those mirrors are finished. They're the priority right now. Sorry," the blond mage apologized to Alys. "Your education is important, don't get us wrong, but—"

"But those mirrors are our protection," Alys agreed.

"Exactly."

"Well, food is important, too," she offered pragmatically. "I'll help Wolfer fetch it, since I don't know the first thing about forging an enchanted mirror."

Both men smiled at her in thanks, making her blush in pleasure.

**O**oh, ripe toska!" Alys pointed at a tree a short distance into the jungle on the northern side of the road.

Wolfer slowed and stopped the magic-driven cart. He peered into the forest, frowning. "I don't see any."

"I did!" Shifting shape, Alys launched herself from the wagon on soft-feathered wings.

There weren't many of the purple-hulled fruits; most were still a dull brownish red, hinting at the sourness of the flesh each hardened rind contained. Landing on a close branch, she nipped at the stem of the ripened cluster, ignoring the bitter-sour sap. Eventually it fell, dropping four purple fruits with a *thump*. Swooping down, she landed, transformed, and worked her way out of the thick underbrush with mussed curls, but thankfully no snagged clothes.

Grinning, she lifted the cluster into the back of the wagon. "I've only had toska less than a dozen times in my life, but it was delicious every single time!"

"You'll be sick of it before we're through," Wolfer informed her, helping to pull her back up onto the bench. "The old orchards definitely went wild after the plantations were abandoned, but toska was one of the more popular fruits grown on the isle, judging by the sheer number of trees. We're after finger-fruit. I know of a stand of them that should be ripe, where the vira-peppers twine around the base of the trees. It's a bit of a walk into the forest," he warned her. "But worth the trek."

"You're the native," Alys agreed. "I forgot—who had the chicken . . . sorry, *citizen*-chicken feeding chore, today?"

He shared a grin with her. "Saber. And I'm happy to let *his* ankles be pecked."

"They are definitely ornery chickens," Alys agreed. A moment later, she laughed. "I don't suppose we could set them on my uncle? They're almost worse than his mekhadadaks!"

"Alys!" Wolfer mock-protested, teasing her much like he used to when they were younger. "I didn't know you could be so cruel. I'm very proud of you!"

Their laughter echoed through the trees, disturbing the birds into winging up into the increasingly cloudy sky.

They weren't laughing that afternoon. Alys sighed roughly as she stared out through the door of the aging boathouse. Rain had caught them just as they were about to cast nets from the edge of the docks. Rain, and a touch of thunder in the distance. There weren't many intact buildings this close to shore; the boathouse had been repaired by the brothers so they could store their enspelled fishing nets on the docks, but it still had gaps in the weather-beaten boards.

"Relax," Wolfer ordered her. "This is a good thing!"

"It looks like it's going to rain for *hours*," Alys stated, wrinkling her nose again.

"Maybe two or three at most. But the fish are usually hungry after a rainstorm," he told her. "We just cast a little bait on the water with a scattering spell, wait a few moments, then toss the nets over the same spot, and just draw them up! Nothing to worry about."

"Tell that to the thunder," she muttered, trying to discern if that was a flash of lightning or just a trick of her eyes; the daylight was doing a good job of obscuring the phenomenon.

"Surely a bucket of chicken innards isn't as scary as whatever you used to feed your uncle's beasts," the man checking the nets behind her offered.

"Chicken, pig, sheep, cattle . . . chicken is bad enough, but mutton smells worse. If Uncle hadn't owned the only butchery on his own property, he would've had a hard time hiding the need for so many meat scraps. Can we get some sheep, too? Along with the cattle?" Alys asked, changing the topic. "I'm not that fond of mutton, but at least we'd have wool for clothes."

Wolfer abandoned the nets, since they looked whole and sound. He wrapped his arms around Alys from behind, resting his chin on her curls. "My domestic goddess. We don't have much use for wool, save in the coldest months. I'm not sure it would be cost-effective to have any, but if you want them, and are willing to take care of them . . . Maybe we should give you the official title of Mistress of the Herds?"

"That'd be nice." She leaned back against him, relaxing as the rain continued to pound down on the roof over their heads. Until she felt his hand caressing the underside of her breast. "Wolfer?"

"Well, we *do* have some time to kill, until the rain subsides," he offered slyly, his deep voice tickling nerves that his fingers couldn't quite reach.

Only the thunder in the distance answered him. Alys was too busy turning in his arms so she could kiss him.

Their kiss lasted through another rumble of thunder. Wolfer broke away from her lips, moving to nuzzle her ear. "Right now," he breathed, "our night-loving brother is undoubtedly roaming around up there, charging himself like a child does when shuffling around on a section of carpet in woolen so—"

Something *cracked* sharply, followed by a sizzling sound that was *not* lightning striking the ground. Orange-red light flared as Wolfer jerked his head up. Alys squirmed around in his arms, both of them peering into the rain as they felt a pulse of energy prickling harshly against their inner senses. The cause of the ongoing sizzling noise wasn't immediately apparent. Not until Wolfer released Alys, stepped out into the rain, and peered around the corner of the building toward the end of the dock.

Mage-fire burned in a rune-etched circle, pulsing with a sickly orange red brilliance. The light arched higher and higher with a rhythm not unlike a heartbeat . . . if that heartbeat was slowing and dying. But rather than dying, the light intensified, forming a dome. A final flair of light, and the dome started descending again.

Filling the ring, an unnatural menagerie now stood on a broad metal surface where there had only been tar-soaked, weather-aged wood. Small, black, multilimbed balls of malevolent hunger, large, dog-like beasts with elongated teeth, slithering serpents scaled in putrid yellow brown, leathery-winged raptors with venomous claws . . . And above them, standing on a floating sheet of metal, a familiar, balding mage. At his feet dripped the corpse of his own brother, red staining him from throat to scalp, since his head and his heels dangled over the magically levitated metal.

The only thing that saved Wolfer from being instantly noticed was an inadvertent effect of the strange transportation spell: Broger of Devries and his magical beasts were all facing the wrong way. The only other thing that saved them from being attacked right away was how slowly the orange red wall of energy was fading back down into the runes scorching the boards of the quay.

Wolfer jerked himself back around the corner, bumping into Alys, who had peered around the corner, too. He grabbed her by the arms, pushing her around the boat-house. "Fly! Fly to the castle, and warn the others!"

"I can't!" Alys hissed back. "He's brought his *wyr-wracks*! They can outfly my owl form, and they'll attack and kill me—run! Run as fast as you can, as a stallion!"

"I can't carry you!" Wolfer shot back tightly, trying to think of a way to get both of them to the safety of the cas-tle. "Not and still outrun those pookrahs!"

Inspiration snapped her eyes wide. "Run without me!"

"No! Alys—"

She transformed even as he protested. Wolfer took one agonized look at the chest-tall canine, and shifted shape as well. Lunging away from his beloved, he galloped across the last of the wooden section of the dock and clattered over the paved stones of the wharf, racing for the road. Alys quickly tucked herself into the boathouse, hiding as the last of the sizzling noise faded.

Her one hope was to mingle with her uncle's army. There were nine pookrahs in his pack. That should be more than enough visually for a tenth to lurk among them unno-ticed. So long as he didn't pause to count them, that was, or notice the diamond still affixed to her breastbone. If he didn't notice, the ruse would work. If he did, she would be in trouble. And, of course, provided his beasts remembered her scent as their primary caretaker, and refrained from turning on her . . .

Of course, she was in danger just for still being alive, too. *Jinga,* Alys found herself praying. *I don't call on You often, but please, please make sure everyone on my side comes out of this mess alive!*

The deep ringing of a bell startled Morganen. He almost ruined the last dregs of magic being poured into the third mirror. As it was, Rydan caught and smoothed out the ener-gies of his youngest sibling. Rydan, who was supplying the

magic for their endeavors, thanks to the storm crackling its
energies along his skin, charging him as they worked in
Koranen's forge outside the base of his tower. Rydan, who
wasn't supposed to be bothering himself with the taming
of those energies any further than converting them into
raw magical energy. It took a lot of attention and control to
turn natural energy into magical energy, after all.

Morganen's estimation of his elder brother's abilities
rose a notch or two, but he didn't have time to dwell on Rydan's multitasking abilities. That bass-voiced chime was no
ordinary sound; it was a warning that the defensive magics
woven into the island and its coastal waters had just been violated. Not breached, not tripped, not invaded: violated.

Someone had just cast a very powerful spell, with a magical signature that did not belong to the inhabitants of Nightfall. There were three possibilities, based on the brothers'
three potential or outright enemies: the Mandarites, whom
Morganen dismissed as too magic-poor to craft such a harsh
signature; the Council of Mages, who had enough power to
do so, but not nearly enough provocation to waste that much
energy; and dear Uncle Broger, who had his own reasons for
hating the eight of them, whatever those were.

Firming his concentration, Morganen resumed smoothing the energies pouring into the spells being embedded in
the third mirror. They wouldn't have time to finish any others, but another handful of minutes would see this particular Artifact ready for the invasion. The island's wards had
been violated at their very perimeter; they had at least that
much time to prepare, perhaps a little bit more. Dear Uncle
Donnock had apparently made it back to his brother's side
faster than expected.

Wolfer didn't bother to open the gates; he leaped, transformed, and soared over the wall in his one bird-shape. The
fear of the incipient attack was more than enough to goad
him through his fear of heights. Speeding on wings to the

far side of the sprawling compound, he raced to the out-building at the base of the southeastern tower, darting in-side. His brothers were just finishing the final spells on one of the proposed mirrors. Fluttering to slow his forward mo-mentum, Wolfer transformed and drew a heavily panting breath to gasp out his message. "Broger—"

"—is here," Morganen finished for him, calmly helping Trevan to seal the wooden frame around the edge of the mirror.

"He brought—" Wolfer panted next.

"—his beasts," the youngest continued for him.

A frown creased Wolfer's brow as he struggled to breathe and speak at the same time. "Alys stayed, transformed her-self—"

"Into something that would hopefully blend in and al-low her to do some sabotage, or at least keep an eye on her uncle's forces," Morganen surmised.

"Would you *stop that*?" Wolfer growled, catching some of his breath as he scowled at his youngest sibling. "You're not a Seer, Morg!"

"No, just very intelligent. Did you see how and where he arrived?" Morganen asked as Saber slipped out of the building, no longer needed to help forge the mirror. The el-dest's voice rose in song for a brief moment, calling to Evanor to warn and guard his wife.

"On the docks . . . some sort of rune-circle. It was an or-ange red fire. He's also murdered Donnock of Devries," Wolfer added breathlessly. "Had the body with him."

"*Shit!*"

The vulgarity made the others in the room jump. Mor-ganen abandoned the mirror to Trevan's hands, raking his fingers through his hair. The act dislodged the band wrapped around his forehead to contain any sweat during their spell-casting efforts. He paced a few steps, making his brothers eye the normally unflappable Mage askance.

"What's wrong?" Koranen asked his twin, hand out-stretched as he killed the forge fires.

"He's crafted a Dark Gate. We're going to have to sanctify and then destroy the docks—and none of us is a priest!" Morganen swore again. "Jinga's Steaming Turds!"

"A what?" Wolfer asked, confused.

"A Dark Gate—it's a pathway through the aether that an evil mage can create by murdering someone who has been to the location where the Portal needs to be opened," Morganen explained. "That's what he meant by Donnock's life being valuable . . . because Donnock had been to our docks—never mind," he dismissed as the others stared at him in confusion. "If it's not sealed properly, if it's not sealed quickly, it creates a weakness in the Veil between worlds. The more intense the sacrifice, the more it weakens the boundaries. The murder of a close family relative means we have a potential doorway to the Netherworlds sitting on that dock!"

"Shit is *right*," Trevan muttered, cradling the mirror. "What do we do?"

"*You* prepare to fight Broger and his beasts. *I* need to do some research!" Turning, Morganen ran—*ran*—out of his twin's forge. The Mage rarely hurried. It unsettled the others.

Wolfer, his breath recovered, cleared his throat. "Alys is still out there, and he's coming up here with a *lot* of beasts. Wyr-wracks, pookrahs, bone monkeys . . . I think he used up all of his wyverns in the last attack, thankfully. We don't have a lot of time to lay traps for them. Who has a mirror, so far?"

"Kelly, of course," Trevan revealed. "Saber has the second mirror, and of course I have this one, though it could go to any one of us."

"Can you carry it in your hawk-form?" Saber asked him, stepping back inside the forge chamber in time to hear Trevan's words.

It was a hand-sized mirror. Trevan shrugged. "Of course; it's not nearly as heavy as the ducks I hunt."

"Then keep it, and try to keep yourself out of the fray," Saber instructed him. "There're wyr-wracks to take care of, but once we clear the skies, you get yourself into a position to swoop down and return any of his offensive spells with that mirror. You're more valuable being a mobile defense for the rest of us. Wolfer, find Alys and get her this mirror; tell her to do the same."

Wolfer grimaced at his twin. "If these mirrors don't work—"

"Then we're *all* in trouble. I'm risking my own wife, here!" Saber reminded him tersely, shoving the mirror into his twin's hands. "Go! The rest of us, spread out, find those beasts, and blast them to pieces. Start with the raptors, if you can. We need those skies clear. Rydan . . . the storm is passing to the south. Can you . . . ?"

One black brow arched upward. Arms folded across his chest, Rydan's mouth twisted into something not quite a full smirk. Rain rattled against the windowpanes, driven into them by a gust of wind.

Saber rolled his eyes. "Stop being so gods-be-damned enigmatic, and start whipping up some lightning, or something! The rest of you, spread yourselves out around the castle, and set some traps for the beasts he'll have brought. I'm going to activate the soldier-stones on the walls; they'll help with some of the defenses, even if they cannot move very far."

I'm afraid we're about to have some very unwanted visitors," Evanor translated for Kelly, as soon as he was finished listening to whoever had called out to him, interrupting his work of prepping vegetables for supper. "Dear Uncle Broger has decided to drop by, and has brought a number of his favorite pets."

Despite his lighthearted words, the blond mage's tone was very unhappy. Kelly dropped the chicken she had been plucking and quickly rinsed her hands at the sink. "How much time do we have?"

"Unknown, but probably not very long—where are you going?" Evanor called out to her as she didn't stop to dry her hands in her haste to leave the kitchen. "Kelly! I'm supposed to stay with you, to help guard you!"

"Then try to keep up with me! I need to lay some traps of my own," she called over her shoulder, hurrying toward the nearest stairwell. "God—why did I leave that chest up in the attic after they left? We need to keep it down in the Great Hall if we're going to keep having visitors drop by!"

"The chest of what?" Evanor asked, hurrying to catch up with her. For a thin redhead who had been nearly skin and bones when she had first arrived just a few months ago, she could move very quickly when she wanted. "What are you talking about? Kelly?"

Alys waited in the shadowed doorway of the boathouse, her jaws slightly agape as she struggled against the urge to pant from anxiety. Any moment now, a host of nasty things would come slithering and scuttling and padding past her position . . . any moment. She blinked as a blurred ripple of air passed in front of her. A largish blurred ripple.

*A concealment spell. He's sneaking up on the castle!*

It made sense. Uncertainty held her still for a long moment, then Alys darted out of the shelter of the boathouse, loping as quickly and quietly as she could into the back of the blur in the air. She passed through the edge of the illusion and almost banged her forelegs against the edge of a metal disc. It was floating about a hand span off the surface of the dock, and it was carrying her uncle's menagerie. Even the wyr-wracks had yet to take flight, still resting on a metal perching-tree affixed to the floating platform. And every last one of the beasts in her uncle's menagerie held itself still in perfect obedience on that platform. Despite the blood of her murdered uncle Donnock dripping down from the smaller metal platform hovering over the center of the larger one, not a single one of the literally blood-thirsty beasts moved.

*Kata . . . I'm not going to be able to hide myself among them until they break ranks!* Not when the pookrahs stood in three rows of three. Only when they started moving would she be able to disguise herself among their milling forms. Until then, she was highly exposed, if Broger of Devries should glance her way.

Her uncle wasn't checking anything behind him, though. She was safe . . . somewhat.

It wasn't easy, keeping herself within the edge of the illusion without banging her forelegs on the platform, though the disc did glide smoothly forward. Keeping a wary eye on her uncle, she followed anxiously until they reached the cover of the jungle. Darting into the underbrush, Alys shifted into her owl shape. Her sharp eyes picked out the blur of her uncle's invasion force easily enough. Alys followed it silently through the canopy edging the winding road that led up to the mountain pass and its walled palace. Part of her watching was made easier by the way the falling rain blurred and wavered as it passed into the illusioned zone, but the rain was beginning to ease, the storm fading as it moved on to the south and west.

The cliff-illusioned wall didn't balk her uncle for more than a moment. The large blur simply paused briefly at the base, then lifted itself up and over. Alys flew over the wall as well, veering toward Wolfer's tower, since she lacked the protective cover of the forest up here. Perching on the blue roof tiles, she watched as the large blur settled onto the cobblestones of the courtyard. After a moment, it broke up, swirling into pieces that moved off in different directions through the courtyard.

There was no sign of Wolfer or the others. She knew he had to have reached his brothers well ahead of her uncle; the disc had moved at the pace of a steady walk, whereas Wolfer had galloped away from the docks as fast as he could race. Unsure which of the smaller blurs to follow, Alys finally picked the smallest of the lot and soared over the ramparts, following as it disappeared into the southwestern gardens. The blur looked too small to contain her uncle; if she could get out of his sight, she could quite possibly contain whatever was underneath that illusion with some of the containment spells she'd learned as the primary caretaker of her uncle's menagerie.

Sweeping down low, she skimmed the blur. There was only an instant in which to see what lay inside; venombeetles and watersnakes. Not all of them, either. Her uncle had apparently broken up his forces into several groups. She swooped down over another blur that was making its way to the south and east, and found a trio of pookrahs. They were heading for the southern courtyard. As she swooped upward, she ran into another blur—a quartet of wyr-wracks. Literally ran into them. The sharp-beaked bird she collided with squawked and twisted, bringing its venomed claws up to attack her.

Alys reacted instinctively, hardening her feathers into thick, tough scales as she and the raptor dropped. Instinct also had her shifting shape out of avian form into a canine one. Pookrahs were jumpers, and her powerful hind legs cushioned the impact of her fall, while her long teeth slashed into the bird, breaking its rib cage. The others shrieked and dove at her in retaliation. Whirling, Alys transformed her shape underneath her hard-scaled skin, casting a spell on the trio. The blur covering them rippled, tearing as the glamour struggled to keep up with the sudden vector-change. Thumping noises hit the white granite wall of the castle, and red blossomed from the impact. More thuds followed as the bodies of the raptors hit the cobblestones lining the edge of the yard, bits and pieces visible through the torn edges of their concealment spell.

A crack of lightning speared down out of the sky, striking something on the far side of the palace from her. Alys bit back a yelp, whirling to look around her. The other blurs were still making their way toward the far side of the compound. If she could get to them and—

All of the illusions vanished as lightning flared and boomed a second time on the far side of the window-rattled castle. As did whatever controlling spell her uncle had cast over the creatures. She found herself abruptly faced with nearly two dozen highly dangerous creatures, half of whom oriented on the scale-hided woman among them. Including that trio of pookrahs, whose muscles were bunching in preparation to leap on her as they turned to face her.

She flinched and cast the first spell she could think of: *"Kai, lusai!"*

They scrabbled to a halt, planting their haunches on the ground. A confused whine escaped one of the bitches, her ears flattening to her skull. It worked! The command to *sit* still worked—Alys bit back her exultation and quickly cast chaining spells on the trio. Then had to leap up into the air in owl-form to avoid the watersnakes slithering her way. The beetles lifted themselves into flight as well, but they were slow. She would have plenty of time to land on the walkway lining the roof of the palace wing, transform, and burn them out of the sky before they could reach her.

Except there was another quartet of wyr-wracks winging her way, now that they were free of whatever compulsion had concealed and compelled them here. A chattering drew her gaze downward in time to see a clutch of bone-monkeys scrambling to climb up the walls and get to her. Her uncle had certainly brought enough of his animal minions to plague a full score of mages, let alone herself, the seven Corvis brothers, and an outworlder woman with no magic whatsoever!

*Though it's not like I have a lot of defenses myself—oh, god, I'm in trouble!* Landing, she twisted and slashed out her hand, throwing a wall of force into the beaks of the wyr-wracks, then twisting to sear the air with fire in the direction of the buzzing horde of venom-beetles. The front half of the lethal raptors hit the wall and dropped, dazed, but the back three swerved aside just in time.

*"Basserfol!"*

The magic-infused shout startled her into jumping, echoing across the compound with enhanced force. She jumped a second time, this time with a squeak, as bodies sprung into existence around her. Clad in blue, dozens of soldiers now lined the battlements edging the castle wings around her. Eyes wide, Alys watched as they brandished their weapons against the incoming beasts, some wielding spears, some swords, and even a few armed with crossbows. She barely remembered the trio of wyr-wracks and spun around to blast at them with the fire-spell, one of the few offensive spells she knew.

A spear thrust past her shoulder as the seared birds tumbled to the roof. Alys shrieked and shied away before realizing the spear had skewered one of the few fist-sized bugs to have escaped her first hastily aimed blast.

"Th-Thanks," she stammered, startled and grateful, but the helmed soldier made no reply.

He whirled to slash his weapon across the crenels, sweeping one of the bone-monkeys from its perch. It shrieked as it fell, but another took its place. Alys flared her mage-fire at the creature, crisping it. If one of those monkeys touched her, it had the power to extract whatever bone lay underneath the flesh it touched, right through muscle, tendon and skin. The beastly, ash gray monkeys loved chewing on fresh bones. She shuddered and cast fire again.

"Alys!" The shout came from down below. A glance over the parapets showed Wolfer twisting and slashing with his sword at something writhing on the ground, off to the eastern edge of the courtyard. At that distance, Alys couldn't tell what it was; venom-beetles, mekhadadaks, and watersnakes weren't the only small yet disproportionately nasty creatures her uncle had kept in his menagerie.

Another bone-monkey leaped up between the crenels, launching itself at her. It was skewered by the silent guardsman that had sprung to life beside her, just as Alys shot another blast of fire at it . . . right through the soldier's arm. It didn't affect the man at all, or his weapon. They were complex illusions, neither real flesh nor real weapons; they were guardian spells wedded to the stones of the palace and enchanted to protect friend from foe. As much as she wanted to join Wolfer, she knew she was safest where she was.

So long as the animals didn't damage the source of the castle guards' illusions, that was.

# EIGHTEEN

❧

I still don't get it."

"Who cares if you don't get it, Ev," Kelly shot back, throwing out more of the marble-sized glass balls. "Just keep activating them! And remind your brothers to make them so they're verbally activated by anyone, like magic-less *me*, next time."

Sighing, Evanor activated the enchantments within each bead clattering onto the floor of the Great Hall. Elegantly clad bodies expanded into existence around them. "Why aren't you activating all of them?"

"Because these are the enchanted courtiers that can do more than just smile, nod and say hello, how do you do, and good-bye," Kelly told him. "I put them away in a specific order after the Mandarites left, so I'd be able to tell which types were which."

"You mean the interactive ones?" the blond mage asked her as she checked through the box to make sure she had enough. "Kelly, there aren't more than twenty of those, and very few of them were based on courtiers who were also warriors. What good will the rest of these do?"

"I don't need them to be warriors! I just need them to take commands!"

"What commands?"

Lightning seared down out of the overcast sky beyond the tall, rectangular-paned windows lining the ordinal sides of the octagonal hall. Thunder cracked, rattling those panes. Evanor didn't even twitch, used to his younger sibling's antics, but Kelly jumped, shoulders hunching. She flinched again as a second strike boomed out there in the courtyard. Around them, the illusioned courtiers stood calmly chatting among themselves, undisturbed by the meteorological display.

"Sounds like the party has started," Kelly muttered, shoving the chest to one side and grabbing an aged but still functional halberd from its brackets next to the archway leading to the northern wing.

Evanor opened his mouth to say something, but movement in the western corridor drew his attention. A ripple, a flutter, and whatever disguising charm had been used up until now dissolved. Leaving a loping trio of pookrahs headed their way. He couldn't see any of them bearing a silver diamond on its sternum, but he couldn't be absolutely sure, either. "Kelly!"

"I see them—Courtiers!" the redheaded woman snapped. "Embrace those dogs!"

"*Embrace* those—?" Shock held Evanor still for a critical moment, and then it was too late to question her oddball, outworlder command. The courtiers, projections of magical energy, swarmed the trio of chest-tall dogs, grabbing and hugging them. Teeth snapped into shoulders and claws scratched through garments . . . but no actual damage was delivered; the courtiers were only sophisticated illusions, after all. And with six to a beast, they were quickly immobilized. Confused, the pookrahs growled, then whined, unable to struggle hard enough to free themselves from so many unaffected, unpoisoned captors.

Kelly peered at sternums, making sure the wardogs weren't their missing friend, then grimly stabbed the spear end of the halberd into each beast's eye, and the brain that lay beyond. Mouth twisted in grim distaste, she stabbed twice, to make sure each pookrah was dead. Doing this was highly unpleasant, but Kelly had heard enough about the old, weekly invasions the eight brothers had suffered to know that killing them was the safest thing to do.

Evanor, more pragmatic about killing the beasts, since he and his brothers had been forced to do these sorts of things for nearly three years, kept his eye on the corridors leading to the central donjon hall. Writhing yellow brown slithered their way. "Kelly—watersnakes!"

Extracting her weapon from the last corpse, Kelly nodded. "Courtiers, set down the dogs and face the snakes!" Ignoring the thumps, she tightened her gut, watching those all-too-familiar serpents heading their way up the western corridor. Gauging the timing of it, she waited until Evanor drew an uneasy breath, then commanded, "Courtiers, stomp on those snakes! Stomp on anything that attacks you!"

"You . . . you . . . are *insane!*" Evanor's expression had crumpled in disbelief. Grabbing his sister-in-law, he pressed a kiss to her forehead as the ornately clad bodies around them started jumping up and down. Blue ichor slimed the paving stones of the floor. She laughed and squeezed him back. No matter how many of the score of snakes tried to bite and inject their venom, it just didn't work on their victims.

Evanor released Kelly long enough to let her slash down with her halberd, severing the head of a snake that had managed to get through the deadly gauntlet of slippered feet. Turning to check the other corridors, he squinted at an odd sight approaching from the eastern wing. It took him a moment to realize it was the wobbling surface of a water-sphere . . . and that within its depths were the lean, lunging bodies of volsnap eels.

"God, Uncle isn't letting anything stay behind, this time!" He didn't think their illusion-courtiers would be suited for this particular threat, but he could handle it.

Thrusting out his palm, he chanted, *"Essska plieth, á pli-ethna!"*

The water of the globe shimmered as the force of his spell struck its surface. A moment later, the sphere exploded outward in a thick wall of steam, force-boiled. Volsnap bodies hit the floor just beyond the entrance to the donjon. They writhed and squirmed, desperately seeking water rather than targets, now.

Kelly scraped the blade of the halberd through some of the watersnake slime, and flicked it at the eel-like beasts. One of them snapped at the blue muck. A moment later, it stiffened, thrashed, and started shriveling as the watersnake venom absorbed the liquid in its body, rather like that florist's gel stuff from her home world.

"Very clever," a baritone voice observed. Kelly and Evanor snapped their gazes upward. "Using illusions to guard and protect yourselves."

"Like you're not?" Kelly demanded, unable to see exactly where that voice was coming from. "Hiding from us like a base-born coward. Or is your face just that shamefully ugly?"

Evanor reaffirmed his decision that his eldest brother's out-worlder wife was utterly insane. And yet, utterly brilliant, for Broger of Devries dropped the illusion cloaking him, pricked by her words into revealing himself. He stood on a metal platter the size one would use to display a whole roasted bull, with the bloodied corpse of his brother draped over its edges in front of his feet.

"I see a woman has come to the isle. How fortuitous; I always wanted to be a Prophesied Disaster."

"Sorry, you missed that by a week," Kelly quipped back, resting the butt of her halberd on the floor as she looked up at him. Her other hand rested itself on her hip. "You're the so-called Count Broger of Devries, I presume?"

"*Count* Broger, not 'so-called Count'!" he hissed back at her, his face reddening a little.

"No, 'so-called' would be correct," Kelly retorted as calmly as she could manage. She was stalling for time, waiting for Saber and the others to catch up with her. Tucked into the back of the belt wrapped around her tunic was the mirror the brothers had given her midmorning. As subtly as she could, she slipped her left hand from her hip to the small of her back, getting ready to whip it out if need be. "You see, you were not invited here. You were not formally introduced into my court, you do not have any papers or presentations to authenticate your claim to being nobility, and until you can actually prove your title was gained legally . . . rather than, say, through murdering the gentleman who was *supposed* to be the interim Count of Corvis during the boys' exile . . . I'm afraid I cannot acknowledge your status as a noble."

Broger's lip curled upward. "Why should I care whether or not some strawberry-haired strumpet acknowledges my rightful title?"

"Because you are an uninvited intruder," Kelly returned. Her courtiers had ceased stomping, now that the watersnakes and volsnaps were dead. In the quiet, she could hear running footsteps in the distance. "Not only are you uninvited, you have committed acts of violence against the persons and property of Nightfall Isle, and I am of a mind to have you arrested, thrown into the dungeons, and punished accordingly for your many crimes." She paused, then tipped her head slightly, fingers tensing around the handle of the hand mirror. "Unless, of course, you wish to apologize thoroughly, make reparations for any damage you and your beasts have caused, withdraw said beasts from our sovereign soil, and get the hell off *my* island."

"*Your* island?" Broger snorted, lowering his floating platform a few more feet so that it hovered at the level of her knees.

"That's right," Saber asserted from behind, making his uncle-in-law whip around. "*Her* island. Or did you not hear that Nightfall has been disavowed by the Council and left to its own sovereignty? Broger of Devries, meet Kelly of Nightfall. Queen Kelly . . . my wife."

"*Jinga's Piss!*" Broger snarled, hands curling into fists.

His middle-aged jowls wiggled as he shook one of those fists at his eldest nephew-in-law. "Why won't you *die*! How *dare* you go from being an exiled Count to being a King? *I* am the one who should be King—and I'll be King as soon as the lot of you are dead!"

"You don't have enough power to be King." That came from Rydan, standing in the shadowed mouth of the northern corridor, wind tugging at the chest-length strands of his midnight black hair, swirling around his body.

"You don't even have enough to be on the Council," Evanor agreed disparagingly.

Broger smirked, a nasty, narrow-eyed, tight-mouthed little smirk. "As soon as you *die*, your powers will be transferred to your kinsman. My son. Oh, yes, I found and modified a spell that will enable me to do that!"

A coppery-colored hawk dropped down from above, landing in a clear patch among the blue ichor still smeared on the floor. It transformed even as it landed, resolving itself into a mirror-carrying Trevan within a heartbeat. "What good would *that* do you, if young Barol had all the power? You would still have almost none, by comparison!"

The smirk broadened into a sneer. "What would stop me from using the same magic on him that I can use on the lot of you?"

"You would kill your own *son*?" Wolfer asked, contempt lacing his voice as he stepped into the archway of the southern hall.

"Of course; you killed your own brother," Koranen observed dryly, making his way between the courtiers on the western side as he joined Evanor and Kelly at the center of the donjon floor. "Why should we be surprised you'd kill your own son?"

Broger shifted his platform in a slow circle, surveying the brothers. "Well . . . All we need are the last two, and the set is complete!—Is that running feet I hear?" he mocked, lifting a hand to his ear. Tilting his head upward, he triangulated on the sound; it was coming from the eastern wing of the palace. "Eager to destroy me, are you? I would hate to run away and leave you targetless in your disappointment.

"Clever paint, by the way," Broger added, nodding at the slowly shifting white of the clouds making their way across the currently blue-hued walls of the great hall. "That's why I couldn't focus the scryings anymore, isn't it? Got tired of my little beasties, did you?"

*"Don't kill him!"*

The shout from above distracted all of them. Morganen appeared at the topmost railing, all but throwing himself over the edge as he peered down at the tableau of his brothers ringing their enemy. He panted for a moment, then jerked his head up sharply, looking at something off to the side at his level of the hall that the others couldn't yet see. A moment later, he looked back down, planted a hand on the carved stone railing—and jumped, chanting something.

Kelly gasped, stumbling back a pace. Koranen caught her by the elbows as she bumped into him. Morganen landed on the platform right behind his uncle-in-law, making it bounce hard, jostling all three bodies on the hovering metal: Morganen's, Broger's, and the corpse that had been Donnock of Devries. They stabilized, but only for an instant. Scintillating light shot out from Morganen's body.

The moment it touched the others, the world wrenched around them. The half-shadowed interior of the donjon hall found itself replaced by the overcast but bright skies of the western cove. Three things happened in rapid succession: Wolfer, Saber, Trevan, and Rydan all yelled—they were *not* supported by the floor of the castle anymore, let alone the planks of the dock like the others—and their startled bodies splashed into the water in the next instant; an owl fluttered down from the sky and landed on one of the posts of the pier near Evanor; and Broger cursed, flinging Morganen away from him with a shove and a burst of magic.

Given how the younger man was the westernmost of the two mages, the blow sent him flying backward over the end

of the quay with a yell of his own, where he splashed into
the salty waters of the cove. That left Koranen, Evanor, and
Kelly still on the pier, facing Broger as he hovered over the
scorched rune-circle etched on the planks of the dock, the
body of his brother dangling precariously over the edge of
his oversized, levitating platter.

Morganen pushed up through the surface of the waves
and gasped a command. "Kor! Ignite the runes!"

The auburn-haired mage blinked for a moment, then
shook it off and flicked out his arm. Flames rose up from
the charred wood, surrounding their relative in dancing
yellow, but not harming him in any way. Broger sneered at
the attempt. "What do you think *that* will do? These runes
aren't meant to contain me!"

"Not exactly," Kelly bluffed. "They're for *me* to use—to
destroy you!" Pulling the mirror from behind her back, she
thrust it at him and started chanting. "Abracadabra, Walla
Walla, bibbity-bobbity-boo! Copperfield, Blackstone, Tele-
mus, and *you*—"

*"Fasherwol!"*

Black energy slashed between them. Kelly braced her
arm, flinching as Broger's attack hit the mirror. The magic
did flash back at its caster. It hit his left arm, but all it did
was make the muscles turn limp. The mirror shattered,
making Kelly shriek and huddle over her hand, clutching at
it as it bled. Broger rebalanced himself on the floating
metal disc. "Is *that* the best you can do?"

Morganen, treading water, scowled. They needed the
bastard to use *lethal* magic! Unfortunately, there was only
one thing he could think of on the spur of the moment.
"Apprentice! Reveal yourself!"

"No!" Wolfer protested. "I still have the mirror!"

It was too late; the owl leapt from its perch on the pylon,
transforming back to her natural shape as she landed next
to Evanor. Broger's eyes widened as he stared at his niece.

"Hello, *Uncle*," Alys greeted him, her face expressionless, but her tone dripping with loathing. This was the
chore Kelly had prepared her for: being able to face her

hated relative with courage, even though she had nothing to protect herself. "You're looking rather fat and bald, as usual."

"Insolent brat!" the balding mage snarled at her. "I wondered why your magics didn't come to me when all my spells said you were dead! An oversight I will correct—*skaren skaroth*!"

A blade of light flung itself from his hand. Morganen clenched his fists, almost forgetting to tread water. Wolfer's eyes widened in horror, as did his twin's. Evanor shifted between Broger and his target. A single, reverberating note, and his magic flexed like a clear, rubber wall, bouncing the spell back at its caster.

The older mage had just enough time to widen his eyes, to start to lift his hand again to try to cast a shield. The blade whipped over his fingertips, slicing deep into his chest. His body buckled and fell without a sound. As it slumped, a dark red bolt—as if lightning had been dipped in blood—arced out of his body and slammed into Evanor, thrusting him backward. The impact knocked Alys over as well, the two of them falling in a bruised tangle of limbs.

"No!" Changing into his hardly used bird-form, Wolfer abandoned the water, fluttering awkwardly up to the surface of the dock on dripping wet wings. He hit the planks on his knees as he changed back, touching Evanor to see if his brother still had a pulse, his eyes meeting Alys' as she blinked and struggled for breath under the blond mage's weight.

The rune-circle shifted from yellow-bright flames to orange red, roaring upward in a fierce conflagration. They seemed to form arms, demonically inhuman arms scaled in living tongues of fire. Arms that reached up, wrapped around Broger's body where it had toppled from its hovering platform, and dragged him down to Elsewhere. The moment his body vanished, the flames died, leaving behind nothing. Not even scorched timbers.

A gesture from Morganen, and the water around the dock calmed, turning mirror smooth. Climbing onto the hardened surface, he gestured again and mounted the steps that rose up out of the water. Saber scrambled out of the water, pushing past his youngest sibling as he hurried up onto the quay. His wife was still huddled protectively over her bleeding hand. "Kelly—"

"Could you, uh . . . find my finger?" the freckled red-head asked him shakily, her aquamarine eyes wide and rather dilated with shock. "I seem to have lost it . . ."

"I'll handle it," Morganen reassured both Saber and her. "A spell to reattach it, some potions to ensure it heals properly, and you'll be as good as new! We've lost and reattached more than a few fingers over the years, in sword practices and botched experiments . . ."

Wolfer was glad his sister-in-law would be fine. He was even more grateful that Evanor was alive; his heartbeat was strong, and his eyelashes were fluttering. Alys finished squirming out from underneath the blond mage just as Evanor roused. His eyes opened, then squeezed shut in a wince; his hands shifted to his throat, and his mouth opened.

Eyes snapping open, Evanor blinked and mouthed something, but only a hiss emerged. Horror dawned in his brown eyes. Only Wolfer and Alys, leaning over him, could hear the thread of breath-based sound that emerged. *"My voice . . . I can't . . . Sweet Kata—I've lost my voice!!"*

He wasn't the only one who was horrified. "Morg!" Alys pleaded. "Evanor's lost his voice! We have to do something!"

"Finger first, voice second!" Morganen retorted. "I've got a narrow window to get this thing reattached before the spell won't work. Trevan, I need you to cast a diagnostic spell on Evanor, find out exactly what's wrong with him."

"There're still beasts at the castle," Rydan reminded the others, mounting the steps his youngest brother had formed from the sea, the last one to reach the pier. "They need to be destroyed."

"Wolfer, Alys, Koranen go with him," Saber ordered as

Morganen chanted over his wife's injury. "We'll catch up to you as soon as we can."

The noise in the donjon told the four mages where most of the beasts had gone, for there was no sign of them in the courtyards of the castle. Instead, the beasts—no doubt geased to attack anything that wasn't Broger—had gravitated to the tempting-looking but utterly frustrating visages of the illusioned courtiers. Who were still following through on their last order from their queen, stomping on whatever attacked them.

Koranen snorted, then glanced over at his brothers and impending sister-in-law. "As amusing as this is, if the three of you can set up a containment shield, I'll torch the lot. A little heat won't hurt the illusions."

One of the bone-monkeys fruitlessly sucking on the foot of one of the lady courtiers released its uncooperative victim, scampering toward Rydan. A dark look, a flick of Rydan's finger, and the primate squealed, flinging back toward its brethren under the force of a sharp *crack* of quarter-sized lightning. Several mekhadadaks swarmed the briefly stunned, smoldering beast. It squealed, grabbed and bit, and it became a race to see which could eat the other faster; the mekhadadaks nipping bites out of its hide, or the bone-monkey sucking the chitin off the squirming, spider-like beasts.

Repulsed, Alys suppressed most of a shudder, focusing on throwing up a globe-shaped shield between her, Wolfer, and Rydan as the three of them spread out, surrounding the melee. She shivered again when Koranen ignited the air inside the sphere. The courtiers burned, but they didn't react like they were burning. They just continued to stomp as the flames seared pale and hot around them. When it was over, Rydan blew away the ashes with a gust of air, and Koranen began deactivating the courtiers, reducing them to thumb-sized glass beads.

Wolfer wrapped her in his arms. "It's all right. It's over."

Rydan snorted. "Not until we've checked the whole castle."

"And the grounds outside," Koranen agreed. "If we had Dominor . . . and Evanor's voice . . . we could do a systematic inward sweep. We'll have to check the castle a different way. And even then, a few beasties might escape our search."

"Seal each room behind you, after you've checked it," Alys offered. She was snuggled against her Wolfer's chest, and very happy that all of them were still alive, even if Kelly and Evanor had been harmed. "That's what I'd do. Check and seal each room as we go, then everyone should be back up here in time to sweep the grounds."

"Supper will be rather late, then," Wolfer observed dryly. "We won't be free to sit down until everything's been certified monster-free."

Rydan looked at his siblings. A disgusted noise escaped him. "You're trying to convert me to live in the daylight hours, aren't you?"

"Oh, yes," Koranen teased mock-solemnly. "You've just proved you can withstand the touch of sunlight, so there's no excuse for you to—eep!" Dodging the swipe of his next-eldest brother's hand, the redhead skipped backward with a laugh. "What? I'm just happy we're all alive!"

*W̶ell?*" Evanor whispered as loudly as he could. He was seated on a stool in Morganen's workroom, with most of the others arrayed around the room. They were waiting to hear the results from a more in-depth study of the problem than the cursory one Trevan had been able to give back down on the docks. The castle and its surrounding grounds had been swept for lingering monsters, leaving them free to attend to less urgent matters. Rydan had retired to the kitchen to fix their supper, and Dominor was still missing, but everyone else was present.

Morganen met his gaze sadly and shook his darker

blond head. "I'm afraid I cannot repair the damage. This requires Healing magic on a level *none* of us has mastered."

"But, you could repair my finger!" Kelly protested on her favorite brother-in-law's behalf. "Why can't you repair his vocal cords?"

"Kelly, your finger was lying on the dock a few yards from where you lost it when the mirror exploded," the youngest mage explained patiently. "It was just a matter of reattaching the severed limb and accelerating the natural healing process. In Evanor's case . . . his voice simply isn't *there*, anymore. No voice box. No vocal cords. There's nothing for me to work with! I can reattach limbs, but the regeneration of lost and vanished body parts is beyond my skill."

Saber fixed him with a hard look. "You're *supposed* to be the most powerful mage in all of Katan, Brother!"

"Power, yes—I have the *power* to restore his voice," Morganen agreed impatiently. "I just don't have the *spell*. Even if I did, I wouldn't dare try to restore something so important as Evanor's voice without having had a lot of practice beforehand. A voice is an intricate instrument of the flesh, and Evanor's doubly so, since it's very much a part of his magical abilities."

*"Leaving me virtually magicless,"* Evanor whispered in the grim silence following Morganen's words.

"Yes. I'm sorry, Ev," Morganen added, running his hand through his ash blond hair impatiently. "I'll see if I can get a Healer to come out here from the mainland. Unfortunately, those that are powerful enough to cast Regeneration Charms are likely to be the kind who make their nests in the money-pouches of the Council."

"Who might forbid any of them to come out here," Saber finished grimly.

Even without vocal cords, the expletive that escaped the fourth-born brother was rather vehement.

"*My* sentiments exactly," Kelly muttered. Her hand was swathed in bandages to keep it from being injured further during the healing process, but it would recover with full mobility, according to Morganen. In that regard, she was luckier than Evanor. "We really need to work on opening diplomatic relations with the Council and the people of Katan, to get over and past this stupid prejudice they have against the lot of you."

Wolfer snorted. "Good luck."

Evanor's lips moved, but whatever he had to say was lost as Koranen spoke up. "Wait—*should* we do anything about Evanor's voice, just yet?"

Evanor wasn't the only one to blink at the suggestion. Saber stared at the second-youngest of them. "What do you mean, Kor?"

"I mean, isn't it part of his 'Song' verse for him to be silent? Or at least 'weep in silence'?" the redhead offered.

That made Morganen nod slowly, thoughtfully. "Yes . . . yes, I can see that. And it is intimated that his powers as the son who is the Song will be restored to him. It's not guaranteed, of course . . . but it's quite possible, Evanor, that your own future bride may have something to do with the restoration of your voice!"

There was a general murmur from the others as hope rose among them. Evanor tried to speak, grew frustrated, and finally fitted his fingers into his mouth, blowing a sharp whistle. That silenced them, and made them strain to hear and understand his words. "*Yes, but what about Dominor? His verse comes first, and in the meantime, I cannot Sing to him to let him know we're still thinking of him, and still seeking a way to bring him home!*"

"*I'm* still keeping an eye on him," Morganen promised. "That will have to be good enough. If your verse in the prophecy does indeed suggest that you will not recover your voice until the conditions for finding your own bride have been met, then you will just have to be patient, Ev. Your twin's Destiny must be decided first."

Once again, the curse that escaped the blond mage's lips passed with little more than a hiss of air.

Alys touched his shoulder. "I do appreciate you stepping

between me and my uncle, Evanor. I owe you my life. Anything you need me to do, just ask, and I'll do it."

"Within reason," Wolfer muttered, and grunted as Kelly elbowed him in the ribs. "What? There are certain things she will not be doing for him, because she's still slated to be *my* wife! Not his."

Evanor had to content himself with a dirty look aimed at his older sibling.

"What *I'd* like to know," Koranen interjected, changing the subject, "is why my twin dragged us down to the docks like that. And what those arms in the flames were, and why I had to ignite them."

"I found a book referencing Dark Gates in my research," Morganen told them. "Since we didn't have access to a priest, I had to improvise with the next-best thing. Sorry, Alys . . . but the next-best thing was to make what the book called a 'justice-sacrifice' of your uncle's soul to the Netherworlds. It requires killing the murderer who created the Gate on the very spot that the Gate was created. Either terminus will suffice, in order to close and seal both ends," he added in explanation, "so wherever he Gated from is now sealed against the Netherhells breaking through into our world, as well as our dockside.

"But there's a catch. It has to be a *just* killing, one that restores the balance wrenched out of place by his original nefarious actions. In other words . . . a self-inflicted death." A wry smile curved his lips. "Which, strangely enough, was exactly how we needed to stop him anyway, bouncing his magics back onto himself to keep his protections from lashing out and killing us—and don't make that face, Evanor. You're still alive. Try to be grateful for that."

"*I am*," Evanor whispered, grimacing. "*I just wish we'd had another mirror ready.*"

No one could disagree with that. Alys cleared her throat. "So . . . uh . . . what happened to my uncle, exactly?"

"The Netherworlds accepted his rotten soul to torment for all eternity, in exchange for letting the weakness in the

Veil Between Worlds heal," Morganen explained. "His death was a just one, and the bargain accepted by the Heavens as well as by the Hells; you saw how the charred marks where the runes had been seared were restored without blemish. Which would have happened if a high-ranked priest or priestess had cast a blessing on that spot, instead."

"So let me get this straight," Kelly interjected, frowning. "This . . . gate-thing that Broger the Idiot cast . . . almost opened up a portal to Hell? On *my* dock? On *my* island?"

"Yes. But it's all healed, now," Morganen reassured her. "He's not coming back, and the demons aren't going to invade."

"Which is a *very* good thing," Trevan muttered.

Kelly rolled her eyes, then looked over at her husband. "Do *all* the rulers on this world have to put up with these kinds of headaches?"

"Thinking of abdicating?" Saber quipped.

She mulled it over for a moment. Her gaze met Alys', aquamarine to gray. A sigh escaped the freckled redhead. "No. I'm still the best woman for the job, and it's a job that needs doing. So I'll do it. We need to try and get a Healer out here to at least look at Evanor, which means we need to either work around or work through this Council of Mages that runs Katan, and in the meantime, we need to pray to Whoever's listening upstairs that Dominor survives his kidnapping and comes back home with a wife really soon, so that Evanor can be healed. Am I missing anything in our list of the monumental tasks ahead of us?"

"Um . . ." Saber hesitated as the others looked at him. He grimaced and mumbled, "I forgot to feed the chickens, today."

Kelly flung up her hands, one bandaged, one uninjured. "I am *so* not doing that chore!"

That made the others laugh. Wolfer cleared his throat. "Alys and I also need to finish arranging our wedding. We *are* getting married soon."

The smile Alys gave him was as sweet as the one she

had given him as a knee-scraped child, after he had let her down from his back the day they had first met. "Don't worry, Wolfer. I'd brave even a Netherworld to marry you. If I absolutely had to. Just, um, make sure I don't *have* to, all right?"

He lifted his hand to cup her face. As he did so, his gaze fell on the bracelet made from a braided lock of her hair. "You bound me to you years ago, Alys, with this little bit of hair. Where you go, I will go. Make sure I don't have to go into a Netherhell looking for *you*."

"Deal!"

"And thus the Wolf is tamed by a chain of Silk," Morganen murmured.

Wolfer frowned at him. "There's no silk in this braid, Morganen. It's just a metaphor."

"Um . . . actually, there *is* silk in the braid," Alys found herself confessing, blushing. "I crocheted a tiny thread of it into an enchanted chain and attached it to the hair behind my ear before I met with you that day. It got braided in with the rest of my hair when I cut it and gave it to you."

His brow arched, and a growl rumbled in his throat. Not a truly angry one, but the confessed manipulation did irk him a little.

"It was Morganen's idea!" she protested.

"Morganen!"

"What? The two of you were perfect for each other!" the youngest of them protested. "Anyone with half a brain and a functional eye could've seen that much."

"Just for that, you're taking over Evanor's chore of helping me sew their wedding clothes!" Kelly ordered Morganen. "Presuming we don't have any more Disasters showing up, we should be ready for their marriage in about a week."

"I'm almost afraid to wait that long, in case there are any," Wolfer muttered, holding his Alys a little closer. "Must we have fancy clothes?"

"Cari says that when a woman gets married, she should make sure she gets the right man for the task the first time around," Alys interjected, returning his attention to her. "She said that I should make absolutely sure you're still the man I thought you were, when I came out here looking for you."

Wolfer remembered that "Cari" was the name of the wench Alys had encountered on the mainland, during her journey to Nightfall. He considered her words, ready to release her if that was what she needed to be able to think clearly. "Do you want to wait longer than a week? I would wait as long as it takes, so long as you do eventually say 'yes.'"

"I'm saying 'yes' right now," Alys told him, squeezing him around the ribs. "Everything I've seen about you through all of this has only proved you're still the man I fell in love with while we were still growing up. But I also did only come here with the clothes on my back. I'd like to look nice for our wedding, and for that . . . I don't want to wear castoffs and borrowed garments. I, um, I want to get it right, the first time around."

Warmed by her shy smile—and driven a little crazy by it as she ducked her blushing cheeks into his chest, this woman who had bravely and boldly disparaged her insane uncle to his face just that afternoon—Wolfer dropped a kiss on her curls. "Anything you want, Alys, anything within my power, and I will give it to you. Even if I have to pick up needle and thread to finish your dress myself."

A wild gesture from the mage on the stool caught their attention. Shaking his head, Evanor hissed as loudly as he could, *"Oh, no—no no no! The last time he tried to use a needle, he bled all over my best shirt!"*

If Evanor said anything else, it was lost in the snickers of the others.

# Song of the Sons of Destiny

*The Eldest Son shall bear this
    weight:
If ever true love he should feel
Disaster shall come at her heel
And Katan will fail to aid
When Sword in sheath is
    claimed by Maid*

*The Second Son shall know this
    fate:
He who hunts is not alone
When claw would strike and cut
    to bone
A chain of Silk shall bind his
    hand
So Wolf is caught in marriage-
    band*

*The Third of Sons shall meet his
    match:
Strong of will and strong of
    mind
You seek she who is your kind
Set your trap and be your fate
When Lady is the Master's mate*

*The Fourth of Sons shall find
    his catch:
The purest note shall turn to
    sour
And weep in silence for the hour
But listen to the lonely Heart
And Song shall bind the two
    apart*

*The Fifth Son shall seek the
    sign:
Prowl the woods and through
    the trees
Before you in the woods she
    flees
Catch her quick and hold her
    fast
The Cat will find his Home at
    last*

*The Sixth Son shall draw the
    line:
Shun the day and rule the night
Your reign's end shall come at
    light
When Dawn steals into your
    hall
Bride of Storm shall be your fall*

*The Seventh Son shall he de-
    cree:
Burning bright and searing hot
You shall seek that which is not
Mastered by desire's name
Water shall control the Flame*

*The Eighth Son shall set them
    free:
Act in Hope and act in love
Draw down your powers from
    above
Set your Brothers to their call
When Mage has wed, you will
    be all*

—THE SEER DRAGANNA

Keep reading for a look at the third book in
Jean Johnson's Sons of Destiny series,

# The Master

Now available from Berkley Sensation!

*The Third of Sons shall meet his match:*
*Strong of will and strong of mind*
*You seek she who is your kind*
*Set your trap and be your fate*
*When Lady is the Master's mate*

Time passed strangely for Dominor of Nightfall. It came and went in muzzy bursts. He had vague, fleeting recollections of the things happening around him: wooden walls that creaked, the tang of the sea ever in his nostrils, voices muttering around him, hands forcing him to get up and walk around when he was too dizzy. He recalled how the floor was too uncertain underfoot to readily stand when he was made to do so, and of being fed minty-flavored food and drink that instinct said he shouldn't eat, yet his captors forced upon him while he was too muddled to resist. And he had memories of eating that herbed food until the world swirled away once more.

He remembered a familiar voice, its source strangely distant yet right there in his ear, desperate to reach him. The voice comforted him with its familiarity, though he couldn't have said who even he himself was most of the time, let alone the name or the face that went with that voice. He was aware of the omnipresent chafe of chains at ankles, wrists, and throat, of a faint memory that he had once worn fine, tailored clothes, not the rough fabric rubbing against his flesh. He hadn't always smelled of sweat and worse things, of unclean things, but that was due to the fact that he wasn't allowed to bathe, nor allowed enough clarity in his wits to tend to himself.

And then it happened. They didn't come with the bitterminty flavored food. The world rocked even more dizzily underneath Dom as he lay chained to his bed; his surroundings swayed and creaked dismally, slanting first this way, then that way at unnerving angles, while his mind slowly woke. The cloud obscuring his senses eased enough that he could hear the shouts and the snapping riggings, smell the rain and the sea, and the captive mage knew he was on board a ship on the ocean.

Dominor remembered the Mandarites and their *falomel*-laced food. He remembered the oddly dressed, arrogantly opinioned Lord and his two duplicitous sons. And he remembered that he was captive on a ship that, from the sound and feel and smell of it, was caught in a bad summer storm, one that seemed to go on and on. Long enough that the last of the mage-confusing drug wore off. As the minutes turned into hours, Dominor became increasingly, uncomfortably aware of how filthy he was, how hungry and thirsty, and most of all how *angry* he was. When Dominor realized that, when his head was clear enough to think, he tested the chains keeping him bound more or less in place on his thin-palleted bunk while the ship surged with each hill-like wave.

The chains were padlocked to thick iron staples set too firmly in the bulkhead walls for him to dislodge physically in his drug-weakened state. He tried a simple unlocking spell next, but the energy just glowed briefly for a moment, then sank into the manacles clamped at neck, hands, and feet. He tried a more complex spell, one that lit up the small cabin he was in, showing the walls, sea-damp from water seeping through the decks because of the storm. Symbols on the stout, silvered metal simply absorbed it. As they did so, the metal clamped around his wrists, ankles, and throat warmed briefly. Warningly.

He didn't know those symbols—magical languages were among the very few things that just didn't translate well without intense study, not even with the aid of the Ultra Tongue spell—but he recognized their effect. They were absorbing his energies. If he threw all of his power at them, they might overload and break . . . and most probably burn off the flesh attached to them. Or, if they were forged with the right sort of enchantments, they could latch onto his powers and drain him to a lifeless husk.

An unpleasant thought.

Then again, so was the possibility of starving to death. Or rather, dying of thirst. That would happen first. His mouth felt like it had been scrubbed with sand, then powdered with dust. The heaving of the ship around him didn't help; it reminded him of the liquid that lay beyond the hull. It was too salty to drink, of course, but it was a form of water, and he wanted water. Preferably without any mind-and-power stealing *falomel* in it.

*Odds are, they'll try to keep me drugged until we reach landfall . . . unless I can talk them out of it,* Dominor offered to himself. It was a slim hope, but not an impossible one. *They're so full of themselves and their males-are-superior attitude that if I pretended to listen and pretended to convert to their ways, they'd probably decide to trust me.*

*Not too quickly, of course,* he reminded himself. His mind was finally clear enough to have the room for cunning, for plotting and laying out his strategies. *They'd not believe a sudden conversion. Not when they've kept me chained like an animal. They'll expect some initial rage—and I have plenty of that! But if I ask the right questions, I can steer the conversation toward the idea of converting-the-prisoner.*

*Like the question of what could they possibly offer me as an enticement to stay, when I'm Her Majesty's Lord Chancellor.*

His mouth twisted wryly. Kelly of Doyle, the woman his eldest brother had married, had made that outrageous claim. The redheaded outworlder had proclaimed herself Queen of Nightfall, the island where he and his seven brothers had lived for three years after being exiled from their homeland, Katan. Her arrival and subsequent romance with his eldest brother, Saber, had fulfilled a prophecy spoken in verse by a woman born a thousand years before. The Seer Draganna had predicted the birth of four sets of twins, all of them mages, all of them with unique Destinies. One of those Prophetic Destinies had been the warning that some unspecified disaster would occur if the eldest ever bedded a virgin.

The Council of Mages of Katan, in their so-called wisdom, had exiled Dom and his brothers to Nightfall to prevent them from meeting any women; if they were the Sons of Destiny, then all of them had to be removed, supposedly "for the greater good of Katan."

The Council hadn't accounted for the meddling of the youngest of them, Morganen, whose predicted Destiny was to match-make all of his siblings. He had hauled in a woman from another universe entirely to argue with, be courted by, and eventually marry the eldest of them. Even if it meant summoning the Disaster foreseen for them so very long ago.

*And the Prophesied Disaster turns out to be the very same misogynistic idiots who have managed to capture me. At least, I hope my presence on this ship was the only Disaster that befell us when Saber married Kelly . . .* It was an ignoble way to fulfill a prophecy, being captured and chained. Still, it only affected himself and his siblings. It wasn't a Disaster that affected all of Katan.

Dominor was glad no one could see him like this. They had taken away his finespun clothes and given him rough homespun that stunk of sweat and sea and the desperate need for a bath. His chains had enough give in them to allow him to check under the pants. No under-trousers. They'd even taken away his shoes and his socks. They had clothed him in ugly, stained, beige leggings and a matching, long-sleeved shirt. At least, he thought it was beige; the storm gray light coming through the one porthole in the room didn't really lend itself toward discerning colors.

A tentative exploration of his hair, once silky-clean, proved it was now rather greasy and tangled, especially at the back. From the growth of hair on his jaw, he judged he'd been drugged for at least a week and a half, if not longer. Dominor grimaced in distaste as he fingered his mustache and beard. He hated facial hair. The mustache, if allowed to grow long, tickled his nostrils and interfered with his food, and the beard just plain itched. Not to mention the males in his family line had never been all that hirsute, which meant that his beard would look scraggly and scrawny even when fully grown. If a man couldn't grow a decent beard, he didn't look respectable, in Dominor's opinion.

*Maybe I can jump-start the "conversion" process by demanding some civilized amenities, like a shave. I could imply to them that I'd be a lot more willing to listen if they were a lot more willing to treat me well . . .*

The door to his cabin opened, startling him. It banged shut again as the ship pitched the wrong way, making someone yelp, then curse and wrestle it open again. The younger of the count's sons fell inside as the ship shifted and tilted the other way, barely hanging on to the oil lamp now lighting the chamber. A waterskin dangled off his elbow, adding to his burdens. Dominor recalled the names of his captors.

*Lord Kemblin Aragol, Count . . . no, Earl of the Western Marches, that was it; representative of King Gustavo the Third. His elder son is named Kennal, and this one is called Eduor. The one who tricked me into drinking that drug-laced alcohol. He still doesn't look old enough to shave.*

"Oh! You're awake."

*Yes, state the obvious, you little whelp.* Dominor leveled him with a firm look and spoke with the lilt of the Mandarite accent, which was how the Ultra Tongue potion he had drunk translated their language. "Yes. And I am not happy with my accommodations. Is *this* how you convince male mages from other kingdoms to work for you?"

A deliberate shift of his wrists made his chains rattle. Eduor flushed. He blinked a few times, cleared his throat, and braced himself as the ship rocked again. Looking around, he hung the oil lantern on a hook next to the door, then faced Dominor again, clutching his waterskin. "Er, well . . . here, you must be thirsty!"

"If it has *falomel* in it, I will shove that bag through your digestive system. In reverse," Dominor added not-quite-blandly, shifting to sit up on the bed. He couldn't go much farther than that, maybe enough to use the chamber pot . . . if there was one in the small cabin. He hadn't seen one, yet. But it was enough slack to lend weight to his threat.

Eduor stared at him, eyes wide. His fingers tapped on the bag clutched to his chest. "Right. I'll, ah, be back shortly!"

The door banged shut behind him. At least the idiot had left the lantern. Not that the yellowish glow of the flame lent much to the dismal décor, but it did shed enough light for him to focus on the planks lining his cramped, closet-sized prison. Unfortunately, counting knotholes was only marginally more entertaining than drifting through a minty, mindless haze.

The heaving swells tossing the ship had eased to an exaggerated rocking motion by the time he was visited again. At least he'd found a lidded chamber pot wedged under his bunk in a small cupboard. Dominor disliked traveling by ship; the facilities were primitive, the opportunity for hygiene less than adequate, and in his case, the accommodations literally stank. Disgruntled, he fixed the man who entered with a hard, unhappy glare and struck first.

"Lord Aragol, I am *deeply* displeased with the way you

have treated me. Not one iota of this situation is disposing me to look *favorably* upon helping you. When we spoke at the palace, you suggested there were enticements for a mage of my abilities. Wealth. Status. Power. Prestige. Where in *any* of that does it include chaining me like a common thief, drugging me senseless, and giving me clothes only the poorest of commoners would be delighted to wear?"

Kemblin Aragol lifted his goatee-covered chin slightly. He had dispensed with the hat and the waist-length jacket, but still wore the rest of his finery, including that ridiculous codpiece-thing at his crotch. "In order to get you far enough away from your homeland that you would be forced to stay long enough to listen to us, it was necessary to keep you drugged and thus cooperative and unable to harm yourself. It really isn't our intent to let harm come to you. But with the drug we use to subdue mages, it tends to relax everything in the body, including . . . digestive muscles," Lord Aragol finished delicately. "Thus it was necessary to remove your clothing and give you something that would not matter if it were . . . stained. Though we have done our best to keep you reasonably clean.

"But, now that you are awake and aware again, we can start treating you like the honored guest you will be, once we reach the shores of our homeland."

Dominor folded his arms across his chest. "Prove it, and I'll believe it. But you have a long way to go to regain my trust," he added in warning. "Starting with *undrugged* food and drink. I am thirsty and hungry . . . and if I detect *falomel* or any other drug in any of it, you will not find my response *civilized*."

The earl unhooked a flask from his belt and tossed it at Dominor. "Water, nothing more. I'm afraid the sea is still too rough for a proper, cooked meal, but I can have some bread and cheese brought to you, and some fruit."

"That would be civilized."

Nodding, Lord Aragol stepped into the corridor, giving a command to someone beyond the door.

Taking his time, Dominor sniffed at the contents of the

flask. He shook it a little, sniffed again, then ventured a small sip. Nothing more than water. Despite the pressure of his thirst, Dominor continued to take only small sips. If the water was drugged, he was not going to let it completely shut down his reactions.

The earl's eldest son, Sir Kennal, entered the cabin. In his hands was a basket with a linen bundle. His father followed him. At a nod from the elder male, the younger one stepped forward and offered the basket to Dominor. "Our apologies, Lord Mage, for any inconvenience caused by the assertive manner we used in our insistence that you visit Mandare. We wish very strongly for you to see the wonders and advantages of our land that await a powerfully gifted male mage like yourself."

*"Assertive manner"? Is that the polite Mandarite version for "kidnapping"?* Dominor asked silently. One of his dark brown eyebrows rose in unquelled skepticism, but he accepted the basket without a word. It had slightly overripe grapes, a quarter-loaf of somewhat fresh bread, and a wedge of soft cheese inside the linen napkin. He wasted a small portion of the water in the flask to dampen his hands, scrubbing his fingers on the linen to clean them, since he couldn't use any spells and there wasn't a washbasin in his cabin. Breaking off a small piece of the bread, he sniffed it carefully, then took a cautious taste.

"It isn't drugged, anymore," Kennal offered with earnest sobriety. "The storm has driven us far to the south and east; we need merely turn north and we shall soon reach the shores of Mandare. Once we have sighted land and discerned our location, we will be able to put to shore long enough to take on fresh provisions.

"If we have not been driven too far east, then we should be very close to the Port of Mandellia, which is but a day's journey from our estates," he continued with rising enthusiasm, as Dominor tested one of the grapes next. "Once we have arrived there, we have a full dozen of the most beautiful slave girls who will bathe you and shave you and please you in any way you desire."

Kemblin touched his son's shoulder, taking over. "In fact, as our most honored guest, you will be pleasured as soon as you cross the threshold of our entry hall. Our slaves are well trained; they will be delighted to kneel before you and give you a most fitting welcome."

Unsure what they were talking about, Dominor eyed them warily. "What exactly is this 'most fitting welcome'?"

"Their mouths," Kennal told him and gestured at the exaggerated lump of fabric centered over his groin. "They are trained to kiss and suckle your masculinity."

For a moment, Dominor felt his groin tighten at the thought of a woman pleasuring him in that way. It had been far too long since his last encounter with a willing female . . . and that was where the heat in his loins chilled. *These men are chauvinists of the highest order. They turn their women into slaves, with no choice and no free will. Even a working wench has more dignity and decision in her chosen career than a slave "trained" to please a man.*

He carefully hid his distaste from the other two, adopting a thoughtful look. "Trained, you say? I could take any pleasure of them I'd like? And they would not say no?"

"Their purpose is to please a man in *any* way he desires," Kemblin Aragol reassured him, smiling through his goatee. "My slaves are well behaved, you have my word. None of that tedious courting is necessary, nor will any of them say 'no' when a man is in the mood for his rightful pleasure."

"And do they wear contraceptive amulets?" Dominor asked him sardonically. He couldn't allow the illusion of caving in too quickly, or they would not believe him. So he added dryly, "Or do you think to have them plowed with my seed, to hopefully reap the harvest of my magical abilities behind my back? No doubt you would have me plow a female mage, to strengthen the possible outcome."

"I will not deny that it would be a good idea for you to spread that seed as far and wide as possible," the earl admitted with a shrug. "Any Mage Lord may sow his seed upon any slave girl of a ripe enough age, whether or not he owns her. It is preferred, however, to have a male mage cast his seed into the womb of a woman without magic; otherwise, that only seems to strengthen *their* lineage, not ours. Mage-bitches wear amulets against bearing fruit for that reason, as well as enchantments and chains to bind their powers. You may rut with any woman at my estate and need not worry; only those who are worthy can be successfully bred."

"I am not inclined to beget bastards," Dominor denied instinctively. Inwardly, he winced; his vehemence against rampant procreation didn't exactly fit in with the Mandarite culture. But Lord Aragol merely nodded in reassurance.

"I can understand why, milord! No doubt you would want to have a hand in the training of any mage-born son you seeded. It is more likely for outlanders to be successful in such endeavors, which is why we seek their numbers so insistently."

"And yet we compensate them most handsomely for moving away from their former lives to live among us," Kennal added quickly. "Your rank would be at least equal to my father's, and you would have the ear of our King, as a Mage Lord!"

"You would not be missing the status you had as Lord Chancellor of Nightfall, I assure you," Kemblin told Dominor, neatening his moustache with the edge of his finger. "Indeed, your status might even be higher, depending on the strength of your magics. You yourself admitted Nightfall is but an island; Mandare spans nearly the whole western edge of a continent. You could be deeded a stretch of land larger than your former isle, with farms and craft shops, villages and villeins working to ensure your prosperity."

"And all the women you could want," Kennal stated, grinning with the enthusiasm of a young man who knew he wasn't going to be turned down. A thought which disgusted Dominor; the youth was good looking enough that he shouldn't have to coax a woman under normal circumstances, yet here he was, gloating that he didn't have to coax at all—to Dom, the prize wasn't worth it, if there wasn't any effort involved. Kennal continued, his hazel eyes bright, "You'll find a lot of your fellow noblemen will want to offer you nubile, luscious slave girls, in the hopes of currying favor with you, slaves trained in a hundred exotic arts, all of them humbled and subservient. You'll be showered with gifts of all kinds, even for the smallest of your spells."

"Or, if you like a bit of spice in your pleasures, you can visit the slave markets, buy an untamed woman and teach her where her place lies," his father finished, his hazel eyes darkening with a hint of cruelty intertwined with his sexuality. "Kneeling at your feet, worshipping you for your Gods-made superiority."

Holding his tongue, Dominor carefully did not point out that, if only the women were being born with magical powers, the Gods of both Mandare and its enemy, Natallia, clearly wanted the women to be considered superior. Of course, he knew that his attitude about magic making one superior came from having been raised in a magocracy, where the most powerful mage was made the King or Queen at each five-year turning of the throne's succession. He also knew that other lands ruled themselves in different ways. True, Aiar-that-was, to the far north, had once been a magocracy much like Katan before its sundering. But the land of the distant Threefold God of Fate was rumored to be a hereditary monarchy.

A knock on the door came as a welcome relief from the awkwardness of the conversation. Kemblin stepped outside. After a moment, his son Kennal followed, leaving Dominor alone in the cabin. With the door shut between them, the chained mage was free to relax his wary vigilance just a little.

Dominor was arrogantly proud of his powers and skills, his civility and his superiority, but he was proud of them because they were facts, not because they were opinions.

There were women mages on the Council of Katan who were roughly his equal in skill and knowledge; there were noble-born sons and daughters who were of his family's rank or higher. Those few who were more powerful than him, he acknowledged their superiority and sought to better himself in strength and stamina for comparison. Those with greater knowledge, he sought to study and learn from them. Those with greater rank and civility, he bowed to when necessary.

It was just that, living on an island with only his brothers for companions and the occasional trading vessel for contact with the rest of the world, he was used to not having his superiority challenged. Morganen was more powerful than all of his older brothers, true, but Morg didn't want to lead anyone. Rydan was more powerful than Dominor, but the sixthborn of the eight of them was strange, reclusive, and disinclined to compete against his siblings. Saber was lesser-powered when it came to magic, and acknowledged that to Dominor, but he had been trained to be the next Count of Corvis before their exile; he was also the eldest and took it upon himself to keep his siblings in line as the head of their exiled family.

The rest of the brothers, Wolfer, Trevan, Koranen, and even Dominor's own twin, Evanor, didn't bother much with ranking themselves against one another. Dominor needed to compete; he was thirdborn and third-powered, and it rankled at times. It was a little irksome that Wolfer, secondborn, hadn't a very strong competitive spirit within him. For the elder male, hunting was its own purpose, not about seeing who brought back the tastier game. And while the shapechanger would still compete for sport with his next-youngest sibling, once he had learned to curb his temper and not grow angry at Dominor's taunting whenever he won a footrace or a knife-toss, Wolfer had treated Dominor with a sort of indulgent good humor that was irritating.

Not to mention Wolfer's magic was average in strength at best.

Trevan's idea of sport and contest lay in pleasuring

women; Dominor had competed with the fifthborn brother to see who could better seduce a certain village girl in their past, but the redhead hadn't cared if a woman was also the prettiest in the village. Dominor liked to surround himself with luxuries, with beautiful things. He added ornamentation to the artifacts he created for the traders. Trevan did make nice things and had a knack for spell-carving wood, but he didn't go out of his way to seek recognition for his talents. The thirdborn of them craved that sort of recognition.

Koranen and his twin, Morganen, had only been twenty when they had left the mainland; moving to the Isle had been more of an adventure for the second-youngest brother than an exile. Kor's affinity with fire meant that it was dangerous for him to indulge in his passions with a woman, too, so they could not compete on that score. As the seventhborn of the four sets of twins, he wasn't even remotely interested in trying to outrank himself socially, since there were six elder brothers in the way, and his powers were indeed attuned more specifically to the element of Fire than the general usefulness of Dominor's own broader-based magic. No competition, there.

As for Dominor's own twin . . . Evanor just didn't bother to compete with his older brother.

Dom had once held ambitions to join the Council and govern Katan; Ev was content to govern a mere household. Dominor loved the feel of silk and velvet on his body; Evanor was content to wear wool and cotton. Dom wanted to have his advice acknowledged as helpful, even wise; Ev was contented when his brothers wiped the mud from their boots after he chided them. They were as different as day and night, as city and village. Dominor loved his twin dearly and certainly missed his presence deeply, stolen far from his home and his kin as he was . . . but they weren't identical twins, by any means.

*Really, of all of us to have been kidnapped, I'm probably the best choice,* he thought with a wry twist of humor. *Evanor is too gentle and guileless to disguise his opinion of these Mandarites and their insane opinions about one gender being superior to the other. Koranen is too . . . young, I guess one could say. Too impetuous and hot-tempered. Morganen might be all right in this situation, but he isn't enough of an actor to seem truly "convinced" by these imbeciles' rhetoric. Rydan, with the way even the most potently spell-locked doors tend to unlock and open themselves for him, would probably have escaped these chains during the storm, and then . . . I don't know . . . flown himself free? I wouldn't be surprised if he had that sort of power. Come to think of it, Morg probably knows a spell to free himself from anti-magic manacles such as these.*

*Annoying little twit.* It irked him that Morganen knew more than he did. Somehow, he knew more than Dominor, had learned more, for all that the thirdborn son had bought the lion's share of magical tomes through the years, and was older by four more years' worth of studying as well. He loved the youngest of his brothers, but Morganen also roused most of Dom's competitiveness. Rydan didn't, but then Rydan didn't play such games anymore.

Dominor returned his thoughts to how his brothers would react.

*Trevan, for all he's a self-proclaimed womanizer, would be appalled at the thought of "slave girls," and would not be able to pretend anything different. Wolfer would be snarling and snapping and growling. No dissembling there. Saber might have the mind and the cunning to dissemble and pretend to go along with his captors, having been trained by our father for the world of Katani politics . . . but he wouldn't have the magical strength to get himself back home again once he was free.*

His brothers were undoubtedly seeking a means to rescue him, even as he sat there on the bunk, nibbling on some of the soft cheese he had been given. Dominor knew he could be annoying, what with his competitiveness, his high opinion of himself, and his need to prove himself better than the rest of his siblings. It was a bid for attention and respect that was as established in his nature as his birth order. But he also knew his brothers cared for him and would back him to the hilt, as surely as he would support them.

*I think Evanor Sang to me, while I was delirious with* falomel *poisoning*, Dom decided. *That was the distant voice I heard in my ear, I'm sure of it. But now . . . I hear nothing. He might be just sleeping, or busy with some task, but it's also possible I'm beyond his range of ability to Sing. Which means beyond the range of most scrying mirrors. It will take all of their craft and cunning to create a means of locating me. Even then, it's not guaranteed the mirror would be strong enough to turn into a Gate over such a long distance, with no paired mirror at my end to stabilize the connection. A pity the aether isn't stable enough for the great Portals to be opened, anymore.*

*Which means I definitely need to work on freeing myself, so that either I can find my own way home, or a way to connect some mirror locally to their efforts, even if the link would only be strong enough to communicate, and not actually cross—*

The door opened and Lord Aragol stepped back inside. He flashed Dominor a broad, quick smile that made the points of his goatee-moustache quiver. His younger son, Eduor, accompanied Kennal as they crowded into the small cabin. This time the youth carried a cut-glass goblet, into which he poured a blush wine from a bottle that his father uncorked in Dominor's presence. It looked like they were going to try to recruit him with the temptation of more of the "finer things" of Mandarite life.

Dominor braced himself to play the part of a slowly, reluctantly convinced potential ally, while the ship continued to heave and rock from the waves caused by the end of the storm.

DON'T MISS THE LATEST BOOK IN THE
SONS OF DESTINY SERIES

"Wildly entertaining."
—JAYNE ANN KRENTZ

THE CAT

FROM NATIONAL BESTSELLING AUTHOR
JEAN JOHNSON

Amara is wary of mages—they chased her out of her homeland. Yet there is something about the mage Trevan of Nightfall that Amara can't resist. But can he be trusted with her most fiercely guarded secret? Courting such a pretty yet prickly outlander won't be easy, but Trevan is determined to try. She may be fierce, proud, and from a different culture, but after all, he is the Cat, and none but the most fascinating and challenging of women could satisfy him . . .

penguin.com

M516T0609